D0649558

THE OTHER EXTREME

THE OTHER EXTREME

T.J. MacGregor

PINNACLE BOOKS
Kensington Publishing Corp.
http://www.kensingtonbooks.com

PINNACLE BOOKS are published by

Kensington Publishing Corp.
850 Third Avenue
New York, NY 10022

Copyright © 2001 by T.J. MacGregor

All rights reserved. No part of this book may be reproduced in any form or by any means without the prior written consent of the Publisher, excepting brief quotes used in reviews.

Pinnacle and the P logo Reg. U.S. Pat. & TM Off.

First Printing: December 2001
ISBN: 0-7394-2351-7

Printed in the United States of America

*With love for Rob, Megan, and Dad,
and many thanks to Carol Bowman,
whose path provided the fodder.*

*A special thanks to Al Zuckerman and Kate Duffy.
Without them, this story would be an orphan.*

"The soul creates the flesh."
                                        —Jane Roberts

"Only when the bond is based on what is
    right . . .
will it remain so firm that it triumphs over
    everything."
                                        —The *I Ching*

Prologue

Thursday, November 1
Tango Key, Florida

Jay Hutchin watched them as they strolled down the dimly lit street, arms around each other, faces as close together as an envelope and a postage stamp. His chest went tight, his throat dried up. He felt as if he might choke.

He sat low in the driver's seat of his wife's Toyota, grateful for the shadows that concealed him. The car was parked in a crowded lot across the street from the restaurant Diane had entered an hour ago. She'd gone in alone and had come out with this man, who must have been waiting for her inside.

I'll be staying at the Peninsula, she'd told him over the phone earlier today. *My manager's in town, we'll have dinner, I'll be back at the Peninsula Motel by midnight. Cabin thirteen.* Even though Hutchin hadn't seen this man's face, he knew he wasn't her manager. He had seen photos of her manager, one of the Hollywood power brokers who was short, squat, balding, mid-fifties. This guy was tall, sinewy, and moved with an undeniable youthfulness. This guy, Hutchin thought, was closer to Diane's age, late twenties or early thirties.

He wasn't sure what had tipped him off that Diane was lying. Experience, he supposed. He made his living sorting truth from fiction. His suspicion had eaten away at him until it had pushed him out of the house and across the bridge to Tango Key, to the Peninsula Motel. This time, he didn't have to make any excuses to his wife, either. She had left for the weekend, a teachers' workshop in Miami, and had gotten a ride with some other teachers. He had taken her Toyota because Diane didn't know this car, had never seen it. He had parked outside the motel just after dark and waited for Diane to appear.

Look at her, he thought, *just look at the two of them,* stopping now on the street, in the shadows of a giant ficus tree, embracing, kissing, their bodies pressed tightly together. He squeezed the bridge of his nose and slid lower in the seat, fighting the hard, relentless pounding in his temples.

Lying bitch. How could you?

For months, they had met whenever she was in town, checking on the home she was building here on Tango Key, haven for the rich and famous, and the nearly rich and nearly famous. Diane belonged to the latter category, an actress whose star was definitely on the rise, a young woman whose exquisite presence had been imprinted on the mind of the American public as supporting actress in an Oscar-winning film last year.

Every time Hutchin had gone to her, he had placed himself at risk. But he had gone because he had to, because her body was his addiction, that eager mouth, those silken hands, those shapely legs, the blades of her hips. He had gone because he had no other choice.

He raised his head once more, raised it just enough to see that they now continued down the sidewalk. Just how had she thought she would get rid of this guy in time to meet him at the motel? What excuse did she intend to give? *Oops, it's midnight, gotta run before I turn into a scullery maid.*

He lost sight of them as they ducked into a dive where the music was loud and the food, greasy. Hutchin waited another ten or fifteen minutes, then he drove out of the lot and headed to her motel, a cluster of old cabins at the south end of the island, the cheapest accommodations on Tango. She had stayed here before because no one recognized her. No one asked questions.

Hutchin had never met her here. They had met at other hotels, off of Tango Key, outside of Key West, and she always left the door key stuck in a nearby potted plant or under a mat, the find-the-key game. He would find the key, all right, and would be waiting in bed for her when she came in.

He parked a block away and hurried along the sidewalk, hugging the shadows, his head down. The cabins were arranged in a square around a swimming pool, with a tall ficus hedge forming the final side of the square that faced the street. Hutchin ducked between the hedge and the corner of the first cabin and walked quickly past the dark, silent row of cabins. By tomorrow, the cabins would be filling up as more snowbirds poured into the keys. But for tonight, it looked as if they had the place pretty much to themselves. Safe enough, he decided.

Cabin 13 stood alone in a corner of the square, shrouded by thick bushes on either side and pines behind it. He found the key under the doormat and let himself inside. He stood for a moment with his back to the door and breathed in her scent—perfumes, soaps, shampoos. A light was on in the bathroom, providing enough illumination for him to make out her bed—sheets rumpled, one pillow on the floor—and her suitcase, the lid thrown open, clothes tumbling out.

How could someone so lovely be such a slob?

Was he with you here earlier?

Hutchin stared at the bed and in his mind, saw her with this man, the two of them rolling through the sheets, breathing hard, their legs intertwined, and began to seethe. *Lying bitch.*

He turned slowly, looking for a second suitcase. But of course the man wouldn't be staying here. Even Diane wouldn't cut it that close. He swept past the bed and went into the bathroom. *Two* towels on the floor, a man's aftershave cologne on the back of the toilet, and a used condom in the wastebasket. Blood roared in his ears, his fingers clenched into fists. He backed up to the wall and just stood there, blinking hard and fast, his heart racing.

They made love in the shower. He saw them, a mental image possessed of such clarity that he perceived details— water pouring over them as they groped at each other, her hair a black waterfall. He pressed the heels of his hands into his eyes, struggling against the tide of her betrayal, his heart splintering into a million little pieces. The next thing he knew, he was at her suitcase, leaning forward, his face buried in her clothes. He breathed in a universe of scents, each with a memory attached.

Lying bitch.

His body snapped upright and he plunged his hands into her clothes, into soft silks and cottons, spilling everything to the floor. Two objects fell out—a pocket-size appointment book and a larger notebook with moons and stars on the front. Hutchin picked them up, tossed the clothes back into her suitcase, and stepped closer to the bathroom door where there was more light.

Heart hammering, he paged through the appointment book. Since February of last year, she had come to the keys at least once a month, her flights as meticulously recorded as her auditions and professional appointments in California, Vancouver, Miami. And every other week or so, a man's initials or name appeared: SP or Steve or, once, S. Poulton. Hutchin could barely think through the terrible pressure in his head, the relentless ache in his temples. He tried to remember when he had seen her, the months and dates, the times. But it was as if his brain had been wiped clean.

He flipped faster and faster through the pages, his hands trembling. Last month, October. Okay, he could remember last month. He had seen her on October 1, a Monday. They had met at the Miami airport, where she had a layover on her way back to California, and had gotten a room just for the afternoon because her flight left that evening and he had to get home.

That square had nothing in it except her arrival time and a red check mark.

In the squares for October 2 through 4 she'd written: *SP, Key Largo.*

Another lie. Instead of leaving, she had gone to Key Largo with SP.

And for this weekend? What had she scribbled in for this weekend? He turned the page. For tonight, November 1: *Dinner with SP.* There was a red check mark beneath it. For November 2: *Steve, Key Largo, 3:00 PM.* No red check mark. For November 14: *Miami, Delta #1256.* No red check.

I'm the red check mark.

A sharp, hideous laugh exploded from his mouth. He pressed his hand over his mouth to stifle it, got a hold on himself, moved over to the bed, and sat down heavily. He slapped the appointment book shut and used the hem of his T-shirt to wipe off the sweat marks that his hands had left, then dropped it on the nightstand. *Let her see it when she comes in,* he thought. *Let her lie her way out of this one.* He wanted to see her face, her lying-bitch eyes.

Hutchin sat back against the headboard, the journal pressed to his forehead. He could almost feel the words inside, the descriptions of her betrayal. *Open it, read it, now.*

No, he didn't dare turn on the light. And he felt too nauseated to stand and move closer to the light that spilled from the bathroom.

For the longest time, he just sat there with the journal pressed to his forehead, his eyes squeezed shut. He suddenly bolted forward, confused, his eyes like grit, and realized he must have dozed off.

He heard footsteps outside, a soft cough. Hutchin swung his legs over the side of the mattress, slipped the journal under the bed, and was rubbing his eyes as the door creaked open.

"Hey," she said in that soft, seductive voice. "Have you been waiting long?"

An eternity. "Just a few minutes." He raised his head, his heart seizing up at the sight of her. "How'd your meeting with your manager go?"

"Okay." She tossed her bag on the other bed and immediately pulled her T-shirt off over her head, her thick, black hair tumbling to her shoulders. "I've got an audition in Vancouver in two days." She unzipped her jeans and stepped out of them as immodestly as a little kid. She left them on the floor with her T-shirt, her shoes, and came toward him in just her bra and panties, her magnificent body stinking of another man. She slipped her arms around the back of his neck and kissed him. He couldn't respond, his body had gone dead. She pulled back, frowning slightly, and sat beside him.

"You okay? You seem kind of subdued, Jay."

"Just tired."

She turned on the bedside lamp and the buttery circles of light fell across the appointment book. He knew she saw it. Even as the reality registered for her, he knew she was struggling to remember if she had left the appointment book on the nightstand. He knew she was also wondering if he had looked at it and what lies she would tell him if he had. Her devious mind churned, but her expression gave no indication of it.

"Work's a bitch?" she asked, running her hand over his hair.

"Something like that."

She unbuttoned his shirt. "You need to relax. I'll give you a massage."

When his shirt was off, he sank back onto the bed and she removed his shoes and then hovered above him, her beauty breathtaking, as always, her hands silken and flawless, as always, her black hair like a dark curtain along the sides of her face. She leaned forward and kissed him again and this time his arms came up to encircle her waist, and he flipped her over on her back. She mistook it for foreplay, her husky laugh seductive. Now he hovered above her—*you lying bitch*—and said, "Tell me about Steve Poulton."

She flinched, he saw it. "Just a friend. A med student, a resident, actually. He works in the burn unit at Jackson Memorial in Miami, where I've done some charity gigs. Why?"

How smoothly she lied, he thought, how effortlessly.

"And that's why you were embracing on the sidewalk tonight outside the restaurant? Out of gratitude?"

"I don't know what the hell you're talking about." She spoke crossly and tried to get up.

But he held her down, held her in place with his large, powerful hands and brought his face right up close to hers. "Is that why his name is all over your appointment book and I warrant just a red check mark?"

She wrenched free of him then and snapped upright, to a sitting position, her face livid. "You're married, Jay. I'm single. I'm allowed to see whoever I want, whenever I want, wherever I want. I don't quiz you about how often you have sex with your wife or why you stay with her. So don't do it to me."

"So it's true. You're having an affair with him."

She rolled her eyes and stood, but Hutchin grabbed her hand, jerking her down to the mattress again. And then everything happened so quickly he could hardly follow the precise sequence of events. It was as if he were standing outside of his own body, watching events unfold over which he had no control. He saw himself shove her down onto the bed, slap a pillow over her face, and hold it there while she struggled and kicked, her screams muffled. He watched himself continue to hold the pillow over her face even when she stopped struggling, even when her legs had gone still. He heard himself murmuring, over and over again, *Lying bitch, lying bitch, lying bitch.*

Then everything snapped into focus and he jerked his hands off the pillow, horrified that Diane didn't move, didn't sit up, that she just lay there. He snatched the pillow away from her face. Her open eyes gazed vacuously at him, the impossibly long lashes like brushstrokes against the egg-shell-colored lids. When he leaned closer to listen for her breathing, he saw himself reflected in those eyes. Those vacant eyes.

No one home. Sweet Christ.

He dropped the pillow over her face and wrenched back, away from the bed, from her, from those terrible eyes.

A tidal wave of panic swept over him. He grabbed his shirt off the floor, jerked it on, his eyes darting frantically around the room. *What did I touch?* Her clothes, he had touched the clothes in her suitcase. His prints wouldn't be on her clothes, but had he touched the lid of the suitcase or had it already been open?

Open, yes, he was reasonably sure it had been open when he'd come in. *Be sure.* He ran into the bathroom, yanked a towel from the rack, paused. Had he touched anything in here? The faucets? The sink? No. No, nothing in here. He hurried back into the bedroom and wiped down the lid of her suitcase, the appointment book, the base of the lamp, the switch. Then he remembered the journal and got down on his hands and knees to retrieve it from under the bed. He pocketed it.

Maybe she had written his name somewhere in the appointment book. He had to be sure. *Take it, too.* He grabbed it, pocketed it, put on his shoes and socks. He hurried over to the door and turned, trying to see this as a cop might. Leave the pillow covering her face or remove it?

Leave it.

And leave the lamp on.

He used the bath towel to turn the knob, to open the door, then quickly rubbed the outside knob, which he had definitely touched. The motel key was still in his pocket. He peered out into the darkness, his terror so extreme now that his body refused to move.

It's okay, no one out there.

The muscles in his legs twitched, he stepped outside, shut the door, and wiped the knob again. Then he darted around to the back of the cabin and through the pines, his chest on fire, her lying-bitch face permanently etched into his brain.

Chapter 1

Sunday, November 4
Sugarloaf Key, Florida

The boy woke suddenly, eyes wide and sticky with sleep, his heart pounding. He clutched the covers to his chin, not daring to move. He glanced quickly around his bedroom, at the shadows that oozed like liquid across the walls, at the blinds that clacked together in the breeze.

He wanted to run into his mother's room, but he knew that if he swung his legs over the side of the bed, something would grab his ankles, jerk him down under the bed and through the invisible black hole in the floor. He screamed. Nothing came out.

Tears scorched the corners of his eyes. He squeezed them shut and tried to pull the covers up over his eyes, his head. His hands refused to move. His dog, where was his dog? She would protect him. *Oro, Oro, come fast, please, oh God, please . . .* The words shrieked through his head. The dog didn't come. He didn't hear the click of her claws against the floors.

Terror swelled in his chest. His breath came in hard, hot gasps. He was alone, totally alone in the dark, with the black hole under his bed getting wider, bigger. He could *feel* it, that hole, feel how big it was now, how it had turned the floor around it to dust. In minutes, his bed would be balanced over the black hole and a hot, stinky wind would begin to rush out of it, to rush upward toward him, toward the bottom of his mattress.

Now, do it now, get out fast, run run run . . .

And suddenly his paralyzed muscles released him and he flew like a stone from a slingshot. He skidded into the hall, his breath shooting from his mouth, his hands balled into fists. No time to get to his mother's room. No time. He raced down the spiral stairs, his bare feet barely touching the steps. Outside, quick. He had to get outside, away from the hole. It wouldn't hurt his mother, it didn't want her. It wanted him.

Ryan Parrish fumbled with the dead bolt on the door. It clicked and he threw it open and ran across the screened porch, through the screen door, out into the yard. Faster and faster he went, through the moonlight, past the palms, toward the fence.

The gate. He couldn't get the gate without help. The driveway gate was wooden, tall, heavy. The latch was new. But the other gate, the sidewalk gate, was old, the wood worn and weak, the latch rusted. He veered toward the sidewalk, not daring to look back, certain *it* was back there, the thing that lived in the black hole. He thrust out his arms, trying to push his body closer to the gate.

He stumbled, nearly went down, but somehow found his balance and burst through the sidewalk gate so hard that he heard the rusted latch tear away from the wood and hit the ground. The gate slammed open against the fence and Ryan loped toward the moonlit field on the other side of the road. *Hide in the weeds. Hide fast.*

He glanced back then, glanced because he couldn't help it, he had to know if *it* was there. And he saw its huge and terrible shadow, felt its hot breath on the back of his neck, and smelled that breath, the stink of old blood. Ryan knew that his mouth opened, he heard the creak of his own jaw, but he didn't know if his scream ever hit the air because just then the shadow fell over him, then seized him like a dog with a bone and dragged him away, faster and faster, across the road and into the field of tall weeds. The weeds slapped at his ankles, stickers clawed at his feet and caught on his pajamas. He shrieked, he sobbed, he begged for it to let him go.

The shadow dropped him on the ground and commanded him to dig. *Dig so deep the sun can't reach.*

Ryan thrust his hands into the weeds and dirt, his fingers hooked like claws, and he dug. Dirt and grit got jammed under his nails, it hurt bad, but he didn't dare stop digging. *Gotta find,* he thought. *Gotta find.*

Dig faster, the shadow snapped.

So he dug faster and faster, dug until he no longer felt his fingers or his hands. Sweat popped out on his forehead and rolled into his eyes. He blinked it away. He didn't look up, didn't stop. *Gotta dig so deep the sun can't reach. Gotta find . . .*

Chapter 2

The first time Kit Parrish heard it, she thought it was part of her dream. But by then she was awake, sitting straight up in bed. Whatever she'd been dreaming had dissolved and the dog's howls filled the darkness. Howls, then a wild, frantic barking and clawing at the front door.

Kit wanted to believe that Oro had caught the scent of a rabbit or raccoon out in the yard. But she knew better. The only thing the retriever liked to chase was a Frisbee, and the only times Kit had heard her howl was when Ryan had gotten into trouble. But Ryan had been asleep for hours.

Kit threw off the sheet and hurried up the hall, grateful for the luminous glow of the night-light that kept her from tripping over her own feet. The instant she glanced through the doorway of Ryan's room, she knew that her son wasn't in bed. She knew, somehow she knew, that he wasn't in the bathroom, either, that he had gone down the stairs and out of the house.

In the middle of the goddamn night.

She broke into a run and hit the stairs with her adrenal

floodgates wide open. Oro was now going berserk at the door, leaping up against it, clawing it, still howling. Kit slapped the wall for the light switch, a dim bulb overhead lit up. Her eyes instantly zeroed in on the disengaged dead bolt.

She hurled open the door and Oro shot out into the dark, Kit close behind her. Across the porch, through the screen door, into the yard. A wind blew in off the lagoon, rattling the palms like castanets and banging the open sidewalk gate against the fence. *Bang,* one two, *bang*, one two, a rhythmic, maddening beat.

Oro raced through the open gate, moving faster than Kit had ever thought it was possible for a ten-year-old retriever to move. Thanks to Ryan and his bike and Ryan and his Frisbee, the dog was still in good shape, trim and athletic. But she moved now like a pup, faster than the wind.

Kit lost sight of her for a moment, then shot through the gate herself—and stopped. No Oro. No Ryan. The strip of asphalt to her right, which eventually led to the main road— the only road—into or out of the Florida Keys, was filled with nothing but moonlight. To her left, the road dead-ended at the seawall that held back the lagoon. Directly in front of her, the tall weeds in the field swayed and rustled like waist-high corn somewhere in the Midwest.

She tore across the road and plunged into the field, shouting, "Ryan, Oro." Her voice skipped through the darkness like some tiny round stone that barely left a ripple in the silence. Burrs pricked her bare feet, scratched her legs, caught on her gym shorts and T-shirt. She paused to brush off the soles of her feet, one and then the other, and shouted again, hands cupped to the sides of her mouth.

Fierce barking erupted off to her left and Kit turned toward it. Moments later, Oro appeared, her coat like burnished copper in the moonlight. She barked at Kit, short, urgent barks, a doggie Morse code that said, *Fast, follow me*. She took off into the weeds again and Kit loped behind her, her mouth dry, panic rising in her chest.

For several terrible moments, she heard nothing but frogs, the wind rustling through the weeds, and a car shooting north or south along the highway half a mile west. Her head snapped right, left. Weeds surrounded her, a field of neglect in every direction. "Ryan, Oro!"

Four sharp yips. They seemed to be coming from the direction of the lagoon. *Shit*. Only a seawall stood between the end of the property and the lagoon. She'd been after the absentee owner to erect a fence, but so far he hadn't done anything. She imagined Ryan getting too close to the seawall and falling into the water. Even though he could swim, it was dark, he might hit his head . . .

She crashed through the weeds and stopped abruptly at the edge of a clearing about three feet from the seawall. She stared at her son and his dog. "Ryan? Honey?"

He didn't seem to hear her. He was kneeling on the ground, in his pajamas, his feet bare, his body hunkered over the hole he was digging with his fingers. The hole was so deep his arms vanished into it up to the elbows. He muttered to himself: *"Gotta find, gotta find . . ."*

Kit moved slowly toward him, speaking softly, not wanting to startle him. She stopped between him and Oro and crouched down. His hands clawed wildly at the dirt in the hole, deepening it, widening it. Sweat glistened on his forehead, dirt streaked his face and arms. She wanted to sweep him into her arms and race back to the house. But she was afraid to touch him.

"Can I help you find what you're looking for, Ryan?"

Such calmness in her voice, she thought. Such falsehood. *My God*. The muscles in her arms twitched to touch him, to grab him, to whisk him away from here and whatever nightmare he was enacting. But her calmness apparently touched him because his hands suddenly stopped their relentless digging. They froze in midair.

"Gottafindgottafind . . ." He gasped the words. "Buried where the sun can't reach."

Oro cocked her head to one side, aware of the inflection in Ryan's voice, puzzled by it. Kit reached out and touched her son's damp hair, brushing it off his forehead. "Let me help you find it, honey." She thrust her own hands into the hole, into the layer of cool sand and the mud just beneath it, and started digging. "Two can dig faster than one."

Ryan's head snapped upward and he looked at her, his blue eyes pale, haunted, and so utterly strange, so *alien*, that Kit wrenched back. Then her son blinked and with one of his muddied hands rubbed at his forehead, streaking it with mud so dark it looked like blood. He frowned slightly and when he spoke, his voice seemed oddly adult. "Kit?"

KitKitKit: her own name bounced like a ball between the walls of her skull. *Where the hell did that come from?* When she finally spoke, her voice sounded tight, hot. "What? What're we looking for?"

Another blink, a deepening frown. Then he looked down into the hole, rocked back on his heels, and pressed his filthy hands to his thighs, leaving imprints on his pajamas. A heartbeat later, a sob exploded from his mouth. "Can't find. Gotta find."

Kit gathered him into her arms and whispered lies, that it would be okay, that everything was all right, that he would be fine. "We'll come out here tomorrow and look for it. We'll find it. I'll help you look."

He gradually relaxed against her and only then did she gently pick him up. His hair smelled of earth, wind, salt. His arms encircled her neck and she kept talking to him, talking softly, lies and truth now mixed.

He fell asleep in her arms before she reached the road.

He would be okay, she thought. He'd been sleepwalking or something, she'd read plenty of stories about kids who sleepwalked. The amazing thing about most of them was the apparent ease with which they made their way to a destination.

But do sleepwalkers dig holes?

Kit moved faster, a part of her hoping that she could outrun the problem and leave it back in the field.

Ryan eyed the darkness that pressed in against the bathroom window. Kit followed his gaze and wished she'd pulled the blinds. "It's late, Mom."

"Past two. You can sleep in. It's Sunday."

"How come I'm in the bathtub now?"

Kit squeezed a sponge over her son's head and wondered what to say. It was apparent that Ryan didn't remember what had happened. "You got dirty."

"In the field?"

"Right. You remember that?"

"I remember digging." He frowned. "Digging down deep where the sun can't reach."

"That's pretty deep, honey."

"I guess curiosity might kill the cat, huh?" He smiled as he said it.

"Curiosity never killed anyone, hon, not even cats. That's just a saying." Her brother used to say that, she remembered. But Ryan had never heard that from Pete. He had vanished ten months before Ryan's birth. "An expression."

He looked at her, his eyes bright with intensity, and took the sponge from her. He rubbed it across his chest, across the crescent-shaped birthmark that went from his sternum to just above his heart. It was several inches long, with pigmentation that always had been darker than an ordinary birthmark. The mark itself seemed more like a scar, elevated somewhat. "Mom, I need to find it."

"Find what, honey?"

He frowned, struggling with something. "I . . . I can't remember." His expression caved in and he started to cry.

"You don't have to remember it tonight, Ryan. It'll come to you."

He sniffled, rubbed his eyes, his little face so consumed with worry that it nearly broke her heart. "Will you help me look?"

"Of course I will."

Oro came into the bathroom, wagging her tail, and rested her head on the edge of the tub, watching Ryan. "Oro will help us, too. She's great at finding stuff," Kit said. "What woke you, anyway? Was it a bad dream?"

And which bad dream? The stone house nightmare? The Bad Man nightmare? The falling nightmare? Or the one about waking up underground? For most of his nine years, her son had been plagued by repetitive nightmares.

"It was the hole under my bed. The black hole. It was getting bigger."

She'd never heard *this* one before.

"Honey, there's no hole under your bed. Really."

"It's invisible."

"Oh." Kit finished rinsing the soap from his body, then handed him a clean T-shirt and underwear and let him dress himself. He always had been picky about his clothes, his body, his habits. Kit figured it was genetic. Ryan's father and her brother had been neat freaks. "If it's invisible, how do you know it was getting bigger?"

"I felt it."

"Felt it how? I don't understand."

He got impatient with her questions. "I don't know, Mom. I just *felt* it, okay?"

"But if you felt it, there must've been something to feel, Ryan."

He jerked on his clothes. "Hot air. I felt hot air."

Good, now they were getting somewhere. "So how did you get outside?"

He walked away from her, out of the bathroom, making it clear he didn't want to talk about it. Oro trotted along behind him, wagging her tail, and Kit hurried after them both. "Ryan?"

"Can I sleep in your bed?" He had stopped at the foot of her bed and glanced back at her now, his eyes pinched with fatigue, his light brown hair still damp, clinging to his skull.

"Sure."

Oro barked and Kit and Ryan both laughed. "Yeah, you, too, Oro."

Once she got Ryan tucked into her bed, with Oro curled up at his feet, a sentinel, she said, "Why did you go outside, Ryan?"

"I got scared," he replied, then turned over on his side, his back to her.

He fell asleep in minutes and Kit sat there, watching him, alarmed and puzzled by what had happened. *Digging like a loony in a field in the middle of the night. An invisible hole under his bed. Hot air rushing out of it as it got bigger.*

Christ, Kit thought, rubbing her eyes. She was an attorney, not a shrink, not a neurologist. Bur she was also a parent and knew what a doctor might ask: what had he been doing before he'd gone to bed, how was his diet, was he taking any medications, was anything unusual going on in the child's life, were there any recent traumas?

Ryan's diet was okay, she controlled his environmental

allergies with homeopathic remedies, and he wasn't taking
any medication. As far as she knew, nothing traumatic had
happened recently in his life. Her schedule had changed last
month, when she'd won a case, and for Ryan that meant
she picked him up from school now, took him to his horse-
back riding lessons, that she was *available*.

What about before he'd gone to bed? What had he been
doing? Sketching, sure, she remembered. She'd been watching something on CNN and he'd been sprawled on the floor,
his collection of miniature horses lined up in front of him
as he'd sketched. Nothing traumatic there, she decided.

In nine years, there had been no traumas for Ryan, she
thought. The traumas had happened prior to his birth, when
his father had walked out before Kit had realized she was
pregnant and her brother had vanished. Perhaps the absence
of a father was the problem.

And maybe he has a little bitty growth in his brain, Kit.

She slammed the door shut on that thought, irritated that
she always presumed the worst, even when it didn't concern
her profession.

Blood work, she thought. She would ask Ryan's pediatrician to run simple blood tests.

She got up from the bed and walked quickly through the
silent hallway to the doorway of Ryan's room. She flicked
the light switch and glanced around. The cool November
air blew through the open window, rattling the blinds. That
was what probably had awakened him. The wind. Kit's gaze
fell to the shadowed area under his bed and for just a moment,
the back of her neck tightened.

Bogeymen under the bed. She had some dim recollection
of Pete frightening her with stories like that when they were
kids. Silly shit, but her body remembered.

She knelt down next to the bed and peered under. Lots
of dust bunnies, but no black hole.

It's invisible.

Right. Of course. The black hole was invisible and when it grew, hot air rushed out of it.

Just a nightmare, she decided. He'd awakened from a nightmare about a black hole under his bed and it was so real it frightened him out of the room and out of the house and across the street to the field. If that was true—and maybe it was, kids had all sorts of weird terrors—how did it explain the digging? And what he'd been muttering?

Gotta find . . . Buried where the sun can't reach.

Find what?

Kit rubbed her eyes. She didn't know, even Ryan didn't know, and she wasn't going to find any answers tonight. She would call his doctor tomorrow, and tomorrow they would have fun—the beach, a picnic, something memorable.

But when she crawled between the covers and shut her eyes, she couldn't sleep. She kept seeing the dense shadows under Ryan's bed, the immense blackness. Then the blackness began to spread like spilled ink, the edges oozing out across the floor, the center of it widening, growing, spreading. And as she watched, the blackness bubbled in the center and the bubble stretched upward like Silly Putty and became a head.

Pete's head.

His mouth opened and she bolted upright, blinking against the brilliant sunlight that streamed through the windows, the chirp of birds outside, and the sound of Ryan's laughter from the yard. *A dream, just a stupid dream.*

(2)

Ryan hurled the Frisbee across the yard and Oro raced beneath it and caught it before it hit the ground. "My turn," called Becky, the eighth grader who lived next door to Ryan. "I get to throw it this time."

But Oro ran for the front yard, the Frisbee in her mouth. "You have to catch her first," Ryan said.

Becky grinned, flashing teeth trapped in braces. "Race you."

They ran after the dog, both of them laughing. Becky was taller than Ryan, with long skinny legs like a colt and a blond ponytail that bounced as she ran. She was fast, too, as fast as Ryan, and she could talk while she ran.

"What was going on last night?" she asked. "I heard Oro howling and then I heard your mom shouting and stuff."

"I guess Oro got out."

She glanced over at him. "Then how come I saw her carrying you out of the field?"

Ryan shrugged and pulled out ahead of her. He didn't want to talk about it—not with Becky, not with anyone. If he talked about it, the black hole would have more power over him.

"Hey, that's rude." She caught up to him and grabbed the back of his shirt, making him stop.

He wrenched away. "Cut it out. You're going to ruin my shirt."

"Then don't blow me off like that. God, I hate it when people do that."

"I just don't want to talk about it."

"Okay, so don't talk about it. I don't care. You don't have to lie, though. I mean, I saw her carrying you out of the field and I was, like, well, curious. You would be, too."

Ryan looked up. Even though the house stood on pilings that raised it from the ground and his room was way up there, it was directly overhead. The black hole might hear them. "C'mon, let's go find Oro." More softly, he added, "I can't talk here. I'll tell you outside the fence."

As soon as they were outside the yard, at the edge of the road, he whispered, "It's the black hole again."

Becky's eyes widened. "This is—what? The third time?"

He nodded. The first two times with the black hole had been more like creepy dreams. Oro had been in the room both times. Ryan was convinced that was why nothing had happened. "The worst yet."

They sat down on the curb. On the other side of the road, Oro stood with the Frisbee in her mouth, waiting for them to chase her. "What happened?"

"I . . . I got scared and ran out of the house. I don't remember too much after that."

"Why were you in the field?"

"I don't know."

Oro dropped the Frisbee by the side of the road and sniffed her way into the weeds.

"Maybe you should tell your mom about the black hole, Ryan."

"I did. I'm pretty sure she thinks it's my imagination. Something lives in that hole, Beck."

"No way."

"It chased me. Into the field." *It made me dig.* He couldn't bring himself to say that part. *Made me dig down deep, where the sun doesn't reach.*

"You're creeping me out, Ryan. Let's go wake your mom and go to the beach."

As they got up, Ryan whistled for Oro. She didn't appear and he suddenly knew she had headed deeper into the weeds, nearer the lagoon where he had been digging. "Let's get Oro first."

"Be careful, here comes a car." She stabbed her thumb toward the end of the road, where a car was turning the corner.

Ryan darted across the road, whistling for Oro, wondering

why Becky made such a big deal about one car. Sometimes she acted like a big sister, as overprotective as his mom. One car hardly amounted to traffic. Most of the time, half the houses were boarded up with hurricane shutters because the people lived up north until Thanksgiving.

Ryan reached the edge of the weeds and shouted for Oro. He didn't want to go into the weeds, not even in the daylight. He was afraid that whatever lived in the black hole was still out there, waiting for him. He moved quickly along the edge of the road, whistling again for Oro. She finally appeared, her muzzle covered with dirt, and Ryan knew she'd been digging.

Maybe digging where he had dug.

"Get your Frisbee, girl. Let's go."

As they crossed the road again, the car that had turned the corner moments ago now slowed, then stopped. A guy wearing sunglasses and a Miami Dolphins cap leaned out the window. "Excuse me. You kids know where thirteen Fly-fishing Lane is?"

Ryan wasn't supposed to talk to strangers. But that was his address. "Who's asking?"

"Ben Webster, FBI."

"Yeah, right," Becky muttered, loudly enough for the man to hear. "C'mon, Ryan." Her fingers closed around his arm. "Let's go inside."

"Here's my ID, see?" He held up a badge, just as Mulder did on *X-Files*. "Federal Bureau of Investigation."

Even though Ryan stood about three feet from the car, he could see the badge. "You come to arrest someone?"

The man smiled and shook his head. "Nope. Just to ask some questions. Nice-looking dog. A retriever, isn't it?"

"Her name's Oro."

Becky leaned close to him and hissed, "Here comes your mom."

And suddenly his mom was at his side, her arm sliding around his shoulders as if to protect him from something. "Morning," she said to the man.

"He's a fed," Ryan told her. "Like Mulder."

"No *X-Files* in my neck of the woods," the man said with a laugh, and held out his ID again.

His mom, being a smart lady and all, took the badge, studied it for a moment, handed it back. "So what can I do for you, Agent Webster?"

He laughed at that. "Actually, I think I'm at the right place. You're Kit Parrish."

Ryan felt the way his mother's muscles tensed and he suddenly felt a little scared. Not the kind of scared he'd felt last night, but a different, stranger kind of scared. Her arm slid away from his shoulders. "Why don't you kids go get your suits and stuff for the beach. I'll be along in a few minutes. Pack Oro's food, Ryan."

"Is he going to arrest you?" Ryan asked, crossing his arms at his chest.

"No, hon. I don't think so."

"Definitely not," Webster said. "Cross my heart."

Ryan still didn't like it. But he said okay and hurried after Becky, who had turned away already. He glanced back once to whistle for Oro and noticed how pretty his mother looked, nearly six feet tall and as thin as a model, the wind blowing her short blond hair into a wild tangle. Agent Webster had gotten out of his car, his sunglasses now sitting on the top of his head, and Ryan could tell that Webster noticed how pretty his mom was, too.

Then he was inside of the gate with Becky and Oro, and Becky was whispering, "What's he want with your mom? Did she do something bad? What's going on, Ryan?"

"I don't know."

And his stomach went tight at the thought of something

happening to his mother. That would be worse than the thing that lived under his bed, worse than spending the rest of his life in the field, digging because the shadow commanded it.

Chapter 3

She was as tall as he was and Webster felt that threw off the balance of power almost immediately. No logical reason that it should, but logic hadn't been his strong point recently. The other detail that threw things off was the way she looked.

He'd seen newspaper clippings of her in Pete Beaupre's file, an attractive woman, certainly, but nothing like this. In person, she was striking. Her features, isolated from each other, might be considered excessive—a mouth that was slightly too large, eyes too widely set, a broad forehead. Yet, put them together and they worked so well that if he had passed her on the street, he would take a second glance.

He figured she was in her early forties now, that somewhere inside those khaki shorts and tank top, there had to be evidence of that. But he sure as hell couldn't see it. She looked as if she kept in shape—running, the gym, yoga, tai chi, something regular and perhaps offbeat. Yes, that most of all. This was the woman, after all, who was one of the top defense attorneys in the state. She hadn't gotten there by thinking like other people.

He suddenly realized that neither of them had said a word, that she seemed to be waiting for him to speak first. So he did. "I just took over the cold cases division in Key West and I'd like to ask you some questions about your brother. If you've got a few minutes."

She frowned, her arms swung to her sides, and she slid her hands into the pockets of her shorts. "I know that the local cops list his disappearance as an open case, but what's the FBI's interest?"

Great, Webster thought. Jerome Banks, who had run the cold cases division for years in the Bureau's Key West office, had told him that he'd contacted Kit Parrish already. Webster realized he should have known better. Banks hadn't been in his right mind when he'd retired. Eighty-one years old, a relic in the Bureau basement who should have retired a decade ago. But because no one else had wanted the job, because Banks—despite his creeping dementia—still seemed to have a nose for the work, the higher-ups had left him alone until the day he had walked into the Bureau not knowing his name.

Webster got assigned to take over until a replacement could be found because, as the newest face in the Key West office, he was technically a floater, filling in wherever he was needed. "Didn't Agent Banks contact you?"

"Nope. I've worked off and on with a number of people at the Monroe County Sheriff's Department. But I don't remember anyone from the FBI ever contacting me."

"Apparently your brother was last seen in the wilderness preserve on Tango Key. That's federal land. That makes his disappearance our jurisdiction."

"Seen by whom?" Her arms came up over her chest again, he noticed, a defensive stance. "I've never heard about this."

"A gardener." Webster leaned back against his car, now

parked on the shoulder of the road. "The guy was an illegal immigrant when your brother vanished. Now he's a citizen and came forward a couple weeks ago. Do you have any idea what your brother may have been doing in the preserve?"

"C'mon. That was ten years ago. That's like asking if I remember if I had Special K or corn flakes for breakfast on my fifth birthday. My brother and I were close, Agent Webster, but we didn't keep daily tabs on each other."

He nodded, feeling stupid now, and flipped through a pocket-size notepad. "According to the file, you last saw your brother on Halloween of 1991. Is that correct?"

"He'd stopped by my place with a load of candy to give out that night. We had planned to go out for a bite to eat, but Pete said he had to work late and wouldn't be able to make it. I later found out he hadn't worked that night, that he'd never gone back to the office after stopping by my place. I called him the next day at work . . . he was working out of the Key West office for the *Miami News* by then . . . and his boss said he hadn't come in, that he was probably out covering a story."

"Had he called in sick?"

"No. After Pete won the Pulitzer in 1990, they cut him a lot of slack. He sometimes didn't go into the office for days at a time. No one thought anything about it. Anyway, I went by his place that evening after work and I got alarmed when I found his dog outside, the house empty, and a bunch of messages on his answering machine. I called several of his friends to find out if they'd seen him, called our folks, but no one had talked to him since Halloween. Finding Oro outside was what alarmed me the most. He'd never just leave the dog outside overnight and that's obviously where she'd been."

"So what did you do?"

A pained look came into her eyes. "I brought Oro home,

38 T.J. MacGregor

waited another day, then reported him missing. And that was it. The police have always treated his disappearance as a homicide, but they never turned up any evidence to support that conclusion.''

Spoken like a true attorney, Webster thought. "So what do you think happened to him?''

Her expression looked resigned. "C'mon, let's go inside and talk.'' They started walking toward the house. "I've had several theories over the years. At first, I hoped that he had amnesia. That he'd fallen or something and when he came to, he didn't know who he was or where he was. Then I thought maybe he had this entire secret life that none of us knew about and had assumed another identity and left the country.'' She shrugged. "Now, I feel he's dead and the particulars are probably going to remain one of the biggest puzzles of my life.''

He heard the regret in her voice. "Was he secretive by nature?''

"No more than any of us, I guess. But he went through periods where he kept to himself. He was in one of those periods when he vanished.''

"Was he involved with anyone?''

She didn't answer immediately. "For a long time, I was adamant that he had no special person in his life. Now I'm not so sure. If he was, none of us knew about it. But it might explain his secrecy.''

"What was he working on?''

"A benign piece on Everglades ecology. Nothing dangerous, no Pulitzer material. His editor confirmed that.''

"Is there anyone else I can talk to who knew your brother well?''

She smiled. "That's not in the file?''

"I've got a few names. But since it's been ten years, I figure I should double-check.''

"Carmela Perez, you should definitely talk to her. She was Pete's source on the Cuban Mafia stories that won him the Pulitzer. They were always close."

Webster checked off Perez's name. "I called your parents' number, but it's been disconnected."

"They've moved and right now, they're overseas. How about Bob Tilden? Is he on your list?"

"Got him. He worked with Pete, right?"

"Yeah. He was one of the photographers for the *Miami News*. Now he runs fishing charters out of Marathon and Bahia Honda. He and Pete went to college together, U of Miami. I'd say he was Pete's closest male friend. But I doubt if any of these people are going to be able to tell you anything new, Agent Webster."

"It'll all be new to me," he said, and starred Tilden's name and glanced at the next name. The last name. "How about his ex-wife? Is she still around?"

"She remarried a number of years ago and moved out of state."

"Do you have Tilden's new address and phone number? What I've got here is out of date."

"Sure, upstairs."

As they came into the yard, Webster caught sight of the kids scampering around the corner of the two-story wooden house, the dog loping after them. "Eavesdroppers," murmured Kit.

Webster chuckled. "How old are your kids?"

"Ryan's mine, Becky lives next door. He just turned nine in September."

"So he never knew your brother."

She shook her head. "He was born less than a year after Pete vanished."

The property spoke tomes about this woman's penchant for privacy. Bordered by water on two sides and a fence on

the other two sides, it was at least half an acre, he guessed.
That was as good as a kingdom in the keys, where land was
nearly as precious as fresh water. The tropical lushness had
been tamed, cut back into manageable islands of plants
and trees. The side yard was covered with white rocks to
compensate for the absence of grass, but was broken up by
tremendous rosebushes with buds in every imaginable color.

"Those are incredible roses," he remarked.

"Pete planted them years ago. He was into roses. Now
my son tends them."

Webster was no expert on kids, but roses seemed like an
unusual hobby for a nine-year-old boy. He had a feeling,
though, that "unusual" was the name of the game in this
family. Pete Beaupre certainly had been something of an
overachiever—with a Pulitzer in his pocket by age thirty-
six. He'd started at the *Miami News* when he was twenty-
four and within twelve years, had his own column and was
the author of two books. His sister had graduated in the top
five percent of her law school class at the University of
Miami and had worked as a criminal attorney for several
prominent Miami firms, building her reputation as a top-
notch defense lawyer.

In 1990, the same year her brother had won the Pulitzer,
she had won a murder case involving a young black man
and a white woman that had cemented her reputation. Not
long afterward, she moved to the keys and opened her own
firm. One look at this property and house, which he guessed
cost well over half a million bucks, told him that she probably
made in a year what would take him eight to ten years to
earn with the Bureau.

He knew she'd been married briefly to a charter pilot and
had gotten divorced the same year her brother had vanished.
He hadn't found any indication that she had remarried and
had noticed that she didn't wear a wedding ring. But when

you looked as she did, he thought, there was undoubtedly a significant other.

Not that he cared. His own ten-year marriage had collapsed like a house of cards six months ago, when his wife had informed him she was leaving to live with her new lover in California. To describe himself as gun-shy hardly captured what he felt. Terrified came close. So did scared shitless.

They crossed the large screened porch and he followed her up a spiral staircase to what was actually the first floor of the house. The longest wall was sliding glass doors that opened onto a screened balcony with a view of the lagoon that blew him away. The view alone was worth the price of the house.

The water, as flat as a mirror and shimmering with morning light, seemed to stretch in all directions. The shoreline in the distance, no more than two or three miles straight across the lagoon, resembled a line drawing, barely more than a suggestion of shape. ''This view is like being on vacation,'' he said. ''It's beautiful.''

''Thanks. We love it.''

She rummaged through a drawer in the kitchen, which was actually just part of the front room, separated from it by a tiled counter with high wooden stools. Unusual art work covered the walls, some of it obviously foreign— framed batiks, oil paintings done in bold colors and impressionistic strokes, and animals sculpted from some sort of metal.

Along the wall opposite the sliding doors was an entertainment center with perhaps half a dozen framed photos on it, family photos, he saw as he went over to it. Mom and son; mom, son, and dog; mom, son, dog, and grandparents; and then sister and brother. That was the one he picked up.

He had seen photos of Pete Beaupre, but only here did the family resemblance really strike him. He and Kit looked enough alike to pass as fraternal twins. The main difference lay in coloring: he was dark-haired to her blond. His eyes were also dark, intense, suspicious, set deeply in the sockets. Kit's were a soft blue, yet piercing.

"That was taken about a week before he disappeared," she said, coming over to him.

"You look like twins."

"People have said that. I've never seen it."

Perception. Webster had learned a few things about perception since his divorce. His friends in Miami hadn't been surprised when his wife had split. They claimed they'd seen it coming. But he never had.

"Here's Bob's stuff—home and work addresses, phone numbers, e-mail. And my numbers and e-mail. In case you have any more questions." As she handed him the scrap of paper, her phone rang. "Excuse me," she said.

Outside, he heard the dog barking, the kids laughing. He turned back to the photos, studying them again as if the riddle of Pete Beaupre's disappearance lay somewhere in these photos.

"Kit Parrish," he heard her say. "Hey, Rita. What's up? . . . You're kidding. Christ. When did it happen? . . . And they've already made the arrest? . . . Okay, hold on. Let me find a pen. . . ." Drawers opening, shutting. "All right, give it to me. . . . Uh-huh. So I think we should take it. What do you think? . . ." She laughed. "Yeah, I figured you'd say that. Call my cell number. Ryan and I will be out. . . . Right. Talk to you later."

As she came back into the front room, she said, "Did you hear about the murder of that actress over on Tango the other night?"

"Sure. Diane Jackson. It's been on the news since the body was found."

"They arrested her boyfriend a couple hours ago, a medical resident named Steve Poulton."

"And you're going to defend him?"

"That's right."

"You don't even know the particulars. Maybe he's guilty."

"Guilty or innocent, he's still entitled to a defense."

"So winning isn't the point."

Her smile struck him as one of the most enigmatic that he'd ever seen. "Winning is always the point."

Which was precisely why he'd never gone to law school, he thought. "I'd better let you go. Thanks for your time and the leads, Ms. Parrish."

"Kit. My name's Kit."

Even though she was a lawyer, he liked being on a first-name basis with her. He didn't want to examine that thought too closely, though. "Ben," he said. "I'll be in touch."

"Great. Thanks."

As soon as he was outside, the kids came tearing around the corner of the house, the dog in hot pursuit. The second they saw him, they all stopped. The boy, the girl, the dog. "Thanks for not arresting my mom," the boy said.

He laughed. "You're welcome. By the way, those roses are incredible. I understand you're the expert."

"He's awesome with roses," the girl said.

"I'd like to grow a black rose," the boy said.

"Is there any such thing?"

"No one's grown one yet. There've been some that are close, but no one's done it yet."

Eerie, Webster thought, how the kid's eyes looked so much like the eyes of the uncle he'd never known. "So how do you know so much about roses?"

The kid shrugged. "I don't know. I just do."

"Well, good luck growing that black rose," Webster said.

"Bye," the girl called after him. "Say hi to Agents Mulder and Scully."

"Will do," he called back, and smiled as giggling broke out behind him.

He always had regretted that children hadn't been part of his marriage. Now, at forty-three, it seemed like a ridiculous regret, but it still bothered him. Right after the divorce, he used to lie awake in bed at night, playing the *what if* game. *If* he and Lynn had had a child, would they still be together? Would he have worked less? Would she still have gotten involved with another man? *If* they'd had a child and gotten divorced, would she have gotten custody? Would he now be like millions of other fathers, seeing his kids only weekends and one holiday a year? The game was futile, of course, because Lynn never wanted kids.

So here he was at forty-three, childless and divorced, with just an older sister who lived in Oregon. His parents had died when he was young, and the grandparents who had raised him and his sister had passed away several years ago. Some of his coworkers envied Webster his "freedom," as they called it, but the last six months had taught him that freedom could also be a prison. It was all a matter of perspective. His dream, at least at the moment, was to quit his job, sell his houseboat, and travel around the world. He couldn't afford it, but even if he could, he eventually would have to come back, his money wouldn't last indefinitely, and then he would have to start over.

So for now, he tried to take each day as it came and to focus on what he had rather than on what he had lost.

Twenty minutes later, Webster walked into Home Fries, the greasy spoon where he'd had brunch nearly every Sunday since he'd been assigned to the Bureau's office in the keys. Eric Moreno had claimed their usual booth in the back, files and notes spread out all over the table, an ashtray holding down one pile of stuff, a coffee mug holding down another. He was on the phone, where he spent nearly as much time as he did on the Internet, communicating with his vast network of acquaintances, sources, friends, and whoever else wanted to join in.

Be off in a second, he mouthed as Webster slid into the booth.

Physically, he was Webster's opposite—short and balding, while Webster was tall, with thick, dark hair. Moreno was muscular from his regular workouts in the gym; Webster was lean, sinewy from regular running. Moreno had been with the Bureau since he'd graduated from college, pushing twenty-five years now. Webster had been with the Bureau for half that time and had held a dozen other jobs since he'd graduated from college twenty-one years ago. But despite their physical differences, a sort of Mutt and Jeff syndrome, as Moreno referred to it, they shared a certain eccentric mind-set and some common experiences—divorce foremost among them.

Moreno had befriended him his first day in the Key West office and was now supposed to shepherd Webster through the labyrinth of the cold cases division. He had worked with Banks for the last five or six months, learning the old man's filing system, which no one else in the Bureau—including Webster—could decipher.

"Shit, man, the wires are humming today," Moreno said as he finished his call. "The Jackson murder is the hottest thing to happen around here since the Mariel boat lift. She was suffocated. Christ, makes my throat close up just thinking about it. She was the next Julia Roberts, that's what they've been saying. You see her in *Run For Your Money*?"

"Three times. So what's the story?"

Moreno launched into a description about where she'd been found, who had found her, and the state of the crime scene. All of this was delivered at the speed of light, as Moreno sipped his coffee and lit one of his putrid cigars and jotted notes to himself on a legal pad covered with his illegible handwriting. "So early this morning, they arrest her boyfriend, a medical resident at Jackson Memorial. How's that for a weird coincidence, *amigo?* Jackson and Jackson. Shit. Anyway, the two of them had dinner Thursday night at Bennino's, then went to Juke's, a dive down near the pier. They had an argument witnessed by everyone in the bar and she left in a huff sometime before midnight. There was a used condom in the wastebasket in her room and they figure the DNA is going to match the boyfriend's."

"So he was arrested mainly because of the witnesses to their argument?"

"Hey, the guy didn't have a fucking alibi," Moreno said. "He claims that after their argument, he drove back to his place in Key Largo and then drove on to work in Miami the next morning. The original plan was that Jackson would meet him in Key Largo sometime this weekend, then he would drive her to the airport in Miami on Sunday or Monday."

"Any idea how long they'd been seeing each other?"

"About two years."

"You think he did it?"

"Right now, that's sure how it looks. But shit, man, who knows."

"He's already got a defense attorney."

"And I'm supposed to guess who it is."

"Humor me."

"Johnny Cochran."

"Kit Parrish."

Moreno let out a soft whistle. "Where'd you hear that?"

"From her. I just left her place."

Moreno snapped his thick fingers. "Right. Of course. Pete Beaupre was her brother. I forgot you were going to take on that case. And she told you she was going to defend him?"

"She got the call while I was there."

Moreno sat back, shaking his head. "Man, are we in for a media circus. You realize that Parrish has lost only one case in ten years?"

Webster shook his head. He didn't keep track of the wins and losses in the legal system, but this news didn't surprise him. "What case was it?"

"A rape case. She lost to Paul Opitz."

Tango County's state attorney. "It obviously didn't hurt her business very much. You ought to see her house. I'm telling you, Eric, we're in the wrong business. We should've gone to law school."

"Yeah, right. And be two more whores in the legion of whores. I don't think so, *amigo*. So did Parrish tell you anything that isn't in her brother's file?"

"Not really."

Moreno leaned forward, his dark eyes glinting with something that Webster couldn't read. "So what's your nose say? That's what Banks would ask."

"My nose says it's been ten years and the trail's pretty cold, Eric."

He waved his hand impatiently and made a sound of disgust. "That's your ego talking. I'm talking about your fucking gut, man. What do you *feel?* Banks always said that with cold cases, you had to feel your way into the past, into those people's skins."

Webster thought about it for a moment. His gut said that Kit Parrish was an attractive woman who looked awfully good after all these months of no women, that she would look awfully good even if his life had been filled with women. But that wasn't what Moreno was referring to. "I don't know what my gut says," he replied, and signaled the waitress to place his order.

Chapter 4

Monday, November 5

"Mom?"

"Yeah, hon?"

They were on their way to school, Kit with a mug of coffee in the dashboard holder and Ryan with a container of Gatorade in one hand, his book bag at his feet. Her head was already at work, racing through her list of things to do today.

"Do you ever hear voices?" Ryan asked.

An alarm sounded at the back of her mind. "Voices?" She looked at him, her beautiful son with his uncle's dark, mysterious eyes, and hoped this was part of some joke or riddle Ryan had heard at school. But she knew it wasn't. His expression and voice were too serious. "What kind of voices? I don't understand what you mean."

"Voices," he repeated, and sucked on the straw in his Gatorade until he was sucking on air. "I don't know. Voices."

"Sometimes I hear a voice that says my son asks me difficult questions."

"Really?"

"Oh, absolutely."

"C'mon, I'm being serious."

"So am I. Give me an example of what you mean, Ryan."

He glanced out the window, offering just his profile, not his eyes. She could read his eyes; she could not read his nose. "When I was digging the other night, before you found me, the voice in my head told me to dig."

Okay, don't leap on this one, take it slow. She braked for a stoplight. "What'd this voice sound like?"

"I don't know. It was just . . . just there."

"Was it the voice of a man or a woman, Ryan?"

"A man."

"Was it a mean voice?"

"Not exactly."

"Then what?"

"It knew what it wanted."

"Determined, in other words," she said.

"Yeah, I guess."

"And the voice told you to dig?"

"The voice kept saying, 'Bury it deep, where the sun can't reach.' "

This was not welcome news. This smacked of schizophrenia, brain tumor, diseases that hadn't been named yet. "The next time this voice tells you to do something, hon, check with me first, okay?"

He nodded. "If I can."

If I can? What kind of response was that?

On one level, it made sense that Ryan would hear a voice that was male and stern. He had never known his father. There was no strong male prototype in his life. In fact, with the exception of her father, Ryan's caretakers were female—

herself, her mother, her partner Rita, and Abuelita, the old woman who had been Pete's source on the stories that had won him the Pulitzer.

"If you can? What's that supposed to mean?"

"Sometimes I don't have a chance to talk to you first. It happens so fast."

"Fast?" She tried to squelch the note of anxiety in her voice. "This has happened before?"

"A couple of times."

"How come you never mentioned it, Ryan?"

He shrugged. "Because I thought you'd take me to the doctor. I'm not sick or anything, Mom. I really don't need to go to the doctor."

"No one said anything about a doctor, Ryan."

He glanced away and she pulled up in front of the school. "Lunch box?" she asked.

"Got it."

"Homework?"

"Got it. You picking me up?"

"I should be able to. In case I can't, though, I'll call Abuelita."

"Love you."

"Love you, too."

He got out of the car and Kit stared after him, puzzled and newly alarmed. It seemed that so much went on inside of Ryan that she knew nothing about. Perhaps most parents felt that way about their kids, but she'd felt this way since the first moment she'd held him in her arms and peered into his eyes. And odd, she thought, that his feelings about doctors had been shared by her brother. Thanks to asthma when he was a kid, Pete had been so terrified of doctors as an adult that the only times he'd gone to one were when he was so sick he could barely stand up and that had been—what? Three or four times that she could recall.

Kit watched Ryan until he neared the door and turned, waving to her one last time. Then he vanished and she pulled away from the curb. She felt the familiar tightness between her eyes that she always felt when something important or dangerous was happening. It was as if the barometric pressure had suddenly surged or plunged and for a while, she knew, that spot between her eyes would ache and throb, trying to communicate something to her. But what? She didn't have a clue. She rarely did. What good, she wondered, was a warning system that didn't define the danger?

Twenty minutes and three cell calls later, the puzzle of her son's remarks and the events of Friday night had receded to the background of her thoughts, making room for the day's crowded agenda—the Poulton case. She headed across the bridge to Tango Key, where her offices had been for the last ten years.

Tango Key measured eleven miles at its longest point and seven at its widest. It was shaped like the head of a cat with some proportion problems—ears separated by knobby hills, a rounded jaw, a face that was excessively long. Between the two towns—Tango to the south and Pirate's Cove to the north—rose the hills, a topographical anomaly in a string of small islands as flat as a sheet of paper.

The town of Pirate's Cove had more wealth per square inch than Beverly Hills and more covenant and deed restrictions than most south Florida communities. Some of that wealth was scattered through the hills, too, where many of the snowbirds had winter homes. But old-timers populated the hills as well and they farmed the same plots of land their ancestors had tilled. The main crops were mangos, guavas, pygmy lettuce, sweet green beans, and Tango citrus.

Then there was the town of Tango at the southern end of the island, where the fishing industry was located and also the bureaucratic hub—city hall, the courthouse, the island's police station and jail, and offices related to those industries. As in Key West and the other islands in the keys, parking was a major problem. The dozen spots that Kit reserved for herself and her employees in the courthouse garage cost her a fortune. But the expense was worth the convenience.

Kit pulled into the garage and nosed her van into one of the firm's spots. *Checklist,* she thought, glancing around the car. Briefcase, purse, cell phone. She'd remembered everything. As she hurried through the garage toward the elevator, someone behind her called out, "Hey, Kit, hold on and I'll walk in with you."

Smiling, she stopped and glanced back, tapping her watch. "C'mon, I've got a crammed day."

Jay Hutchin laughed and broke into his Charlie Chaplin walk, feet turned outward, one hand to his mouth, fingers holding an imaginary cigar. He looked comical, this tall, attractive judge in his expensive suit, clutching a briefcase and waddling like Chaplin. At fifty-one, he was nine years older than Kit and his résumé was about three times as long and more impressive than anything she could ever hope for.

After graduating from Harvard Law in 1977, Hutchin had spent two years in Tallahassee, as staff director of the Judiciary Committee of the Florida House of Representatives. In 1979, he'd gone into private practice with one of Miami's largest law firms and two years later, had become one of the youngest criminal law professors at the University of Miami—and Kit's professor.

In 1984, the governor had appointed him state attorney for Dade County. He was voted back into office after that, then left Dade in 1991 when the governor appointed him to step in as state attorney for Tango County. Six years ago, he was appointed and later elected as one of two circuit court judges assigned to the criminal division of Tango County.

In the course of his career, he had instituted job programs for newly released inmates, passed laws for more humane treatment of Cuban and Haitian refugees, pressed for better education for gifted and handicapped kids in Florida, and had challenged the Florida Supreme Court on the constitutionality of the electric chair. She didn't just admire this man; she revered him. He had talked her out of leaving law school during her second year, when a kind of existential despair had seized her, and had come to represent all of her idealism about the law and democracy.

Yet, their relationship remained entirely professional. Although she knew that he and his wife, an elementary school teacher, had been married for twenty-five years and had a daughter in college, she didn't know much else about his personal life. His personal life didn't interest her.

"How can your day be crammed this early?" he asked as he reached her.

"New case."

"Just one?" he teased.

"Actually, we're juggling almost more than we can handle. But this one may be very big."

"Music to an ex-law professor's ears."

"You hear about the Jackson homicide?"

"Quite a shock. Did you see her in *Run For Your Money*?"

"Didn't everyone?"

"You think she was *that* big?"

"Jay, c'mon. The movie won an Oscar. Her career picked up big-time after that."

"You keep up on that stuff?"

"Not really. But the news on Jackson was hard to miss."

The elevator doors slid open and Hutchin, ever the gentleman, stepped in after Kit did and punched the button for the ground floor.

"So what do you think about the arrest of Jackson's boyfriend?" Kit asked.

"Do I think he's guilty?" Hutchin shrugged. "That's not for me to say. Do I think he'll beat the rap? That depends on his defense."

Spoken with the heart of a true attorney, she thought. No direct answers, just questions and facts. Oddly, he didn't seem to have made the connection, however, between her potentially "big" case and Poulton. "We've been hired to defend him."

Hutchin's reply coincided with the final jolt of the elevator, which jarred her. "And *when* did *that* happen?"

"Yesterday, not long after his arrest."

"Should I congratulate you or send you to a shrink for counseling?"

Kit laughed. They were outside now, in the bright morning light, waiting at the corner to cross to the courthouse. "C'mon, Jay. When you were a defense attorney, you took cases like this."

"Yeah. And I was a lot younger. Has Opitz already indicted him?"

Opitz was the state attorney for Tango County, a little shit of a guy, at least in Kit's opinion, but she was hardly unbiased. Opitz was the only prosecutor in her years in the keys to beat her in court. "Even Mr. Opitz doesn't move *that* fast. But right now, at least from what we've been able to determine from the paperwork, they have a very strong case against him and I suspect Opitz will be handing down an indictment in the next few days." She glanced at him, suddenly realizing that he might have asked because he was in line for the next case.

Criminal cases in Tango County, as in some other Florida counties, were assigned to a specific judge at the point that the state attorney filed an indictment. The clerk of court assigned these cases on a rotational basis. In the event that a judge couldn't hear the case because of illness or some other reason, then a substitute judge—usually from Monroe County—was brought in.

"You next on the schedule, Jay?"

"Yeah, I think I am." He frowned, looking worried now. "Opitz hasn't handed down an indictment yet, but just to be safe, we shouldn't be talking about this case, Kit." He paused, then added, "I'd think twice about it if I were you."

The light changed and they crossed the street. "I thought we weren't supposed to be talking about the Poulton case."

"I'm just giving you some personal advice."

She remembered how he had stood up there in front of her criminal law class, igniting a fire in her heart and idealism in her soul, and she smiled and shook her head. "Ha. You'd snatch it in a heartbeat."

Something changed in his expression, but she couldn't say what, exactly, it was. Regret? Concern?

"I don't know if I would take it. I always weighed every case against my personal ambitions."

"Weighed it in what way?"

"By asking three questions. How good are the odds that I can win the case? Will the time I have to invest in the defense investigation be better used on another case? And can I offer the client a top-notch defense even if I believe the person is guilty?"

A mini lecture in criminal law, she thought. "I'll keep the questions in mind, Jay. Thanks."

They went their separate ways then, Hutchin heading off toward the courthouse and Kit turning in the opposite direction, toward her office. She ran through the questions and realized it was too early to answer them. She had no idea what the odds were about winning the case. Although Rita had spoken to Poulton yesterday, Kit hadn't met him.

However, with every case she'd taken in her years of practicing law, she always had gone into it assuming she would win, not lose.

She couldn't guess how much investigative work she and her team would have to do. But the only reason that would be an issue was if she didn't think the client could pay the legal fees. She had no worries on that score. Rita had discovered that Steve Poulton's sister could afford to pay off the debt of some third world countries. Part of her money was inherited, the rest came from real estate investments. She was putting her younger brother through medical school and was apparently devoted to him. So scratch the second question.

Then there was Hutchin's third question. If she came to believe that Poulton was guilty, could she still offer him a top-notch defense? It was a thorny area, always had been. In the rape case that she had lost to Opitz, she'd believed absolutely in her client's innocence and it had made her loss a crushing one—both for her and for her client. In a celebrated murder case she'd taken, she'd come to believe halfway through the trial that her client was guilty. By then, it was too late to back out and when the man was acquitted, she'd felt utterly sick inside for weeks.

But with the majority of the clients she'd defended, she had managed not to allow herself to consider their guilt or innocence; she simply cut that issue out of her life and had focused on her job—*to defend.* That was how it would have to be with Poulton as well, she decided.

(2)

Hutchin's hands trembled as he turned on the faucet and cupped them under the flow of water. He stood at a sink in the men's rest room in the courthouse, his stomach churning with anxiety, his temples pounding. He splashed cold water on his face, but it did nothing to abrade the sinking sensation in the pit of his stomach.

When he finally raised his head and looked at himself in the mirror, Diane's body was superimposed over his own image, her body motionless. He could see those long, lovely legs, bare and open to the scrutiny of everyone who had entered the room after he'd fled. He could see the pillow that covered her beautiful face. And he could still see those spooky eyes staring up at him when he'd taken the pillow off her face. *Jesus God.*

And now Kit Parrish would defend Poulton.

Kit, who had lost only one case in the last ten years. Kit, a woman he had trained for criminal law.

He yanked towels from the dispenser and rubbed them over his face. A wave of nausea swept through him. He squeezed his eyes shut and gripped the edges of the sink, struggling against the images of Diane that had haunted every hour of his life since Thursday night.

It's done. Get over it.

The wave passed and he looked at himself in the mirror again. Dark circles nestled under his eyes, but other than that, he didn't think his anxiety showed. The telling moment would be when he saw his wife this evening. Isabel had left the conference early this morning and had driven straight to work at the elementary school where she taught gifted fifth graders. If he passed her scrutiny, then he would look normal to his staff and to anyone else who knew him and he would be able to get through this.

Lying bitch. She deserved it.

Right. Justifiable homicide. It wasn't even murder one, he thought, jerking more towels from the dispenser and drying his hands. It wasn't premeditated. She'd purposely tantalized him, mocked him, and his rage had gotten away from him. He regretted it, yes. But he couldn't change it, couldn't take the moment back.

It's done. Get over it. That was the bottom line.

He ducked into his office through the back door, thus avoiding his secretary, his assistant, and the rest of his staff. He felt a deep relief within the familiar walls of his office, his home away from home for the last six years. Here, he commanded. Here, he controlled everything. Here, he was God.

Hutchin sank into the large black chair behind his desk, rubbed his eyes, and saw one more image of Diane and Steve Poulton as they'd stopped under that giant ficus tree that night to embrace, to nuzzle each other.

Get over it. His eyes snapped open. He was next in line for cases. So unless another indictment was handed down this week, he would be sitting on the bench for the trial of the man accused of killing the woman whom he had suffocated. The irony, the grotesque irony.

Focus, he thought. He needed to focus. He glanced at his schedule for the day: three arraignments, a pretrial conference for a case to be tried in early January, and a mountain of paperwork to get through. Pretrial motions, sentencing hearings, plea negotiations . . . a paper nightmare.

He reached for the stack of pink phone messages on his desk. Three calls from the state attorney's office, two from the Tango County PD, one from his wife . . . Then his vision blurred, words melting together like wax, and he was suddenly inside cabin 13 again, rushing around with the towel, frantically wiping here, there, struggling to eradicate every trace of himself.

He had done this in his head dozens of times since Thursday night, seeking any detail he might have overlooked that would connect him to the crime scene and, in a broader sense, to Diane. He knew he had been meticulous about getting rid of evidence. But in retrospect, he worried. Even when murder was premeditated, when every detail was planned, shit happened. Murphy's Law reigned supreme.

And he might well be sitting on the bench for this trial. He had no grounds for recusing himself, and if he pretended to be sick, then it had to look very convincing; otherwise it might look suspicious.

The buzzer on his phone rang and he hit the intercom button. "Yes, Louise?"

"I wasn't sure whether you were in or not, Judge Hutchin. You have a call from a Mr. Godwin. Do you want to take it?"

"Who is he?"

"I don't know, sir. That's the only identification he offered. Would you like me to ask who he's with?"

"No, forget it. I'll take the call. Thanks, Louise."

Taking a call, even from a stranger, would distract him from thoughts about Diane. The phone rang and he picked it up on the second ring. "Judge Hutchin."

"Judge, this is Charles Godwin," said a booming car-salesman voice. "President Baker's chief of staff. How're you this fine Monday morning?"

The President Baker? U.S. President Baker? Struck mute, Hutchin simply sat there clutching the phone, trying to think of something intelligent to say. If not that, then something courteous and not too fawning. "What can I do for you, Mr. Godwin?"

"Your name is one of three the president has submitted for possible appointment as attorney general. Before we proceed, the president would like to know whether you're interested in the position."

If Hutchin hadn't been seated, he would have collapsed into his chair. As it was, a strange sensation swept through him and it took him a moment to recognize it as elation.

"Interested? You're a master of understatement, Mr. Godwin."

Godwin laughed. "It's part of my job description, Judge Hutchin. The president will be delighted to hear that you're interested. We'll be in touch soon. Thanks again and have a great day."

"You, too."

The line went dead and Hutchin just sat there, gripping the receiver, the hollow emptiness echoing in his ear. *Sweet Christ.* Attorney general. The most powerful prosecutor in the free world. *Nope, sorry, Charlie, I'm not interested.* He dropped the receiver in the cradle, shot to his feet, sat down, and got up again, grinning like a loon.

His wife, he thought. He should call Isabel, interrupt her class, and invite her to dinner tonight at Diego's and tell her the news over dinner. A romantic dinner like they used to have in the days before . . .

. . . *before Diane.*

His elation hissed out of him like gas from a balloon.

He stepped back until the edge of the desk cut into his spine, and he ground his fists into his eyes. *Can't risk it.* Once that short list was handed over to the FBI, the feds would be sniffing around in his life like a pack of hounds, looking for anything—any reason—to cross his name off the short list. *Get out now.* He would call Godwin back, tell him he'd changed his mind. . . .

No. No, he couldn't act rashly. He had to think about this, sort it out. Since he was a married man in a public job, he had been scrupulously discreet about his affair with Diane. They had never spent the night together anywhere near Tango or Key West, had come and gone alone from the motels where they'd met, and the rooms had been in Diane's real name or a name she'd made up. He didn't know whether she had paid in cash or by credit card, but either way, nothing could be connected to him. Poulton, after all, had been her public lover, and investigators would assume he had stayed with her or she had been alone.

Just how closely would the FBI investigate him, anyway? Would they spy on him? Talk to his colleagues and employees? How deeply would they probe? *Deep, Hutch, deep. Don't kid yourself.*

Would they investigate Isabel as well? If so, how deeply would they look into *her* life? This made him as uneasy as the feds probing into his own life. On the other hand, why should they probe deeply into his private life when his public life had been so exemplary?

This thought instantly relieved his anxiety. He sat down at his desk, spun the combination on his briefcase, popped the lid open. From a pocket in the lid, he withdrew the journal and the appointment book he had taken from Diane's suitcase. He would have to find a safe place for these things somewhere at home. He'd been carrying them in his briefcase since Thursday night and, until this moment, hadn't been able to open the journal, much less to read anything she had written. But he opened it now, opened it to the very first page.

5/8/99

    I'm 26 years old today. I have one Oscar nomination, more work than I could even imagine five years ago, and I'm being touted as the next Julia Roberts. I have a home in Beverly Hills, a ranch in Wyoming, and I've bought property on Tango Key where I plan to build a hideaway. By Hollywood standards, my star is brightening by the second.

    According to my family, however, I'm living a life thick with sin and corruption and they don't know the half of it! None of them communicate with me anymore.

They've written me out of their lives. Suits me. I don't need them. I am reinventing myself daily.

One of my inventions is mistress to a man nearly twice my age. Another invention is as a lover to a medical intern. A third invention is as a spokesperson for disadvantaged and handicapped children. My manager came up with that one and it actually fits how I see myself. I like kids, I want kids, my heart bleeds for kids who can't walk or breathe on their own.

Steve wants kids, too, but not right away. He's applying for a residency at Jackson Memorial in Miami, specifically in the pediatric burn unit. His idealism speaks to me on a level I don't understand yet, but which I find infinitely seductive. Jay is a judge. I have never liked judges, never liked attorneys, never liked any of those assholes. But I like Jay. In him, I see another kind of idealism, even though his idealism seems to be pretty jaded. But there's a lot to be said for a man whose résumé reads like a who's who. He's a wonderful lover, too. I guess married sex gives you plenty of practice.

Jay doesn't know about Steve. Steve doesn't know about Jay. That's another one of my inventions. I like the separateness of these two distinct parts of my life. I like the risk, the thrill, the threat of discovery. I like living on the edge and

Hutchin slapped the journal shut. When he'd seen Diane with Poulton Thursday night—and Hutchin hadn't known his name then—he mistakenly had believed that Poulton was a new addition to her life. But he was no newer than Hutchin himself.

He had met her in the Key West airport on New Year's Day 2000, almost two years ago. He'd taken his daughter to the airport for a flight back to her freshman year at Amherst and, as he'd turned away from the gate, he literally had run smack into Diane. He hadn't recognized her immediately.

She'd been wearing faded jeans and shades, her luxurious hair drawn up off her shoulders. They'd murmured apologies simultaneously, laughed simultaneously, and leaned forward simultaneously to pick up the change that had spilled from her wallet.

"Serves me right for thinking about how fast I could get out of here and away from my cousin," she said.

"That sounds like Catholic guilt," he remarked.

"For sure. You think confession would do the trick?"

"I doubt it," he replied, and they laughed again and he handed her a handful of the spilled change and they both stood.

"How about a cappuccino?" she asked, nodding toward the Starbucks booth just ahead.

"Sounds good."

They talked as they stood in line, as they found a spot in the airport to sit, talked for the next two hours, exchanging stories and personal histories, electricity flying between them. He kept telling himself that she was young enough to be his daughter, but that argument hadn't prevented him from driving with her to Tango Key, to take a look at the property she recently had purchased.

They had walked into the trees on her acre of paradise, into the deep shade and the luscious scent of pine, and he had sensed what would happen and had done nothing to stop it. They had made love in the leaves, in the thick shade, in the sweetness of that pine-scented air, and all of it had smacked of destiny.

In the twenty-five years that he'd been married, it was the first time he had been unfaithful to his wife. He hadn't felt guilty about it, why should he? He suspected that Isabel had been unfaithful as well. But even if she hadn't, it wouldn't have changed what had happened between him and Diane.

In time, he learned to slice his life down the middle, with one half belonging to Diane and their secret life and the other half belonging to his wife, his daughter, and his career. And for that first year, he'd been able to maintain this schism. Then the balance had shifted and Diane consumed his thoughts. He became obsessed with what she did when she wasn't with him, with whom she spent time, what she did on movie locations, who her friends were, whether she slept with other men.

One day in the grocery store, he had seen her photo on the front of a tabloid, Diane embracing some hot Hollywood hunk, the headlines screaming that the two were headed to the altar. He nearly lost it right there in the store and had taken the first of what eventually became a string of dangerous risks. He had called her from his cell phone and she just happened to be home. He could no longer remember exactly what he'd said to her, but knew that it had been so abusive and cruel that he'd reduced her to tears.

After that, they hadn't seen each other for several months and he felt sure now that her relationship with Poulton had heated up during this time. She had broken the impasse first by calling him at work on his private line, the line that didn't go through his secretary or assistant. She had rented a cottage on Big Pine for a couple of weeks and of course he had gone to see her. Not once, not twice, but almost daily.

But eventually she had left Big Pine and he had descended into obsession again and it was this same obsession that had prompted him to follow her Thursday night. His obsession had killed her.

Get over it.

Right. He had to move forward. If he kept moving forward, the past would not catch up to him.

He picked up the phone to call his wife and invite her to a celebration dinner.

Chapter 5

Kit and Rita Vasquez walked parallel to the dock, beneath a splendid November sky that simply begged to be celebrated. In the distance, the soft green hills loomed like camel's humps.

"Did I ever tell you that I got married to my second husband on a day as gorgeous as this one?" Rita asked.

Rita, who had recently turned forty, had been married and divorced three times and Kit couldn't keep the ex-hubbies straight. "Refresh my memory. Hubby number two was the gaucho?"

"Please. Husband number two was the Argentine rancher."

"Oh. Right."

Rita made a face and reached behind her head to lift her shining black hair off her shoulders. She fixed it there with a clip and now the bold lines of her jaw and the long sweep of her neck were visible. She was Argentinean by birth and American by marriage to hubby number one, a Manhattan businessman twenty years her senior whom she'd married when she was eighteen. He had sent her to college and then to law school, and halfway through law school they had gotten divorced. Her second marriage—to the Argentinean rancher—had been brief, Kit recalled that much, and the marriage to hubby number three had died a couple years after she had become Kit's partner.

She often reminded Kit of a flamenco dancer—the same kind of lithe, quick body and innate grace, the same flair for color and style. She attracted men the way certain flowers drew butterflies and pity the fools who mistook her for nothing more than a pretty face.

"Poulton's sister called four times before you got in this morning," Rita said. "She wired the retainer fee at eight A.M. and at nine, I called to verify that it's been deposited."

"She called us four times to tell us that?"

"Actually, she wanted to speak to you directly."

"I hope you told her rule number three."

Rita laughed. "Absolutely. 'Whatever you have to say to Kit can be said to me, Mrs. Courtland. And vice versa.' "

"So did she?"

"Yeah, she wanted to know when one of us was going to see Steve."

"Where's she live?"

"Martha's Vineyard. She's got MS, so she won't be coming down here."

"Is she prepared to put up a substantial amount of money for bond—if we can even get bond?"

"Whatever it takes. Those were her exact words. Despite the fact that Poulton is a medical resident, I don't think we're going to get a bond with a murder one charge. *If* that's how the indictment reads when Opitz hands it down."

"You talk to Opitz yet?"

"That proverbial bear shit in our woods about half past eight this morning. He wants to meet, discuss things, you know, the usual Opitz bullshit."

Ever since Opitz had beat her in court, his attitude toward her had been one of patronizing courtesy, a sort of gloating demeanor that he tried to disguise with a false openness.

"I have a weird feeling about this case, Rita."

"Yeah? Weird how? Weird good? Weird bad? Weird as in, we shouldn't take this case?"

"I don't know. An odd thing happened with Ryan Saturday night," she said, and gave Rita the abbreviated, three-sentence version of the incident. "That may have something to do with how I'm feeling."

"So what do the stars say?" Rita asked, referring to Kit's closet passion for astrology. "I mean, is the sun retrograde or something?"

"The sun and moon don't go retro."

"Mercury, I meant Mercury. I think I meant Mercury. When it's retro, communication, travel, and contracts are fucked, right?"

"Right. And no, it's not retrograde. But Jupiter and Saturn are."

"Luck. And Saturn is authority, rules, Dad, older men."

"Hey," Kit said with a laugh. "You actually remember the stuff I talk about. What's Poulton's birthdate?"

"He's a Scorpio. I don't know where he was born or when."

"Guess we'll have to ask."

"I was actually asking what the stars say about Ryan."

Kit didn't know. When it came to reading her son's charts for information, her knowledge seemed to go the way of the dodo bird. Abuelita, who had taught her astrology, blamed this failing on emotional ties. The closer you were to the person whose chart you were interpreting, the more difficult and erroneous that information often tended to be.

"I don't have a clue."

They neared the Tango County police station and jail, a

two-story structure with a wooden front that had stood here since the early 1800s. The inside of the jail had an oddly homey feel to it, like an old bed-and-breakfast—knots in the pine walls, tall windows in the lobby, throw rugs on the wooden floors. They went through the metal detector and their briefcases, bags, and laptops went through one of the county's new X-ray machines.

They were subsequently escorted into the conference room, where the furniture smelled new and the walls had been freshly painted a pale celery green. While Rita set up the laptops and a portable printer and the videocamera, Kit tested the recorder and brought out writing pads and pens.

Two cops brought Poulton in a few minutes later. Kit jotted the time and date on one of the pads: *11/5/01, 10:26 A.M.* Poulton didn't speak; he merely stood next to one of the cops while the other unlocked his handcuffs. He looked younger than his twenty-eight years, Kit thought, a boyish face with blue eyes that scrutinized and absorbed everything around him without seeming to do so. He had the long, beautiful hands of a pianist or a surgeon. He was several inches taller than Kit, definitely not overweight, and at the moment his expression gave away nothing about what he felt.

Although he was attractive, he wasn't handsome in a Hollywood way. He was no Russell Crowe, a tabloid link to Diane in the past.

"Would you like one of us to remain inside, Ms. Parrish?" asked the taller of the two cops.

"It's not necessary."

"Sit down, Poulton," snapped the shorter cop, and jerked the chair over to him, then pressed his hands against Poulton's shoulders, forcing him into the chair. Kit started to protest, but Rita cast her a sharp, warning look that clearly communicated that a confrontation wasn't in the best interest of the client.

"We lock the door and you can . . ."

"I know the routine," Kit said curtly.

As soon as both cops had left, Rita started the video camera, Poulton pulled his chair over to the table, and Kit introduced herself. "Since you and Rita have already spoken, Dr. Poulton, you know what to expect from here on in. But we're going to need quite a bit of information. Do you have any objection to the video camera? Or to the recorder?"

"No. Whatever it takes."

Kit recorded the data. "Today is Monday, November fifth, 2001. It's now 10:42 A.M. Present are Kit Parrish, Rita Vasquez, and Steve Poulton."

"How long had you been seeing Diane Jackson?" Rita asked, joining them now at the table.

"Since December fifth, 1998. We met at the University of Miami medical school. She was there doing research for a movie. I showed her around, we hit it off . . ." He paused and a look of excruciating pain flickered like shadows across his features. "Just for the record, I didn't kill her. I . . . I loved her, for Christ's sake. That night . . . we had an argument, she got pissed, and left."

"We'll get to that part in a moment, Dr. Poulton," Rita said. "Let's try to keep this chronological for right now. It'll make our investigation easier."

Kit noted the fissures in his composure, that raw emotion leaking through, and decided he was either a very good actor or innocent. "How often did you see her?" she asked.

Poulton rubbed his wrists, where the cuffs had made the skin nearly raw. He had regained his composure again, just as Kit would expect a doctor to do. This guy wouldn't fall apart in the midst of a crisis; his training was too ingrained.

"We saw each other as often as we could. She was busy, I was busy, and we lived on opposite coasts. . . ."

"I meant in the beginning," Kit said. "How often did you see her while she was doing research?"

"She hung around the hospital for a week, observing autopsies, sitting in on a few classes. We saw each other a lot."

"When did you become lovers?"

It was immediately obvious that he didn't want to answer such intimate questions. But it was also obvious, Kit thought, that he knew the score. He realized that his best defense lay in utter and total honesty. "By the second day."

"Who initiated it?" Rita asked.

"She did."

"So she stayed at your apartment during that time?"

"Yes. Then she had to fly back to the west coast and we talked nearly every night for a couple of weeks and we exchanged a lot of e-mails. I still have them. They're on my computer."

"Which is where?" Kit asked.

"At my place in Key Largo."

He ticked off the address and Kit jotted it down. "So after that, when did you see her next?"

"We spent Christmas together, dividing our time between my place in Key Largo and my apartment in Miami. On New Year's Day, I had to work, so she took a flight to Key West to check on her property on Tango Key. She was building a home there. She was supposed to fly back to LA that night. She was also supposed to call me before she left and she never did."

"Did she ever say why?"

"She said she forgot."

"You sound doubtful," Kit remarked.

Poulton rubbed his beautiful hands over his face, sat forward, then back, then got up and began to walk around the room, hands jammed in the pockets of his prison blues. "She had an incredible memory. You've got to have a good memory to memorize lines in a script. After the weeks we'd spent together, it's not likely that she would *forget* to call me."

Rita had gone over to the videocamera, moving it so that it followed Poulton's restless movement around the room. She leaped in with another question. "So what do you think really happened?"

"I don't know."

"Was she seeing other men, Dr. Poulton?"

He stopped, glanced over at Rita, then at Kit. "Look, my name's Steve, okay?" He spoke crossly, color flaring in his cheeks. "If you two are going to defend me, I have to know you as well as you know me. So let's just dispense with the *doctor* shit."

Passion, fire, a temper. Interesting, Kit thought. "I'm Kit."

"I'm Rita."

The three of them looked at each other, none of them speaking. Then Poulton said, "Me Tarzan," and they all cracked up.

It was better after that, questions and answers coming more rapidly, more fluidly. She and Rita no longer had to pull teeth to get information out of him. He talked with a distinct urgency. "Every so often I'd see her name linked in the tabloids with different guys. But she always said those were publicity stunts."

"So you think she was committed to her relationship with you?" Kit asked.

"In one sense. I mean, when we were together, she was fully *there*. And yet, there were parts of her life I knew nothing about. So yes, it's possible that she was involved

with someone else. I became a lot more suspicious about
that possibility last year. We would have plans and she'd
call at the last moment and change the plans or say she
couldn't make it. I don't know. I think I knew there was
someone else, but I just didn't want to think about it too
closely.'' He reached into his shirt pocket and withdrew a
folded sheet of paper. ''Last night, I jotted down a time line,
as nearly as I can remember it.''

Kit unfolded the sheet, which was covered with Poulton's
small, legible printing. Apparently the scrawl on physician
prescriptions, she mused, was something that doctors learned
once they practiced medicine. Poulton's precision with dates
and places astonished her. ''This will definitely help. How
do you remember all this stuff? It goes back two and three
years.''

''Intense emotions, I guess. On my computer, you'll find
a journal that has more detail about dates and things. Diane
and I both kept journals. She took hers everywhere.''

''Did she have it with her at the Peninsula Motel?'' Kit
asked.

''Sure.''

''You saw it?''

''Yeah, we were joking that we should turn our respective
journals over to each other.''

Kit jotted: *check property list for journal*. Rita apparently
had the same thought, because she quickly paged through
a sheaf of papers, then shook her head. ''There's no journal
on the property list, Kit.''

''It was in her suitcase,'' Poulton said, sitting forward.
''I remember seeing it there, half buried in her clothes.''

''We'll check with the police,'' Kit assured him.

''So you were at the motel with her?'' Rita asked.

''Yeah, earlier in the afternoon, not too long after she

checked in. I got off work early, but not early enough to pick her up in Key West. I met her at the Peninsula.''

"There was a used condom in the motel wastebasket, Steve." Kit finished scrolling through the notes on her laptop, then looked up at him. "Forensics is running tests on it. I'm assuming it was yours."

"Yeah." His gaze dropped to his hands again. "That's what we argued about."

"A condom?" Rita exclaimed.

"Well, that's what started it. She wanted kids in the worst way. I wanted to wait until I was finished with my residency. It was a long-standing bone of contention between us. But I just wasn't going to take chances. That afternoon, though, it wasn't an issue and she never brought it up during dinner, either. It was just later, when we went to the bar. That's what we argued about, about when to have children. I don't know what set her off. I was thinking last night, going over it all in my head, and it seems like she provoked the argument."

Kit scribbled more notes. "About what time was that? Do you remember?"

"I happened to look at the clock behind the bar just as she stormed out. It was eleven twenty-two."

The time went into her notes as well. "Did you go after her?"

"No. She made it pretty clear that if I did, we were history."

"Did she have a car?"

"She walked to the restaurant and I drove over there."

"Why did you go separately?" Rita asked. "You were at the motel that afternoon."

"I left the motel around five, I guess it was, to pick up my car. I was having some work done on it. At Harrold's Garage over on White Street. As it turned out, I had to wait awhile, so I called Diane and told her I'd just meet her at the restaurant. Anyway, I left the bar around a quarter of twelve and walked back to the public lot across the street from the restaurant. My stuff was in the car because I knew I was going back to Key Largo that night. I headed out of town and got to Key Largo around two-thirty, I guess it was. I had to stop for gas. I slept for a few hours, then got up the next morning and was at work by eight.''

Rita made notes of her own, then asked, "Did you talk to anyone during the trip or in Key Largo?"

"No. I bought the gas with my ATM card."

Finally, Kit thought. *A bit of proof.* A receipt would show the time and the name of the gas station. "Do you have the receipt?"

He shook his head. "The printing thing was out of paper."

Get ATM records, she wrote. "I'll need the name of your bank. This could be the thing that establishes your whereabouts. About what time did you stop? And where was it, do you recall?"

"Marathon. I'm not sure of the time. I'm guessing it was one-thirty, maybe one forty-five."

"Do we know Diane's time of death yet?" Kit asked Rita.

"Dr. Luke promised he'd have something today."

"So you were at work by eight," Kit said. "I'm assuming that's documented, that there are witnesses."

"An entire hospital filled with witnesses," Poulton replied. "The police came to the hospital around noon, told me Diane was dead, asked me a lot of questions. I . . . I was a fucking zombie. . . . At some point, after they left, I realized I might need an attorney. That's when I called my sister. The cops arrested me Sunday morning."

"Your sister is willing to pay whatever it takes to get you out on bond, Steve," Kit told him. "But frankly, with a murder one charge, we're not very hopeful about getting bond at all.''

He paused in his relentless pacing and rubbed a hand over his face. "Look, my sister is a wonderful woman. But she's a control freak. I'd rather sit in jail than have her put up her money.''

Now *that,* Kit mused, was mighty interesting.

"What's my defense going to cost?'' he asked.

"A lot,'' Kit said, and told him the cost per hour.

She felt him figuring this, that, the angles.

"Jesus,'' he murmured. "Does that come with guarantees?''

"Nope,'' said Rita.

"I don't have that kind of money.''

"Your sister is paying for your defense.''

"Then I definitely don't want her to pay for bail, even if I *can* get it.''

"What's the arrest going to do to your residency?'' Rita asked.

"Nothing good,'' Poulton said softly.

Kit made a new file on her laptop, then set it in front of Poulton. "Before we leave, we need a list of things: the name of your bank, the address for the house Diane was building, everything you can recall seeing in her room, no matter how insignificant it seems, the names and addresses of members of her family—''

"She was estranged from her family.''

"For how long?''

"Ever since she split for Hollywood. Eight, nine years.''

"Any particular reason?''

"Yeah. They're hillbillies and she wasn't.''

"We also need the exact address for your place in Key Largo, the name of your supervisor at Jackson Memorial, the address for Harrold's Garage, the names of the restaurant

and bar where you and Diane were on Thursday night, and
anything else that might helps us in our investigation. Oh,
by the way, do you know your exact time of birth?''

"Seven twenty-two.''

"A.M. or P.M.?''

"A.M.''

Sun close to the ascendant, she thought. Good. "What
date and which place?''

"October twenty-four, 1973, Miami, Florida. Why?''

"Just curious,'' she said, and turned to Rita. "Make sure
you read his list aloud so we have a video record as well.
I've got to make some calls. I'll be right back.''

Minutes later, she sat on a bench outside the police station,
where the air smelled of pine and ocean, and called the
county coroner's office to find out if the autopsy on Jackson
would be done by the end of today. Dr. Luke, she was told,
was in the middle of the autopsy now and would be finished
by one. Kit left her cell number and asked that he call her
as soon as he was finished.

Her second call was to Carmela Perez—Abuelita—the
old Cuban woman who had been her astrology teacher, her
brother's primary source on the Cuban Mafia stories that
had won him the Pulitzer, and the woman who looked after
Ryan when she got tied up. The old woman herself answered
the phone, her melodic voice soft against a backdrop of
chirping birds.

"Carmela, it's Kit.''

"Ah, *mí amor.* I was just thinking of you.''

"Would it be too much trouble for you to pick up Ryan
and Becky from school today?''

"It's never trouble. You're taking the Poulton case,
right?''

Abuelita always unnerved her. "How'd you know that?''

"I woke up this morning feeling its certainty. Be careful, Kit. I have an uneasy feeling about all this."

First Hutchin, now Abuelita, she thought. "I should be able to pick up Ryan around dinner."

"Don't worry about it. We'll probably go up to the beach at Bahia Honda. We'll take Oro, too."

"Carmela, if you get the chance, talk to Ryan about the voices he hears," she said, and gave her a quick rundown of the events Saturday night and their conversation on the way to school this morning.

"He didn't know what he was looking for when he was digging?"

"No."

"I'll certainly talk to him, *mí amor.* And don't worry about the time."

"Thanks, Carmela, I appreciate it."

"Kit?"

"Yes?"

"Get the birth data for Poulton and the young woman. We need to look at their charts."

"He's a Scorpio." Kit rattled off the birth data. "Diane's birth data should be public record."

"We'll need the time of her death and his arrest."

"I'll do what I can."

"See you then."

When Pete had vanished, she wasn't good enough—or objective enough—to use astrology to find him or to determine what had happened, but Abuelita was. She believed that Pete had been murdered, possibly by someone he knew, and that a woman was somehow involved. Kit had never shared that information with the police because she knew how it would look. She didn't intend to lose business over it. But perhaps she would pass the information along to Webster.

Kit returned to the conference room, where Rita was now reading aloud what Poulton had written. He stood at one of the windows, gazing out at the park across the street. She couldn't tell whether he was listening or was off in a world of his own.

"Do you happen to know anything about Diane's will, Steve?" Kit asked as she joined him at the window.

"I don't even know if she *had* a will."

"Did she have a bank account here in the keys?"

"She opened one at Tango Sun when she bought the property."

"Who's building her house?"

"Guy named Craig Farmer."

No surprise. Farmer & Brothers Construction built a lot of the homes on the island, especially at the northern end, where homes started in the millions. "If you think of anything else that might be useful in our investigation, Steve, here're my phone numbers." She handed him a card. "They can't keep you from calling your attorney."

His face softened as he pocketed the card. "Thanks. I feel more hopeful now than I did an hour ago."

"Don't talk about this case to anyone unless Rita or I are present."

He nodded.

"I still have to talk to the state's attorney. They may try to go for a deal, Steve. What're your thoughts on that?"

His expression hardened. "I'm not interested in any deal. I didn't kill her."

Kit's and Rita's eyes met across the room and Kit knew they both believed him.

* * *

"She was involved with someone else," Rita said as soon as they stepped outside. "I mean, when a woman is cheating on her significant other, she *forgets.*"

"The voice of experience."

Rita shrugged, an admission that she had been in that position with at least one of her husbands. "And that argument in the bar. It sounds to me like she had other plans for the rest of the night and instigated the argument to get rid of Steve."

"I agree."

"So all we have to do is find the other guy."

"You make it sound easy, Rita."

"Not easy, but it gives us a direction. We have to keep in mind that the killer was smart enough to frame Poulton."

"Or lucky enough."

"Interesting thought. That it wasn't premeditated."

Interesting—or wrong? Kit wondered.

Jackson's property, a lush, rolling acre just outside of Pirate's Cove, stood among half a dozen homes at the edge of a cliff that overlooked the Gulf of Mexico. Hidden behind thickets of pine and clusters of banyan trees, the partially constructed house didn't look to Kit as if it intended to be just a weekend getaway.

"Five or six thousand square feet, that'd be my guess," Rita said as they walked the periphery. "I bet the piece of property alone cost her a million or more."

"No telling what Farmer was charging her for the house. Probably upward of five or six million."

"Even if she has a will, it's probably a California will. He's going to have to get in line with her other creditors."

They reached the back of the house and walked on a bit

farther, following a footpath through the weeds and deep shade. Birds twittered from the trees, dragonflies darted through the November air. The closer they got to the edge of the cliff, the stronger the wind blew. The air here smelled of mystery, of Gothic novels. But in this novel, the heroine wasn't old-fashioned. She was independent and rich, famous and recognized, and this place had been intended as her refuge, her sanctuary.

Kit suspected there was a message in that thought for her, given the privacy of her own home on Sugarloaf. She remembered what the media attention had been like following Pete's disappearance—microphones in her face, flashbulbs flashing, cameras clicking madly, the crush of journalists. Multiply her brief exposure a thousand times and that was what life had been like for Diane Jackson on a daily basis.

No wonder she had needed a place to hide.

They stopped several yards from the edge of the cliff, where the wind swept up off the gulf and threatened to whisk them away. Kit held on to a nearby branch, but Rita ventured forward, head bent into the wind, the hem of her skirt flapping wildly, her hair blowing around despite the clip that tried to hold it all together. She stopped no more than half a foot from the edge of the cliff, so close that Kit felt dizzy just looking at her. Rita, a classical Aries, thought Kit, just had to see how the land dropped away at the edge—the violence of the jagged rocks, the grand sweep of flawless blue sky, the crash of waves against the shore way down below.

Rita slowly raised her arms and her head dropped back and she stood there a moment, a silhouette against a sea of blue, her hair now loose and tumbling darkly down her spine. She looked like someone paying homage to some ancient goddess. Then Rita shouted into the wind and the wind hurled the words back toward Kit. *"Hey, fucker, we're on to you."*

* * *

Dr. Luke's offices, tucked away in the rear of the Key West Hospital, were as eccentric as the man himself. No drab colors here, Kit thought. Nothing to remind you this was death's kingdom. The walls shimmered with pastel colors and were covered with eleven-by-fourteen photographs of island scenes—beaches, windsurfers, sailboats, conch houses.

His secretary, a sweet young thing as bright and colorful as the walls, told Kit to go on into the lab. Dr. Luke was hunched over a microscope, only the tufts of his gray hair visible. He was so intent on whatever he was doing, he didn't realize she had entered the room until she said, "Hey, you need a break, Aaron."

He raised his head and peered at her over the rims of his bifocals, his smile quick, brilliant. "What I need is a hug, kiddo."

Luke was a small, compact man whose head, when they hugged, barely reached her throat. Like Hutchin, he was one of those people who had circumnavigated the periphery of her life for years. The difference was that she knew him personally—his wife, his kids, his grandchildren. He and her father, a retired pathologist, had worked together in the Miami coroner's office during the eighties and still played chess at least once a month, when her parents weren't traveling.

"I want you to see something." Luke took her hand and led her over to the counter where half a dozen microscopes were lined up.

Kit peered through the microscope at what appeared to be a blood sample. "What am I looking for?"

"It's what you're looking *at*." The excitement in his voice was palpable. "It's fetal blood."

"Fetal?" Her head snapped up.

"Diane Jackson was about ten weeks pregnant." Luke straddled another stool and rubbed his hands over his jeans. "She had type O blood. So does Poulton. That means the baby should be an O. But the baby was A negative. It wasn't Poulton's child."

Kit threw her arms around his neck and bussed him soundly on the cheek. "You've just given me the foundation of a defense, Aaron. How'd she die?"

"From suffocation, just as it appeared. There were no bruises on her body, no skin or blood under her nails. No struggle, in other words. She knew the man, that'd be my guess. I'm still running DNA tests on the semen in that condom, but I don't expect any surprises on that count. Odd about the condom, though. Does that mean she didn't know she was pregnant or that she knew and didn't want to change the routine with Poulton because he might become suspicious?"

"Interesting points. You think like a lawyer, Aaron. What's the estimated time of death?"

"This is where it gets tricky. According to what I know, she left the bar sometime before midnight. Her body was found around eight the next morning. Based on the serotonin levels in her blood, I'd have to place time of death between midnight and four A.M."

Not good enough. If Poulton bought gas in Marathon between 1:30 A.M. and 2:00 A.M., the prosecution could make a case for his having killed her shortly after midnight. It wouldn't be a stretch for him to make it to Marathon in a little over an hour, not at that time of night, when traffic was minimal. One way or another, she would get around it. The most important thing was the fact that the baby couldn't be Poulton's, therefore Diane had been involved with someone else. All Kit had to do was prove beyond a reasonable doubt that the someone else killed her.

Chapter 6

Maybe she doesn't want me anymore.

The thought kept running through Ryan's mind, scaring him so deeply that he bit his lip to keep from crying. He craned his neck, looking anxiously for his mother's blue van in the long line of cars that moved slowly toward the pickup area at the front of his school. But he didn't see the van. His mother had said that if she couldn't pick him up, Abuelita would, yet he didn't see her car, either.

She left me.

His nails dug into his thighs, he swiped at his eyes. *No crying.*

He sat with other fourth graders under the canopy at the front of the school, the cars snaking along like some giant and colorful anaconda. Maybe he would be sitting here when it got dark because his mother had moved out of their house and left him, and Abuelita couldn't take him because she was too old. No adult wanted a kid who did what he'd done Saturday night, digging like a loony in the field.

He remembered digging, his hands clawing at the hole to

make it bigger, dirt jammed up under his nails. He dug to find what he'd buried, but he didn't have any idea what he had buried or when or why. He didn't remember burying anything. This burying and digging, he knew, came from the thing that lived in the black hole. From the Other.

He rubbed his eyes and forced himself to page through the art book in his lap. He tried not to think about his mother leaving him, about who the Other was or why It made him do things like go off in the middle of the night to dig in a field. He needed to be more careful.

He turned the pages of the art book until he reached the section on van Gogh. His art teacher had told his class that if you really wanted to be a good artist—and Ryan did—then you needed to study the masters. He studied the three paintings—of sunflowers, a bridge in a meadow, and the third, a self-portrait. Did you have to be crazy to paint like this?

As soon as he thought this, the page blurred and everything around him melted like wax, colors running together. . . . *And he's standing in a museum, staring at the bridge in the meadow painting, at van Gogh's signature down there in the right-hand corner. He's with a lady, a very pretty lady with curly hair. Elation fills him like air in a balloon. . . .*

"Hey, Ryan."

At the sound of the voice, Ryan's head snapped up. His heart pounded like he'd been running, sweat poured from his hands, but the world looked okay again. Becky Landress waved as she made her way toward him through the crowd of students. Her long, dark hair fluttered in the breeze. This year, the gifted seventh and eighth graders had their own building at his elementary school because there wasn't room for them at their middle school. It meant he saw Becky sometimes during the day, like at lunch, and that they could still carpool in the afternoons.

"Hi, Beck."

"I'm riding home with you today, remember?"

He felt a sudden relief. If Becky was getting a ride home with him, then his mother definitely hadn't abandoned him. She or Abuelita would be here. "My mom's late."

"There's Abuelita's car."

Becky pointed at a shiny old diesel Mercedes coming out from behind an island of trees, the hood shimmering in the heat. Ryan picked up his backpack and hurried after Becky, past the kindergartners and first graders and out along the curb to where the older kids sat. He kept his left arm close to his side so no one could see the rash that covered his arm from the wrist to the elbow.

The rash had broken out just after he'd gone into the field to dig. He hadn't shown it to his mother; he didn't want to go to the doctor. He hoped maybe something in the dirt where he'd been digging had caused it. But in his heart, he knew better. It was the act of digging that had caused the rash. But he still didn't have any idea what the connection was about. It was like electricity. He could plug a lamp into the socket and a light came on, but he didn't understand *why* it happened.

The back door of Abuelita's Mercedes swung open. He and Becky tossed their packs onto the seat and piled in. Oro, in the front seat with Abuelita, barked a greeting, then climbed over the seat and into the back, where she promptly covered Ryan's face with slobbery kisses. Abuelita laughed. "Ready for the beach?"

"We don't have suits," he and Becky said at the same time.

"Not true." She tossed two bags into the back. "I stopped by the swim store. The sizes should be about right. Get the door, Becky."

Becky shut the door and off they went, the Mercedes

darting around cars, cutting back into line, darting out again. As soon as they were on the open highway, Abuelita let down all the windows, popped in a CD, and the Mercedes flew along the highway with "Born to Be Wild" blaring from the speakers.

Driving anywhere with Abuelita was always an adventure. She was as old as Stonehenge, but wasn't like any other old person Ryan had ever met. She wore glasses only to read, occasionally used a cane, but she still drove, shopped, and did her magical work, as his mother called it, about thirty hours a week. Ryan knew she was very rich, yet she didn't live like a rich person. She knew a lot of important people, yet she wasn't a snob. She was, in fact, one of Ryan's favorite people in the world.

Sometimes when he was with her, the Other stirred around inside him, but not in a threatening way. He didn't know what that meant, either.

They sped into Bahia Honda, dust flying up behind them. Abuelita waved at the guy in the toll booth, who thumbed them on through without having to pay, and Abuelita said, "See? There are benefits to being a senior citizen." Then she laughed to herself, a quiet, private laugh, like she'd made a joke.

The wind had whipped her hair loose and, as they got out, she reached back and removed combs and clips so that her hair fell free, a thick waterfall as white as her shirt, capri pants, and sandals. She looked as wild as the music that had blared from the speakers, Ryan thought, the wind blowing through her hair, one hand shading her eyes against the sun as she watched Becky run off to change, Oro trotting along after her.

"Está bíen, mi amor?" She slipped an arm around his shoulders. *"Dígame la verdad."*

He never had studied Spanish, but it seemed he had understood it for most of his life, a fact that bothered his mother. Whenever the Spanish issue came up, his mother would call him an *enigma* and run her fingers through his hair and try to smile. But he always saw the truth in her eyes, her worry.

"*Estoy bíen*," he replied.

Abuelita leaned down and touched his shoulders. "I don't hear *bíen* in your voice, Ryan. I hear . . . hmmm. . . ." She turned her head to one side, listening to a voice he couldn't hear. "Secrets. Yes, that's it. I hear secrets."

Sometimes she knew things just by looking at him. Other times she read the cards for him or tossed cowrie shells or small, smooth sticks and read the patterns they made. His mother said that was part of Abuelita's magic. But she didn't know the half of it. Ryan had seen Abuelita do things that were really magical. He had seen her move objects without touching them. He had seen her make things disappear and then reappear somewhere else. His mother said Abuelita was like Houdini or David Copperfield, an incredible magician. But Ryan knew better. He knew Abuelita's kind of magic was *real*.

Even when she touched him, as she was doing now, with her hands just resting against his shoulders, he could feel her magic singing through him. It came out of her hands and went into him and everything around him blurred. In another second or two, the air would go silent and he would feel her inside his thoughts. Once, he'd seen a movie about an alien that could get information out of people just by touching them; that was how Abuelita's hands would begin to feel in another few seconds.

"Don't," he said crossly, and wrenched free of her hands.

She stepped back, frowning, and pushed her sunglasses back into her hair. Her eyes, clear and dark, were like tiny mirrors in which Ryan could see miniature reflections of himself. He didn't like what he saw, a skinny kid who looked scared.

"You're right," Abuelita said. "I must stop doing that. Go change. We'll head over to the Atlantic side. It's calmer."

He stood there staring at her and suddenly wanted to tell her everything, about the digging and the black hole under his bed and the thing that lived in the hole. He wanted to tell her about the voice of the Other. "Help me," he whispered, and then, to his complete horror, he started to cry.

Abuelita put her arms around his shoulders, holding him so closely against her that he could breathe in the sweet smell of her skin. Then she took his hand and they walked over to one of the huge sea grape trees and sat in its shade, on a big piece of driftwood.

"Tell me what you feel when these things are happening to you. Or when you hear the voice."

"It hasn't happened that many times." Well, that wasn't exactly true. The black hole sensation had happened twice before Saturday night and there had been other things before then that were only now coming back to him. Things like what had happened when he'd been waiting at parent pickup and had seen himself with the pretty lady, at a museum. "I feel scared. I don't know what else I feel because . . ." *I'm someone else.*

"Because why?"

"Because I don't feel like me."

"Who do you feel like?"

"A big person."

"Does this big person have a name?"

Yes, but I can't find it. "I don't know."

"Is this person a man or a woman?"

"A man."

"Tell me more about this man, Ryan."

Just then, Becky came skipping across the parking lot. "We'll finish talking later," Abuelita said softly.

They walked over to the Atlantic side, where the beach was wide and the water was shallow for such a long way that when he looked over his shoulder, Abuelita wasn't any bigger than an ant. After a while, he and Becky returned to where Abuelita was sitting. She gestured at the pile of shells she'd collected.

"Pick twelve," she said to Becky.

"For what?"

"Go on. This is fun," Ryan told her.

Ryan usually picked his shells slowly, passing his hand through the air just an inch above them until he felt heat or cold or a *zingy* feeling that meant he should choose a certain shell. Becky, though, picked her shells fast.

"Now what?" she asked.

"Toss them."

Becky tossed them and Abuelita, already on her knees in the sand, leaned forward, studying them.

"You want your mother back. You love your father very much, but he is not your mother. Some day, you will forgive your mother for leaving as she did."

The blood drained from Becky's face and she looked accusingly at Ryan. "You talked to her about me."

"I did not."

"The shells talk to me, little one."

"What else do you see?" Becky asked.

"Little pictures. Drawings. Sketches, yes, they're sketches. Not your sketches. You and this other person, the artist, keep them secret. There will come a time, though, when the drawings can no longer be kept secret. Do you understand what I'm saying?"

Ryan's stomach knotted. *Don't tell, please don't tell*, he thought at Becky.

"Yeah, I understand," Becky replied, and didn't give anything away by even looking in Ryan's direction.

"Oh, one other thing," Abuelita said. "You're going to be on some sort of team." She paused. "I see colorful things. Strips of paper on a stick."

Becky giggled. "Pom-poms."

"And a red and white uniform."

"Cheerleading," Becky exclaimed.

"You make that team."

Becky let out a delighted whoop. "What else?" she asked eagerly.

"That's it for now, little one." Abuelita gathered up the shells and dug her cell phone out of her bag. "I have a few calls to make."

"We're going swimming," he said, grateful that the reading had ended and that Abuelita hadn't asked him to toss the shells. Now he wished he hadn't started crying in front of her, that he hadn't told her anything. "C'mon, Beck." And as soon as they were far enough away from Abuelita, he said, "Becky, you got to promise me something."

"What?"

"Don't ever tell anyone about the drawings." For three years now, he'd kept his sketch pad at Becky's house because he didn't want his mother to see it. "You have to swear."

"I swear, you know I do. But it sounds to me like we're not going to be able to keep them secret much longer. You heard what she said. The drawings are important and—"

He grabbed her arm. "Promise me," he hissed. "Promise you won't tell."

"Pinky promise," she said, and hooked her little finger around his.

Even though he knew Becky would never do anything on purpose to hurt him, he worried that his mother would find out about the sketches. If she did, she would think he was going bonkers and take him to the doctor.

Please, Beck, don't tell.

(2)

Ben Webster stood on the dock outside the snack bar at Bahia Honda, looking around for a man who had described himself as a conch with a face like leather. He'd said he would be wearing a red baseball cap. Considering the number of men around here who had faces like leather and wore dark caps, it wasn't much to go on. But only one of them, a guy scrubbing the deck of a fishing boat, wore a red cap.

He strolled over to the boat. "I'm looking for Bob Tilden."

The guy glanced up, the bill of the cap pulled low over his dark shades, and leaned against the mop he held. "You Webster?"

"Yeah."

"You don't look like a fed."

"What's a fed look like?"

"You know, coat, tie, white shirt . . ."

"Too damn hot."

Tilden laughed, dropped the mop, and motioned Webster aboard. They sat in canvas chairs, beneath a canvas roof, a cooler between them. Tilden didn't waste any time flipping open the lid of the cooler and digging two beers out of a load of ice. He tossed one to Webster, popped open the other, and tilted the can to his mouth, drinking down half of it before he said a word. Then he cut right to the chase.

"So what do you want to know about Pete?"

"Anything you can tell me. But for starters, what do you think happened to him?"

"I don't know, man. For a while, I figured he assumed another identity and took off."

"Why would he do that? It seems to me life was pretty good for him."

"Life was great for him. He had an incredible amount of freedom at the paper. It didn't matter what he wrote, as long as he got his weekly column in. He had two books published, had another in mind, and was doing better financially than he ever had. But you got to understand something about Pete. He didn't think like normal people think. He was intellectually eccentric."

"In what way? Give me an example."

Tilden didn't drink his beer. He guzzled it. Like so many natives of the keys whom Webster had met, Tilden drank too much. Maybe Hemingway had started the trend. Maybe it was the weather and the Jimmy Buffet laid-back lifestyles. Whatever Tilden's reason, Webster recognized the symptoms. His ex-brother-in-law was an alcoholic. A functional alcoholic. He was able to work at his high-powered job in the banking industry in the Northwest, but he started every day with a glass of OJ spiked with vodka, had several more drinks at lunch, several more with dinner, then continued drinking after dinner until, around eight in the evening, he passed out. Tilden crunched his empty beer can, tossed it into a nearby trash can, and reached into the cooler for another.

"An example. Okay. Pete and I were partners for a long time at the paper. He was the journalist, I was the photographer. It was close to Halloween and we were brainstorming in this Cuban café, looking for a spooky story. So he says how about if we spend the night in this hotel up the coast that's supposedly haunted? By 'up the coast', I figured he meant Lauderdale or maybe Palm Beach. But no, this guy is talking about St. Augustine. Hell, that's a good eight-hour drive from Miami, more depending on traffic. Eight hours up, eight hours back, no thanks.

"Not a problem for Pete. He simply charters a Cessna and a pilot to get us up there and back. *He* pays for it. He somehow convinces the management to give us the room that's supposedly haunted, even though the room was already taken for the night, and it turns out to be one of his most popular columns." Tilden leaned forward. "This is *not* the way most journalists think, okay?"

"So did you meet the ghost?"

Tilden laughed. "We met something, but damned if I know what the hell it was. I got all kinds of weird shit on film. The film was analyzed by experts who couldn't prove fraudulence. The story about the analysis of the film was another one of his wildly popular columns. I mean, the man had a flare for the work."

"Around the time that he vanished, was he involved with anyone?"

"What'd Kit tell you about me, Agent Webster?"

"That you were Pete's closest friend. You went to college together, worked together, that's about it."

"Did she mention that she and I haven't seen each other since she was pregnant? That I've never even met her kid?"

"No."

"Oh, we've talked, traded e-mail, but it's mostly just a courtesy. We move in very different worlds now. Even when Pete was around, she didn't like me much. I think there was some sibling jealousy there. Pete confided in me about certain things that she knew nothing about. That bugged her."

"Things like his relationships with women?"

"Yeah."

"So he *was* involved with someone?"

"That's what he said. I never met her, he never even told me her name. But there was definitely a woman and he was nuts about her. When I told that to Kit after he disappeared, she refused to believe me. I believe her exact words were, 'If there was a woman, I'd know about her.' She completely dismissed the possibility. When the cops came around asking questions, I told them what I thought, which Kit disputed, so that was that. Her word carried more weight with them than mine, her being an attorney and his sister."

"Why was he so secretive about this woman?"

"Beats the shit outta me, man. Maybe she was married, maybe she wanted it that way, maybe he wanted it like that. Who knows? Like I said, Pete didn't think like ordinary people. She lived somewhere in the keys, I know that much. Pete said their relationship was complicated, but never said how it was complicated."

"Had you met other women in his life?"

"Sure. Just not this one."

Webster gazed off toward the trees and the campground to the right and some distance beyond the snack bar. The ground rose steeply there, ending finally at the old bridge that used to reach to the next island and that had been blown up during the filming of *True Lies*. He suspected there were a number of true lies in this complex picture that was emerging of Pete Beaupre. A woman, but who was she? Secrets, but why?

He thought back to his own marriage, to his ex-wife's periodic absences, her indifference toward him sexually, to his growing sense toward the end that she was seeing someone. If he hadn't been so involved with work, he might have noticed the symptoms earlier. Then again, maybe not. People tended to see what they wanted to see. The most likely explanation for Beaupre's secretiveness was that his mystery woman had been married.

"Is there anything else you can tell me about Pete? Any other people I should talk to?"

"His ex. His former editor. His folks. The old Cuban woman who—" He stopped suddenly and leaned forward in his chair, watching something off to the right. "What the hell. Is that a kid? I don't have my glasses on."

Webster glanced in the direction that Tilden was pointing. He started to say he didn't see anything when the kid shot out of the trees and headed straight up the slope toward the old bridge. The bridge that had been blown up. The bridge that had ended abruptly a hundred feet out over the water and seventy feet up.

"Jesus," Webster whispered, and leaped up and over the boat railing in a single, clumsy movement.

He tore away from the dock, Tilden tight at his heels. The kid vanished behind the trees again, but Webster caught sight of a dog racing behind the boy. Webster ran faster, crashing through the thick underbrush and pines that covered the steep slope. The boy appeared again, his arms tucked in close to his sides, his legs moving so fast they seemed to blur. Then, some distance behind him, Webster saw an old woman and a girl running after the boy.

He recognized the girl. Becky someone, the Parrish neighbor.

(3)

Ryan's breath exploded from his mouth, Becky kept shouting at him, Becky and Abuelita, shouting at him to stop. He heard Oro barking. Then he heard nothing but the voice of the Other, demanding that he run, pushing him faster, faster so that he could catch the lady, grab her hand, whip her around, hold her in his arms.

He saw her, the lady on the bridge, hurrying away from him, her strides long and fast, her arms swinging at her sides. His heart was breaking. The farther she moved from him, the deeper the ache inside of him. *"Wait!"* he shouted, but she didn't wait, she broke into a flat-out run. . . .

(4)

Webster reached the beginning of the bridge. He could see the kid clearly now, Ryan Parrish, his dog not far behind him. He tore up the bridge, waving his arms and shouting, "Hey, Ryan, hold on. . . ."

Behind Webster, the old woman and the girl screamed at Ryan to stop, but he kept on moving. He didn't seem to realize that the bridge ended in an abrupt and perilous drop. Webster closed the gap between them and, twenty feet before the end of the bridge, he hurled himself at Ryan and tackled him and they both crashed to the ground.

Webster struck the concrete first, using his body to shield Ryan's. He rolled onto his side, Ryan now kicking and sobbing and before he could get to his feet, the retriever sprang at him, her fierce snarls and barks sundering the air. She snapped at Webster's sleeve, tearing the fabric, then Tilden threw himself between the dog and Webster, buying him precious moments, giving the old woman and the girl time to reach them, to pull the dog away.

Webster rocked onto his knees, the boy crying softly, limp in his arms. "Ryan, hey, it's Mulder." Webster smoothed his hand over the boy's hair. "It's Agent Mulder. You okay?"

Ryan, sniffling, opened his eyes and looked at Webster. He blinked. "You're not Mulder. You're Agent Webster."

Reality check: he passed. Webster set him on the bridge,

Ryan ran his hand under his nose, looked at the dog, the old woman, the girl, and at Tilden. He suddenly scrambled to his feet and ran over to Tilden and threw his arms around Tilden's legs. "Bob," he said. "Bob."

"What?" Tilden muttered, and looked helplessly at Webster, then at the old woman.

She let go of the dog and swept past the girl to Ryan, pulling him away from Tilden. The retriever barked and raced around them and seemed as confused by the whole thing as Webster was.

Bob. Bob. Hadn't Tilden told him he'd never met Ryan? So how did Ryan know his name? *What the fuck's going on here?*

Before he had the chance to think about any of it, the old woman was hugging Tilden, murmuring, "You have made yourself a stranger, Roberto."

Words were exchanged in Spanish spoken too rapidly for Webster to understand. But he did catch the word *Abuelita*, and suddenly realized who this woman was. When she came over to him, he was still standing there stupidly, trying to sort through the intricate connections.

"You saved his life, *señor*." She took his hand in both of hers and held on tightly. "I am immensely grateful. I . . ." She paused, her dark eyes narrowed, and she whispered. "Pete. You have questions about Pete? You are . . . ?"

She let go of his hand and he felt the sudden absence of whatever had passed between them when she had touched him. "Agent Webster. Ben Webster."

"Agent?"

"He's a fed, Abuelita," said Tilden. "He's investigating Pete's disappearance."

Her eyes held Webster's for a long, uncomfortable moment. Then she fumbled in her fanny pack, brought out a business card, handed it to him. "Call me, señor. We must talk."

With that, she returned to the boy, the girl, the dog, and Tilden, leaving Webster alone and confused on the bridge that led nowhere.

Chapter 7

Tuesday, November 6

Hutchin ran along a jogging trail on Tango Key. Gulls pinwheeled, screeching, through the buttery morning light. All night, it seemed that he had hovered at the edge of sleep, haunted by images of Diane, of cabin 13, and of a possible life in the corridors of power. He'd awakened at five, his wife sleeping peacefully beside him, her conscience apparently as clear and unencumbered as a baby's. Last night at dinner, he hadn't told her about the call from Chief of Staff Godwin and wasn't sure why.

He ran harder and faster, his shoes pounding the path. Within, he felt like Humpty Dumpty after the fall and he didn't know if he could put the pieces back together again. He didn't even know where to begin. So he kept running, as if to outdistance his terror.

When he finally stopped, his sides on fire and his lungs heaving for air, he was shocked to find himself in front of the Peninsula Motel. His feet had brought him to the crossroads of his life, to the very opening between the hedges that allowed him an unencumbered view of cabin 13. He stood there with one hand pressed to his side, trying to catch his breath and struggling not to look toward the cabin. But in the end, he had to look, was *compelled* to look.

Even from here, he could see the yellow crime ribbon, the evidence of travesty. His mind filled, again, with those final images of Diane, prostrate on the bed, her eyes gazing upward. Those eyes, he knew, would haunt him the rest of his life.

He turned quickly away and jogged off in the direction from which he'd come, terror biting at his heels like some rabid dog. He glanced anxiously around, certain he would see an unmarked car parked nearby, a fed inside of it, watching him, taking notes.

He didn't stop running until he reached his car. He scrambled inside and drove fast across the bridge, clear at this hour of the morning. By the time the front gate of his home clattered shut behind him, he nearly collapsed from adrenaline exhaustion. He tore off his running shoes and sat down at the edge of the swimming pool, his hot, tired feet submerged in the water, his hands covering his face.

Get over it. You can't take it back.

If he failed to move forward, if he became mired in the past, then sooner or later he would make a mistake so huge that his travesty would be discovered. Look what had happened just now, his feet leading him back to the Peninsula. What might it be next time? Coming to in the bed where he'd smothered her? Wandering across her property on Tango Key? Weeping as he watched her movies?

Today is the first day of the rest of your life. Wasn't that how the adage went? Hokey, but he had to make it true. And he had to begin this first day of his life by telling his wife about Godwin's call.

"Hey, handsome."

"Hey, hon," he replied automatically, wondering how his wife had approached so silently.

Hon and Handsome, two peas in a pod, the result of nearly twenty-five years of marriage. He glanced back to see Isabel standing in the doorway, her timing so impeccable, it seemed like cosmic design. Her auburn hair, chin length and curly, shone in the early light. She still wore the clothes that she'd slept in—gym shorts and a T-shirt with a toucan on the front. Even at this hour of the morning, she moved with the ease of a woman born into a state of grace.

"You took an early run," she remarked, sitting beside him at the edge of the pool.

"I woke up early and couldn't go back to sleep."

He felt her eyes searching his face for what he wasn't saying, for the underlying reason for his restlessness. Isabel, psychological probe. "Last night at dinner, I got the feeling you wanted to tell me something. What was it?"

Embrace the present, he thought, and asked, "What would you think about moving again?"

"Let's see, this would be move number . . . what? Thirteen?"

A disturbing coincidence, Hutchin thought. Cabin 13, move 13. "Is that what it would be? I've lost count."

"Where would we be moving?"

Another woman might ask, first and foremost, *why* they should move. But Isabel wasn't like other women. It was one of the many traits that had attracted him to her way back when he was at Harvard and she was at Vassar.

"Georgetown. Northern Virginia. Southern Maryland."

"I like the weather here better."

Naturally. She was a Florida girl, a Tango Fritter, as natives of Tango Key were called.

"Why one of those places?"

"Just curious."

She laughed, a wonderful sound, filled with life and energy. The first time he'd heard her laugh, he'd been in a restaurant in Cambridge, having dinner with his parents and his fiancée. That musical laughter had exploded around them, each piece a separate note that contained the whole, as though the laughter itself were holographic.

Hutchin had whipped around in his chair and seen a slender young woman with waist-length hair, rising up onto her bare toes years before Kate Winslet had done it in *The Titanic*. Young men surrounded her and they started clapping and then the jukebox came on, some wild Mick Jagger tune blasting from it, and the young woman balanced exquisitely on her toes, her entire body weight of maybe a hundred pounds poised there.

He'd started clapping, too, clapping as his fiancée and parents looked on with utter disdain, and the young woman had started to spin like a ballerina on her strong little toes. People around them stood up to see better and Hutchin did the same, then pushed his way through the crowd to watch up close. By the time the spectacle wrapped up, his parents had left, his fiancée had stormed out, and he was having drinks with this delicious young woman, the sparks exploding between them. Six months later they were married.

For a long time, through the birth of their daughter and half a dozen moves and career promotions, their marriage had retained that wonderful spark. But as his commitment to ambition deepened, so did his love of power. He discovered that he was very good at what he did and that the law really was his mistress. A demanding mistress. To satisfy her, something had to go and what went was his personal life—not all of it, but enough so that he wasn't around for his daughter's ballet lessons and piano recitals, her school functions and homework problems.

And he wasn't around for his wife, whom he suspected had gone elsewhere.

Maybe, in the beginning, Diane had been payback for his suspicions that his wife had strayed. But only in the beginning. Then his obsession had subsumed him.

Get over it.

"Okay, I can't stand the suspense, Hutch. What's going on?" she asked finally.

"I've made the short list for attorney general."

There. He'd said it.

"What?" Her eyes widened and she threw her arms around his neck, then rocked back, hands at the sides of his face, her astonishment surpassed only by her joy. "My God, Hutch . . . you've worked your entire career for a chance like this."

"I won't do it without your support."

"Of course you have my support. Why would you even doubt that?"

Because we have issues, Isabel. Because I killed a woman Thursday night. Because I held a pillow over her beautiful, despicable face and didn't let go until she was dead. Because the feds and then Congress and then the media are going to put me—and you—under a microscope.

"Because it means our lives would be completely different. More public. Political."

"I'd still be able to teach, right?"

"Absolutely."

"And Barb can still continue at Amherst."

"Sure."

"Tell me what the attorney general oversees."

"Well, for starters, he or she oversees the budget for the Justice Department. That's somewhere in the vicinity of twenty-two billion. The attorney general's jurisdiction includes the FBI, immigration and naturalization, the DEA, federal prosecutors and marshals, and federal prisons.''

"And we wouldn't have Secret Service people following us around or anything." She paused, then added, very softly: "At least, not until you get into the White House."

Hutchin realized she was asking him a question: would this appointment, if he won it, become a stepping stone to even greater power? "Hey," he said with a laugh. "The only thing that's happened is that I'm on the list. There are two other candidates."

"Who are they?"

"I don't know."

"Well, whoever they are, they can't be as qualified for the job as you are."

Birds swooped into the yard, the sun crept up over the horizon, the sounds of traffic increased. And still they sat there at the edge of the pool, talking quietly about what if. What if he won the appointment, what if it led elsewhere, and what if that elsewhere was the White House? How would she feel about that?

"I'd love it," she said.

In the old days, before life had gotten very complicated, he and Isabel used to talk like this in the dark, after they'd made love. They used to voice their ambitions, their dreams. Politics had been among those dreams. They even had laid out a strategy, that they would both go to law school, perhaps create their own firm, then branch out into local and state politics, then the larger arena of national politics.

But when it came down to it, down to everyday life, Isabel had quit law school after her first year and switched to a master's education program and he had gone on alone. Her involvement in politics had been truncated, expressed primarily through her involvement in the teachers' union. This arrangement had worked for years.

Yet, now, the old dream haunted him. He could taste it against his tongue, its spice and seduction, and moved it around in his mouth like a sip of cognac. *President Hutchin.* Christ, yes, he loved the way that felt.

"So what's the first thing you would find an answer for if you were president?" she asked.

This, too, was an old game. But the answers were new. "Who really killed JFK?"

"That's a good one."

"What about you?"

She thought about it a moment. "I'd request the UFO files."

Hutchin burst out laughing. "For real?"

"Yup. Then I'd ask for the files on the Philadelphia Experiment. I mean, I'd have to keep it interesting since I wouldn't be able to dance on my toes in public anymore."

He laughed again and slipped an arm around her shoulders and she leaned into him, the two of them more content together in that moment than they had been in months. Hutchin didn't understand this strange and sudden shift in their marriage, the way the old issues abruptly had evaporated, the way the past no longer seemed to matter.

It didn't surprise him when they ended up in bed, but it scared him a little. He hadn't touched her for at least a month, an eternity in their marital scheme of things, and he feared that he would confuse her body with Diane's. Habit saved him, however. Habit kicked in. His body recalled how his wife liked to be touched, what she enjoyed, what turned her on.

He thought, suddenly, of the Clintons during the Lewinsky mess. He remembered seeing Bill and Hillary on CNN one afternoon at a military function, and how she had looked so completely consumed by a barely subdued rage. Would he and Isabel come to that? Would they reach unspoken agreements in return for power?

No. The difference between himself and Clinton, he realized, was that he would not get caught.

(2)

Neither of them said much over breakfast. Kit knew that Ryan knew Abuelita had told her what had happened at Bahia Honda. But he hadn't brought it up and neither had she. She intended to wait for him to mention it first. Otherwise, he would clam up and refuse to say anything at all.

Ryan cleared the dishes from the table, rinsed them off, put them in the dishwasher, all very uncharacteristic. Oro, Kit noticed, tagged his heels more than she usually did. Perhaps she feared that if she let him out of her sight, there would be a repeat of yesterday.

"Are you picking me up today, Mom?" he asked.

"Becky's dad will be picking you guys up. We've decided to alternate days, if we can."

"Can I come over here after school to get Oro?"

"She's going with me today. I may try to get to Key Largo."

"You going to put her to the sniff test?"

"Something like that."

"This is about that dead actress, right?"

"Yes. I'll tell you about it tonight."

He got his lunch out of the fridge. "Mom?"

"Yeah, hon?"

"You mad at me?"

Kit realized this was her opportunity. "Of course not. Have you done something I should be angry about?"

"Well, I thought that after Abuelita told you what happened, you would say something and you didn't and . . ."

"I was waiting to hear your side of it, Ryan."

"That's the problem. I'm not sure what happened." He sat at the table again, nervously rubbing his hands over his jeans. "Becky and I were building a sand castle down by the beach and I heard the . . . the voice. It told me to look up toward the bridge. That's when I saw her."

"Saw who?"

"This lady. I knew her, see. And she was hurrying away from me. I . . . I didn't want her to go, I needed to talk to her. So I ran after her. And then suddenly Agent Webster tackled me and we crashed to the bridge and . . . and when I opened my eyes, I saw Abuelita and Becky and . . . and Bob."

"Bob Tilden." Whom he'd never met.

"I didn't know his last name."

"You've never met him, hon."

"Then how did I know his name?"

"You probably heard Abuelita say it. Or Agent Webster."

"But when I looked at him later, after we'd left the bridge, he didn't seem familiar to me."

The most reasonable explanation, Kit thought, was that Ryan and Becky had been eavesdropping when she and Webster were talking inside the house Saturday and that was when he'd heard Tilden's name. But that didn't explain *recognition*. Abuelita had clearly heard Ryan say Bob's name. Had Ryan seen a picture of Tilden in one of the family photo albums? She couldn't recall any photos of Tilden around the house here, but her parents had stacks of albums. It was possible that he'd seen a picture, of course it was. There was no other explanation.

"Later, Becky asked me what had happened, why I was trying to run off the bridge. I . . . I didn't see the bridge like it is now, Mom. I saw it like it *used to be*. I thought the lady was just going to keep walking right up the bridge to the next island.''

Hallucinations. What can cause hallucinations? A chemical imbalance? A brain abnormality? A tumor? She struggled to keep alarm out of her expression and her voice. ''Who is the lady, Ryan?''

Obviously miserable now, he just shook his head. ''I don't know. The Other knows her.''

''The Other,'' Kit repeated. ''By that you mean the voice?''

''Yeah.''

She felt, suddenly, like a nonswimmer who had ventured too close to the water and been jerked under by a riptide. She clearly needed advice, but from whom? A pediatric shrink? A counselor? Ryan apparently sensed what she was thinking because he leaned toward her, his expression skewed with such earnestness and fear that it changed the way he looked to her, actually changed the topography of his face.

''I'm not sick, Mom.'' He grabbed her hand and held it tightly in both of his own. ''I'm not. Promise you won't take me to a doctor. Please, promise me.''

''I know you're not sick.'' She pressed her free hand against the top of his. ''But I need help to understand what's going on with you. I ... I don't have the experience or knowledge to be able to help you cope with this.''

He looked so frightened, so utterly alone, that Kit got up quickly and put her arms around him, her need to comfort him as great as her need to understand what was happening to him so that she could help him. ''How about a compromise? Would you consider talking to Doc Luke?''

''He's like my second grandpa, Mom.''

''But he's a doctor.''

"So's my real grandpa."

"Yeah, but he and Nana are away."

"I'll think about it."

While he was thinking about it, she would talk to Dr. Luke. "Hon, let's make a pact. The next time you feel the Other around, before he starts telling you what to do, tell me."

"Suppose it happens at school?"

"Call me. You have my cell number."

"But I have to go to the office to call, Mom. By then it might be too late."

"I'll give you a cell phone. I have an extra one here that we sometimes use for work. Keep it in your backpack." Then she grinned and poked him playfully in the chest. "But you have to promise that you won't use it to call all your friends."

He laughed at that, gave her a hug, then pointed at the clock. "We need to get moving or I'll be late for school."

"Let me get that cell phone."

When they left the house a while later, Oro delighted that she could tag along, Kit felt that she had averted a crisis—at least temporarily. She'd bought herself a little time to mull over her options while keeping Ryan's fear of doctors in mind. Yes, there were plenty of parents she knew who would consider her irresponsible for not whisking her son off to his pediatrician the day after the digging incident in the field and certainly after yesterday's episode. But she respected her son's feelings. As her father had once said, *Kids are just little people with feelings. And we have to respect those feelings.*

But she also needed advice and Dr. Luke would give it to her.

* * *

As soon as she pulled out of the school parking lot, Kit turned on her cell phone and saw that she had five messages. She intended to return them, but first she wanted to call Webster again and thank him. She'd left a message on his machine last night, but that hardly seemed appropriate, in light of the fact that he had saved Ryan's life.

She tried his cell phone first and was surprised when he picked up on the first ring. "Hey, Kit."

That threw her. Of course he would have Caller ID on his cell phone, just as she did. Hell, Bureau cell phones probably had all the bells and whistles. "I just wanted to thank you for what you did for Ryan yesterday." *For saving his life.* "I'm so grateful you saw him in time."

"I'm just glad I was there. How's he doing today?"

"Okay. Some weird stuff has been going on with him, but he seems okay. Anyway, thanks again. If I can help you at all with your investigation about Pete, just holler."

"I'd really love the opportunity to go through his notebooks, journals, anything he might have kept of that nature."

It disturbed her that she felt a fluttering in the pit of her stomach at the thought of seeing Webster again. It had been a long time since she'd felt any visceral attraction toward a man. The last guy was a Miami attorney with whom she'd been involved for six or eight months. That had ended the night he'd shouted at Ryan and then told her that she spoiled her son. *Yeah? Good-bye, asshole.* But she didn't sense that kind of arrogance about Webster.

"Most of Pete's journals and things are in my storage closet on the porch downstairs. You can come over any time to go through them."

"Great. I'll call you beforehand."

"Talk to you soon."

As soon as she disconnected, the phone rang. "Kit Parrish."

"Paul Opitz here, Kit. Hope I haven't caught you at a bad time."

"I don't have bad times, Paul. What can I do for you?"

Opitz was the last person she wanted to talk to before her second cup of coffee. Everything about him grated on her, particularly his rolling southern accent, that stab at a downhome simplicity. He led other people to believe that he was one of those the-cup-is-half-empty kind of guys when he was actually a go-for-the-jugular kind of guy. In her years in the keys, she had come up against him in court several times, but the only time that mattered was the Henderson rape trial, which he had won.

"I hear you're defending Poulton," said Opitz.

"Really." She picked up her speed, darted around three cars in front of her, and settled back, doing 65 mph toward Tango Key. "And who'd you hear that from, Paul?"

"Scuttlebutt."

Sure. It smelled like spies at the Tango Key jail to her. "What else do you hear?"

"That Poulton's sister has a ton of dough and that Poulton doesn't have a chance in hell of getting bond."

"Then you're better informed than I am."

"So you're not defending him? Is that what you're saying?"

"Actually, Paul, what I'm saying is that my cell phone isn't secure. I'll call you back as soon as I get to work. You in your office?"

"I'll be here until noon."

As soon as Kit hung up, she checked in with Rita. The news was good. She had procured a copy of Poulton's ATM withdrawals, which clearly showed that he had bought gas at a station in Marathon at 1:52 Saturday morning. Diane Jackson had paid the builder half a million on the house, with another million due next week. They would have to go through official channels to get copies of Diane's bank records, but the president of the bank, a personal friend of Rita's, had told her that with CDs and money markets, Diane Jackson had about two million on deposit.

"What about the property inventory?" Kit asked.

"I'm on my way over to the PD now."

"Good. Get a piece of Diane's clothing. I need something with her scent on it for when we go to Key Largo."

"Oro's going to do her thing?"

Kit glanced at the dog, her head poking out of the passenger window, snout lifted into the wind. "If there's anything of Diane's there, she'll find it."

"I'll meet you at the airfield in an hour," Rita said, and hung up.

Twenty minutes later, Kit stood in Opitz's office, the element of surprise in her favor because he had expected a call, not a personal visit. He was about her height, with a gaunt face, stooped shoulders, and dark, deeply set eyes that, when the occasion called for it, could become inflamed with passion. At the moment, however, those eyes looked merely nervous, unsettled by her visit.

"I was in the vicinity," she said. "So let's talk."

"So you *are* defending him."

"Yes. Your sources got that much right."

He plucked a file off his desk and they moved to a plush sitting area at the other end of his spacious office. He fussed around with the file, pulling out papers, rearranging other papers. Kit didn't bother opening her briefcase. "If I'm not mistaken, I think that Judge Hutchin is next on the rotational schedule," Opitz said.

"I don't have a problem with Hutchin. He's fair."

"We're going to recommend that bond be denied."

"My client doesn't want bond. We're not even requesting it."

His brows arched. "I see."

"No, I don't think you do. Your office jumped the gun on this one, Paul. The murder occurred sometime between midnight and four Friday morning and my client was arrested about thirty hours later. That's maybe one of the speediest arrests on record."

"We had everything we needed. Probable cause, an alibi that couldn't be confirmed by anyone else, witness statements about their very public argument, a used condom in the wastebasket . . ." He shook his head. "We didn't act prematurely."

"She was seeing someone else."

"Not surprising, given who she was."

"It's possible this someone else killed her."

Opitz laughed and made a dismissive gesture with his hand. "Anything's possible. But there's no proof of that."

"Actually, there is. If you'd bothered to wait for Dr. Luke's autopsy report, you would know that Diane Jackson was pregnant and the blood types involved make it impossible for the kid to be Poulton's."

In the moments after the blood drained from Opitz's face, Kit could almost hear the wheels turning madly in his head as he tried to figure the various angles—how she might use this information in Poulton's defense, the doubt it might seed in the collective mind of the jurors. "All the more reason for him to kill her," Opitz said.

"If he knew, why would he have used a condom, Paul? The last time I checked, a woman can't get pregnant when she's already pregnant. What it shows is that Diane Jackson had at least two lovers. Reasonable doubt, don't you think?" She smiled as she said it and felt Opitz seething inside.

His desk phone rang and he excused himself to take the call. He spoke in a hushed voice for several moments, then returned to where she was and stood there, hands in the pockets of his slacks. His body language suggested that he felt relaxed and confident; but the expression on his face said otherwise.

"How open is your client to a deal?"

"Out of the question. You've charged him with murder one. He says he's innocent and that's how his plea will be entered."

Opitz paused behind the chair in which he'd sat earlier and leaned against the back of it. "Then I'm afraid this will be a repeat of the Henderson trial, Kit. You should think about that."

She recognized the remark for what it was, an attempt at intimidation, and just smiled and got up. "That's what I like about you, Paul. Such humility. See you in court."

Chapter 8

The art room smelled like home to Ryan, safe, protected.

The second he walked through the door, he could smell the crayons, chalks, glue, paints, even the paper and the easels and scissors. The sounds in this room always seemed friendly and inviting. Chairs scraped against the floor. Sketch pads rustled. The pencil sharpener whirred. Everywhere he looked, he saw color—bright colors, pastels, earth tones. One wall had been sponge-painted in sea greens and pale blues, another was as red as a radish. Drawings, sketches and half-completed projects filled the low shelves. He belonged here.

"Okay, class," said Ms. Cannon. "Listen up."

And everyone did, naturally, because they loved art and they loved Ms. Cannon. She was probably his coolest teacher, with her frizzy red hair and freckles, and her jeans and colorful shirts. She had only two rules in her class: to be creative and to do the best that you could. She didn't care if you talked, as long as the talk was creative. She didn't care if you didn't complete an assignment by the end of the class because, as she always told them, creativity didn't happen on demand. She constantly reminded them that their most creative times were when their minds were in a dreamlike state, relaxed, not thinking too much. Ryan knew that state of mind really well. He lived in it most of the time.

''Today I'd like you to get out your sketch pads and draw a place that's important to you. It can be funny or serious, pretty or special, it doesn't matter, as long it's a place that *matters* to you. You'll need your number-two pencils, *sharpened*, please, we always do better with *sharpened* pencils, and an eraser. The assignment doesn't have to be completed today. But it's fine if it is. No rules. You've got five minutes to get your supplies.''

Ryan was back at his seat in less than five minutes, his number-two pencil sharpened and ready. He turned to a clean page in his sketch pad, closed his eyes for a moment, and saw the stone house that he'd dreamed about several times. Saw it in detail. He held the image in his mind, then opened his eyes and stared at the sheet of paper. The trick was to get the image onto the paper in exactly the way he saw it in his head.

Ryan put the pencil to the paper, shut his eyes, and willed his hand to move, to take the image in his head and translate it onto the paper. After a few minutes, his fingers twitched and tightened around the pencil and his hand started to move. Relieved, he opened his eyes.

Shapes began to emerge on the paper, a dirt road lined with trees, an old wooden gate with some sort of emblem on it, huge trees in an overgrown yard, and there, behind the trees, the first hint of the stone house. His fingers paused, reached for the eraser, drew it across the lower part of the branches, as if to let more light into the yard so that he could see the house more clearly. But the house wasn't finished yet. Windows, he thought. It needed two windows downstairs and a couple of windows upstairs, where the loft was. But first, he finished the house, every stone as he saw it in his mind, all the swirling tones, the shifting shadows. As he added windows, he included the reflection of the trees in the glass, a spooky effect, but true to the image in his head.

The door didn't seem quite right and he decided to sketch it so it was open. Now the winding spiral staircase could be seen. He picked up the eraser again, removed the closed door, and sketched in a door that was partially open, light falling through it, revealing a spiral staircase made of— *what? Wood? Iron?*

He darkened the staircase with the side of his pencil, certain that it was very dark and made of iron. He didn't allow himself to think about how he knew this.

Then he turned his attention to the front porch. *What's on the porch?*

A chair, one of those special wooden chairs named after mountains somewhere in New York State. He sketched it, the slats wide at the back of it, the arms wide. In his mind, the chair was green, but the sketch wasn't in color, so he shaded it to suggest that it was a dark color. And a table, he thought. The image in his mind had a table on the porch, too. A low wooden table as square as a die.

Now he added detail to the trees, lowering the branches, texturing the leaves and the bark, creating shadows under them. Banyan trees, he thought. These were banyans. In the mental picture, he saw a hammock strung up between them, a rainbow-colored hammock with a woman inside.

Who's the woman, Ryan? whispered a small, distant voice inside of him. *Find the woman's name and everything will fall into place.*

His hand stopped and his fingers were pressing down so

hard on the pencil that the point suddenly snapped, startling him. For several terrifying moments, as he stared down at the sketch, it seemed that he could see a man standing in the shadows of the trees, as if he were spying on the woman. It scared him and he quickly flipped pages down over it.

Who was that?

He lifted the corners and peeked. The man was gone.

Ryan let the pages drop and set his pencil aside, his heart beating fast and furiously. Ms. Cannon, who was walking around the class and glancing at the sketches, strolled past his desk and stopped. ''That sketch is awesome, Ryan. I can tell it's very special to you. Where's it located?''

I don't know. ''I'm not sure.''

She leaned closer. ''The stone has swirls in it, like marble.''

He nodded.

''Tango stone, that's my guess. And it looks old. There're a lot of historic places on Tango. Maybe it's one of those. Excellent job, Ryan.''

Tango stone? Was this house on Tango Key? But where? *Where? And how can I find it?*

During his English class in fourth period, they went to the library and Ryan searched the shelves until he found a book on Tango Key history. He paged through it, studying the photographs, looking for the stone house that he'd sketched.

He noticed immediately that Ms. Cannon was right about the swirls in the stone. It was called Tango stone and when it was polished, it resembled marble. The oldest part of the Tango Key Lighthouse, now a library, was built from Tango stone and so were many of the historic buildings.

Early in the island's history, almost the entire town of Tango was built of this stone and withstood hurri-

canes and floods in a way that even the best of current construction does not. Geologists speculate that eons ago, the island was pushed upward from the depths of the ocean during some type of upheaval. While the stone is not volcanic in origin, it is as strong as volcanic rock. In a highly polished state, it resembles marble.

Some of the most notable examples of Tango stone construction are the island lighthouse, the Pirate's Cove Cliff Hotel, the Tango Art Gallery, the Tango Key Museum, Calypso Farms, and the Baker Homestead. All of these structures are more than a century old.

Ryan flipped to the index and looked up the page numbers for each of the places mentioned. Each page showed a large photo, with a long description about the building's history. The lighthouse awed him, but it wasn't what he'd sketched. The Pirate's Cove Cliff Hotel was too big, the Tango Key Art Gallery didn't feel quite right. Although Calypso Farms had the same mysterious feel that the house in his sketch did, he sensed it wasn't the same place. That left the Baker Homestead and the museum.

Both places had huge banyan trees out front; neither had a hammock. Both had a wooden gate with some sort of emblem on the front and both had front porches, but without any furniture. Both had windows in the front and smaller windows on the second story. The Baker Homestead had been around since the late 1700s. The building that housed the museum had been built in 1821.

He read about the history of both places, looking for clues, something that felt right to him. The Baker Homestead had been built by—who else?—the Bakers, who had come to Tango from Boston in 1772 and homesteaded fifty acres of land. They had eight children, six of whom were born on the homestead. The place had remained in the family until 1961, when the last surviving Baker had sold the house and the remaining ten acres for five million. It was now a bed-and-breakfast inn, one of those ritzy places where rooms went for several hundred a night.

The museum started out as a one-story cottage, which a wealthy Miami farmer, James Mecca, built in the middle of twenty acres. He found Tango's soil much richer for the crops he grew. Mecca, read Ryan, had five children, and to accommodate all of them, he built a loft in the house. The loft was destroyed in a fire in 1870 and also killed Mecca's wife, who was asleep upstairs at the time. In 1872, Mecca himself died and the property passed to his oldest son, Wayne Mecca.

"Blah, blah, blah," Ryan murmured, running his finger down the page, looking for the building's more recent history.

He found it, but wasn't sure what, if anything, it meant for him. From 1961 to 1993, the Mecca Homestead was owned by the Schuller family, longtime Tango residents. Granger Schuller bought the twenty acres of land and sold it off, bit by bit, over the years, until only two acres were left in 1993, when it was sold to Tango County. It was declared a historical landmark in 1984.

So who're the Schullers?

He went through the index again, looking for an entry for the Schullers. One page, that was all, just one lousy page was listed under Tango's "Important People."

Granger Schuller was a Tango fritter, born in 1921 in the Tango Key clinic. His father was a citrus farmer, his mother a teacher. In the stock market crash of

*1929, Schuller's father bought up cheap stocks and
and was a millionaire within three years.*

*By the time Schuller's parents died, he'd inherited
enough money to buy the Mecca Homestead. For many
years, the Schuller Farm produced the best grapefruit
in the state. It also produced papaya and oranges.*

*In the early 1980s, Schuller's wife died. Not long
afterward, he ran into financial problems and sold off
acres of his property to pay off debt. With his death
in 1990, only two acres remained. They and the house
passed to his five daughters, who used them off and
on until they were sold to Tango County in 1993.*

Five daughters, Ryan thought. What were their names?
Who were they? Were any of them still alive? Were any of
them the woman in the hammock?

He went through the index again, hoping he had missed
other entries on the Schullers, but he hadn't. There wasn't
anything at all. Frustrated, he began to search the other local
history books, but their teacher told them they had five
minutes left to select their books and get in the checkout
line.

But at least he had found something, he thought. It was
a start.

(2)

The Bonanza lifted into the impossibly blue sky and
headed north along the gulf coast toward Key Largo. Kit
peered down at the dots of land, at the tiny houses, at the
lines and curves that were highways, bridges, and beaches.
Up here, she thought, everything snapped into perspective.

She'd been flying with Rita ever since they'd opened the
firm and felt safer with her than she did in a commercial

plane. That aside, the Bonanza would get them to Key Largo in less than half the time it would take them to drive the distance and, ultimately, this saved the client money.

"We should've gotten up here yesterday," Rita said. "Let's hope that Opitz hasn't beaten us to the punch."

"Opitz is too busy preparing indictments."

While Oro settled in the backseat with a bone, Kit exchanged her skirt for slacks, her heels for a pair of sling-back sandals, and took off her jacket. Given her druthers, she would go to work every day in jeans and a T-shirt. But even in laid-back Key West, people in the legal profession dressed formally. For their search of Poulton's house, however, more comfortable clothes were in order. Even Rita had changed before they'd boarded the plane.

They touched down in Key Largo around 11:30, rented a car at Hertz, and pulled up in front of Steve Poulton's place shortly afterward. The house, elevated on pilings at the end of a dirt road, looked old and weathered, as if it had been built before snowbirds had discovered the keys. Parked under the house was an old VW Bug, circa 1965. Kit found the key to the house stuck to the underside of its bumper, exactly where Poulton had said it would be.

"Doesn't look like the cops have been here," Rita remarked.

"No reason for them to be since the murder happened elsewhere. Paul Opitz will think of it sooner or later, but he'll send his lackeys to check things out and by then it'll be too late."

"Shit, it wouldn't surprise me if Opitz himself had taken the journal."

"Maybe this time Diane left it in LA."

"I doubt it. Not from the way Poulton talked."

Kit didn't really expect to find Diane's journal here. But she hoped they would find something in the house that would support Poulton's innocence. She reasoned that since Diane had spent time here, she might have left behind personal belongings that would connect her to another man. Granted, it was a long shot. People who cheated on their lovers and spouses were probably very careful about not leaving incriminating evidence behind. But Diane had split her time between Hollywood, the keys, and wherever she happened to be on location, so perhaps she'd gotten careless.

Oro bounded up the steps, then stopped at the door, waiting for Kit and Rita. "Okay, let's have that article of clothing, Rita."

She wagged a Baggie with a shirt inside that had belonged to Diane Jackson. "Got it right here."

"Sit, Oro."

Oro sat and waited expectantly, her eyes on Kit.

Kit took the Baggie and opened it. "Smell, Oro. Find this smell."

The dog sniffed at it, barked, sniffed some more, and Kit unlocked the door. When they stepped into the house, Kit repeated the command and for a few moments, Oro stood where she was, snout lifted into the air. Then she trotted down the hall, tail wagging, nose to the floor.

"You follow her," Kit said. "I'm going to look around."

She supposed she had expected a masculine sort of place, sparsely furnished and without much character. She was obviously biased in that respect. The house was beautiful inside, with shiny wooden floors, skylights, a spacious kitchen, and a living room that overlooked the woods out back. The only bedroom on this floor had been converted into an office, its walls lined with medical books—and books about movies and Hollywood. A computer was in here as well, the PC where Poulton had kept his journal.

Kit booted it up, found the journal folder easily enough, and went into it just to make sure this was what she was looking for. It was. She poked around in the folders, but most of them appeared to be related to medicine and Poulton's residency. Her next stop was Poulton's e-mail: a queue of twenty-seven new e-mails and sent e-mails that numbered in the hundreds.

She went through the new ones and found an e-card from Diane, from Blue Mountain Cards, sent the day after she was murdered. Blue Mountain offered an option about when to send the cards, so this one obviously had been prepared in advance, with a send date the day her body had been found. Kit accessed the card, a cute little thing that amounted to an apology.

The card, Kit thought, smacked of design. She had the distinct impression that Diane had decided she and Poulton were going to argue that evening so that she could leave him and meet with her other lover. But just to cover her ass, she had prepared the Blue Mountain Card in advance, knowing, of course, that Poulton was madly in love with her and would forgive her in a heartbeat.

Ironic, she mused, that the card had sailed off into cyber-space right on schedule, inadvertently giving her enormous insight into Diane's capacity for duplicity. It also would strengthen her defense. *Prove beyond a reasonable doubt that your client is innocent because the prosecutor is going to be proving beyond a reasonable doubt that your client is, in fact, guilty as charged:* Hutchin's words, in his criminal law class. But who the hell was he kidding? *Reasonable* was one of those vague legal idioms that really meant *Get it right or your client is fucked.*

Kit disconnected the monitor, keyboard, printer, and box, and carried everything into the front room. This was going with them. She returned to the office to finish searching it, but didn't really expect to find anything. This room clearly had belonged to Poulton, not to Diane. The desk drawers yielded several framed photos of Poulton and Diane, a handsome couple by anyone's standards, but little else of interest. Same with the closet.

She went through the kitchen, looking for a junk drawer, that black hole where stuff went that didn't fit anywhere else. But Poulton appeared to be an organized man. He didn't have any junk drawers. Eventually, she thought, they would have to search his Miami apartment, too, but from what Poulton had said, it seemed that Diane had spent more time in this house than in his apartment.

"Hey, Kit," called Rita. "Get up here and bring flashlights. I'm in the loft."

Kit plucked two flashlights out of a drawer that held hurricane supplies, and hurried upstairs to the loft. Rita was crouched at the farthest wall, peering through a narrow opening where only Oro's tail showed.

"What the hell," Kit murmured.

"She was going crazy right here, trying to dig her way through the wall. That's when I found this panel. It appears to be some sort of storage area."

"Let's take a look."

Oro had crept in so far now that Kit didn't see even her tail. She got down on her knees and ducked through the opening, Rita right behind her. Almost immediately, Kit felt short of breath, her heart fluttering wildly in her chest. The walls seemed to press in against her like huge, hot hands. The ceiling was so low that she had to get down on her hands and knees and practically shimmy across the floor like a commando. Cobwebs stuck to her face, caught in her hair. The center of her chest tightened unbearably. Motes of dust drifted in the beam of her flashlight. She crawled faster through the crawl space, panic crouched just below the surface of each breath she took.

Just when she didn't think she could stand it any longer,

the crawl space emptied suddenly into a room large enough for her to straighten up in. She couldn't quite stand upright, but it was close enough. She inhaled deeply, the panic subsided, and the beam of her flashlight struck Oro. The dog was sniffing along the base of boxes piled nearly as high as the ceiling.

"Lights," Rita said, and flicked a switch on the wall.

An overhead bulb winked on, a naked bulb of about forty watts, covered in cobwebs. The room seemed to be located under the eaves along the side of the house and obviously had been used strictly for storage.

"Christ, is this all Poulton's stuff?" Rita asked, going over to the boxes.

"Judging by the way Oro is acting, I'd say some of it belongs to Diane."

Kit and Rita moved simultaneously to the boxes and shifted them around, creating an opening between the stacks. Oro darted through it and sniffed around the edges of an old steamer trunk. "Looks like the real McCoy to me," Rita said. "And Diane's name is engraved on it." She shone her flashlight at the words engraved in silver.

Kit struck the lock with her flashlight, Rita kicked it, but the lock didn't give. "Let's just take the damn thing with us," Rita said. "I mean, there's no law against that. He's our client. We have his permission to be here. Hell, he probably doesn't even know about the trunk."

Kit wasn't about to argue legalities. "Good idea."

She called for Oro and the dog hurried over, tail wagging, and Kit handed her a doggie biscuit and congratulated her for a job well done. Oro hurried back up the passageway, the biscuit bone in her mouth. Kit and Rita then proceeded to push the trunk along the narrow passage. For moments there where the ceiling was lowest and the walls too close, the near-panic returned. Kit forced herself to take deep breaths, pushed harder on the trunk, and felt enormous relief when she and the trunk popped through the hole and into the loft.

"You okay?" Rita asked, combing the cobwebs from her luxurious hair with her fingers.

"Yeah. It's just ... a little tight in there for me."

Rita chuckled and poked her in the ribs. "By God, girl. I think you're claustrophobic. I'll go back and turn off the light."

They had to make three trips to carry everything down-stairs. The trunk, though it wasn't very big, felt as if it had bricks inside. After they got it into the trunk of the car, Kit found a large rock in the yard and slammed it against the lock. It fell apart.

Rita raised the lid. The trunk was stuffed with clothes and shoes. "Imelda Marcos would be green with envy."

Kit picked up one of the shoes and whistled softly. "These are Italian, probably two hundred bucks a pair."

"There's got to be more in here than clothes and shoes."

They dug through the silks and cottons, the dresses and skirts and blouses, and under it all found a shoe box jammed with a stack of e-mails, some from Poulton, the rest from what appeared to be fans. Under these were several pocket-size notebooks. She and Rita paged through several of them. They seemed to be mostly notes that Diane had kept while on location or when she was auditioning or researching acting parts. No journal, Kit thought, but all this stuff would come in handy in one way or another.

"We can go through this more thoroughly later on," Kit said.

"Good idea. I'll go lock up."

Kit closed the steamer trunk, shut the lid of the car trunk, and took Oro across the street to go to the bathroom. She wondered how many other trunks Diane had stuffed with clothes and keepsakes and where they were. LA? A storage unit somewhere? As soon as they got Diane's financial records and canceled checks from the Tango Key bank where she'd had an account, they would have a more complete picture of where else to look for personal items. But such a search could take months and she had an uneasy feeling they weren't going to have months.

As they emerged from the field, Oro started barking and a moment later, Kit saw why. A navy blue Explorer had pulled alongside her van. Paul Opitz, accompanied by one of his lackeys and a cop, strode up to Rita.

Shit. Opitz came himself. Once again, she had underestimated this guy. Fortunately, she and Rita had packed everything in the trunk of their rental car, out of sight. "Paul," Kit chirped, and he turned around. "We really have to stop meeting like this."

He didn't look amused. He hooked his thumbs in his belt and drew himself up to his full height. "We have a search warrant."

"You shouldn't have gone to all that trouble. Nothing in there is going to be of much interest to you. C'mon, Rita, let's get moving." Kit looked pointedly at the officer, a newbie cop she didn't know. "Keep him honest, officer."

"Just a minute, Kit," Opitz snapped. "I need to know if you took anything from the house."

"Nope." She opened the back door of the car for Oro and noticed how Opitz and his lackeys eyed the empty backseat.

"Just the key," Rita said, and held it up. "Should I unlock the door for you, Paul?"

The implication was clear: *we've got nothing to hide.*

"That won't be necessary. We have the means to make a key," Opitz said coolly.

With that settled, Kit slid behind the wheel and Rita got

in the passenger side. "Y'all have a nice day now, hear?"
Kit called, and waved as she drove off.

"Jesus," Rita muttered. "What the hell does his wife see
in him?"

"He's on his third wife."

"Frankly, I'm shocked that three women would find him
appealing."

"He's cunning, Rita."

"So are we."

"Not like he is. Suppose they find something?"

"No way. I checked the loft and the bathroom up there.
The storage area was the only place that had anything interesting."

"He wanted to check the trunk," Kit said. "I could see
it in his face."

"Ha. Fat chance. He'd need a warrant."

"We need to be really careful around him. I don't have
a good feeling about Opitz."

"I've never had good feelings about Opitz."

"That's not what I mean."

She had lost to this man once and she needed to remain
alert and several steps ahead of him not to lose again.

Chapter 9

Ben Webster sat on the back deck of his houseboat at the Mile Zero Marina, watching a gull some fifty feet above him. It screeched as it made increasingly tighter circles through all the blue; then it suddenly fell silent and spiraled downward. It vanished into the water about four yards from the houseboat and surfaced seconds later with a fish wiggling in its beak.

This was the sort of vision, Webster thought, that he needed to make any headway with the Beaupre case. He needed a bird's-eye view.

He pressed the print button to finish printing out the information he had so far on the Beaupre case—what he had culled, what had been in the Bureau file, and what he'd gotten from the file at the local PD this morning, shortly after Kit had called to thank him for yesterday. That file was appallingly thin, even after ten years, and it wasn't clear to him whether it was the result of indifference or just that there was nothing left to uncover.

The last local cop to work on the case had managed to

fill in some of the gaping holes in Beaupre's life during the last forty-eight to seventy-two hours before his disappearance. Webster had added these details to what he already knew and now arranged the information on one of two large corkboards so that he had a visual depiction.

On the second corkboard, he'd arranged a list of Beaupre's assignments, columns, and professional activities for the *Miami News* during the last eight months before his disappearance. Beaupre's former editor, eager to help and delighted that the FBI had gotten involved, had faxed and e-mailed the material to Webster and added some personal insights about Beaupre:

> *Pete wasn't just about words. He always backed up his beliefs with actions. He believed, for instance, in journalism as an honorable profession and accepted a lot of invitations to speak about his profession. After he won the Pulitzer, the invitations really poured in— from community and civics groups, from schools and private organizations. He tried to accommodate most of them. I've included an attached file that lists those I found in my records, with dates where they were noted. Hope this helps. If you need anything else, Agent Webster, don't hesitate to get in touch.*

Webster printed this list as well and posted it on the second corkboard. Then he stood back, studying the boards, his equivalent of the bird's-eye view, the bigger picture. Somewhere in here, he thought, swam the fish. But where?

Beaupre's public appearances spanned the gamut from press luncheons and local writers' groups to Kiwanis and Toastmasters. He had talked at various public schools about journalism as a profession, had been a guest lecturer at four different colleges, and had appeared at gatherings that were largely Hispanic. Using the date of Beaupre's disappearance as ground zero, Webster arranged the appearances backward through time. If Tilden was right that Beaupre had been seeing someone during the six months before his disappearance, then perhaps he'd connected with the woman at one of his appearances.

On the other hand, maybe he already knew the woman— a colleague, a peer, a friend—and the relationship changed. In that case, nothing on these boards would prove helpful. But he had to start somewhere, with some theory. So, starting in January 1991 until Beaupre's sister had last seen him on Halloween of 1991, the appearances for which Webster had dates numbered thirteen. This broke down to two engagements a month for January, February, and March; three in April; one in May; none in June, July, or August; two in September; and one in the month he disappeared.

Based on what Bob Tilden had told him, he selected March and April 1991—six and seven months before Beaupre had vanished—as the place to start. On March 6, he'd appeared at the Sugarloaf Key Middle School for their job roundup day. On March 22, he was a guest speaker at the Key West High School job roundup day. On April 2, he had spoken at the Kiwanis Club; April 9 put him at a local writers' group; and on April 20, he'd been the guest speaker at a press club luncheon. In each instance, a contact and a phone number were included.

The schools seemed like a dead end—job roundup days usually involved the entire student body. So he tried the contact for the Kiwanis, but no one was there by that name. The number for the contact at the local writers' group had been disconnected. The absurdity of the situation struck him. People moved, married, got divorced, died. It had been ten years, and in a state of transients, where things changed by the second, a decade was as good as a century.

The most reliable information about Beaupre's disappearance probably had come immediately after it had happened, when the trail was still fresh. Webster looked through the file again and copied down the name of the cop, J.R. Dexler, who initially investigated the disappearance and apparently kept at it for the next two years, until another cop took over. He started to call the Key West PD to find out where Dexler was, but decided he probably would get the information faster in person.

His cell phone rang as he was carting everything back onto the houseboat. He dug it out from under a pile of papers. ''Webster.''

''Señor Webster. This is Carmela Perez. I apologize for not returning your call sooner.''

''No problem.''

''I want to thank you again for what you did for Ryan.''

''I'm just glad he's all right. Do you have a few minutes? I'd like to ask you a couple of questions about Pete.''

''Of course. I imagine your first question is whether he was involved with anyone at the time of his disappearance.''

Either the woman read minds or she had been questioned so often by police that she knew the routine. ''Actually, that *is* my first question.''

''Of course he was involved with someone. He was a young, virile man who was passionate about everything. Unfortunately for us, he could also be incredibly secretive. My own feeling—and Kit may differ on this—is that Pete got involved with someone early in 1991. I believe he was very much in love with her, but I'm not at all certain that she had anything to do with his disappearance.''

''Everyone I talk to refers to his 'disappearance.' But the initial investigation treated it like a homicide. Do you think he's alive or dead?''

"I think the man we knew as Pete Beaupre is dead. That he was killed. But there are larger forces at work here."

"Larger in what sense?"

"A spiritual sense."

"I'm not sure I follow."

"You saved Ryan's life, Mr. Webster."

Everyone, he thought, seemed to be making a bigger deal out of yesterday's events than was warranted. He simply happened to be in the right place at the right time. "I don't understand what that has to do with spirituality."

"Perhaps that's the wrong word. Think, for a moment, about how improbable it was that you should be at Bahia Honda, speaking to Pete's closest friend, at the exact time that Ryan did what he did. Think about the odds against events coinciding in the exact way that they did. An order exists in the greater scheme of things that we can't even begin to perceive."

Jesus, Webster thought. He wanted to talk about Pete and this woman was out there in the cosmos. The improbability had occurred to him, certainly, but only briefly. After all, any number of events and experiences in a person's life could be viewed in this light. His move to the Bureau's Key West office, for instance, had been that sort of event.

He'd heard about the opening two days after his wife had left and had applied immediately. Openings in the keys were rare, coveted, and usually went to the agent with the most seniority or to the agent whose talents and abilities best fit the job. Two other agents besides Webster had applied for the job. Both had more seniority and were better suited for the job. And yet, within two weeks of his application, one of the agents had gotten assigned to a special case in the Southwest and the other had ended up in the hospital with a bullet wound to the chest. So Webster had gotten the job.

Up until this moment, he had considered it an incredible stroke of good luck, had marveled at how things had worked out, and occasionally had wondered how it fit into the larger scheme of his own life. But he hadn't attached any cosmic significance to it. Yet, if he correctly understood what the old woman was saying, it all smacked of a larger design.

"Mr. Webster?" she said.

"Still here," he replied. "Just thinking about it."

She laughed softly. "Mark my words, one day you will be deeply grateful to your wife for walking out."

Of all the things she might have said, this surprised him most.

No, this shocked him. Shocked him because he hadn't mentioned his personal life to anyone the old woman might know—not to Kit, Bob Tilden, or Ryan. In fact, the only person who knew anything about his ex or all the Miami shit, as he had come to think of it, was Moreno.

"And why is that?" he asked.

"Because her departure brought you to your path, Mr. Webster. You don't see it yet, but you're on that path."

"If you can provide those kinds of details for me, a guy you were with for less than thirty seconds, then why can't you see who killed Pete?"

He blurted the question. He didn't mean to, didn't intend to, but that was how it came out. And she didn't come back with some quick, glib reply. Moments ticked by in which neither of them said anything. When she finally spoke, her very soft voice seemed impossibly distant and not quite real.

"In some ways, people like me are cursed, Mr. Webster. We can see things for strangers that we can't see for the people whom we love most. I don't know who killed Pete. For me, that knowledge is blocked. But I can perceive the connections to that knowledge and you are intimately a part of it."

Webster suddenly couldn't think of anything else to ask her. It was as if his mind had been wiped clean. He felt as if he were slogging through mud or shit, with no clear memory how he'd gotten there. He stammered that he had another call, thanked her for her time, and hung up.

Only then did he remember that he'd wanted to ask her how Ryan had known Bob Tilden's name.

Webster headed across the Tango Bridge, curious about how a retired cop could afford to live there. The address for J.R. Dexler that the Key West PD had given him took him deep into the emerald hills, to a dirt road lined by farms and pastures. The house itself lay at the end of a curving driveway, a single-story stone house that looked as if it belonged in New England somewhere.

Two dogs announced his arrival, yapper poodles that raced the length of a fence. They snarled and barked as he got out and walked up to the door. It opened before he rang the bell and a slender black woman in jeans and a cotton shirt said, "Now let me guess. You must be Agent Webster." Then she laughed at his startled expression. "Personnel always calls me when they give out the address."

"You're J.R. Dexler?"

"Joy Ramona. Now how could I get any respect in a predominately male PD with a name like that?" She laughed again, then hushed the dogs. "Personnel tells me you're assigned to the Beaupre disappearance. How'd that come about? Last I heard, it was a local case."

He explained how he'd come to get the case, probably explained more than he had to, and she suggested they talk inside. Before he went in, Webster retrieved what he needed from his car. They finally settled on a back porch that overlooked the hills. By then, they were on a first-name basis.

Her easy, flowing style wouldn't have it otherwise. Webster guessed J.R. was in her sixties, but she talked, moved, and thought like a younger woman.

"I left the department because I wanted to write full-time," she explained. "Pete was actually instrumental in my wanting to write. I belonged to a local writers' group for years. We'd get together once a month or so and critique each other's work, offer suggestions and advice, that kind of thing. Then in the spring of 1991, Pete was our guest speaker. He was just great. I felt so inspired by his talk that I put in for two weeks of leave to finish the book I'd written.

"We ran into each other in May, I guess it was, and he asked how my rewrites were going. I was shocked that he remembered. But he had that kind of charm about him, you know what I mean? Anyway, I told him I'd finished it and he offered to take a look at the manuscript."

"Was it a novel?"

"No, a memoir. My folks were very active in the civil rights movement in the late fifties and throughout the sixties. I was in my twenties and thirties then, so my memories of that period are still vivid. Pete and I met once a week or so for a month after that. He helped me hone and polish the manuscript. Then I started submitting it to agents and editors.

"On Halloween day, I got my first positive responses. Both an agent and an editor were interested. I must've called Pete's place a dozen times. He was never in. Two days later, Kit reported him missing. I took the case and spent the next two years driving myself crazy. I interviewed dozens of people in an attempt to reconstruct Pete's last few days. What I realized is that some people live their real lives in utter secrecy. That was Pete."

"Did you find any evidence that he was involved in something illegal?"

"No. But I never discounted the possibility because he

was so secretive. I do know there was a woman. I was never able to find out who she was.''

"I heard that from Bob Tilden." And from Abuelita, he thought.

She made a face. "Tilden. Please. He never told me much of anything useful. I got my first inkling about this woman from Pete.''

Webster listened closely now. "You'd better explain that one.''

"We were pretty tight during the time we worked on my book. We started exchanging bits and pieces of our personal lives. Sometimes when we got together, he was high, buoyant, on top of the world. Other times, he was in the pits. One day, a down day, I half jokingly told him he needed Prozac. I believe his exact words were, 'No, I need a commitment from this woman I've been seeing.' He said she was married, that it was complicated. I told him that people get divorced all the time, that if he really wanted her, then he needed to push her to make a choice. He listened but didn't comment. I asked him how long they'd been seeing each other and he said several months, then clammed up and refused to talk about it anymore.''

Webster sat forward, fascinated. "Do you think he and this woman disappeared together?''

"For a while, that's exactly what I thought. Then about eighteen months into my investigation, my book sold. The editor wanted me to change some things, so I went back through the notes Pete had made on the manuscript. He used to write on yellow legal pads. And I found something. Hold on. I'll get it.''

When she returned, she held a yellow legal pad covered in small, neat printing. "Pete's notes," she said. "You can tell from his writing that he was a meticulous man, at least when it came to his work. He even dated it.''

5/16/91.

A kind of chill went through Webster, one of those chills he experienced when he knew for sure that he was on to something. The night he first had suspected that his wife had been seeing another man, he'd felt this chill. He'd also felt it the day his folks had been in a car accident, the day before he'd been hired by the Bureau, and a full week before his transfer had been accepted to Key West. Every so often on a case, he also felt it. Moreno referred to it as Webster's gut feelings or his "spooky shit," but there was nothing spooky about it. Webster thought of it as the result of a perfect blend between his left and right brains. The left brain collected facts and the right brain processed those facts through his imagination. A hunch. Nothing more, nothing less.

"It's on the tenth page," J.R. said.

Webster turned to the tenth page, where Beaupre had written:

> *I can't continue like this, never knowing when I'll see you or what's going on. You need to come to some decision about your marriage. Until you do, I can't see you anymore. I love you, but I also love myself. If you want to talk, I'll be on Tango at the usual time.*

"Do you think she lived on Tango?"

"Or Key West. I have no idea if he ever sent her a note like this, but it's very clear that he loved her, whoever she was."

"And that she was married."

"My guess is that she had kids. That could be the complication he referred to. Anyway, after that, I just couldn't believe that the two of them had run off together. I think they split up for a while sometime in May of that year, then perhaps got back together.''

''And then?''

''I don't know.'' She spoke softly, with resignation and regret. ''Maybe the husband found out. Maybe Pete told her he would go to her husband if she didn't make a choice. Maybe he killed himself. Maybe this, maybe that. I just don't know. We're complex creatures, Ben. None of us ever really knows another. We can only guess.''

Webster got up and looked at the time line on his corkboards. ''By May, when you two started working together on your manuscript, he said he'd known the woman several months. So that would put their meeting around February or March.''

''That sounds about right.''

He put red check marks next to those two months. He made a mental note to check out Beaupre's appearances at the school and the press club luncheon in March and two appearances at a local country club in February. It seemed like a very long shot that anything would come of these avenues of inquiry. But he reminded himself that if he planned to head down this route, he had to do it completely.

''If you can reconstruct his last two days,'' J.R. said, ''then you should have a pretty good shot at figuring things out. But even ten years ago, I had a tough time doing that.''

''What do you think the reference to Tango Key means? Did the woman live there? Was there some particular place they met?''

''Beats me. I canvassed every bar and restaurant on Tango during the last six months I worked for the department. I never turned up anything.''

She made a copy of Beaupre's notes on her book and his note to his lover. When he asked her the title of her book, she gave him a copy of the first book and the second, and said that with any luck, her third would be finished by Christmas. "And none of it would have happened without Pete," J.R. said to him as she walked him out to his Jeep.

"May I ask you another question?" He hated to impose anymore, but he needed one more answer.

"Of course."

"What did Kit Parrish tell you about her brother?"

"She refused to believe he was involved with anyone. She said he would have told her about it."

Interesting, Webster mused. That was the same thing Tilden had said.

He promised J.R. he would be in touch and left with an uneasy feeling in the pit of his stomach.

The preserve where Beaupre had last been seen, the sighting that had thrown the case to the feds, covered about a hundred acres of the island, most of it in the hills. The jogging trail, the specific spot where Beaupre had been seen on the afternoon of October 31, 1991, was in the northwest corner, a three-mile track through a small park. Beaupre's home at the time was in Key West, some fifteen miles from the park. So why had he been jogging here? *I'll be on Tango at the usual time.*

Where on Tango? Beaupre had written the note in May and had vanished five months later. Webster had no way of knowing if what had been true for him in May had still been true by the time he had disappeared. But if Beaupre still had been meeting this woman on Tango during the final days of his life, then perhaps the place where they'd met had been somewhere near the park.

County records would tell him what businesses and homes had been standing in this area ten years ago and who owned them. The task would be daunting, no question about it. But at the moment, it looked like his best bet.

As he was leaving the county offices an hour and a half

later, Moreno called him on his cell phone. "Hey, Ben. Call me back ASAP from a pay phone."

"Why? What's going on?"

"Our job descriptions are about to change. Call the office number."

"Got it." He disconnected and hurried back inside the county offices, to the bank of pay phones near the rest rooms. Moreno answered on the first ring. "You know who Jay Hutchin is?"

"Criminal court judge. What about him?"

"He's made the short list for attorney general. You and me, amigo, are supposed to make sure he's up to snuff. Vogel says we're to meet him at Steamer Charlie's on Tango in thirty minutes. You know where it is?"

"Near the docks. Why're we meeting him there?"

"Beats the shit outta me."

"You have any idea what this is going to entail?"

"Probably not much. Hutchin's résumé reads like a squeaky clean who's who. But I suspect boss man will fill us in on the specifics. See you in thirty."

Steamer Charlie's was an island landmark that had been around, in one form or another, for a century. It looked as if it had been slapped together with driftwood and dried mud and topped with sheets of aluminum. It stood on stilts at the edge of the gulf, had been battered and damaged during numerous hurricanes in its hundred years, but it never had been flattened. In Webster's opinion, it served the best seafood in the entire Florida Keys and he expected they would have to wait an hour to get a table. But apparently Bernie Vogel had friends in high places at Steamer Charlie's; the hostess led Webster to a table outside, on a deck that overlooked the gulf, where Vogel sat alone, a cell phone pressed to his ear.

He motioned for Webster to have a seat and mouthed that he would be off in a minute. He was a large man, muscular, with skin the color of charcoal. His deep, quiet voice inspired trust, but his dark, intelligent eyes warned you not to be fooled by the voice. Everyone who worked under him knew that if you fucked with Vogel, you quickly found yourself transferred to Bismarck, North Dakota, or Billings, Montana, to Detroit or Chicago or some other outpost. Or so office legend claimed.

Personally, Webster didn't have a problem with the man. But he wondered, as most of his colleagues did, how Vogel had gotten where he was. Instead of working his way up through the Bureau to his position as director of the FBI's office in the keys, he had been brought in eight years ago from another agency. Speculation about which agency ranged from the CIA and NSA to some covert intelligence faction. Whatever the truth, the man was well connected— he had information that simply didn't come through normal channels.

By the time Vogel finished his call, Webster had ordered coffee and Moreno had arrived, griping about the traffic on the bridge. "Damn cars are lined up for five miles in both directions. I may take the ferry back."

"Snowbirds," Vogel said. "They always start arriving in droves a couple weeks before Thanksgiving."

"So how come we're meeting here, Bernie?" Webster asked.

"Because I hear they've got a new garlic sauce with their steamed clams and shrimp."

Moreno snickered. "Yeah, right, Bernie. Since when do you spring for meals?"

"Who said I was springing for it now?" Vogel shot back.

"Okay, okay, so it's Dutch treat. Why're we really meeting here?"

"No walls." His immense arms opened, as if to embrace the sea air. "No walls means no ears."

"Yeah? We've got spies in the Bureau?" Webster asked, amused.

Vogel leaned forward, his arms resting against the edge of the table. "What we have, gentlemen, is a situation in which we're supposed to determine whether a candidate for the office of attorney general is fit for such a position. I don't know how agents in other areas are going to determine this about the other two candidates, but I *do* know how we're going to do it."

"C'mon," Moreno said. "It happens with every change in administration. There's a protocol for it."

"Sure, there's a protocol. You talk to people who know the candidate. You poke around in the candidate's past. You flush out the Anita Hills, the—"

"That was for the Supreme Court."

"Supreme Court, attorney general, it's all the same goddamn thing. You find the weakest point and let someone else—the president, Congress, whoever—determine if they can live with that weakest point. The challenge here is that the president wants a determination on his three candidates by the Thanksgiving holidays and he doesn't want any surprises. We get Jay Hutchin."

Moreno made a face. "I may take early retirement."

"I want to know the intimate details of Hutchin's life—him, his wife, his daughter," Vogel said. "Who are these people? Who is Hutchin when he's not sitting on the bench? Who is he inside his own head?"

Webster and Moreno glanced at each other and Webster felt sure that Moreno was thinking the same thing he was: *Don't like the sound of this.* "Yeah, so, short of being psychic,'' Moreno said quietly, ''how the hell are we supposed to determine this kind of information about Hutchin?''

Vogel gave him a scathing look that would have sent a lesser man running for the hills. Moreno simply shook his head and glanced away, rubbing a hand over his jaw. Then he whistled a refrain from *Mission: Impossible.*

The waitress came over with a platter of steamed clams, another of steamed shrimp, and three bowls. She set down a basket of hot rolls, butter contained in large shells, and three Coronas. When she left, Vogel picked up his beer. ''Cheers, gentlemen,'' he said and tipped the bottle of beer to his mouth.

Webster liked independent thinkers. He liked rebellion. He liked social movements. But he did not like what was merely implied. That, he thought, was too much like his failed marriage. Besides that, he knew that Vogel had an ax to grind with Hutchin. Years ago in Miami, Vogel's nephew got arrested for possession of cocaine. Webster didn't know what federal organization Vogel worked for in those days, but Hutchin, who was state attorney at the time for Dade County, hadn't taken that into account. Nor had he taken into account that it was the kid's first offense for anything. He'd thrown the book at the kid and Vogel's nephew did seven years. So perhaps Vogel saw a way to get even.

''Excuse me, Bernie. But spell it out.''

Vogel speared a shrimp smothered in sauce. ''You do whatever is necessary to find out who Hutchin really is. You tap his phones, his car, his bedroom. You intercept his e-mail, his snail mail. You tell me when he shits and who he shits with. You turn his life inside out and bring it to me on a platter.''

Webster nearly choked on a sip of beer. ''In other words, we violate his civil rights.''

''That, my friend, is exactly right.''

Moreno scooped a clam out of its shell. "Yeah? And what do we get in return for putting our asses on the line, Bernie? Comp time? Great evaluations?"

"I'm putting my own ass on the line, too. We're talking about the individual who will be in charge of the Justice Department and will be our next boss. You want a repeat of Waco? You want to repeat Elian Gonzalez? As long as we're all working for the Bureau, your stake in this is just as high as mine. And like I said, the president doesn't want any surprises."

Neither of them said anything.

"As for compensation, there isn't any. It's part of your job."

The implication was clear: do the job or hit the highway. "Yeah? And suppose we're caught?" Webster asked.

"C'mon, Ben. You've both had sufficient training not to get caught."

"*If,*" Moreno said.

"You're on your own."

"In that case," Moreno said, "I want a house in Tahiti and a couple of mil in the bank."

Vogel snorted. "Put it in the wish box, Eric."

"I want my houseboat paid off," Webster said. "And six weeks' vacation, all expenses paid to wherever I want."

"Get real," Vogel replied.

Webster pushed to his feet. "Then find someone else, Bernie."

Moreno also got up. "Yeah, ditto."

They stared at Vogel and he glared back. "Ten days' extra leave and a five percent bonus," Vogel finally said.

Webster and Moreno glanced at each other and exploded with laughter. "Sure," Moreno said.

"Two weeks of leave."

"And a ten percent bonus," Webster said.

Vogel rolled his eyes. "Okay, okay."

"We're pimps." Moreno shook his head and sat down again.

Webster sat again, too. "You're not authorized to do this kind of thing on your own, Bernie. You're acting with the blessing of some higher authority."

Vogel pointed his index finger at Webster. "Very good, Ben. Are you in or out?"

"In, but I don't like the notion of legal bills."

"There won't be legal bills," Vogel replied. "Because I'm going to tell you how to do it so that none of us is caught."

Chapter 10

Ryan and Becky settled in her room with their homework, their books spread out across the floor, the TV tuned to Nickelodeon. Becky motioned to his backpack, where the cell phone stuck up from a pouch in the front. "Wow, you have your own cell now? When did that happen?"

"This morning. Because of what happened at Bahia Honda. I told my mom about . . . about the voice I hear sometimes."

"The Other's voice, you mean."

"Yeah. She said if I feel the Other around, I should call her immediately."

"Exactly what did the voice say to you at Bahia Honda?"

"It told me to look toward the bridge."

"And that's when you saw her? This lady?"

"Uh-huh."

"But no one else saw her, Ryan."

"So what're you saying? That I'm crazy?"

"No, I just think you see things that other people don't. That doesn't mean you're crazy. It just means you're . . .

well, different. Better to be different, Ryan, than just like everyone else. Hey, I'm starving. How about a snack?''

"Sure." He pretended not to notice the way she changed the subject so quickly. Maybe she thought she might catch whatever he had if she heard too much about it.

When she left, he went on-line to look for more information on the Schuller family. A number of entries appeared and Ryan clicked on the first one about Granger Schuller. Some of the information differed from what he'd found in the library. This article, for example, said that Schuller had bought the Mecca homestead in 1957, not 1961. Schuller quickly discovered that although Tango Key had all the natural beauty and simplicity he was looking for, it lacked certain amenities—like a school. At that time, kids were bused to Key West. So Schuller solved the problem by raising half a million dollars that he donated to the county. They matched his donation and in 1960, the school was finished.

Schuller's two youngest daughters, Izzie and Mishka, were in the first class to attend the school from kindergarten through high school.

Ryan scrolled through the rest of the list, hoping to find the names of Schuller's other daughters, but couldn't find anything. By then, Becky had returned and she wanted to know what he was looking for. He told her about the sketch and what he'd found in the school library.

"The Tango Museum looks like the place I drew, but I won't be sure until I see it."

"Ask your mom to take you over there."

"She's too busy." Besides, if it *was* the right place and he did something weird, his mother might decide that he *really* needed to see a doctor.

"Abuelita would take you."

"Yeah, maybe."

He would have to think about it. Maybe it would be better for him and Becky to go to work with his mom one day and ride their bikes over to the museum. Would they let a couple of kids into the place?

Becky had brought in a plate of cheese and crackers and they settled on the floor with their snack and school books. She switched the channel to CNN and explained that she had to report on a current event for social studies, any event that appeared on CNN today.

They sat through boring reports on the stock market, the president's travel overseas, and then a pretty broadcaster came on and said, "Only two months ago, the attorney general of the United States had to step down for health reasons. CNN has learned that President Baker has narrowed his search for a new attorney general to three possible candidates, all eminently qualified for the position. . . ."

"Perfect," Becky said. "I'll do this current event."

Three photographs came up on the screen with a heading above them that read CANDIDATES FOR ATTORNEY GENERAL OF THE U.S. Ryan, frowning, leaned closer, staring at the photo of the man in the middle. JUDGE JAY HUTCHIN, read the name under the middle photo. The name didn't mean anything to him, but the longer he stared at the man's picture, the more uncomfortable he felt.

"Ryan? Hey, Ryan. You look sick."

"I know him." Ryan could barely spit out the words. He scrambled across the floor and stabbed his index finger against the screen. "*Him.* I know him. He's . . ."

A bad man. . . .

Ryan slapped his hand over his ears and squeezed his eyes shut. "Stop it," he hissed. "I won't listen to you. Stop it."

Bad man. . . .

He shot to his feet and ran out of the room with his hands

pressed to his ears. And suddenly he found himself outside, in the bright afternoon light, racing across the road, running until he stumbled and sprawled in the weeds. He lay there, waiting for the sound of the Other's voice, waiting for that voice to demand that he do this or that, go here or there, waited for the voice to snap orders. But his head had filled with silence.

Ryan rolled onto his back, his heart still hammering. He was in the field where he had been digging last Thursday night, but across the street from Becky's house rather than his own. Any second now, she would come running out with her father. *Get up. Now.*

He sat up. *I know that man, but from where? And why is he a bad man?*

"There he is, Daddy," Becky shouted, pointing, and she and her father ran across the road to the field.

"Are you okay, Ryan?" Mr. Landress asked, helping Ryan to his feet. "Are you hurt?"

"No, sir. I'm all right. I just stumbled. Becky and I were, uh, playing hide and seek and I forgot we weren't supposed to leave the house." He looked at Becky, his eyes begging her not to say anything.

"I thought you said he freaked out," her father said.

"Well, he did. He freaked out because it was his turn to hide. I was shouting at him that it wasn't fair to hide outside."

Mr. Landress, Ryan thought, didn't look as if he believed a word of it. But to Ryan's surprise, he said, "So why don't you kids extend the boundaries to the backyard, within the fenced area?"

"Good idea, Daddy," said Becky. "Right now, I think we'll go back upstairs and finish our snack."

"Just give me another hour to wrap up what I'm doing," her dad went on. "Then we'll go out in the boat for a while."

A few minutes later, when Ryan and Becky were alone in the backyard, she got angry at him. "You almost got me into big trouble, Ryan. I thought you'd freaked out and shouted for my dad."

"I *know* that guy. The judge."

"Your mom's a lawyer. You've met a lot of judges."

"No, I've never met him. I'd remember."

"You *are* remembering."

Ryan shook his head. "It's not the same thing. This isn't *my* memory."

Becky looked puzzled now. "So are you saying it's, like, the Other's memory?"

"I don't know."

"How do you know for sure that it's not *your* memory, Ryan?"

"It doesn't feel like it belongs to me. That's the only way I can explain it. When I saw the lady on the bridge . . . that wasn't my memory. Whatever I was digging for the other night—that wasn't my memory, either."

They had reached the dock and sat at the edge of it, bare feet dangling over the side. Ryan could tell that Becky was thinking hard about what he'd said. She would come up with something, he knew she would. She was in the gifted program and was one of the smartest kids he knew.

"The kid in *The Sixth Sense* saw dead people all the time—"

"I'm not seeing dead people. The lady on the bridge wasn't dead."

"I'm just thinking out loud. Let me finish. The man in *The Dead Zone* was so psychic that he picked up stuff from everyone he touched—"

"That's not how it is for me."

She made an impatient gesture with her hand. "Then there was the kid in *The Shining*—"

"Who also saw ghosts."

"Yeah, he did. And he was psychic, too. But remember, he had an imaginary friend who turned out to be himself, as an adult, in the future."

Ryan considered this. "So maybe the voice in my head is the voice of myself in the future?"

"It's possible, Ryan." She sounded excited now. "The voice belongs to the adult and he's trying to warn you about something that's buried and involves a woman and that judge. In *The Shining*, the kid's adult self was trying to warn him about the Overlook and how his father was going bonkers and had started drinking again and about the threat to him and his mother." She snapped her fingers. "Maybe that's it! Your adult self is trying to warn you that your mother is in danger, maybe because of this guy she's going to defend."

It didn't feel quite right, but it felt a whole lot more right than what his mother probably thought about now, that he was sick in the head. That he needed to see a doctor. "Maybe we should try to find out more about this judge."

"Great idea. The Internet. There should be something about him on the Internet, right?"

They jumped up and ran into the house, to Becky's room. The TV was still tuned to CNN, but to a different story, and the computer was still on Becky's home page. Ryan plopped down in front of the computer and Becky pulled a chair up next to him.

Ryan went to work, narrowing the search phrase until he found a list of criminal court judges in the Florida Keys. Was Hutchin a judge in Monroe County or in Tango County? He clicked Tango first, found Hutchin's name, and clicked it. His photo came up, a little thing that didn't tell him much. Ryan clicked it to make it larger and as it scrolled into view, his stomach felt like he was on a plane that suddenly had dropped a mile through the sky.

"He scares me." He whispered the words.

"Why?" Becky whispered back.

"I don't know why."

"He kinda looks like Harrison Ford."

Ryan touched his fingers to the screen, against Hutchin's face. *Talk to me,* he thought at the Other. But the voice remained silent now.

"Scroll down," Becky said. "Maybe there's something about him that will give you clues."

They read through five pages of stuff about how Hutchin ruled on cases in his six years as judge, but Ryan didn't understand very much of it. He didn't think Becky did, either. Even though she was smart, you had to go to law school to understand this stuff. He kept scrolling down the screen and got to the part about what Hutchin had done before he'd been a judge. Only one part of it made sense to him, the part about how in 1981 he'd been teaching at the University of Miami Law School. "That's the same year my mom went to law school," he exclaimed. "Maybe Hutchin was her teacher."

"Ask her. Since she's a defense attorney, I bet she's tried cases where he was the judge. That's another connection."

"Probably. But what does it prove? Does it mean he's a threat to my mom?"

"I don't know. You're the one who's hearing the voice, not me."

Becky got up to turn off the TV and Ryan just stared at the computer screen, struggling to find another search term for Judge Hutchin.

"Ryan, hey, it's your mom! Look."

Ryan glanced around and Becky turned up the volume.

"In a new development in the homicide of actress Diane

Jackson, CNN has learned that the accused, Steve Poulton, with whom Jackson was romantically involved, is to be defended by a prominent South Florida law firm, Parrish and Vasquez. Kit Parrish, the firm's founder, is the sister of journalist Pete Beaupre, who vanished ten years ago.

"Jackson, the Oscar-winning actress of *Run For Your Money*, was building a home on nearby Tango Key, and met Poulton, a medical resident in pediatrics, when she was doing research for a movie that will be released early next year. Her body was found on the morning of November second, at the Peninsula Motel on Tango Key, where she was staying. She and Poulton were seen arguing earlier Thursday evening in a Tango Key bar. Parrish and Vasquez declined comment on the case. . . ."

The image of his mother's face lingered in Ryan's mind even after it vanished from the screen. He quickly found his cell phone and dialed her cell number.

"Kit Parrish."

"Mom, I just saw you on CNN."

"Oh. That happened a while ago. Don't pay any attention to what they're saying. Are you at Becky's?"

"Yeah, her dad picked us up."

"I should be home at five. I've got to scoot, Ryan."

"Wait. Mom."

"Yes?"

She sounded impatient. He could hear phones ringing in the background, voices. "Do you know Judge Hutchin?"

"Sure. I know all of the criminal court judges in the keys. Why? How do you . . . oh, you must've seen the news on TV, right? About the attorney general position?"

"Uh-huh." *Be careful around him.* "He's . . ." *Say it. Warn her.* "Mom, be careful. Love you." Ryan disconnected before he could blurt out that Hutchin was a bad man.

Chapter 11

Silence. A strange and blissful silence had descended over the courthouse. Hutchin reveled in it, embraced it, welcomed it. He rolled around in it like a pig in shit. He poured himself two fingers of Scotch on the rocks and moved restlessly around his quiet office, hoping that he had done the right thing.

He hadn't expected an announcement of the list of possible appointees for the attorney general position. He wasn't even sure at this point whether there had been an official announcement or whether the news had been leaked intentionally to CNN. Either way, the end result to him had been the same: chaos.

Finally, two hours ago, he had stepped outside and said that he was honored to be selected as one of the candidates. But until the matter was decided, he would appreciate it if the news vans left because they were blocking access to the courthouse. It had done the trick, the media had left. Congratulatory calls had poured in, but he'd instructed Louise to tell people he wasn't available. Every now and then, his phone rang, but he didn't bother answering it. He didn't want to talk to anyone.

At one point this afternoon, he had considered making an announcement that although he was honored by his candidacy, he had been elected by the people and felt obligated to finish out his term. Then the FBI wouldn't poke around in his life, Congress wouldn't scrutinize him, and he would surely get away with murder.

But he felt confident that he would get away with it even now. Nothing connected him to Diane, nothing at all. Even the necklace he'd bought her had been paid for in cash. No witnesses and no paper trail, except for her journal and notes, which he had in his possession. He'd gone over every piece of their relationship, every encounter during their months together, every call, every treacherous touch. And he felt confident that he wouldn't be discovered.

Nearly every time he'd called her, it had been from a pay phone; she had claimed the same was true for her. Whenever he'd seen her, it had been away from Tango and Key West, except for Thursday night. They never had gotten together with other people, either her friends or his. Their relationship had existed in a social vacuum, exclusive and isolated.

But in whom had *she* confided?

Probably no one, he decided. Diane herself had been as secretive as he was, or more so, and it seemed highly unlikely that she had mentioned their relationship to anyone. In public, her man of the moment had been Poulton, although even that relationship was private enough so that Hutchin hadn't known about it until he'd seen her with Poulton. But Poulton, he suspected, had met Diane's friends and vice versa. Their relationship hadn't existed in a social vacuum because Poulton wasn't married and they were about the same age. So Poulton had been charged and arrested, and Kit Parrish and her partner would defend him. Innocent until proven guilty was bullshit; the jury would find Poulton guilty because there was no proof otherwise.

Therefore, he had decided to make the statement that he had.

He walked back over to his desk and picked up the rotational schedule for cases. No mistake about it: his name was right there, next to the State vs. Steve Poulton. This would be the next major challenge, getting through the trial without blowing it, losing it, exposing himself in some way. But how many surprises could there be? Opitz didn't have to prove conclusively that Poulton had killed Diane. He merely had to prove it beyond a reasonable doubt and, with a little help from Hutchin, help that was clearly within his judicial powers, he could do that.

There would be no surprises in court. Both Opitz and Kit knew the rules in his courtroom. At pretrial conferences, defendants and counsel had to be present unless excused by the court. At these conferences, he had a specific list of issues that had to be discussed: order of selection of juries, order of trial, evidentiary problems that needed the attention of the judge, the length of the trial, and jury instructions. Pretrial motions had to be heard prior to the pretrial conference or, in lieu of a conference, prior to jury selection. The only exceptions to this were motions in limine, which requested that the court not allow certain evidence that might prejudice a jury. Plea negotiations were provisionally accepted when made subject to review of presentence investigations, evaluations, score sheets, and other relevant matters. All plea agreements had to be in writing, in the form approved by the court.

But all of that aside, he thought, there would be no surprises because on the bench, in the courtroom, his word was law. He was God.

He gathered up the stack of papers on his desk to take

home with him. As he raised the lid of his briefcase, his gaze fell on Diane's journal. He kept meaning to stash it somewhere safe in the house, but every time he started to do so, he felt uneasy. Perhaps the journal was safest right where it was, in his briefcase, which was usually locked and in his possession.

He picked it up—*lying bitch*—and opened it at random.

7/2/2000

We finished shooting yesterday and Steve met me in LA, then today we drove up the coast to Carmel. It's one of my favorite spots on the planet, lush and romantic, magical. People here are so accustomed to seeing celebrities that no one bothered us.

I'm happy when I'm with Steve. He accepts me as I am, paradoxes and all. With J, all the rules are different and most of the time when I'm with him I feel such angst that it's all becoming unpleasant. I think it's time to end that part of my life.

"Jay? Hello?"

Hutchin's head snapped up and there stood Paul Opitz in the rear doorway, materializing like some apparition at the gates of hell. He quickly slipped the journal under a pile of law journals on his desk. *Did he see it? Could he see it from the doorway?*

"Paul. You startled me."

Opitz, dressed in his usual natty attorney attire, stepped inside, briefcase in one hand. "I hear that congratulations are in order."

"Thanks, but right now I'm just a name on a list."

"A very short list. The way I hear it, you're a shoo-in."

Hutchin surreptitiously drew one of the law journals closer toward him to cover the edge of the journal. "So what's on your mind, Paul?'' *What is it that warrants a personal visit after hours?*

''Not much. Just wanted to say I hope you get in because then I can say I knew you when.''

''How about a drink?''

He tugged at his tie. ''Sounds good.''

They settled near the windows, Hutchin with his Scotch and Opitz with a cold beer, two men whose lives had crossed many times over the years. Opitz had taken over as state attorney for Tango County when Hutchin had been appointed to the bench and subsequently had been elected. He pushed for speedy trials, had a flair for inflammatory courtroom oratory, and had been cited for contempt several times. But he was also the only attorney in ten years to beat Kit Parrish in court and Hutchin suspected that he intended to prosecute the Poulton case himself rather than assign it to one of his underlings. And why not? A high profile case like this one could make Opitz's career.

''I ran into Kit at Poulton's place in the keys. We'd gone up there with a search warrant, but she'd already been into the house.''

''We shouldn't be discussing the case, Paul. The rotational schedule puts me on the bench for this one.''

''I'm not saying anything the defense doesn't know about. As far as I could see, she hadn't taken anything from the house. But I couldn't very well check the trunk of the car. Anyway, I think Kit is griped because Diane supposedly kept a journal that Poulton says was in her suitcase at the Peninsula, but property doesn't have it listed.''

The air behind Hutchin, specifically in the area where the journal was hidden, suddenly seemed heavier, weighted. ''Kit told you that?''

Opitz gave a weird little laugh that exposed his crooked front teeth. ''Shit, no. She doesn't let anything out of the bag. The cop in property told me. He also said she checked out an article of clothing that belonged to Diane and since Kit had her dog with her, I'm assuming she was looking for something of Diane's in the house.''

Hutchin sipped at his Scotch and wished he had burned the goddamn journal. ''Is Poulton going to waive his right to a speedy trial?''

''I hope not. The longer we wait, the bigger the media circus.''

Translated: *the longer the wait, the more time Kit Parrish would have to prepare her defense.* Opitz detested losing and he knew the media attention on this case would be considerable. Hutchin, of course, realized it would be to his own advantage if Poulton went to trial quickly.

''You're undoubtedly right about the media attention, but the court would need a better reason than that, Paul. Even O.J. had to wait his turn. I understand Poulton doesn't want bail.''

''Yeah, well, that's not all.'' Opitz now lowered his voice. ''The coroner is supposed to release his official report tomorrow morning, but get this. Diane Jackson was pregnant and the baby can't be Poulton's.''

Opitz continued talking, but to Hutchin his voice sounded like a high-pitched hum. *Jesus God, the lying bitch told me she couldn't have kids, that her tubes had been tied.* And he had believed her. It never had occurred to him not to believe her.

''Jay?''

Jay Jay Jay. ''How far along was she?'' It took enormous effort to form the words, to pronounce them, to speak them in a tone of voice that bore any semblance of normalcy. ''Do you know?''

"Dr. Luke says she was between eight and ten weeks pregnant."

September, that means it happened sometime in September. He had seen Diane only twice in September—over Labor Day weekend when they'd met for a night in Miami and again about two weeks later in Vero Beach. That Vero meeting had been disastrous, he remembered. They had argued most of the time they were together and he hadn't touched her. He was suddenly sure she'd gotten pregnant that night in Miami, when they'd stayed at a romantic place on the beach. *My baby. I killed my own baby.*

His chest went tight, the room spun, he felt as if he might puke. *Not here, not now, not with Opitz sitting there, taking it all in. No.* With enormous effort, Hutchin set his glass of Scotch on the table and rubbed a hand over his face. "I should eat something before I drink Scotch."

"I was thinking the same thing about this beer. How's Isabel taking the news about your potential appointment?"

He noticed how easily Opitz shifted the conversation away from the case, totally uncharacteristic for him. Usually, he simply kept at something with the relentlessness of a mosquito seeking blood. It bothered Hutchin, but his head ached so badly now that he couldn't think it through. He kept seeing Diane struggling for air, trying to get the pillow off her face, but the image was even more horrendous now that he knew she'd been pregnant with *his child.*

He took a calculated risk to plant a seed in Opitz's devious little mind. "Off the record, the pregnancy sounds like a motive. She told Poulton she was pregnant with another man's child and he lost it."

Opitz emitted a soft, commiserating chuckle. "My thoughts exactly, Jay."

(2)

The motel in which Diane Jackson had died hardly qualified as the best on Tango Key. From the looks of it, Kit figured it rated two stars out of four. But for a woman with secrets, she thought, it had served its purpose.

She parked in front of the Peninsula Motel, promised Oro she would be back shortly, and went into the front office. The young woman behind the desk, a Florida suntan babe with thick blond hair, flashed a perfect white smile. "Evening, can I help you with something?"

"Yes. Is Mr. Cintrella in?"

"He's taking his supper break."

"I really need to talk to him. I'm Kit Parrish, the attorney representing Steve Poulton in the—"

"Yeah, I know. I'll be right back."

She disappeared for a few minutes and returned with a guy in his forties who wore polyester slacks and a yellow guayabera shirt. A spot of ketchup bloomed in the corner of his mouth. "Evening, ma'am. I'm Kevin Cintrella."

A hint of Georgia or Alabama in that voice. She went through her spiel again, dropped her ID on the counter. He glanced at it, pushed it back across the counter. "So what can I do for you, Ms. Parrish?"

"I understand you found Diane Jackson's body."

"I did, ma'am. Terrible thing. She was just . . . just lyin there, a pillow over her head, her legs bare, her arms bare . . ."

"What prompted you to go into her room?"

"She'd left a message with the desk for an early wake-up and—"

"How early?"

"Six A.M. I called several times and when I didn't get an answer, I went down there and knocked at the door. I didn't

know it was her, you understand. I mean, when I checked
her in Thursday—''

"At what time did she check in?"

"Ten A.M."

"Under her own name?"

"No. As Dionne Johnson. I knew she looked familiar,
but her hair was different, she wore sunglasses, a cap—''

"Did she use a credit card?"

"Yes, ma'am. Let me get this information for you." He
went over to the computer while the suntan babe stood
there shuffling papers, pretending that she wasn't listening.
Cintrella's fingers tapped the keys, then he glanced up,
frowning. "I don't know if I'm s'posed to give out this
information."

"Let me put it this way, Mr. Cintrella. Either we do it
like this or I subpoena all your records."

"I'm not trying to be difficult. I just don't want to get
into trouble."

"You're not going to get into trouble by cooperating with
the courts."

He hit the print button and a few minutes later, Diane
Jackson's entire bill spat out of the printer, complete with
times, charges, phone calls, room service, credit card receipt
in the name of Dionne Johnson, the whole nine yards. With
this information, she could run a credit check and find out
where else and when the card had been used.

"Had she ever stayed here before?"

"The cops asked me the same thing, so I did a computer
check and I found that she stayed with us a number of times.
I understand she was building a house here on the island.
You want those bills, too?"

"That'd be great. Thanks."

While this information was printing, Kit asked if she

could see cabin 13. Cintrella looked very unhappy about this request. "The crime tape is still up."

"The defense is permitted to see the crime scene."

"Yes, well . . ."

"I need to videotape it."

"I guess it'd be all right, long as we don't break the tape."

"Great. Let me get my videocamera." *And my dog*.

She met Cintrella in the courtyard, the videocamera over her shoulder, Oro on her leash. "A dog?" he balked.

"She's police trained." Actually, Pete had gotten her when she was about six months old, after she'd washed out of police training. Apparently Oro hadn't wanted to spend her entire life sniffing for drugs in high school lockers. "She won't disturb anything." Kit removed the Baggie with Diane's blouse in it. "Sniff, Oro. Find this scent."

"She can do that? Out here? After all this time?" Cintrella asked.

"Imagine, Mr. Cintrella, that a single scent would provide us with the history of whatever the scent belongs to. That's how I think it is for retrievers. Watch." She leaned close to Oro. "Find the smell, girl," she said again, and unfastened the leash.

Oro darted forward, nose to the ground. Kit and Cintrella hurried along after her. She went right, left, straight, then left and right again. It took her a few minutes to single out Diane's smell, but once she had it, she made a beeline for cabin 13. She stopped at the door, barked, and glanced at Kit, who tossed her a dog biscuit.

"That's incredible." Cintrella sounded genuinely astonished. "But what can she possibly find in the cabin? The cops went through it meticulously for two days."

"Maybe she won't find anything. But I'd like to try."

"You sure she won't knock over anything inside here?"

"Positive."

He unlocked the door and they went inside the cabin. Nothing too special about the place, Kit thought, glancing around. Double bed, bureau, the usual motel stuff. She offered Oro another sniff of the blouse, then got out her videocamera and moved slowly around the room.

"It's November sixth, five-fifteen P.M. I'm in cabin thirteen at the Peninsula Motel, where Diane Jackson was killed." She aimed the camera at Oro, who was coming out of the bathroom, tail wagging, following Diane's scent throughout the room. The dog paused near the bed, then turned ninety degrees and stopped next to the air conditioner, an old-fashioned unit that rested under the window, close to the floor, and had dials for temperature adjustment. Oro pawed at one of the control panels.

"I'm going to turn the camera off for a minute to check out whatever Oro is picking up on here."

"What's she doing?" Cintrella asked. "The air conditioner doesn't move or anything."

"I don't know." Kit flipped open the panels, but didn't see anything. She knelt and pressed her fingertips down between the slats of the air conditioner, then moved to the side of the unit, opened the curtains for more light, and peered into the narrow space between the unit and the wall. Oro whined and kept pawing at the unit, trying to get under it.

Kit pulled a flashlight out of her purse, shone it into the crevice. Something glinted in the light. "I need something long and flat."

He hustled over and handed her a metal tape measure. She pulled it out about two feet, stuck it down between the wall and the unit, moved it back and forth rapidly until she felt something come loose. As it struck the floor, Oro whined and pawed at the carpet, trying to reach it. "Good dog," Kit said, patting her. "Let me get it."

She got down on her hands and knees, reached under the unit, and brought out a silver, rectangular-shaped object. It reminded her of a cigarette holder, one of those things that had been in vogue when smoking was fashionable, except that it was much flatter and fit perfectly in the palm of her hand. She popped open the delicate lid. A gold heart on a chain lay inside of it. A very expensive gold heart, she thought, on a very expensive chain.

"What the hell," Cintrella murmured, peering over her shoulder. "How'd the cops miss that?"

"They didn't use a dog."

Kit set the delicate silver box on the windowsill, slipped a small fabric pouch from her purse, unzipped it, withdrew a pair of tweezers. She pinched the edge of the heart with the tweezers, turned it over. The writing on the back was very small. She had to bring out a magnifying glass to read it: *love, the centaur.*

"A centaur?" said Cintrella. "Isn't that a mythological creature that's half man and half animal?"

"Yeah. It's also the symbol for Sagittarius."

Poulton was a Scorpio, not a Sagittarius. But maybe "centaur" had a different meaning to whoever had given her the heart.

"That's a weird place to put anything, much less something valuable," Cintrella remarked.

"Do you have a security box where guests can put their belongings?"

He seemed insulted by the question. "Of course we do."

"Diane might have been in a hurry when she stashed it back there." Kit snapped the silver case shut, pulled a Baggie from her fabric pouch, and put the silver case inside of it. She gave Oro another dog biscuit and wondered how many biscuits that was for the day. Pete, she thought, would have a fit. He'd been meticulous about Oro's diet, her exercise, her moods.

Kit picked up the videocamera again and finished walking through the room and into the bathroom. She didn't mention finding the silver case. It might prove to be just the ace in the hole that Poulton needed and she didn't intend to turn it over to property, not until she and Rita had the chance to run down where it had come from—and, if possible, from whom.

Chapter 12

Thursday, November 8

The small stone house sits on a hill that overlooks a body of water. Ivy snakes across the front of the house, twisted vines with leaves as large as his hands. The vines even outline the pair of windows on the second floor, where lights are on. Those upper windows look like luminous eyes, gazing out into the greater darkness, where he stands.

In the dream, he unlatches the gate and moves silently up the curved stone sidewalk, through the trees, the deep shadows, beneath an overcast sky. He doesn't have to ring the bell. He knows she is waiting for him inside the little stone house.

There's a story about these stones that he can't remember now, some island legend that he has heard somewhere. Perhaps she told him about it. He touches the knob on the heavy wooden door, turns it, steps inside, listens. Maybe he will hear her humming to herself. Maybe he will hear her breathing somewhere close by.

He hears something, a distant, isolated noise that seems wrong somehow, and he is suddenly filled with fear. It grabs him by the throat, this fear, and won't let go. It screams at him, screams for him to run now, while he still can. He spins around—

—and spun right out of the dream, the covers tangled around him, his chest on fire. His screams came out as hoarse, rasping whispers, ''Help me, someone help me. . . .'' Not even loud enough to wake his dog, asleep at the foot of his bed, and definitely not loud enough to wake his mother down the hall.

Ryan untangled himself from the covers and stumbled out of bed and raced through the hall to his mother's room. He dived into bed beside her and buried himself under the covers.

''Jesus, what . . .'' his mother murmured, and gathered him in her arms. ''Ryan.'' She ran her fingers through his hair. ''You scared me, kiddo.''

''Scared myself.'' His mouth moved against her shoulder. He wanted to get lost in the smell of her shirt, wanted to hide in that smell.

She rolled away from him, but reached for his hand under the covers, held it tightly. ''Bad dream?''

''Can I sleep in here, Mom?''

Two quick squeezes on his hand. That meant it would be okay, Ryan thought. The first squeeze meant that she believed his dream had been one of the usual nightmares, and the second squeeze meant that he would be safe here, next to her, and they would talk about it in the morning.

His mother fell back to sleep immediately, he could tell by the way she breathed and by how the pressure on his hand got lighter. Ryan lay there, huddled next to her, to his mother, and heard Oro's claws tapping the floor as she came into the room. The dog sighed as she flopped to the floor on his side of the bed.

Safe. I'm safe. Oro and his mother would keep him safe.

He shut his eyes, saw the little stone house, and his eyes snapped open again. He knew that if he fell asleep, he would fall back into the dream inside the house and this time the noise that he'd heard would take human form and it would hurt him. So he lay there, pressed up against his mother, and stared upward at the ceiling fan and then at the book-cases, and deep inside himself he felt the Other coming alive.

Much of the time, the Other seemed to sleep inside of him. But when It came awake, It clawed at his insides, demanding to be freed, and It hurt so much that Ryan couldn't fight it. And he couldn't fight it now. It demanded that he sit up, so he sat up. It demanded that he get out of bed, that he find a pencil and a piece of paper, that he go into a room where there was light.

He did everything the Other told him to do, but this time Ryan was aware of what he was doing. This part, he understood, was new. It was as if there were two Ryans, the boy who heard the Other's voice and did what the Other told him to do, and the boy who watched it happening.

He found a pencil and a notepad on his mother's dresser and went into the bathroom, where a night-light glowed. He sat down on the floor and allowed the Other to seize control of the pencil and then he went away for a while. When he came back, he felt so tired he could barely stand. He picked up the pad and the pencil and dropped them on her dresser and rolled into her bed.

He slept like the dead.

Ryan woke suddenly, sunlight pressing against his eyes so that the world seemed to have been wiped clean of color.

No Oro, no mom, the bed was empty. But he smelled coffee and heard morning sounds that told him his mother was getting breakfast. Ryan padded into the kitchen—and watched his mother rushing around, putting out plates, feeding Oro, pouring cereal into bowls, popping bread in the toaster oven.

"We overslept?" he asked.

"We did."

"How bad?"

She glanced over at him, her hair wild, uncombed, her dressy blouse hanging loose over gym shorts. "You're going to be at least an hour late for school."

Bad, that was bad. "I'll be ready in fifteen minutes," he said.

"Let's call in sick," she said.

What? His mother had never, ever said that before. "Okay."

They looked at each other, he and his mom, and they both laughed and he sank into the chair and poured milk into his cereal. "So if we're both calling in sick," he said, "what're we going to do today?"

"We're going to Tango."

Good, he thought. He would ask her to take him to the Tango Museum. Ask casually, so she wouldn't suspect anything. "And maybe have lunch at our favorite place on the pier?"

"And hang out. Like tourists."

Ryan gave her a quick hug. "I'll be ready in five minutes."

They drove across the long bridge to Tango Key and turned north into the hills. Ryan lowered his window and the sweet, clean air blew into the van. Fields covered in brightly colored flowers stretched off to his right. Clouds of yellow butterflies appeared and disappeared. A hawk rode invisible currents just above the road and Ryan leaned forward, watching it through the window.

The sight of it, long wings extended against the blue sky, reminded him of another hawk he'd seen a long time ago. Now the hawk seemed to be circling the car and Ryan scrambled into the back of the van to watch the bird through the rear window. As it came around toward the front of the van again, he climbed back into the passenger seat. "It's following us!" he exclaimed.

"You know what the hawk's message is?"

"I'm hungry?"

His mother laughed. "No, I meant the deeper message."

Ryan shook his head.

"Well, according to Native Americans and people who know about these things, the hawk's message is to remember who you really are."

"How?"

"That's different for each of us. I think the hawk's message for me pertains to doing the very best job I can to defend Steve Poulton."

"But you always do your best in court."

She smiled at that. "I try, hon, but with this case, I have to pull out all the stops."

"What's the hawk's message for me?"

"I think that's something you have to figure out, Ryan."

When he peered up through the windshield again, the hawk was gone.

His mother turned off the main highway through the hills, onto a narrow two-lane road. "Where're we going, Mom?"

She reached under the seat and brought out his sketch pad, the one he'd taken from her dresser last night when he couldn't sleep, when the Other had ordered him into an area where there was some light. He recognized the pencil strokes as his own. And he recognized the house that he had sketched as the one he had seen in the dream, a continuation of the sketch he'd done in art class. The viewpoint was different, not straight on, but from the side so that part of the front grounds and part of the property at the back of the house were visible.

"Look at the next page," his mother said, and he flipped the page.

Here was an almost exact duplicate of the sketch he'd done in art class. The stone walls. The ivy. The front door wide open so that the spiral staircase was visible. Both sketches were the stone house, but he had no memory of drawing them. He knew that he had sketched *something* in the bathroom last night, but he had been so tired when he'd finished that he hadn't looked at it. He'd left it on his mother's dresser and had fallen into bed.

"These are astonishing drawings, Ryan." His mother spoke very softly. Ryan didn't look at her. He couldn't. His eyes wouldn't move. His eyes stayed glued to the sketch. "The detail is beautiful. The stones on the front of the house . . . I can almost see the cracks and fissures in them. The ivy looks alive; I can see it growing, arranging itself around the windows. And the gate. It looks really heavy, like iron, and there's some sort of emblem on the front of it. And behind the house, in that first sketch, I can just make out the edge of the cliff."

She stopped. Ryan knew he was supposed to say something, but he had nothing to say. He just looked up at her and shook his head, trying to tell her he didn't know how he had drawn this house, why he had dreamed about it. He had no answers.

"When I look at this drawing, hon, I see incredible talent. It's also obvious that you've seen this house. I think it's the

Tango Museum, yet as far as I know you've never been to that museum, unless you went with Nana and Grandpa. Or maybe you went there with Abuelita. But I called Abuelita and asked and she said she's never taken you there. I e-mailed Nana and asked the same thing. She and Grandpa have never taken you there, either. Maybe you saw it in a book of photographs. Do you think?''

"Only after I drew it in art class Tuesday. But in the book at school, it didn't show the back of the house.''

"Maybe you saw it on TV.''

"No.''

"The only place in the keys where houses are built of stone, Ryan, is on this island. Oh, there're places built of coquina stone, but this stone isn't coquina. This is two-toned stone. Only Tango has stone like that.''

"It's the Tango Museum, I'm sure of it.''

"How can you be so sure?''

"I . . . I . . . *feel* it.''

"Feel it how, hon? Help me out here. Is the voice telling you this is the right one?''

Ryan shook his head, glanced at her. "No. I *feel* it, Mom. The Other is . . . is asleep.''

Huge banyan trees rose up on either side, their branches growing together overhead so they formed a tunnel of green. Light and shadow danced across the windshield. Ryan shifted in his seat, uneasy now.

His mother pulled into the museum parking lot. "As Pooh would say, let's go take a look-see.''

"It looks like the kinda place Pooh and his buddies might like.''

"For sure.'' She took his hand as they started up the walk. "Hon, if you feel uncomfortable when we get inside, just tell me, okay?''

"I'm fine, Mom.''

But he wasn't fine. He had nervous flutters in the pit of his stomach, and his hands started to sweat. He wanted to tell his mother he had changed his mind, that he didn't want to go inside, but then he remembered the hawk. *The hawk's message is to remember who you really are.*

The building was stone, all right, two-toned Tango stone, each block like a work of art. It was two stories, with tall windows on the lower floor and shorter windows on the second floor. It had a porch, just as he'd drawn, with an Adirondack chair on it, that was what his mother called it. The banyans stood at the front, a pair of them, proud and ancient, their huge branches braided together overhead so they formed a canopy of green. But no ivy covered the front of the museum. No hammock was strung up between the banyans. No other furniture was on the porch.

These small differences bothered him, caused him to doubt his feelings about the museum being the place he had drawn. But if Becky was right and the Other was his future self and that self had used his hands to make the sketch, it made sense that in the future, the buildings would be changed.

He suddenly wasn't so sure he wanted to remember anything. Remembering scared him. But he also knew that if he didn't try, things would get more confusing for him, more mixed up. He might even do something stupid again, like the digging or racing along the bridge that went nowhere.

He had to go inside the museum. "Where's the gate?" he asked.

"Down there." His mother pointed off toward the far right corner of the property. "It looks like that used to be the driveway. We'll take a look at it on our way out."

His mother paid at the door. Inside the museum, the floor was wooden, that seemed right, and when he raised his head, he saw the spiral staircase, iron, old, just as he had seen it in his head. *It's the right place, changed but the same.* For moments, he just stood there, looking around, soaking it up, a part of him braced for the Other to come shrieking to life as it had in the past. Instead, the fluttering in his stomach was now wild and fast. His mouth went dry. He felt slightly dizzy.

"Let's take a look over here," his mother said, moving to the left, toward an exhibit of some kind.

Ryan started to follow her, but he felt a sudden tug in the opposite direction, almost as if someone were pulling on his arm, and he turned toward it. His feet moved fast now and he realized they were *remembering*, just as his hands had remembered that night in the field. It scared him, but he couldn't stop now, couldn't call out for his mother's help, couldn't do anything except let his feet lead him.

Remember who you really are: the hawk's message.

Your future self, Becky had said.

But how could his feet be remembering something that still lay in the future?

Now he was running, his feet tearing down a hall, and he couldn't stop, he had no control over his feet. He threw his arms out in front of him, to protect himself, and his mouth dropped open to scream for help. He crashed through a swinging door and stopped, looking around, confused. He seemed to be in some sort of utility room.

A woman in a uniform stood at a utility sink, washing something, and she glanced around. "You're not supposed to be in here, young man."

"I . . . I'm sorry. I . . ." And then the right words popped into his head. "There's supposed to be another room in here." He pointed to his right, at a wall that wasn't stone. "Right there. And there were stairs, old wooden stairs, not iron like the spiral staircase . . . back stairs that went to the loft. . . ."

The woman's eyes got big. Very big. "Actually, that

room was walled off in 1992 and they never reopened it. It's used for storage now and—''

His mother exploded through the swinging doors. ''Ryan?'' She glanced quickly at the woman. ''I'm really sorry that he intruded back here. I didn't realize that he wandered away from me.''

''That's quite all right, ma'am. Your son seems to know quite a bit about the museum.''

''Really.''

''He knew there's a room back here with wooden stairs that lead up to the loft. It was walled off in 1992. It's not on the museum map. Hey, would you like to take a peek inside?'' the woman asked Ryan.

''Sure.''

She unlocked the door and as it swung inward, a light came on automatically. Ryan stepped cautiously into the room, his mother right behind him. He looked around, taking in the wooden stairs, the bare stone walls, the boxes of stuff. His breathing speeded up, he clenched his fingers, his vision went sort of fuzzy, as if he were peering at the room through a lens that was out of focus. And suddenly, he tore toward the stairs. . . .

(2)

Kit saw the shift in her son's face, the moment when he was no longer *here,* the moment when his mind went *elsewhere,* to the other extreme. Subtle changes tipped her off, a tightening at the corners of his mouth, the way his lower lip quivered, the sudden clenching of his fingers, the squint to his eyes. Just as she moved toward him, he lunged for the stairs and the museum woman snapped, ''Hey, you can't go up there, it isn't safe, the steps . . .''

Kit lurched after him, but he was halfway up the stairs

by then. The old wooden steps obviously had rotted in places and they creaked and moaned with her weight. But she kept moving, moving. She shouted for Ryan to stop and the museum woman shouted at them both from the bottom of the stairs. The stairs curved gently upward, not a helix like the wrought-iron staircase, but more of a gradual, lazy S, and then she reached the top and blinked against the strange light that filtered through a stained-glass window.

Her son stood in the middle of the room, turning slowly, tears streaming down his cheeks, his arms flung out at his sides, as if to catch or to embrace whatever he was seeing. "She doesn't love me anymore," he whispered, and Kit rushed over to him and picked him up and his small arms closed around her.

"I love you, hon." She cradled the back of his head in one hand and the other pressed against the small of his back, holding him in place. His legs scissored around her hips. He didn't fight her, didn't struggle to get away from her. "I love you bigger than the universe," she whispered.

She carried him over to an old couch under the stained-glass window and sat down, Ryan still clinging to her. He was crying, but there was no terror in these cries, no panic, only heartbreak. The museum woman appeared at the top of the stairs, winded from the climb, and had the wisdom not to interrupt.

"It's okay, hon," Kit said over and over again.

A lie, it was all a lie. Nothing was okay and it was her fault. She should have filed the sketch away and waited until he was ready to talk about it. Instead, she had forced the issue and still didn't have a clue what the issue was about. What was she dealing with here? Who didn't love him? And how was he able to draw a place he had never seen?

What the fuck's going on?

Ryan finally lifted his head from her shoulder, knuckled

his eyes. "It's all wrong. The rooms are all wrong." He climbed off her lap, unaware that the museum woman was in the room. "This window . . ." He pointed at the stained-glass window. "It used to go from the ceiling to the floor and only the upper part was stained glass. There was a desk over there."

"That's right," the museum woman said softly. "He's absolutely right."

Ryan didn't seem to be aware of the museum woman or of Kit. "Over there was an old-fashioned rolltop desk, like Nana has. And over here . . ." He turned, pointed at the left corner. "There were bookshelves. She had a lot of books."

"Who, Ryan? Who're you talking about?" Kit asked.

He pointed at the ceiling. "A crystal prism hung from up there and in the afternoons, when it caught the light, it used to fill the room with rainbows and—"

"Excuse me, ma'am," said the museum woman. "I don't know what's going on here, but you and your son need to leave. This area really isn't safe, the floor has already rotted through in certain spots and—"

Ryan spun around. "You tell her. The window used to be bigger, didn't it? And down that hall was a bathroom and the toilet never flushed right and—"

"Yes," the woman said, nodding, backing away from Ryan, obviously startled by his intensity. "You're right. The window . . . they took it out last year . . . and the toilet was leaking, it had leaked for probably fifteen years, a slow leak that caused the ceiling in the room downstairs to start crumbling. . . . We really need to go downstairs. I can lose my job over something like this."

Questions raced through Kit's mind. She wanted to quiz her son, to interrogate him, to cross-examine him. But not here. She stood. "We're going."

"But, Mom . . ."

Kit shot her son the sternest look she could muster and he followed her, reluctantly, down the stairs. They didn't speak until they were in the car and then it was Ryan who broke the silence, who asked her to pull up to the gate. "What for?" she asked.

"I need to see if the emblem is still there."

She parked to the side of the road, left the engine running, and they both hurried over to the gate. What had looked in his sketch like an emblem was actually a family seal. It read THE SCHULLERS. "I don't know that name," Kit said, more to herself than to Ryan.

"I know some stuff about them. But not enough, Mom. I need more. It's really important. I have to know more."

Kit glanced at her son, who was now rubbing his palm over the seal, cleaning it, shining it. *I don't know him. I don't know who this kid is. I don't understand what the fuck's going on. What happened in there? How does he know all that detail? And who doesn't love him anymore?*

"Ryan, what's going on?"

His hand fell away from the seal and he raised his eyes, those huge dark eyes like Pete's. "I don't know."

"Who doesn't love you anymore?"

"The lady who lived here."

"Who was she? Was she a Schuller?"

"I don't know. I can't see her face yet."

She crouched so they were eye to eye and touched his arms. "Hon, I'm not following this."

"I'm not sick." He looked defiant as he said it.

It was like some existential dilemma, she thought. A scene out of Kafka or Dostoevsky. It was *The Sixth Sense*, except that her son wasn't seeing ghosts in the traditional sense, whatever that was. She suddenly felt giddy, unhinged, and nearly overwhelmed by the whole thing. "I know you're not sick, Ryan. I didn't imply that you are. It's just that I don't know how to help you because I . . . I don't understand what's going on.''

Then he put his arms around her neck and hugged her. ''I don't understand, either,'' he whispered. ''But it scares me less now.''

Then he pulled back, stuck his hands in the pockets of his jeans, and walked across the road, a little guy with his head bowed and an unspeakable weight on his shoulders.

Chapter 13

At 4:13 Thursday afternoon, the fire alarm went off, a loud, shrill, and continuous sound that silenced everything in Hutchin's courtroom. It went on for about thirty seconds, stopped, and two courthouse security guards and a pair of cops rushed into the courtroom. "Ladies and gentlemen, please evacuate the building in an orderly manner. Take your things with you. Exit right through here. This is not a drill."

The alarm shrieked again. Hutchin quickly removed his robes and draped them over the back of his chair. Then he gathered up the papers and files on the bench, shoved everything into his briefcase, and followed the others—attorneys, clerks, clients, cops, court reporters, all of them shouting at each other to make themselves heard over the shrieking of the alarm. Hutchin didn't smell smoke, so this couldn't be related to a fire. That left a natural disaster, a riot, or a bomb threat.

His mind raced. Was Diane's journal in the briefcase? He thought he'd glimpsed it when he'd shoved the papers inside, but he couldn't be absolutely sure. And what about the files in his office? Sensitive files, correspondence, cases, judgments. And in the safe . . .

He turned away from the others to head through the courtroom's rear doors that led to his chambers. But one of the men in gear—SWAT team, bomb squad, fed, Hutchin didn't know what the hell he was—blocked his way. "Everyone has to leave *now*."

Over the man's shoulder, Hutchin saw his staff being herded out the back door of his chambers. "I'll go out that way," Hutchin insisted, trying to push past the man.

"No, sir, you're going out *that* way."

And he had the gall, the unmitigated gall to grab him by the shoulders, whip him around, and nudge him toward the front door of the courtroom. Fuming, Hutchin wrenched free of the man's grip and spun around. "Now just a goddamn minute. I—"

"We've got a bomb threat on our hands," the man hissed. "Get moving. *Fast*."

He then blocked Hutchin's way to his chambers, leaving him no choice but to leave through the same doors as everyone else. The alarm abruptly fell silent and a voice blared over the PA system: "Please evacuate the building now."

As soon as he was outside, cops herded him across the street with the rest of the crowd, past the barricades that had been erected. Choppers hovered overhead, sirens sundered the air. He ended up on the steps of a house, watching the chaos, anxious to open his briefcase to check if Diane's journal was inside, but afraid to do so out here.

Off to his left, he saw cops leading prisoners out of the county jail, which was connected to the courthouse. His attention fixed on the only prisoner with three escorts. A current of recognition sped through him. Poulton, that man was Poulton.

Hutchin maneuvered through the crowd for a closer look at the bastard. In the moments before Poulton was hustled into a waiting van, he got that look. A handsome young man, but not extraordinary looking. What the hell had Diane seen in him?

With Steve, I can be myself, she had written.

Bullshit, he thought. Diane had been her press releases, her image, the characters she had played. She hadn't had any idea who she was.

Poulton suddenly turned his head and gazed straight at Hutchin, almost as if he sensed that someone was watching him who would make a very big difference in his personal scheme of things. Hutchin gazed back, hating the prick for his youth, his intelligence, and ultimately, for his innocence. Then he vanished into the truck and Hutchin sank back into the crowd, taking refuge in the hot press of bodies, the stink of their excitement, their fear, the very things that, only minutes ago, had repelled him.

His cell phone rang and when he answered it, Louise Reese sounded a bit frantic and frayed at the edges. "Judge? Are you okay?"

"Sure, fine, Louise. I got herded out the front of the courtroom. How about you?"

"I'm fine. Just fine. Standing out here on the sidewalk, trying to see what's going on. But I wanted to tell you that at one point, I was able to get back into our offices for some files and I swear there's something very strange about all this."

Hutchin stopped where he was and leaned against a light pole, listening. Listening hard. When Louise talked about "strange," then he needed to listen. "Strange about the bomb threat? The evacuation? What?"

"Frankly, I thought a fire had broken out somewhere, but since I didn't smell smoke, I didn't think it was hazardous to go back into the office for some files. I managed to get back in, but when I got there, I saw that the doors to your chambers were closed. This struck me as very odd, considering how these feds were rushing everyone out of the building. I decided to go in and have a look, but the door was locked.''

"*Locked?* Who the hell locked it? I wasn't even allowed to go back into the offices or my chambers.''

"That's the big question, isn't it, Judge Hutchin? I pounded on the door, demanding that it be unlocked, then one of those bomb squad men came in through the courtroom door with a dog and practically carried me out of the building.''

"Did you see his badge? Did you get a name?''

"Yes, sir, I sure did. His name was Webster. Ben Webster, FBI.''

"Good job, Louise. I'll take care of it from here. Get out of that crowd, you hear? Rent a car and go home. The office will pay the expense.''

"Thanks, Judge Hutchin. I think I'll do just that.''

As soon as Hutchin disconnected, he walked quickly away from the crowd, from the courthouse, walked until he reached a restaurant. He ducked inside, felt an enormous relief when he saw it was practically empty, and slid into a booth. He set the briefcase beside him, against the wall, so that his body shielded it from the view of whoever might pass, and dialed in the combination. The instant he raised the lid, he saw the corner of Diane's journal.

Safe. Christ, it's in here and it's safe.

Insanity. He couldn't keep carrying it around with him. But so far, he'd been unable to hide it anywhere because to hide it would mean letting it out of his possession.

Forget about that now. Think about that locked chamber door. Think about those guys in the bomb gear. Think specifically about the fed, Ben Webster. Would the feds stage a bomb scare and evacuation just to get into his chambers? Was that how candidates were investigated, for Christ's sake? It seemed so far over the top that he nearly laughed out loud.

But the longer he mulled it over, the more plausible it became. As plausibility increased, so did the depth of his fear that he would be discovered, that the process of discovery was under way even now. It ate away at him, this fear, like some savage parasite intent on devouring him from the inside out. If he went to the FBI and lodged a complaint about Webster, what purpose would it serve?

He was a candidate who was being investigated by the FBI and who would subsequently be placed under a microscope by Congress and he'd better get used to it. On the other hand, if the bomb threat was bogus, staged just as a means to get into his chambers, then the agents who were responsible needed to be held accountable. They had broken laws . . .

So did you, whispered the vestige of his conscience.

No, it wasn't the same thing. The lying bitch had taunted him.

Just what did they intend to find in his chambers? What sort of incriminating shit were they looking for? Abuse of judicial powers? Clinical depression? Bribes, bankruptcy, and babes? Even if he'd been guilty of all of the above, he wouldn't keep incriminating evidence in his office . . .

Except for the journal. And that was *with him.*

A waitress came over with a menu, but Hutchin didn't bother with the menu. He ordered the salad bar and a coffee and when she went away, he called Isabel's cell phone.

"Hey, hon."

"Jesus, Jay. I heard the news and called your cell phone, but it wasn't on. Are you okay?"

"I'm fine. They evacuated the courthouse and I'm sitting in a restaurant on Tango until I can get to my car."

"I'm on Tango," she said. "I came over here after school to do some Christmas shopping. They say the bridge is backed up for miles, so how about if we just stay here for the night? Things should be clear by morning."

His wife was here, on the island. He was here, on the island. He couldn't possibly tell her he preferred to be alone for a while or that he would meet her in a couple of hours. He couldn't say what he felt because he knew it would hurt her and, Christ knew, he had done enough to hurt her already.

"Traffic around here won't be easy to get through. Let's meet at the Tango pier, in front of Geraldo's."

"In the meantime, I'll make us a hotel reservation somewhere."

"I just ordered, so I'll meet you in about thirty minutes."

"Love you, handsome," she said.

After he'd helped himself to the salad bar and the waitress had brought his soup and coffee, Hutchin unlocked his briefcase and removed the journal.

October 10, 2000
Vancouver

I've been feeling weird for a while. Physically weird. My breasts ache sometimes and I've been feeling nauseated in the mornings. I bought a pregnancy kit today and can't quite bring myself to do the test.

I'm on location here. Tomorrow we'll shoot my final scenes, then I'm free. I want to see S. I wish he were here. I called him this evening, but got the machine. He must be pulling double shifts. I'd like to call J, but the rules say that I can't. So many goddamn rules. He's never met any of my friends, has never been a

part of my life in LA or anywhere else, for that matter.
We meet in secret, like thieves. I need to end this.
  Later.
  Okay, it's later now. I did the test.
  It's positive!!!!!!!!!!!!!

My baby, Hutchin thought, and slapped the journal shut.
When were you going to tell me? Never.

He squeezed the bridge of his nose, dropped the journal
into his briefcase, spun the lock.

Get over it, get on with it.

Thirty minutes later, he paid his bill and walked purpose-
fully toward the Tango Pier to meet his wife, walked fast,
as if he could outdistance the weight of the journal in his
briefcase. But the relentless pressure of the past remained
strong, powerful, a force that couldn't be squashed or van-
quished just because he deemed it so.

At every step, his treacherous heart offered up visions,
images, memories of Diane. He remembered her as she had
been in the beginning of their affair, that first time in the
trees on her otherwise vacant Tango Key property. He
remembered how, one night up the coast, she had danced
alone on a moonlit beach, the waves breaking at her feet,
danced in a way that had reminded him of his wife that
night years ago in Boston. He remembered Diane as an
enchantress, mysterious, elusive, the very paragon of a goddess. He loved his wife, but she was not Diane.

She would never be Diane. And if his life were going to
move forward again, he would have to learn to live with
that reality.

The Tango Pier stretched for several miles along the
island's most southern coast, a hub of shops, restaurants,

and tourists. This evening it was so crowded that Hutchin couldn't walk a straight line without being bumped or jostled.

He spotted his wife before she saw him, a slender, attractive woman standing outside Geraldo's Bar & Grill. She wore jeans that fit her like a glove, a lavender T-shirt tucked in neatly, high-top sneakers, and a denim jacket. She carried herself with grace and certainty and looked, he thought, a decade or more younger than her forty-nine years. But she wasn't Diane.

Forget Diane. She's the past.

Isabel was now and she was also the future, the long-range future, the future that loomed in his mind as Washington, DC, attorney general, then perhaps the Senate, then the White House. Suddenly, it all seemed possible. It was as if he had only to open his arms and embrace the possibility and it would be his.

Isabel turned her head and saw him and waved. He hurried through the crowd, eager now to see her, touch her, be with her. "Hey," he said, and caught her hand, squeezing it tightly.

She hugged him hello, hugged him in a way that she hadn't since they first had started dating. "I was so terrified when I heard about the bomb threat," she said softly.

"Hey, I'm not going anywhere unless you're with me."

She laughed at that and held up a bag. "I bought us some overnight stuff and we've got a reservation at the Hilltop Inn."

"Sounds great. Let's have dinner there. I should call Louise and alert her to the traffic situation."

"Down here where it's quieter."

Isabel led the way down the steps to the beach and they ducked under the pier, into the shadows. Hutchin called the office and she was there, they had just been allowed back into the building. He said what he had to say, said it some distance from his wife, so that she couldn't hear the conversation, and as soon as he disconnected, he sank into the cool sand next to Isabel. He took off his shoes, just as she had done, and dug his bare toes into the cool sand, and wondered how such simple pleasures had escaped him for so many months.

They sat in silence for a few minutes, her arm hooked through his, watching a guy on the beach tossing a Frisbee to his dog. Lights from the pier spilled across the sand and touched the edge of the waves as they broke gently against the beach.

"When I was a kid," she said, "I used to come down here with my dad to watch the sun rise on weekend mornings. It was great because it was just the two of us. Everyone else was at home still sleeping. One Sunday morning, we were walking along the water's edge when Daddy suddenly gasped and doubled over at the waist and threw up in the sand. I must've been about twelve. It scared me and I . . . I got down on my knees and asked him what was wrong, did he want to go back? He was clutching his chest and his teeth were gritted with pain, I remember. He said I needed to call nine-one-one, that he was having a heart attack."

Odd, Hutchin thought, that he'd never heard this story before. He figured that after twenty-five years, he had heard all the minidramas and small stories that composed the larger story of his wife's life. "So what'd you do?"

"Well, I was terrified of leaving him and it was so early no one else was around. This was in the days when Tango's year-round population was maybe fifteen hundred people, cell phones were nonexistent, and the only medical facilities were the Tango Clinic. So I made sure he was comfortable on the sand and then ran like hell for the nearest pay phone. The paramedics told me what to do and about twenty minutes later, a medical chopper landed on the beach here and air-lifted him to a Miami hospital that had a cardiac unit.''

''He didn't die until the early eighties,'' Hutchin said.

''Yeah, but one second we were walking along the beach, eager to watch the sunrise, and the next second, he was clutching his chest and puking in the sand. That day I learned how temporal life is, Hutch. What seems stable and secure one moment may be yanked out from under you in the next moment.''

For the space of a single, horrifying breath, Hutchin believed that his wife knew about Diane—about the affair, that he had killed her, the whole nine yards. He believed that she had paused to give him the chance to confess before she laid it out, a blow-by-blow description of what had happened and when it had happened and how she intended to deal with it.

Then he stole a glance at her and saw that tears glistened in her eyes, on her cheeks, and realized this wasn't about him or his infidelity. This was something else, something private and separate from him. ''What?'' he whispered. ''What is it?''

She swiped at her eyes with the back of her free hand and glanced off to the right, away from him. In the light, he saw the way her lips trembled, as if she could barely hold back a flood of tears. As she regained her composure, her knees came up against her chest, her arms hooked around them, and her bare feet dug into the sand. Everything about her just then suggested containment.

''When I finally saw Daddy in the hospital, he was connected to five million tubes and I wondered if it would be kinder to just jerk the tubes out and kill him. I think I could have done that, Hutch. I think my greatest capacity for evil, like my greatest capacity for good, stems from a sort of twisted compassion.''

Hutchin suddenly wanted to grab her by the shoulders and shake her until the truth spilled out of her. *You know, I know you do, so just say it.* . . .

But habit saved him. Habit told him that he had no facts to support his conclusion that she knew about Diane. "No one ever knows their capacity for good or evil until it comes right down to the wire, Isabel. We might think we know, in the abstract, as a concept, but thinking about something and doing it are two separate entities entirely."

I know, believe me, I know. Up until the moment when he actually had slapped the pillow down over Diane's face, the thought of killing her had never crossed his mind. Even when he'd done it, he had the choice to whip it off or to press down. And he had pressed. He had held the goddamn pillow in place, fought to keep it there. After a certain point, the pressure had been all that mattered. Maintain the pressure, apply more pressure. Even now, he could feel the tension in his hands, his fingers. He could feel the tension of all that pressure in his own body.

Did that single act of murder make him a *bad man?*

Did it mean he was *evil?*

No. Of course not. He was still the same man, Jay Hutchin, husband and father, judge and community player, a man who, in the course of his life, had done mostly good things. No single act amounted to the sum total of who you were. No single act corrupted a man. Even though he wasn't an innocent, neither was he heinous, corrupted at the core. He wasn't a Manson, a Bundy, a Boston Strangler. He wasn't like the scum that passed through his courtroom.

"When I was the Dade County prosecutor, I had a case where a young black man had killed his bedridden father. The old man had ALS—Lou Gehrig's disease. For months, the son was there for him, day and night, Isabel, through meals and bedsores, through vomiting and bedpans, and a creeping paralysis. The kid didn't have a life. And one night, he put Drano in his old man's dinner and the guy was dead in a couple of hours. He showed no remorse during the trial. The only thing he said in his own defense was, 'You do what you gotta do and when you can't do it no more, you do what you shouldn't do.' ''

She was rocking then, her arms still hooked around her knees. "I don't remember this case."

"It was a long time ago." Lifetimes ago. Their daughter was young, Isabel had been caught up in being a mother. PTA. Carpooling. Field trips. "Anyway, the jury could have found him guilty of murder one and recommended the death penalty. Instead, they found him guilty of manslaughter. He did less than three years."

Isabel, still rocking, glanced over at him. Her cheeks and eyes were dry now. The emotional crisis, he thought, had passed. "What's your point?"

"The point is that the jury believed he had done the compassionate thing. But because he'd taken a life, they felt they had to find him guilty of *something.*" Hutchin paused. "We're all guilty of *something.*"

She considered this, her eyes on the dark gulf waters, then gave a small nod, as if to say that she agreed with his basic premise. "Shit, how'd we get on this depressing topic, anyway?" With that, she rocked onto her feet and then to a standing position, and reached out to pull him up. "Let's go check in and get a bite to eat."

He caught her around the waist and they stood there in an uneasy embrace, their long and convoluted history together like a third presence between them.

Save us, he thought, and wondered for whom or what the thought was intended.

Chapter 14

At 6:45, the courthouse was deemed to be bomb free and the employees were allowed to go back inside. By then, Ben Webster and Eric Moreno were waiting for a replay to come through the small TV in the surveillance van, which was parked in the Tango hills about two miles from the courthouse.

"The feed we'll get momentarily should start from the moment they allowed everyone back into the courthouse," Moreno said, his fingers tapping steadily at the keyboard. "If we installed everything correctly."

"*If?* I thought you knew what the hell you were doing."

Moreno withdrew a cigar from his shirt pocket, lit it. The stink quickly permeated the air. "Relax, man. There won't be a problem. Hey, here we go. Our first images of the chambers and office."

Webster got up and leaned over Moreno's shoulder, watching as Hutchin's staff returned to the office to gather up their things. Moreno hit another key and the image zoomed in on a plump woman who waddled around the room, peering into drawers, a closet, either looking for something or checking to make sure everything was as she'd left it.

"That's Louise Reese, Hutchin's right arm," Webster said. "She tried to get back into the chambers after we'd secured them."

Moreno puffed on his putrid cigar. "How do you know who she is?"

"I made it my business." A cloud of smoke wafted toward Webster. "Jesus, do you have to smoke in here?"

"Hey, man, I'm the one who's going to be living in here for the next few days. How long's she been with him?"

"Since he was appointed to the state attorney's office on Tango Key. Loyalty, Eric. If he makes attorney general, she probably will go with him."

"She looks like the female version of the Pillsbury Dough Boy."

"She's probably a nice woman."

Moreno laughed. "Shit, Ben. That's probably what you were saying about your ex as she was walking out the door. You're too willing to give everyone the benefit of the doubt."

Am I? Was that the central problem of his life? "We need sound."

"Coming right up." Moreno's hands flew across the keyboard again and the sound came through loud and clear, with Louise Reese barking orders, her little mouth pursed as if she'd bitten into something inordinately sour.

"Make sure the security system is working in here. Get those files back into the cabinet. Tell Alfonso to get in here tonight with a cleaning crew. They tracked dirt all over the place. Just look at the rug."

"Bossy little bitch," Moreno remarked.

Now Louise went over to the chamber door, touched the knob as if she expected it to be locked, turned it, and stepped inside. Moreno tapped the keys again and the picture switched to Hutchin's chambers, tracking Louise as she went over to the judge's large oak desk. She stood there for a few moments, unmoving, her back to the camera. Webster sensed that she was looking for anything out of place. But neither he nor Moreno had touched the top of the judge's desk—they'd searched the drawers.

She turned, her tiny dark eyes moving slowly around the room, and waddled over to the counter—a mini kitchen counter with a sink and small fridge and bookshelves above it. Louise tipped several books forward and reached into the space.

"This could be a safe," Moreno said. "We'll bring it up again on the videotape and freeze it."

"She's not removing anything. She's just checking it," Webster said.

The phone rang and Louise went over to the desk and answered it. "Chambers."

Now the bug on the line kicked in. Moreno fiddled with dials, raising the volume. "Louise, it's Jay. I just wanted to let you know there's a two- to three-hour backup on the bridge and on the ferry. If you need to stay overnight on the island, charge it to the office. Isabel and I are staying at the Hilltop Inn if you need me for anything."

"Thanks, Judge Hutchin. I'm checking your chambers now to make sure nothing was disturbed."

"First thing tomorrow, I want our security personnel to sweep the chambers."

"Good idea, sir. I'll leave them a note tonight."

"Thanks, Louise. See you tomorrow."

Vogel, who had made the actual phone call about the bomb, had assured them that the courthouse equipment wouldn't be able to detect the sophisticated devices they had planted in Hutchin's office—or that Vogel himself had planted in Hutchin's home. But Webster still felt distinctly uneasy about this. The fact that Hutchin had instructed Louise to bring in the security people meant that he was suspicious about the evacuation. He did *not* intend to spend twenty-five years in the slammer. He would leave the country before it came to that.

"Since we know where Hutchin is staying for the night," Webster said, "I'm going to drive over to the Hilltop and see what he and the missus are up to." He slung his pack over his shoulder. "Besides, the cigar smoke is choking me. My cell will be on. Let me know when you want a break."

"You kidding? This is the easiest job I've had in twenty years. You do the pavement bit, amigo. I'll be here. If you can't get home before the dead of night, there's an extra bunk in here. With the cigar smoke and my snoring."

It was a relief to get outside, into the fresh air. The night was clear and, up here in the hills, the temperature was at least ten degrees cooler than Key West or the town of Tango, probably in the mid to upper fifties. Webster zipped up his lightweight jacket and drove his Jeep three miles east to the Hilltop Inn.

The inn had a prime spot overlooking one of the Tango reservoirs. Built in the shape of a half-moon, all of the rooms faced the water and overlooked the open deck dining area and the pool beyond it. Webster figured the dining area would be jammed to the hilt because of the traffic delays. But he was seated almost immediately in a corner of the deck, where the breeze that kicked off the reservoir smelled sweetly of the surrounding woods.

One glance around told him he was the only lone diner, a fact that made him feel strangely conspicuous. The world, at least on Tango Key, seemed to consist of couples and families. Even now, months after his wife had left him, he still hadn't adjusted fully to being single. He missed a warm body next to him at night, missed sharing life with someone, missed the companionship. And if he kept thinking along these lines, he was going to leave here so depressed that a cot in a van stinking of cigar smoke was going to look good. He picked up the menu, determined to treat himself to a good dinner at the Bureau's expense.

"Hey, Agent Mulder!"

Webster laughed and glanced up from the menu. Ryan Parrish stood there in jeans and a sweatshirt, grinning. What a far cry, Webster thought, from the kid he'd tackled Monday afternoon at Bahia Honda. "Hi, sport. I told Scully you sent your regards."

"Oh, c'mon. Really?"

"Sure did. Had to tell her by phone, though. She's off in Arizona, investigating another X-File. Grab a seat. Where's your mom?"

Ryan plopped down in one chair and dropped his backpack on another. "She's at the desk, getting the last room. I guess you heard about what happened at the courthouse, huh?"

I was there, kid. "Sure did. I'm stuck here, too. But what're you doing on the island?"

"Mom and I played hooky today. Listen, thanks a lot for tackling me at Bahia Honda."

"I'm just glad I was there. What was that all about, anyway?"

The boy shrugged and fingered the salt shaker, turning it this way and that, as if he'd never seen one before. "I'm not sure. So where were you when the bomb scare came down?"

Webster noticed how deftly the kid had turned the conversation away from himself. "I was in there evacuating people."

Ryan's eyes widened and he leaned forward, the salt shaker forgotten. "For real? Was it scary?"

"No time to be scared."

He launched into a story, half truth, half fiction, about the evacuation. Before he got very far, Ryan spotted his mother and waved her over. Webster watched her, couldn't help but watch her—the poetry of her movements, the way her jeans and denim jacket fit her, those long legs.

"You not only found us a table, you found company," Kit exclaimed, touching her son's head, but her eyes went to Webster. "Good to see you, Ben."

"Mom, he helped evacuate the courthouse," Ryan said, excited.

"Any idea who made the call?" She set Ryan's pack on the floor and claimed the last vacant chair. "Or is it too soon?"

"Too soon."

"The lobby in there is jammed with people. Probably eight out of ten of them are stranded. You planning on going back to the mainland tonight?"

"I doubt it. I'm staying with a friend." *On a cot in a van that stinks of cigar smoke.*

"So tell me more about the evacuation, Ben," Ryan said, sitting forward.

"Well, we brought in dogs and the bomb squad . . ."

Throughout the telling, he had the full attention of both mother and son. Much of what Webster related was taken straight from his one and only bomb squad experience when he worked for the Bureau's Miami office. He had to tailor some of the details to fit the Tango Courthouse, then winged the rest of it.

Ryan interrupted frequently with questions that usually concerned some weird technicality or detail, offering Webster a glimpse of how the kid's mind worked. At some point, he realized that while he was talking, Ryan's perceptions weaved the story into visual images, as though he were watching a movie. When he questioned Webster about something, it was as if he had paused the film to scrutinize it for fine inconsistencies or details that he needed to flesh out into images.

The waitress arrived in the nick of time, just as Webster was getting to the part where he and Moreno split, and she took their orders. Afterward, Webster questioned Kit about how her investigation was going and he did it before Ryan could press for more information about the evacuation. He was too polite to interrupt, so he colored on the kid's menu while they talked.

Ryan finished eating first and asked his mother if he could feed the catfish down on the pier. Then he was off, moving like the wind. "If I blink too fast, he's gone," Kit remarked, staring after him.

"He said you two played hooky today."

"Something weird is going on with him and I don't have a clue what it means or what I can do to help him. He sees things. Sometimes he hears a voice in his head that tells him to do things." She laughed, a sharp, truncated sound that sounded dangerously close to desperation. She spoke faster and faster, one incident blending into another, as if she hoped to spill everything before Ryan returned from the pier.

When she got to the part about what had happened this morning at the museum here on Tango, Webster held up his hands. "Wait a minute. Are you talking about the Tango Museum?"

She nodded.

"Last owned by the Schullers?"

"Yes, why?"

"Now *that*," he said, "is intriguing."

"What is? You've lost me."

He told her about his visit with J.R. Dexler, about the note Beaupre had written in Dexler's legal pad when they were working on the revisions of her book. "So I figured that since Pete was last seen in the wilderness preserve here on the island, maybe he used to meet the woman somewhere near the preserve. I got a list of homes and motels within one square mile of the jogging trail in the preserve." He unzipped his pack, reached inside for the printout, and smoothed it out on the table so she could see the listing. "There aren't many. But the museum is one of them." He pointed. "See? And in 1991, when Pete vanished, the house belonged to the Schuller family."

She glanced at it, then at him, obviously puzzled. "So? What's that have to do with Ryan?"

"I don't know. But until this week, I'd never heard of the Schullers and now that name has come up twice in as many days. I've learned to pay attention to coincidences like that."

"Do you know anything about the Schullers?"

"Not yet. Haven't had time to check."

She no longer looked puzzled or skeptical or whatever the hell she had been looking while he'd been talking. Everything about her suddenly softened. "Does your neck ache when you're stressed out?"

"What?" he said with a laugh, confused by the sudden shift in topics.

"Your neck. Does it ache when you're stressed out?"

"Yeah, doesn't everyone's?"

"You're a good cook, stubborn as hell, slow to anger, relentless in your pursuit of what you want, slow to change your opinion, athletic, and probably an anarchist at heart."

Bingo. She reads you like the Sunday funnies. "Anything else?"

"You were born in May, deep into May. You're not an early Taurus."

Totally intrigued now, he leaned forward. "You're psychic."

"I'm an astrologer."

"I thought you were an attorney."

"That, too. But astrology is my closet hobby. Do you know what time you were born?"

"Five-twelve A.M., May seventeenth, 1957."

"First house sun," she murmured to herself, nodding. "The weird and the strange interest you. Mystical things. Mystical spiritual beliefs."

The woman was beginning to spook him. "Yes."

"Where were you born?"

"You don't know?"

"Hey, I'm an astrologer, not a seer."

"Gainesville, Florida."

"A Florida boy. Were your folks with the university?"

"Both of them were professors. My mother taught criminology and my dad taught psychology. So are you going to do my horoscope?"

"I've got my laptop in my room. Let's find Ryan and have coffee upstairs."

No arm twisting to be done on this count, he thought, and picked up the bill.

As they got up, Webster saw Hutchin in the doorway, gazing out over the crowd, probably looking for a free table. Kit saw him, too, and waved and Hutchin waved back, weaving his way through the crowd. Webster thought this connection was also quite interesting. He had come here hoping to get a lead on Hutchin and his wife, had run into Kit and her son instead, and now she was the reason Hutchin came over to them.

Except for the fact that he wasn't wearing his judge's robes, he didn't look much different than he had this afternoon when Webster refused to let him exit the building through his chambers. He'd been wearing a helmet that covered his entire face, so it seemed unlikely that Hutchin would recognize him. Still, he felt distinctly uneasy in Hutchin's presence.

"So you got stranded here, too?" Hutchin asked.

"Got the last room. Jay, this is Ben Webster. Ben, Jay Hutchin."

They shook hands and in the moments when their palms touched, Webster felt chilled to the bone.

"Are you staying here tonight?" Kit asked.

"Looks like it. My wife happened to be over here, too, so she nabbed the room. She's on her way downstairs."

"Take our table," Kit said. "We're just leaving." She glanced around. "As soon as I find my son. Excuse me, Jay. I need to see if he's down by the reservoir."

She walked off, leaving Webster alone with Hutchin, a rather interesting situation, Webster thought, all things considered.

"You seem familiar to me," Hutchin said, not bothering with the usual amenities. "Have we met before?"

Webster knew that he should stick to the methods that were Bureau tried and true, the ones that cautioned agents to keep their own counsel. But an impulse told him to do otherwise. "It's possible our professional paths have crossed. I'm with the FBI."

The change in Hutchin's face was subtle, but only because practice had taught restraint. This was a man who couldn't allow his inner feelings to show when he sat on the bench. But Webster glimpsed astonishment and recognition in Hutchin's eyes. He suddenly realized he'd been wearing his badge during the evacuation and that Louise Reese probably had seen it when he'd prevented her from reentering Hutchin's chambers. She probably had told him about it. But perhaps he was wrong about all that and Hutchin was simply reacting to *FBI,* the agency that was investigating his candidacy for attorney general. If that was the case, then it would make sense to Hutchin that Webster was quizzing Kit, an attorney who had come up against Hutchin in various legal situations and who had known him as a law professor.

"We've probably met in court." Hutchin slid his hands into the pockets of his trousers. "That would make sense."

"Yes, that was probably it."

"Unless you were evacuating staff from the courthouse this afternoon. We might've met then."

Fishing? Was he fishing? "Actually, yes, I was."

"So do you people have any leads on the bomb threat?" Hutchin asked.

"There're plenty of rumors, but I'm not in the investigative end of it."

"How long have you been with the Bureau, Mr. Webster?"

It's none of your goddamn business. "Years."

Just then, Kit returned, Ryan trailing behind her. "I don't think you've ever met my son, Jay. Ryan, this is Judge Hutchin. He's . . ."

And suddenly everything collapsed into the weird and the strange, that was how Webster would remember it later. He would remember how Ryan's head raised up slowly and how he gazed steadily at Hutchin as the judge extended his hand and smiled and how Ryan just stood there, motionless. Kit, obviously embarrassed, said something to her son and his arm flew up and he pointed accusingly at Hutchin.

"You! I hated you. Jay will pay, Jay must pay, bad man, bad man . . ."

His voice lifted into a terrible shriek, the words echoing out across the deck, "Badmanbadmanbad . . ." People turned to look, to gape. Kit, her hands balled at her mouth, looked too shocked to speak or move, and Hutchin stared in horror at the boy, who kept moving back, shrieking, a stream of words pouring from his mouth, the same words, over and over again. Then Hutchin lurched forward—Webster couldn't tell if he moved in the boy's direction, his viewpoint didn't allow him to see that, but Ryan thought so and he spun around and crashed into a table.

The table tipped. Plates, glasses, and silverware slid off the table and crashed to the deck. Ryan scrambled over the railing, screaming and sobbing, and dropped to the ground on the other side. He tore through the bushes and shrubs, across a bed of flowers, and raced into the darkness before any of them had even moved.

Then they all moved at once. In fact, it seemed to Webster that the entire deck moved—waiters and waitresses ran over, a man whom Webster assumed to be the manager barreled through the crowd, diners shot up from their tables to see what was going on, where the boy had gone, and Hutchin pointed and shouted, "There! There he is!" And he vaulted over the railing, with Webster right behind him and Kit behind the two of them.

Webster caught up to Hutchin and for moments they ran neck to neck. "Stay out of this!" Webster snapped, and pulled out ahead of Hutchin, his shoes pounding the grass, his arms tight at his sides.

Ryan weaved into the trees, vanished, and reappeared again, a solitary figure in the starlight, racing along the edge of the reservoir, his terror fueling him, driving him on. As Webster narrowed the gap between them, he glanced back and saw Kit closing in on them and behind them, Hutchin climbing into a golf cart that had pulled alongside him.

When he looked for Ryan again, the boy was on the ground, sprawled there on his stomach, trying to get up. Webster reached him, dropped to his knees beside him, but didn't touch him for fear he would scare him.

"Your mom's coming, Ryan," he said quietly, gently.

Ryan rolled onto his side, knees tucked up close to his chest, his tear-streaked face turned toward Webster. He pushed to a sitting position, knuckled his eyes. "I messed up, didn't I?"

"You got scared. That's not messing up."

Kit didn't just reach her son, she skidded to a stop in front of him, on her knees, and slid her arms around him. She spoke too softly for Webster to hear. Moments later, the golf cart pulled up, Hutchin and the hotel employee inside. "Is he all right?" the hotel employee asked as he jumped out of the cart.

Before Kit could reply, Hutchin marched over to Kit and Ryan. Even in the dim light of the stars, Webster could see that Hutchin's face was bright red. "Your son must be ill, Kit. I think he needs psychiatric help and I'll make sure that he gets it. . . ."

Kit shot to her feet before Webster could move and grabbed Hutchin by the front of the shirt, her expression livid, her body tensed with something so primal that the very air around them seemed thick, viscous, changed at some fundamental level. She jerked him forward and hissed, "Don't you *ever* threaten my son, you son of a bitch."

Hutchin wrenched back, breaking her hold on his shirt, and his arm flew up, fist clenched, and Webster leaped between them, taking the blow on his shoulder. He grabbed Hutchin's wrist before he could strike again. "Get outta here."

The judge, breathing hard, looked to be on the verge of a stroke, the redness seeping up around his eyes, veins standing out in his temples. "I'm filing a complaint about you, Webster."

"You threatened a kid, Hutchin. That's why he ran. I'll be filing my own complaint."

"You had no right to block my assistant from returning to my chambers during the evacuation."

So that's what this is about. Webster ignored him, walked over to the hotel employee, and flashed his badge. "You mind if I drive them back to the hotel? I'll leave the cart out front."

"Sure thing. Not a problem. The keys are in the ignition."

Hutchin gave Webster a homicidal look, then turned abruptly and started walking back toward the hotel. Webster hopped into the cart and drove over to where Kit and her son stood talking quietly. "Hop in, guys. Your taxi's here."

Ryan sat in the passenger seat with his mother and Webster put the cart in gear. He drove along the edge of the reservoir, avoiding Hutchin. The cart's soft hum mitigated the thick, uneasy silence, which Ryan finally broke. "He's a bad man."

"He's one of my colleagues." Kit spoke sharply. "My God, Ryan. He's the judge who's going to be hearing the Poulton case. The things you said to him, the—"

"Is that all you care about?" Ryan jerked his hand away from his mother's. "Your work? Is that all that matters? He's a bad man and I don't care if you don't believe me, I don't care!"

"Stop the cart," Kit said. "I need to walk."

Webster stopped, Kit slid out, and Ryan sat back in the seat, arms crossed at the chest, and refused to glance her way. He started the cart again, continuing along the edge of the reservoir. In a soft, choked voice that nearly broke Webster's heart, Ryan said, "She doesn't want me anymore, does she?"

"Don't be ridiculous. She just needs some time alone. It'll be okay. Trust me."

"He *is* a bad man, you know."

"Hey, I'm with you. I haven't liked the man since I set eyes on him."

"Really?"

"Absolutely. He was just acting like a judge. See, the problem with judges is that in their courtrooms, they're like God. Some of them—people like Hutchin—forget how to act any other way. Do you remember what happened back there on the deck?"

"Not really." He sniffled and Webster reached into the pocket of his jacket and brought out a couple pieces of Kleenex. Ryan blew his nose. "I just remember that when Mom said his name and I . . . I looked up at him, I was afraid."

"Do you know what you said?"

"Not really."

"You said, 'You. I hated you. Jay will pay, Jay must pay, bad man, bad man . . .' "

"I remember the bad man part, but not the rest."

"You'd never met him before?"

"Never."

"Then why do you think you said 'hated' in the past tense?"

"I don't know."

"What do you think the other part meant, Ryan? 'Jay will pay, Jay must pay . . .' "

Ryan shook his head and rubbed his palms over his jeans. "It's not me saying those things, Ben. I know that sounds really weird, but it's the truth. The night my mom found me digging in the field, the day on the bridge, even when my mom and I were in the museum today . . . all of that . . . it's not me. It's like, I don't know, it's like I have someone else's memories and that person's memories tell me that Judge Hutchin is a bad man."

He talked fast, very fast, and Webster stopped the golf

cart on the far side of the reservoir, where the water caught the reflection of the moon. An owl hooted from the nearby trees, the breeze carried the scent of water. He let Ryan finish, then waited, gathering his thoughts.

"When I was a kid, about your age," Webster said, "I used to get cold right before something was going to happen. I would tell my mom or dad and as I was telling them, I would see pictures in my head, like a movie, of what was going to happen.

"One summer night, I woke up freezing. My parents had gone out and left my sister and me with a baby-sitter. I went into my sister's room and woke her, complaining about how cold I was. And then these pictures started coming into my head, and I knew something had happened to my mom and dad."

"Were you right?"

Webster gazed off in the distance, where the trees on the far side of the reservoir loomed darkly against the starlit sky. Even after all these years, he thought, the painful emotions of that night remained. "Yeah, I was right. My parents had been in a car accident. They died a couple of days later and my sister and I moved in with our grandparents."

Ryan took Webster's hand. "That's terrible," he said softly. "I'm really sorry."

Webster, astonished that the boy could offer comfort to someone else when he was so badly in need of it himself, gave his hand a quick squeeze. "It was a long time ago, Ryan. But see, other people have these feelings and experiences, too. I'm not saying your feelings are exactly like mine, but I think there are similarities."

He started the golf cart again and turned so they were headed back toward the motel.

"Do you still get those feelings?" Ryan asked.

"Mostly about my work."

"Do you get those feelings about the judge?"

"Yes."

He was quiet then and Webster sensed he was mulling over everything they'd talked about. "Your feelings *belong* to you. Mine don't. I mean, they do in one way, because I feel them, but they don't belong to me. It's kinda confusing."

"How do you feel when these things are happening?"

"Scared. Angry. I told Abuelita that when this stuff is happening, I feel like a big person. Like a man, not a boy. Becky thinks it might be my future self trying to warn me about something—about the judge, that he's a threat to my mom. I don't know anymore."

Webster hesitated, reluctant to suggest something that might not be related at all to what Ryan had been experiencing. But Ryan himself had said he felt like a big person, like a man, when these incidents happened, so perhaps what he had to say would help. "Suppose these feelings and memories are those of someone you used to be, Ryan?"

"Mom talks about that sometimes when she's doing astrology charts. But is it possible to actually remember?"

"There've been a number of cases of children remembering past lives, through spontaneous recall, where the memories surface in bits and pieces. Sometimes it's because the person died suddenly or without finishing something, and in the present they begin to remember so they *can* finish whatever it was."

Webster pulled up in front of the building, where Kit waited with the hotel employee. Hutchin, he noticed, was nowhere in sight.

"We rode down along the reservoir," Webster said.

Ryan went over to his mother. "You better now?"

"I am." She slipped her arm around his shoulder. "How about you?"

"Me, too."

"How about some coffee upstairs?" Kit asked Webster. "I'll do your chart."

"Yeah, c'mon, Agent Mulder." Ryan winked at him. "I want to show you this cool thing I have."

Of course he nodded.

Chapter 15

During his walk back to the hotel, Hutchin felt as if he were on an emotional roller coaster, one of those rides that turns you upside down and inside out, then spits your remains onto the dusty ground. He went from rage to near panic to utter despair. Then, finally, habit clicked in and he began to figure the angles. If this happened, if that happened, what this might mean, what that might mean . . .

By the time he reached the lobby and spotted his wife at the house phone, he knew exactly what he had to do and what he had to do before he could initiate his plan. They would have to eat first, he and his wife. They would have to talk. They would make love. All of that would have to be lived through, gotten out of the way. Then, when she was asleep, he would seek out Rico and call in favors.

As soon as they stepped into the elevator and Isabel saw that they were alone, she said, "I only caught the tail end of that fiasco downstairs. What'd the kid say to you, Hutch?"

He peered into me, Hutchin thought, and nearly exploded with laughter. *Peered into me and saw my blackened soul.*

But Ryan Parrish couldn't possibly know about Diane. So why had he said what he'd said? Hutchin couldn't think of a reasonable explanation, but at least two illogical possibilities occurred to him: the boy was clairvoyant or his mother suspected that Hutchin had killed Diane and had said as much to Ryan. Both possibilities were absurd.

The only other explanation was that the boy had psychiatric problems. He desperately wanted to believe this because it would mean that the actual words Ryan Parrish had shrieked were nothing but a fluke and he, already paranoid, had attached personal significance to them. He didn't tell Isabel this part, but told her everything else, including his suspicions about the bomb scare and Webster.

"You think he's one of the feds investigating you for the attorney general position?" she asked.

"Absolutely."

"Christ," she murmured. "Where the hell do they get these Gestapo tactics? Isn't there anything you can do about it? I mean, I understand that they investigate potential appointees, but c'mon, Hutch."

"We're going to have the office swept for bugs. If anything turns up, I'll launch an investigation that will make Webster's head spin. But if they don't find anything, there isn't much I can do."

"Until you get the job. Then you can fire his ass."

"Or send him to the worst spot I can think of."

"North Dakota."

"The heart of Mississippi."

"Northern Alaska, where his balls will freeze eight months out of the year."

They looked at each other and laughed. "But none of it's really funny, is it?" She unlocked the door to their room. "It's intrusive. It's a kind of insidious voyeurism."

"I may ask Vic Blake to look into it." Blake was sheriff

of Tango County, a laid-back homeboy from a family of laid-back homeboys, but he was also an ambitious prick. Hutchin had known him for years. "What do you think?"

Isabel, now making drinks at the minibar, glanced back. "I think it's a great idea. Vic can be discreet when it suits him. Call him tonight. Get him over here. In the meantime, I'll order room service."

Within an hour, Blake showed up, a pale, sinewy man about Hutchin's age, whose expression always seemed masklike, as though his facial muscles were atrophying. While Hutchin voiced his suspicions about the bomb threat, he could see interest in Blake's eyes, spurts of lights, like solar flares. Hutchin took it as a good sign and suspected that Blake was thinking that if he took care of Hutchin, Hutchin would take care of him when he became attorney general. It was Florida politics, the old way.

"That's going to be mighty hard to prove, Hutch, without some evidence," Blake drawled. "I'll have our unit come in and sweep your chambers and the courtroom tomorrow."

"Thanks, Vic, I'd appreciate it."

"You said an agent blocked Louise's way. Any idea who he was?"

"Webster, I think she said his name was. Ben Webster."

"He's new here. Been working the Beaupre disappearance for the Bureau cold cases division. Lives on a houseboat down at Mile Zero Marina outside Key West. Not to worry, Hutch. I'll look into this."

Hutchin felt better after that, less burdened, less angry, but no less determined to carry out his plan.

He and Isabel ate by candlelight out on the terrace, overlooking the reservoir. Over shrimp scampi, they shared a bottle of Chilean wine and quiet talk. For Hutchin, it smacked of their early days together, except back then they'd had no money and the wine was some cheap California rotgut and the sex had been spontaneous and passionate.

The wine set his libido on fire and he and his wife made love as they had in the distant past, before his life had gotten so complicated. Afterward, sprawled on their backs on the huge bed, under the soft whir of the ceiling fan, they held hands and he drifted into a kind of half sleep. Images blazed against his inner eye, images of Diane, of Isabel, of Webster and Kit and the kid, effluvium of the last several days that meant nothing. The images faded quickly and reformed into a carnival of shapes and colors that collapsed into a swirling vortex and threatened to suck him in. His eyes snapped open and a moment later his wife said, "Truth or consequences, Hutch. Remember when we used to play that game?"

Yes, he remembered. They had played that game frequently during the six months of their courtship. "Sure."

"Okay, I have a question."

"Shoot."

"Have you had an affair since we've been married?"

Shit. Not now, Isabel, don't ask me that now. Don't make me lie. And he thought, just then, of Bill Clinton on national TV, insisting that he hadn't had sex with "that woman." Never mind that it hadn't been anyone's business. The issue had been truth or consequences, just as it was now, for him. So of course he lied. He had to lie. He had no choice.

"C'mon, what the hell kind of question is that?"

"An honest question."

"No affairs," he said.

She lifted up and gazed down at him. In the soft light that filtered through the windows, she looked younger than she was, maybe a decade younger. But she didn't hold a candle to Diane, he thought. "Sex?" she asked. "Have you had sex with anyone else?"

"Hey, it was my turn."

"Oh," she said. "Okay, so ask a question."

"Have you had sex with anyone else during our marriage?"

Hesitation, then: "Yes." And: "You?"

"Yes."

Silence.

Her fingers flexed against his. Hutchin turned his head away from her and knew he was really splitting hairs here, that he was like Clinton, trying to make legal distinctions between sex and a blow job. He hadn't just had sex with Diane; they'd had a full-blown affair.

Maybe the same was true for Isabel and she was just trying to spare him the same thing he had tried to spare her. He wasn't about to go into it. He knew she would more readily accept it if he'd had sex with another woman than if he'd had an affair. The latter implied a commitment, emotions, entanglements, layered lies.

Isabel surprised him. Instead of quizzing him about the woman, about the sex, she said, "Why did we go elsewhere, Jay? That's what bothers me."

He rolled onto his side, his arm draping her waist, her cool skin. "I don't know."

And it was the truth. In that moment, in the exact moment when he answered the question, he really didn't know why he had gotten involved with Diane. There didn't seem to be any glaring reason; she had been there. She had made the first move. It was as simple as that. It didn't matter that nothing after that had been simple. The first embrace, the first press of her body, that first kiss: from that point on, the relationship had been complicated, intense, beyond his ability to understand.

"I don't know. But I know that I like this better." He lowered his face to hers and her arms went around his neck, answering him, sealing the inexplicable.

(2)

Always, the chart was the most telling moment for Kit, the most intimate glimpse into another person's soul. The chart hid nothing. It simply was. Webster's chart confirmed much of what she had sensed about him, but raised questions as well.

"Was there some sudden and unexpected event in your childhood that caused you to be separated from your parents?"

He looked shocked. "Did Ryan tell you about the talk he and I had?"

"No."

"Then where do you see what you just said?"

"Two places. Uranus on the cusp of the fourth house and the asteroid Ceres in the first house. The fourth house relates, among other things, to one of the parents, and Ceres in the first is about separation during early childhood."

"My folks were killed in a car accident when I was nine."

My God. I hit it on the nose.

"So go on."

She was in the flow now, allowing her intuition to speak through her. His physical proximity—arm occasionally brushing hers, the soft cadence of his voice when he asked a question—worked on her like a drug. She felt loose and fluid, as though her body could be poured into a vessel that would give it shape and form.

It got too cool on the porch where they were sitting, so they moved into the living room of the suite. Kit put the laptop on the coffee table and they both sat Indian style on the floor, their knees touching. Arms, knees, and once, when he leaned close to the screen to look at something, their faces were so close she could almost feel the heat that radiated from his skin.

As she described the focused energy of his Capricorn moon, she was thinking about the sensuality of his Taurus sun and Taurus rising. She was admiring his strong and beautiful hands. They happened to turn their heads at the same time and for a moment, they were nose to nose, eye to eye, and Webster touched her chin and brought his mouth to hers. It was the single most sensuous kiss she had ever known.

Then his hand slid under her hair, so that his palm warmed the back of her neck, and the kiss became something more, something deeper, a promise. She broke the embrace first. ''I'm coming up for air,'' she said, and he laughed.

''I've been wanting to do that since the day I met you.''

Kit leaned back, the chart forgotten. ''I don't understand what you're doing in the FBI.''

''It's not in my chart, huh?''

''Not really.''

''Before I went into the Bureau, I was teaching psychology, just like my old man. I hated it because I wasn't allowed to teach it the way I really wanted to.''

''Which was how?''

''No Freud, no Adler, just Jung and the real mysteries.''

''So Ryan was right. You're Agent Mulder.''

She laughed and poked him in the ribs and he caught her finger and brought it to his mouth. He ran his thumb from the knuckle to the tip of her fingernail and kissed her again. They both leaned back against the couch and his hands moved over her shoulders and down her arms, a long, sliding touch so strangely erotic that she felt like tearing off her clothes right then. Her long-deprived libido slammed into overdrive and started screaming.

Now his hands moved from her waist, up her sides to the curves of her breasts. Through the fabric of her cotton shirt, his thumbs slipped over her nipples and they instantly responded, betraying her desire. After that, it seemed that everything happened very slowly, as if time itself had contracted, and yet when she thought about it later, she couldn't remember the exact moment when they got the business of clothes out of the way. She couldn't remember either of them getting up to shut the door to the bedroom, where Ryan slept, yet she knew that one of them had. What she remembered most clearly was that he turned her body to liquid fire.

"Show me how you use astrology in your work," he said a long time later.

She was wearing a T-shirt and a pair of shorts she'd bought in the hotel lobby; Webster wore the gym shorts and T-shirt he'd had in his pack. Both of them were barefoot, sitting on the floor again, in front of the coffee table, their bare toes playing.

Kit brought up the charts for Poulton and Diane and explained the similarities, the points of fatal attraction. "Poulton has a Scorpio sun, moon in Libra, Libra rising. This indicates an intense man with a need to balance everything in his life, but he isn't able to find that balance. That Libra moon so close to the rising means he'll come before the public in some way—I'd say that has happened. The phase of his moon is balsamic, which in astrology is the most karmic phase of the moon, indicating a life in which the individual has to tie up loose ends with people he's known in other lives—"

"You can see past lives in charts?"

Something in his voice, an excitement, an intense curiosity, told her this was one of the "real" mysteries he'd mentioned earlier. "I can't tell you that you were King Tut, but I can see broad themes that are brought into this life from other lives. For Poulton, one of the themes surrounds intimate relationships and the balance of power within those relationships.''

''What about Diane? What themes did she bring in?''

She brought Diane's chart up next to Poulton's, studied it. ''The ability to influence the masses in a big way, through the arts, specifically through movies. Her battle cry is 'my freedom or die.' Her most profound transformations happen through her intimate relationships.

''But the rest of it is shit on a stick. It doesn't *prove* anything. Her relationship with her siblings should have been good, but Poulton said she was estranged from her family. She died suddenly, which fits, but it should have been an easy death. I mean, how easy can suffocation be? She may have had father issues.'' She pointed at Saturn in the fourth house. ''But Poulton doesn't know anything about her relationship with her father.''

''So some pieces fit and others don't.''

''Exactly. That's the problem with astrology. Nuances, free will. If you buy the basic premise of astrology, that every soul chooses to incarnate with a specific potential, then Diane might have been an artist, a writer of speculative fiction, or even a religious martyr of some kind. Poulton might have been a minister, an authoritarian parent, a professor with rigid precepts. But none of that happened. Instead, she was a famous movie actress and he had almost made it out of residency as a pediatric physician who specialized in burned children. If they knew each other before, in other lives, then they sure made a mess of things this time around.''

''What about Ryan?'' Webster asked. ''What do his charts tell you about stuff going on now with him? What past life themes do you see in his chart?''

The question surprised her. But then, Webster seemed to be full of surprises. ''I have trouble reading the charts of people who're close to me. After Pete vanished, I spent hours poring over charts and I couldn't see a damn thing. But Abuelita looked at the same charts and said flat out that he'd been killed, that a woman was involved, and that it would be years before any of it was resolved or understood.''

"She could tell all that from his birth chart?''

"No, we used a variety of techniques.'' She gave him a minilecture on progressions, solar returns, transits, horary charts. "Anyway, Abuelita could read them, I couldn't.''

"Can you bring up charts for Ryan and Pete side by side?''

"Sure.''

She did and Webster leaned forward, looking at them. "They were born on the same day,'' he exclaimed.

"Yeah, both of them Virgos with moons in Sagittarius, but born thirty-five years and nine hours apart.''

"Exactly nine hours,'' Webster pointed out. "Pete at nine minutes past noon, Ryan at nine minutes past nine P.M.''

"You make it sound significant,'' she remarked with a smile.

He shrugged. "I don't know much about astrology, but I recognize patterns. What's that?'' Webster asked, pointing at a fixed star on Ryan's chart, then at one on Pete's chart.

"Ryan's has the fixed star Toliman conjunct with his moon. Basically, it's a star that addresses some cause or issue that needs healing either privately or collectively.''

"And in Pete's chart?''

"He's got several fixed stars, just like Ryan does. Antares is rising with Pete's Saturn. It means an obsession with success and also indicates his work will live on after he dies.''

Kit began to feel that aching pressure between her eyes that warned her to pay attention. This was important. The problem, though, was that she already understood the importance but didn't want to probe too deeply into it. She was too close to it. "What're you implying, Ben?"

"I'm not *implying* anything." He pressed his fingertips to his forehead, as if to squeeze away a headache. "Do a chart for the incident this evening."

"Okay. What time do you figure it happened?"

Webster thought about it for a moment. "I'd guess around eight-thirty."

Kit typed in the date, the time, and the Tango Key coordinates. After the transit chart came up, she erected a biwheel chart, so that Ryan's natal chart was on the inner wheel and the transit chart in the outer wheel. What struck her immediately was the position of the moon's nodes. The nodes weren't actual planets, but were considered by many astrologers to be karmic points in a chart. She pointed them out to Webster.

"In a birth chart, the north node is considered to be the future we have to move toward in this life to evolve spiritually. The south node represents the patterns we bring in from other lives that we have to release. Ryan's natal north node is in Sagittarius in the ninth house. That's all about looking for the big picture, the higher truth. What's interesting here is that the transiting south node is conjunct with the natal north node to the exact degree, indicating that something has to be released before he can move forward in his life."

"Memories," Webster murmured. "The memories are being released."

Kit looked over at him, startled that he used those words. "Did he talk to you about all this?"

"Yeah, he did. After you got out of the golf cart. Look, I'm not a shrink, I don't even have kids. But I think you should consider the possibility that what Ryan is experiencing might be spontaneous recall of past-life memories."

As an astrologer, she believed in reincarnation, believed

that the soul chose its time and place of birth and the circumstances into which it was born, circumstances that were most conducive to whatever lessons the soul needed to learn this time around. She believed that certain proclivities, talents, and issues were brought forward from other lives and, to some extent, she could see these things in natal charts. But this belief was intellectual and related to astrology. Other than inexplicable feelings of attraction or revulsion toward certain people, places, and ideologies that *might* be related to her own past lives, she'd never had anything as specific as a *memory* or names that could be checked against existing records.

Even so, the absence of such experiences hadn't made her skeptical. When she thought about reincarnation separate from astrology, it excited her. It felt visceral, intuitive, and somehow *right.* And it was finding support in the world of consensus reality, through a growing body of empirical evidence.

"I don't have any problem admitting that possibility, Ben. But what the hell do I do about it? Have him hypnotized? If these memories are surfacing because he suffered some terrible trauma or painful death in another life, then hypnosis might be too traumatic for him."

"I agree. Maybe you should just let things unfold and look for the patterns. You're good at that. You can see patterns in charts, you can see patterns in the law, Kit. So start looking for patterns in what Ryan is experiencing."

Kit sat back, staring at the screen, but not seeing it. "If all these strange incidents are related to a past life, then Hutchin must be related to this past life of Ryan's, too. Otherwise there's no reason he would react so violently to a man he's never met."

Webster stood at the sliding glass doors now, gazing off into the darkness. "It would seem so."

"It doesn't make sense."

"Not if we use the rules of consensus reality. But consensus reality, at least in the western world, says that reincarnation is a crock, Kit, so we can't use those rules."

"How come I get the feeling you know stuff you're not saying?"

He looked over at her then, his smile sort of cockeyed, as if he couldn't decide whether to smile, frown, or laugh. "Hey, I'm just a guy stumbling around in the dark like everyone else."

No, she thought. There was more to it than that. She sensed that everything in this little scenario was personal for Webster and that Hutchin—and her son—were central to whatever he was seeking. She got up and walked over to him.

"If you know something that I don't about Ryan, please tell me. I need all the help I can get right now."

He combed his fingers back through his hair, then stuck his hands in his pockets again. "Look, I don't like bursting people's bubbles. You obviously admire Hutchin. But he acted like a fuck. He thinks your son needs psychiatric help."

"Bullshit," she snapped.

"There were a lot of witnesses. It happened in a public place. Ryan broke plates and glasses. I could easily see Hutchin going to a family court judge and that judge putting a bug in the ear of social services and some social worker coming around to inform you that your son has to undergo psychiatric evaluation—"

"And I'd sue the shit out of them. They have no legal ground to stand on."

Webster smiled. "I'm playing devil's advocate, Kit, but you see my point here. Why would Hutchin even say something like that?"

"Are you asking my opinion or do you already know the answer?"

"You know him, I don't."

"Well, I may know him, but I don't have a clue why he'd say something like that."

Silence. Moments ticked by. Somewhere distant, downstairs in the real world, a horn blared. Webster went over to the couch and sat down.

"By the way, I thought you were going to slug him," Webster said.

"I nearly did." And then it suddenly made sense to her. Of course. "You're investigating him for the attorney general position."

"You got it."

"And you're seriously considering information about Hutchin that comes from a nine-year-old boy who'd never met him until tonight?" She burst out laughing. "C'mon, Ben. That's ludicrous."

He didn't look the least bit amused. If anything, she thought, he looked angry. "It goes back to the same old thing, Kit. It's ludicrous by the standards of consensus reality. And those same standards would say that Ryan is in the midst of a nervous breakdown or schizophrenia or some other goddamn thing. So if those are the standards you want to go by, be my guest."

He never raised his voice, but it seemed that he had and she simply stood there, hands on her hips, her head aching with possibilities. If he was right, if Ryan—somehow, in some way—knew something about Hutchin, if her son's episodes were connected in some way to Hutchin, then she needed to pay very close attention.

"Could you show me how horary charts work?" he asked, returning to their original topic.

"Give me a specific question."

"You pick the question."

She should ask something about the murder, she thought, but what? She brought up Diane's chart again and her eyes were drawn to that Saturn in the fourth house. Saturn represented dad or the authoritarian parent, yes, but it also represented an *older man.*

"Shit, this is it. This is what I didn't see earlier."

"What?" Webster leaned forward, peering over her shoulder. She pointed at Saturn and gave him a quick synopsis of what the planet represented. "An older man might be able to afford that silver box with the gold heart inside. An older man might be married, with a life of his own, and might have been fitting Diane in on the side, at the periphery of his life. Older, okay? The lost father, the little girl's daddy."

"Then that's your question: Was Diane killed by an older man?"

Kit glanced at the clock, then cast a chart for her question.

"So explain to me how this works," he said.

"It works on the same premise as any other predictive system. In the moment the chart is cast—or the cards are laid out or the coins or runes are tossed—a pattern is formed that's intrinsic to that moment."

"So it's like a snapshot that freezes a single moment in time and it describes the nature of the question."

"Right."

"Jung's synchronicity."

"Yes. The problem is that there're a lot of stringent rules that have to be applied and you work only with the original seven planets known to the ancients—Sun, Moon, Mercury, Venus, Mars, Jupiter, and Saturn."

It took her a while to apply the rules and figure out the planetary rulers that represented herself as the person asking the question, Diane as the person about whom she was asking, and the killer. Since she was asking about an older man, she assigned Saturn to represent him.

Virgo rising represented Kit, and Virgo's ruler was Mercury. On the opposite side of the chart, Diane was represented by the sign of Pisces on the cusp of the seventh house, so Jupiter—the ancient ruler of that sign—symbolized Diane. Death traditionally belonged to the eighth house of a chart and in this chart, Mars ruled the eighth. The "yes" and "no" parts of the question would be found in the aspects—the geometric angles that Mercury, Jupiter, Mars, and Saturn made to each other. Trines—120-degree angles—and sextiles—60-degree angles—would mean yes. Squares or 90 degree angles and oppositions—or 180-degree angles—would mean no. To count as a yes, the positive aspects would have to be applying or approaching each other rather than separating.

"So what's it say?" Webster asked when she finished explaining all that. "Is it a yes or a no?"

"Hold on." With everything in place, Kit brought up the aspectarian where the aspects were depicted in a graph. Her heart caught in her throat: Mercury formed an applying trine to Jupiter at twenty-three minutes. "A definite yes. Even more intriguing, Mars—which symbolizes Diane's death—forms a separating trine of one degree and thirty-seven minutes with Saturn, which symbolizes the killer. This indicates that the death happened about a week ago."

"What else can you tell?" Webster asked, now on the floor beside her.

"Power and a heated argument about Diane's freedom to live as she sought fit may have preceded her death. Her pregnancy was unplanned and there may have been some uncertainty in her mind about who the father of her baby was. Her death happened away from the place she called home, it wasn't due to an accident, and sexual issues may have played a prominent role.''

"What else? What's that planet up there?" he asked, pointing at Saturn in the ninth house.

Everything inside of her went utterly still. Then the stillness exploded suddenly in an inner resonance so powerful that she shot to her feet. "Jesus," she whispered. "The ninth house represents higher education, the law, the judicial system, long journeys, foreign cultures, and people. It's government, the judicial process, and everyone involved in that process. If this chart is correct, then this is a profile of Diane's killer."

"He's older than she was," Webster said.

"Maybe considerably older. He works in higher education, the law, government, the judicial system, or in the legal profession. He may be foreign born or has a liking for foreign travel or foreign cultures."

"Now all you have to do is find the bastard."

Chapter 16

Friday, November 9

Hutchin woke suddenly in the darkened bedroom, his mouth as dry as straw, the dream burning through his brain. The dream about Diane, rising from the dead.

He got up slowly, quietly, so he wouldn't wake his wife, and blinked against the dark. His mind came awake, a beast reluctantly shaking off sleep. He dressed quickly in the dark, retrieved his cell phone from the dresser, and dug through the endless paraphernalia in his wife's purse, looking for the car keys and the room key. He pocketed both, picked up his sneakers, and crept out of the room.

In the hall, he put on his shoes, his mind fully awake now, alert, thoughts spinning on out in front of him. He took the freight elevator, which let him off at the side of the inn, so that he could get to the parking lot without passing through the lobby.

He worried that Isabel might wake up and find him gone, but if she did, she probably would think he was in the bathroom. Twenty-five years of marital habits didn't include his sneaking off in the middle of the night, so that would be the last thing that occurred to her.

As he drove north into the hills, his plan took on greater clarity. His atrophied conscience managed to get out a pathetic squeak or two, but his need proved greater than what remained of his conscience. Some risk would be involved in this because he would be bringing someone else into the picture. But the risk, he decided, was a calculated one. The plan would work. It would work because it was *his* plan.

He entered the wilderness preserve, which at this hour was a vast darkness, an undiscovered continent where dozens of dirt roads twisted through hundreds of acres. There wasn't much out here, just trees and wildlife and occasional poachers who trapped the wild peacocks and plucked them bare of feathers. Rico was one of those poachers, a shrewd, wiry guy in his late forties who had a record a mile long. Years ago when Hutchin was state attorney for Dade County, Rico had been arrested for shoplifting and Hutchin had given Rico the money for restitution—$625.45—and the store had dropped the charges. That six hundred bucks and change had given Hutchin a fairly reliable street source over the years. He always had paid Rico for that information, but now he intended to call in the favor that had kept his miserable butt out of jail and he wasn't about to pay for it.

Rico's place stood about three hundred yards short of federal land, a ramshackle hootch surrounded by a barbed-wire fence. Inside the fence were chickens, pigs, dogs, and peacocks, whose feathers brought about fifty bucks apiece on the open market. The dogs launched into frenzied barking as soon as Hutchin pulled up in front of the place. The headlights of the Mercedes struck a hand-painted sign that read ELIAN MUST STAY!

The outside security lights came on, blazing like the noonday sun, and Rico sauntered out onto the porch with a rifle cradled in the crook of his arm. He was a short, skinny man, compact and solid, with dark, curly hair that he wore in a ponytail. He whistled shrilly and the dogs fell silent.

Hutchin killed the engine of the Mercedes and got out. "Hey, Rico, Elian went home months ago," he called out.

The security lights dimmed and Rico stepped off the porch and came over to Hutchin. "Mr. Judge," he said in his thick accent, so that it came out as "Meester Hoodge." He grasped Hutchin's hand in both of his own and pressed hard. "It warms Rico's heart that you visit. *Por favor, entra.*" He swept the rifle toward the hootch, a grand gesture for such a shack. "It is early for *cafecito,* no? We will have some tequila. Rico has excellent tequila."

"It takes a special man to be a gracious host in the middle of the night, Rico."

Considering the state of the outside of the hootch, the inside was surprisingly comfortable, clean, orderly—and somewhat eccentric. Peacock feathers fanned across an entire wall, hundreds of peacock eyes staring at them, watching them. "That must be worth a small fortune," Hutchin remarked as they settled in with glasses of tequila.

He grinned, his capped teeth lining up in his mouth with dazzling perfection. "My retirement, Meester Hoodge. You, of course, do not have to worry about peacock feathers for retirement. As a hoodge, as the next . . . big general . . ." The last word rolled off his tongue and he opened his hands, as if to catch bits of falling sky, and grinned again.

That grin, thought Hutchin, was getting old fast. "Where do you stand these days on parole, Rico?"

The grin faded. "Eight more months. Just for a little B and E, *me entiendes?* Every Friday, Rico meets with his parole officer, a *maricón* of the first order."

"What's it worth to you to get out of that time, Rico?"

He sat forward, eyes narrowing, his eagerness undisguised. "That, my friend, would be paradise. You tell Rico what you need, Rico get it."

"Two things."

Rico knocked back half a glass of tequila. In the muted light in the room, his dark eyes seemed moist and glassy, as though they weren't quite real. "I do almost anything for you, Meester Hoodge, 'cept kill or kidnap." He shook his head and knocked back the rest of the tequila. "Not those two things."

"I wouldn't ask you to do either of those two things, Rico." *I'd do them myself.*

"Then tell me."

Hutchin told him.

Rico sat back. Maybe Hutchin imagined it, but the little guy actually seemed relieved. "That's it?"

"That's it."

"And no one has to die?"

"Of course not."

"I can choose my own time to do these things?"

"Yes, but it has to be done in the next seventy-two hours."

"And when will you get me off parole, Meester Hoodge?"

"I'll start the paperwork in the morning and will have it put through when you're done."

"Señor?"

"Yes?"

"You would like more tequila?"

Hutchin held out his glass. "Love some, Rico."

He refilled their glasses, then touched his glass to Hutchin's. "*Salud,* my friend."

(2)

Ryan woke early that morning, a pale light coming through the window, and his stomach rumbling with hunger. His mom was still sound asleep in the other bed, so he walked out of the bedroom and into the little kitchen to find something to eat.

There wasn't much, just some stuff his mother had bought in the inn's market before they'd come upstairs. A couple of bananas, four little boxes of cereal, a pint of milk, and an apple. He fixed himself a bowl of Fruit Loops and went out into the living room to watch cartoons, but there was a body on the couch. And suddenly the body sat up and startled Ryan so badly that he leaped back. Milk sloshed over the sides of his bowl.

"Agent Mulder. What're you doing here?"

"I had an X-File to look into," he said, his voice sleepy.

"Yeah, right."

"Your mom was generous enough to let me use the couch. What time is it, anyway?"

"I don't know. Early. The sun's barely up."

Ben Webster stretched his arms above his head, then swung his legs over the side of the couch. "You think it's okay if I use the shower?"

"Sure. My mom can sleep through anything. I'll start the coffee."

"You know how to do that?"

"If I wake up first, I start the coffee for my mom. If she gets up first, she makes my breakfast. You like your coffee strong?"

"Absolutely," Webster said. "I can smell it already." He stood, grabbed his pack, slung it over his shoulder. "How're you getting to school today?"

"I think Abuelita is coming to get me. Mom called her last night when we checked in."

"Well, if she doesn't show up, I can drive you," he said, then walked off toward the bedroom.

Ryan, already at the kitchen counter, measuring out coffee, stepped back a little, trying to see into the bedroom. He couldn't remember his mother ever offering a couch to a guy for the night and there had been a lot of guys in the last few years. Some guys she went out with, some guys she worked with, but he didn't think there had been any special guy. Till now.

Through the crack in the door, he saw Ben leaning over his mother, his face close to hers as she slept. He must have said something, because she rolled onto her back and her arms went around Ben's neck and then Ben glanced toward the door and saw Ryan.

Ryan quickly returned to the coffee machine, poured water into it, turned the machine on. He added more milk to his cereal and thought about his mother and Ben. He had noticed the way they looked at each other over dinner and he felt okay about it. He liked Ben, he could talk to him. He liked the way Ben treated his mother.

On his way into the living room, he glanced toward the bedroom again. This time, his mother was standing up, brushing her hair, wearing the gym shorts and T-shirt she'd slept in. She came to the door.

"Hey, I smell coffee. Thanks, hon. Did you get something to eat?"

"Cereal. What time's Abuelita coming?"

"Probably around seven. As soon as you finish eating, we have to hustle."

She came out into the kitchen for coffee. Ryan heard the shower come on and wondered if his mother and Ben had had sex.

He flicked through the TV channels, about a hundred of them, movies and cartoons and news. He wanted to call Becky to find out how Oro was, but it was too early. Becky didn't get up until seven. By seven he would be on his way across the bridge with Abuelita. They would stop at the house so that he could change clothes, get his backpack, and bring Oro home. He couldn't ask Abuelita about sex. He could ask her about other things, but not about that. It would embarrass him too much. So all day, he would wonder about his mother and Ben. If they had sex, would they make a baby?

His mother and his father must have had sex at least once, since he was here. After that, his father had left. Did that mean Ben would leave, too? This thought made him sad. He didn't want Ben to leave. He needed to talk to Becky about it. Becky knew about these things. Her father had told her about sex, about how things worked with men and women, about how babies were made, and Becky had told Ryan. He still didn't really understand it.

But when he had been big, he had understood. When he had been big, he'd had sex with the pretty woman he had glimpsed on the bridge at Bahia Honda. And he hadn't left her. He had loved her, she had loved him. Then something had gone wrong. Very wrong. He didn't understand that, either.

He didn't understand a lot of things. But for the first time ever, he knew he was getting closer to understanding. He knew because the Other didn't come shrieking out of nowhere as it had done before. He knew and for right this second, that was enough. *To know,* even if he didn't know why.

His mother came over to him and hugged him good morning, the scent of her coffee getting all mixed up with the smell of her hair and skin. "You feeling better today?" she asked.

"Yeah, I'm fine. I'm sorry that I broke all those dishes and glasses and stuff."

"I'm more worried about you than about a bunch of plates and glasses." She lowered herself to the floor beside him. "I'm really sorry I got so angry at you last night. I was feeling frustrated, I guess."

"It's okay, Mom. Really. If I were you, I'd have gotten mad, too. But Judge Hutchin is still a bad man."

She didn't say anything to that.

"Do you like Ben, Mom?"

"Yeah, he's a nice guy."

"No, I mean, do you *like* him? Is he special?"

"I think he could be, yes. But only if *you* like him, too."

"I think he's the best."

She gave him another hug and stood. "I need to get ready for work. You'd better hurry up and finish your cereal."

"Mom, do you think I might be remembering a past life? Ben and I talked a little about it last night."

He could tell by the expression on her face that his mother had given the idea some thought, but hadn't decided yet what she believed. "I don't think we should dismiss the possibility. But this is new terrain for me, hon, and I need to get some advice about how to help you, if that's what's going on."

"No doctors," he called after her. "Except for Dr. Luke."

"I promise," she called back.

Abuelita arrived a little early and spent a few minutes talking to Ben and his mother while Ryan finished showering and got dressed. He could hear their voices through the bedroom door, which wasn't completely shut, and he moved closer to hear what they were saying.

Ear to the wood, he listened. His mother and Ben were telling Abuelita what happened last night and Abuelita listened, as she always did, but didn't say much. Ryan knew that she sensed his presence behind the door. He sometimes wondered if she had X-ray eyes or something, and moved quickly back into the room.

When he came out, they were really quiet, all three of them watching him like they expected him to do something sudden and strange. Ryan just stared back at them and said, "You don't have to whisper behind my back, you know."

His mother said, "No one's talking behind your back, hon. I've got to fly to Miami today with Rita and if you call me on your cell phone, I won't be able to do anything. Abuelita said she'd stay at the house and pick you up from school."

"And I've got to be there in the afternoon," Ben said. "To go through some stuff in your mom's storage closet."

"That's all we were talking about, *mí amor,*" Abuelita assured him.

In other words, Ryan thought, an adult would be keeping an eye on him from the minute he got home from school. "I'm not going to freak out again."

"Good." Abuelita stood. "So there is no problem. *Vamonos,* Ryan. Or we'll be late."

Ryan blew his mother a kiss, flashed Ben a thumbs-up, and took the old woman's hand. It wasn't until they were alone in the elevator that Ryan realized Abuelita's magic sang through her touch, the heat of her palm. A part of him wanted to take his hand away from hers, but another part of him hoped she would be able to guide him somehow.

"You were a big person again," she remarked.

He noticed it wasn't a question. "A little person with big-person scary things going on."

She smiled at that. "These big-person memories can't hurt you, Ryan."

"Then why was I so scared of the judge?"

"Because you're remembering emotions. If you were bitten by a snake when you were a baby, you might not consciously remember being bitten, but you might have a terrible fear of snakes for a long time."

"Was I someone else, Abuelita? Is that what you think?"

"We all were other people. But not all of us remember. Sometimes these memories surface on their own when we're confronted with people we've known before or with events similar to what we've experienced before."

"Like the snake."

"Exactly."

"Do you think the judge is a snake?"

"I don't know him. Besides, your opinion is the only one that matters."

He felt frustrated because no one gave him definite answers—not his Mom, not Ben, not Abuelita. He knew they meant well, he knew they were concerned, but he needed direction, guidance. He needed someone to take him by the hand and lead him into the place where the answers were. But he had a terrible feeling that none of the adults in his life could do it. Even though they were older and smarter than he was and seemed to believe other lives were possible, the reality was as new to them as it was to him.

If that was what was happening.

In some ways, talking to his mom and Ben and Abuelita was like playing doctor. *Here are my symptoms, Doc. What's wrong with me?* Maybe nothing was *wrong*. Maybe what was happening to him had happened to other people, ordinary people, kids like himself. He decided that today in computer lab, he would go on the Internet and look for information. As his mom always said during a trial, *Information is power.*

The elevator opened into the crowded lobby, where people who had gotten stranded on the island last night were now trying to get checked out. Ryan felt very small in the crowd, almost invisible, and clung tightly to Abuelita's hand as she made her way through the crowd, to the door.

Someone stepped on his toes. He was bumped from behind. The press of bodies, the noise and activity, made him hot, dizzy. Everything started to shift to one side, as if he were in an airplane that was banking steeply to the right. It seemed that everything in the room slid toward him, people and suitcases, lamps and desks and rugs, and then the light turned milky, sound vanished from the world, and everything slammed into slow motion.

Ryan turned his head, but even this seemed to happen so slowly he could hear the muscles in his neck stretching, the joints creaking. When he blinked, the blink took forever, his eyelids coming down, down, down, his lashes brushing his cheeks like the wings of a bird. And now his eyelids began to open again and fire surrounded him. Flames climbed through the air, but didn't touch him. He couldn't even feel the heat of the fire. But it was there, in front of him, at his sides, behind him, everywhere, a fire burning in slow motion.

And at that moment, his hand slipped out of Abuelita's. Panic roared up behind him and hurled him forward. Ryan pushed through the crowd, but even this happened slowly, as if he were in a dream. He clawed at the blur in front of him, trying to make space so he could get out. He sucked air through his mouth, tried desperately to scream for help. Nothing came out except weird, gasping sounds.

A woman looked down at him and her mouth opened like that of a fish and the words that came out sounded the way noises did underwater, elongated, stretched out.

"Heeeeyyyyy. Thaaat's myyy skiiirt yooouu'rree jeerrk-iing oonn. . . ."

Ryan looked up at her and everything inside of him went still. The fire was gone, the crowd was gone. It was just him and the woman, the two of them staring at each other. Then the crowd sucked her away and spat him out and he stumbled and fell to his knees.

He pulled the sweet, fresh air into his lungs and rocked back on his heels, shaking his head to clear it. People hurried past him, just their legs visible to him. "Up you go," said a friendly male voice, and strong, capable hands took hold of his arm and pulled him to his feet.

"Thanks," Ryan said, and looked up at Ben. "Where'd you come from?" he asked.

"I was trying to get through the mess in the lobby. Where's Abuelita?"

"Right here." She hurried up behind them, her cheeks red, strands of her white hair fallen loose from her braid. "What a nightmare. What happened to you, *mí amor*? One moment I had your hand, the next moment, you were lost in the crowd."

I saw fire.

I saw her. The woman from the bridge.

He was sure of it. But he couldn't speak it.

Ben walked with them out to Abuelita's Mercedes and Ryan, between them, looked back toward the front entrance of the inn, hoping to see the woman again, hoping he hadn't imagined her. Hoping.

The next thing he knew, the Mercedes was speeding across the Tango Key Bridge, under the bluest of skies and above water so clear that when Ryan looked down, he could see almost to the very bottom. In the distance, fishing boats headed out into the gulf, flocks of gulls following them. He wished, suddenly, that he were a gull and could fly away into all the blue and forget about everything here on the ground.

But if he did that, he would never see the woman again. So he drew his gaze away from the gulls and the sky and rested his head against the back of the soft leather seat and shut his eyes.

Chapter 17

Kit had gotten about four hours of sleep and it wasn't enough. Not nearly enough. Her eyes felt as if they'd been scrubbed with sand, her thoughts seemed sluggish. But as the Bonanza lifted into the air, her fatigue lifted with it, and by the time they reached altitude, she felt almost normal.

"We've got a nice tailwind," Rita said through the head-set. "We should be in Miami in about an hour. How much driving do we need to do once we get there to check out all of Diane's credit charges?"

Kit reached into her briefcase for a map of Miami and the list of charges that Diane Jackson had made to her credit card as Dionne Johnson. The credit card records listed five charges at the Mizner Hotel on Miami Beach between the months of March and September. These charges included six or seven thousand dollars' worth of charges for hotels, meals, shopping, and other purchases. Kit hoped to find someone who remembered Diane and who might be able to tell her whether Diane had been alone or with someone. A long shot, perhaps, but she was used to long shots by now.

"In August and September, it looks like all the charges were made on or around Miami Beach. Let's focus on those two months. They're the most recent."

"Are they within walking distance of each other?"

"Except for a charge at the Lincoln Mall. I think that's a bit of a hike on foot from the beach."

"I stopped in to see Poulton last night after the fracas at the courthouse and showed him the necklace. He says he didn't buy it. Despite his sister's money, he says he can't afford gifts like that. And he doesn't have any idea who 'centaur' might be. I've contacted just about every jewelry store on Tango and in Key West, but none of them sell the silver box. The heart is a standard issue found in most jewelry stores—eighteen-karat gold, worth between eight hundred and a thousand bucks. But none of the stores did the engraving on the back of it. A couple of jewelers said the silver box is worth as much as the heart, or more, because of the quality of the craftsmanship. So maybe we're talking about a gift worth between fifteen hundred and two thousand dollars, which adds credence to your horary theory about an older man with an expendable income."

"Or a Brad Pitt type for whom money is no object. We're closer, but not close enough."

"She's only been dead a week, Kit."

And next Thursday or Friday, would their litany be that Diane had been dead for only two weeks? At what point did the "only" get dropped? The longer it took, the colder the trail would be.

They rented a car at the airport and Kit drove because Rita was the better navigator. On their way into Miami Beach, the office called Kit's cell phone twice about details in one of Rita's cases. When the phone rang a third time, Rita griped about incompetent office help and answered the phone with a curt "Vasquez. Oh . . . uh, yes, hold on a second, Agent Webster."

She lifted her brows and mouthed, *Sexy voice*, as she handed the phone to Kit.

"Hey, Ben."

"Hi. You in Miami yet?"

"On our way to Miami Beach."

"I never got a chance this morning to tell you how much I enjoyed last night."

The surface of her skin lit up, as if he were touching her all over again. "Me, too. And thanks for talking to Ryan last night."

"I'm glad I could help. He's a nice kid. Listen, you sure it's okay if I rummage through that storage closet on your porch for Pete's journals and notebooks?"

"Positive. You've got the key. His stuff is on one of the back shelves. With any luck, I should be back at the house by five or five-thirty. Abuelita will be there most of the day."

"Great. See you then."

As soon as Kit disconnected, Rita had comments and questions. "That was the agent who's investigating Pete's disappearance?"

"The same."

"And now sexual abstinence is in your past."

Kit smiled and glanced in the rearview mirror to switch into the right lane. She spotted a beige car that she thought she'd seen earlier, when they were leaving the car rental place. *Yeah, and so what?* South Florida probably had thousands of beige four-door cars. Maybe hundreds of thousands.

"And afterward he spent the night on the couch," Rita went on.

"You know me too well, Rita."

"Ryan likes him?"

"Ryan's crazy about him."

"And he talked with Ryan about all the weirdness last night?"

"They apparently talked at some length."

"Christ, it sounds ready made, Kit. Look, if he's half as good-looking in person as he sounds on the phone, find out if he has any single friends."

"Fine," she said with a laugh. "Now get us into Miami Beach."

She glanced in the mirror again, but the car was no longer in sight.

The Art Deco district was just about a mile square, yet included more than six hundred buildings listed on the National Register of Historic Places, most of them architectural gold mines from the 1920s and 1930s. The Miami Beach that Kit remembered as a youngster was a far cry from the trendy Miami Beach of the twenty-first century. Now it was a kind of American Riviera, winter home to jet-setters and celebrities.

Some of them had bought a piece of the action—Madonna and Stallone had lived here and both had had part interest in businesses. At one time, novelist Anne Rice occasionally was spotted having coffee at the News Café. The six-million-dollar mansion that Versace had renovated still stood, an icon of grandeur now owned by someone else. No wonder Diane had stayed here. She'd been just one pretty face among many, Kit thought, and probably hadn't attracted inordinate attention, a real plus if she'd been with a secret lover.

They found a parking space between 12th and 13th Streets, fed five bucks of quarters into the hungry parking meter, and headed down Ocean Drive toward the Mizner Hotel. Roller bladers, babes in string bikinis, models on photo shoots, and the usual variety of hot flesh, beautiful trendsetters, and ordinary snowbirds crowded the sidewalks. People spilled out of the cafés and restaurants, where lines for lunch were already forming, even though it was barely eleven A.M.

The traffic on Ocean Drive was even worse, bumper-to-bumper cars crawling forward through the pleasant November air, horns blaring, tempers short. Too many cars, too many people, not enough parking spaces or restaurants or hotel rooms to accommodate the crush of humanity, she thought. Thunderheads stacked up in the distance, still out over the Atlantic, but moving inland. In a few hours, people would scatter for cover as the rains arrived.

Just before they reached the Mizner, Kit thought she saw the beige car again, turning out of the traffic on Ocean. "Hey, I think that beige Pontiac is following us," she said to Rita.

By the time Rita glanced around, the Pontiac was gone. The hoods of other beige cars glistened in the light. "You're getting paranoid in your old age, you know that, Kit?"

Maybe, she thought. And maybe not.

The Mizner, just three buildings down from Versace's place, dated back to 1933. It was classic Deco, painted a dove gray and pastel pink, with streamlined corners and tiny windows. The lobby boasted walls of inlaid tile that depicted birds and butterflies in flight, a tile floor that looked to be composed of Mayan or Aztec symbols, Deco sofas and chairs in pinks and blues and pale yellows that Kit found somewhat nauseating. Deco didn't do much for her, but Rita loved it.

At the desk, a tall woman with an angular face and small, white teeth like Chiclets greeted them with a public relations cheerfulness. Her name tag read COKIE DAVIDSON, MANAGER. When Kit explained what she wanted, Davidson replied that she couldn't release that kind of information. "We respect our clients' privacy and they—"

"Maybe you didn't understand me. This concerns a murder investigation. I can subpoena the hotel's records if I have to, but right now I'm not requesting access to your records. I'm simply asking you to tell me how many days Dionne Johnson stayed here, if she was alone, and if any calls were made from her room," Kit said.

Davidson, like so many people, Kit thought, seemed to feel she had to protest first, as if to legitimize her job or her belief in the democratic way or some other damn thing. But the bottom line was that she realized it would be simpler to cooperate. "Why don't we go into my office."

A computer and desk took center stage in Davidson's office, which was barely large enough to accommodate the three of them. "The only reason I'm going to give you the information you've requested is to avoid publicity," Davidson said as they sat down. "Because of who, uh, *Dionne* was."

"We know *who* she was." Rita's voice held a sharp, impatient edge. "We appreciate your cooperation, Ms. Davidson, and understand this puts you in a compromising position. We'll respect that. Now can we get on with it?"

Davidson swiveled her chair around and typed in *Johnson, Dionne.* Five dates came up. "Which stay would you like?"

"All of them," Kit replied.

"This will take a couple minutes." She pressed the print button.

"Was Diane ever with a man when she was here?" Rita asked.

"I work from eight to five. Diane was rarely seen before five. I saw her only once, when I had to stay past five. She was with a man then."

"This man?" Kit slipped a newspaper photo of Poulton out of the file on her lap. "Was it this man?"

She glanced at the photo of Poulton and shook her head. "No, absolutely not. I saw him on TV. Steve Poulton. It wasn't him. The guy she was with was at least twenty years older.''

Rita's eyes met Kit's and seemed to say, *You were right about an older guy.* ''Can you describe him?'' Rita asked.

''Not specifically. I saw him at a distance, across the lobby, as they were leaving. He moved quickly. He wore a baseball cap pulled low over his face.''

Not enough, Kit thought. ''Then how do you know he was older than Diane?''

''I deal with people all day long. And when I'm not dealing with them, I'm watching them. I knew this man was older because of the way he carried himself.''

''How was he built? Was he heavy? Slender? Tall, short, what?''

''On the slender side. Tall, but not inordinately tall. Five-ten, maybe six feet.''

Rita scribbled notes as Cokie Davidson spoke, but so far, everything she said probably fit fifty percent of the forty-and-over male population in south Florida.

''How did he dress?'' Rita asked.

''How does anyone here on the beach dress? Some guys stroll around in Versace's casual best. Others wear strictly jeans. I honestly don't recall how he was dressed.''

She removed the printed pages from the tray, stacked them, then stapled the bills for the separate stays. Rita took the pages and immediately started flipping through them, comparing the phone numbers Diane had called with a list of known phone numbers for the people in her life.

''Is there anything else you can tell me about this man, Ms. Davidson? Is there anything unusual you noticed about him?'' Kit asked.

''No. Other than the apparent age difference, that's about it.''

Rita glanced up from her phone log. "Did you ever see the car he drove?"

"No. And she never listed a car on her room card. According to the evening staff, she usually went out alone around suppertime; then she would return a couple hours later and a man would be with her. I don't know if it was the same man."

"Who *would* know?" Kit asked.

"The evening staff. They don't come on until seven."

"Who cleaned their room?" Rita asked.

"Excuse me?"

"Take Labor Day weekend," Rita said. "Who cleaned the fourth floor rooms over that weekend?"

"I really don't know. That's the housekeeping department."

"Housekeeping should have schedules, right?"

"Well, yes, but like I said, that's not my department."

Laziness, Kit thought. This was laziness and not intentional evasion. Cokie Davidson was a Very Busy Person and simply couldn't be bothered. "Can you access housekeeping's records from here?"

"Look, I really don't have time to—"

Rita sat forward, chin resting in the palm of her hand. "Would you do that, please? We'd like to talk to someone else who might have had contact with Diane and this man."

This elicited a prissy little sigh from Davidson, but she did as Rita had asked and the housekeeping schedule for the month of September appeared. "Okay, Labor Day weekend. Consuelo Rodriguez had the suite on the fourth floor. I wasn't working that weekend. Let me call housekeeping and see if she's in today. She doesn't speak much English."

"Not a problem," said Rita.

Consuelo Rodriguez was a shy young woman with the high cheekbones and skin coloring of someone whose gene pool came from the Mayans—Guatemala or Mexico, Kit thought. She spoke softly as she answered Rita's questions. Kit's spoken Spanish was marginal, but she understood it fairly well as long as Rita and Consuelo didn't speak too quickly. Yes, Consuelo remembered the beautiful actress. Even if she hadn't been an actress, however, Consuelo claimed she would remember her because she hung a DO NOT DISTURB sign on her door that rarely came down before midafternoon.

Over Labor Day weekend, she couldn't remember exactly which day, the actress had forgotten to put up the sign. Just the same, Consuelo had knocked and when no one had answered, she assumed the señorita had gotten up early. So she unlocked the room and walked in and immediately heard the shower. Before she could duck out, a man came out of the bathroom with a towel wrapped around his waist. He was rubbing another towel through his hair and he didn't see her immediately. Then he looked up, as shocked as Consuelo was.

"Can you describe him?" Rita asked in Spanish.

Her soft, dark eyes narrowed, as if she were peering into that morning more than two months ago, when she'd walked into Diane Jackson's room. "His body was that of an older man. A good body, compact and hard, but not a young body."

"What did he look like?" Rita asked. "What color were his eyes? His hair?"

"I did not see his hair. He was rubbing it with the towel. I do not remember about his eyes. I was too surprised."

"Could we use a room for a while?" Rita asked Davidson. "I'd like Consuelo to work with me on a police sketch program I have on my computer."

"Fine, that's fine." Davidson sounded really impatient now. She stood, brushed the wrinkles from her otherwise impeccable skirt. "I really need to get back to work. You can use room 101 down the hall."

While Rita worked with Consuelo, Kit walked a block west and two blocks north along Penna Avenue, looking for a clothing shop where Diane had charged a bundle. A Cuban shop had racks placed out on the sidewalk, where guayabera shirts in Deco colors hung swaying in the rising breeze. Kit had to step off the curb just to get past them and nearly missed Dominica's, the shop she was looking for.

Inside, Latino music blared from speakers mounted in the four corners of the shop, a Gloria Estefan piece, the kind of rocking beat that made you tap your feet and snap your hips from side to side even if you didn't like to dance. Kit glanced at price tags as she made her way to the area where several Latino women chatted away in Spanish far too rapid for her to understand. Everything was incredibly expensive, from the $50 T-shirts that announced you'd been to Miami Beach to the $300 shoes and plain cotton blouses for a hundred and change.

The sales clerk she spoke to was helpful. She spoke a combination of Spanish and English—Spanglish, as the natives called it—but she didn't need to speak at all for Kit to discern that she had known Diane Jackson. As soon as Kit showed her the photo, the woman's eyes widened. "*Ah, sí, sí, una lástima.* She be so young, so talented, so pretty."

"What did she used to buy in here, señora? She was here over Labor Day weekend and purchased nearly eight hundred dollars' worth of clothes."

This short, corpulent woman, Francesca, turned to another short, plump woman and rattled off something in Spanish. The woman replied, then Francesca touched Kit's arm. "Come, I show you our private *colección*, yes?"

The private collection she referred to occupied a back room with a single barred window. It was filled with lingerie that would put Frederick's of Hollywood to shame. "Diane, she buy many things from our private collection. She says her men have different tastes, yes? Different passions."

Kit ran her fingers over a lace teddy with the nipples cut out and a pair of attached panties that had no crotch. She tried to imagine herself wearing a getup like this and nearly laughed out loud. In many ways, places like this echoed the repressive fifties, when women got what they wanted through seduction and sex. "She discussed her men with you?" Kit asked.

"I tell her I am filled with lust for Brad Pitt, no? And she shakes her head. 'Don't be. He's not that great.' And she tells me about other actors she knows and we laugh and laugh because now she is trying on clothes and calling out, 'Hey, Francesca? Who would like this? Brad? Russell Crowe? Dennis Quaid?' And while I know it is a game, señorita, I also know it is not a game, *me entiendes?*"

"What about this man?" She showed Poulton's picture to Francesca. "Was he ever here with her?"

"No, I see his picture on the TV news and I can't believe it. This man, he is no movie star. He is a doctor. No doctor come here. Once, I see her with an older man. He wait outside, on the sidewalk, his head down. And Francesca thinks to herself that it is strange, no? Why not he come in? *Tiene verguenza?" Did he feel shame?*

"*Quizás,*" Kit replied. *Maybe.* "Can you tell me anything else about him?"

"He pace. He pace back and forth in front of the store. I never see his face too good."

"Did you ask her about this man?"

"*Claro, que sí.* And you know what she does? She puts her finger to her mouth and laughs. It is a small laugh, ha-ha, and she says he is married, but this is a secret she must keep."

Kit didn't have to coax Francesca to talk. She obviously loved to talk and she especially loved to talk about her experiences with the famous Diane Jackson. When Kit finally left the shop, the sky looked threatening. Dark clouds sagged over the beach, the sun hid behind a thunderhead, the smell of rain hung in the air, a threat or a promise, depending on where you happened to be when the heavens opened up. She decided to find a little something for Ryan and walked a ways up the street, checking out the shops. And there, sandwiched between two clothing shops, was a jewelry shop, a rather expensive shop from the looks of it. Since Diane had shopped on this street, perhaps her lover had shopped here or around here.

An elegant woman waited on her. "Morning, may I help you with something?"

Kit brought out the delicate silver box. "I hope so. I was wondering if you have any idea where something like this might be sold around here."

"This looks like one of ours." She took the box, opened the lid, removed the heart and chain, and pinched the piece of felt on the bottom between her long, polished nails. She fixed a jeweler's loupe to her eye. "I knew it. Take a look." She handed Kit the loupe and turned the box so she could see it.

Kit peered through the loupe and saw a numerical and letter code etched into the right-hand corner, numbers and letters so small that only a Lilliputian could have done it. "An identifying code?"

"We bought six of these from an estate sale in Palm Beach and added the codes ourselves so that we could distinguish these from any copies that might be made. They belonged to the Flagler family."

Kit could almost taste her excitement. "Do you have a record of who bought this?"

"These were sold over our Internet site, in a private auction. We sell a lot of our estate jewelry like that."

"But there are records, right?"

"May I ask what this is about?"

Kit introduced herself and explained the circumstances. She probably explained more than she should have, but she sensed this woman might be an ally.

"Well, as far as records are concerned, they aren't here. Our auction is conducted by a private outfit in New York. These items were on display here for most of the summer."

"How much was this sold for? Do you remember?"

"Like I said, I don't have anything to do with the auctions. We set the bottom-line prices and I believe we priced these at between five and seven."

"Hundred?"

The woman smiled. "Five and seven thousand."

Seven grand? It suddenly occurred to her that Diane may have bought the silver box herself and used it to store the heart and chain. "What about the engraving on the heart? Is that something your store does?"

"Most jewelry stores do engraving. There's no way to tell if we did this or not. We don't keep records on this kind of thing."

"At the moment, this is our strongest lead."

"I can give you the name and address for the auction company, but you'll have trouble getting the information. They pride themselves on their privacy policy. There is a woman at the company with whom I'm friendly. I'll e-mail her and ask if she'll get me that information. I don't know if she will, but I'll try. In the meantime, let me get you the company's card."

When Kit left the store ten minutes later, it had started to rain. She pulled an umbrella out of her shoulder bag and thought she would duck into a Cuban coffee shop just up the street before she returned to the hotel to get Rita. But when she started walking, the hairs on the back of her neck began to prickle and the area between her eyes started to ache the way it had the night she'd awakened to find Ryan gone. She had the uneasy sensation that she was being watched. Or followed.

Kit glanced behind her, but the sidewalk was filled with umbrellas now, all of them bobbing up and down like painted ponies on a carousel. She glanced right, where traffic moved slowly north and south, and saw the beige Pontiac. The windows were too darkly tinted for her to glimpse the driver, but if she slowed down and let the car move ahead of her, she could get the plate number.

She stopped at a storefront and, as she pretended to be looking at something in the window, reached into her ubiquitous and bottomless shoulder bag for the videocamera. Years ago, she and Rita had agreed that the camera should be a permanent fixture in their attorney paraphernalia and this particular model was not much larger than her hand. Her thumb slid the switch on and she brought it out of the bag and held it against her chest, watching the traffic's reflection in the storefront window.

As the Pontiac came into view, the driver's window came down and the man behind the wheel checked out the sidewalk, apparently trying to locate her in the sea of umbrellas. *Gotcha, sucker,* she thought, and turned, the camera aimed at the car.

In the moments before his window went up, she zoomed in on his face, capturing minute details—his dark shades, his unshaven jaw, his cruel mouth, the way his dark hair fell across his forehead. He was just ahead of her now and she zoomed in on the license plate, but doubted if she got anything because it was so dirty.

Suddenly, the Pontiac swerved to the curb and another

man leaped out of the car and started across the street, darting between cars, headed straight for her. "Jesus," she whispered, dropping the camera back into her bag, and moved quickly down the street.

The umbrella caught the air and slowed her down. She closed it and rain poured over her. When she looked back, the man was now on this side of the road, a tall, heavy brute of a guy, a bouncer type, the sort of guy who banged heads for a living. He maneuvered his way through the press of pedestrians, and Kit broke into a run, grateful that she was wearing flats instead of heels, slacks instead of a tight skirt, and flew into the Cuban clothing store.

Francesca was still at the register, chatting away with the other clerk, when Kit shouted, "Call the police, a man's chasing me!"

"*Cierra la puerta!*" Francesa barked at her companion. *Shut the door.*

Her companion lurched forward and Francesca grabbed Kit's arm and motioned her into the back. "In the private collection, señora. The rear door opens into an alley. *Apúrate.*"

Kit raced into the private collection room, her wet clothes dripping all over the rug, and threw back the dead bolt. She ran out into the wet alley, where rain now fell in slanting sheets. Right or left? Neither. She raced across the alley and plunged into a thick hedge. Branches scratched at her arms and face, clawed at her clothes. She popped out of the bushes into yet another alley. Instead of shops, this one was lined with small apartment buildings in various states of disrepair.

She loped toward the closest building, into its small parking lot, and raced into a dirty stairwell that reeked of urine. She ran up two flights of stairs, the rain now at her back. Her sides ached, she was drenched to the bone. She ducked into the building's laundry room, dismayed to find it occupied.

An elderly woman, hunched over in front of a dryer, looked up and muttered something in what sounded like Yiddish. Kit patted the air with her hands and, between gasps for air, explained that a man was after her, could she shut and lock the door?

The woman straightened up, a load of clothes in her arms, and looked Kit over from head to toe. She knew she looked worse than the proverbial drowned rat, hardly a threat to the old woman or anyone else. The woman nodded and Kit shut the door, slammed the dead bolt into place, then peered out one of the barred windows. She saw him now, coming into the parking lot, through the rain, a cell phone pressed to his ear. She got out the camera, zoomed in on his face, then turned the camera off and backed up. Cell phone, she thought, and dropped the camera into her bag and dug out her cell phone to call Rita.

"Vasquez."

"It's me."

"Hey, where the hell are you?"

"Someone's after me. A guy from the beige Pontiac. I'm holed up in a laundry room at . . . I don't know the address."

"The Majorca Building," the old woman said in perfect English, and spat out the address.

Kit ticked it off.

"I'm calling the cops," Rita said.

"Move the car. They'll go back there when they don't find me."

"I'm getting in as we speak. Are they in the car?"

"One is, the other's on foot." She peered through the window again. "I don't see him now. Just get over here. I'll mute my phone."

"Right. I'm on my way."

The old woman said, "Hey, over here." She dropped her laundry on the sorting table, grabbed a child's blanket, and limped over to the far corner, where she unlocked a door. "Quickly."

They went into a bathroom with ancient fixtures, a tiny sink, and a toilet intended for midgets. The old woman pressed her hand against a lower section of the wall and it swung inward. "A laundry chute. It's like a slide, you don't just drop straight down. It goes to the garage. You can unlock the door from the inside. You'll be safe. You're so wet, though, you should sit on this. So you will slide." She thrust the blanket at Kit.

Kit reached into her bag and pulled a fifty-dollar bill from a side pocket. She pressed it into the woman's hand. "Thank you."

Outside, footfalls echoed on the stairs.

"Go now. Fast."

She held the panel open while Kit set the blanket on the chute, the slide, whatever it was, then squeezed inside and sat on it, one hand gripping the low side. As the panel swung shut, she heard pounding on the laundry room door, and the old woman shouted in Yiddish and closed the door.

Kit, squashed into a tight, dark space, felt the familiar tightening in her chest that signaled an attack of claustrophobia. She couldn't see a damn thing, didn't have any idea what shape or how large the chute was, and she didn't have a flashlight or even a goddamn match. The old woman's voice got louder, Yiddish spewing from it so fast it sounded like gibberish, and now she heard a man shouting.

Go, fast, while he's up here.

With the strap of her bag still over her shoulder, but the bag itself clutched against her chest, she lifted one arm up to test the height of the chute. Nothing but air. She touched either side, trying to get a sense of the height; six inches. *Shit, it's not enough. One sudden turn and I'll fall out.*

But she couldn't stay where she was.

She wrapped her arms around her knees, and shoved off.

The blanket she sat on was dry when she started off and she moved fast and picked up speed by the second. Air bit her eyes, making them tear. The slide curved sharply and she turned into it and nearly lost her balance and toppled over the side. Distantly, like noises in a dream, she heard a shouting match upstairs. These sounds were drowned out by noises on other floors as she sped past them.

Her claustrophobia reached nearly epidemic proportions—the wild fluttering of her heart, the relentless pressure in her chest and throat, and the almost overpowering need to hurl herself out of here. Then the chute ended and the abruptness caused her body to list slightly and she landed hard on her right side. She lay there for a moment, arms still wrapped tightly around her bag. Her breath came in ragged, erratic bursts.

She managed to sit up and blinked against the darkness. Gradually, her eyes became accustomed to the dark and she could detect cracks of light off to her right. A window? A door? She couldn't tell. But the light grounded her, gave her some sense of direction, of up and down.

Cell phone, she thought, and fished it out of her bag. She checked her messages; Rita had called twice. She raised the volume, punched out Rita's number.

One ring, Rita had been waiting. "I'm on the move, Kit. You okay?"

"Get over here fast." She didn't dare speak above a whisper. "Come around to the back of the building, at least I think it's at the back, where the parking lot is. Honk once. I'll be coming out of the garage. Did you see the Pontiac?"

"Nope. Not yet. Keep talking to me. What're you doing in the garage?"

As Kit told her, she moved slowly toward the cracks of light, hoping she didn't stumble over anything. She found the door, pushed back the dead bolt, pressed down on the handle. The door creaked, opened a crack, and she shut it again. "I'm ready. Where are you?"

"On top of you. Get out here."

Kit pushed the door open and darted through the rain, to the rental car, and scrambled into the passenger seat. Just then, the Pontiac screeched into the lot behind them and the hulking brute who had followed her exploded out of the stairwell. Rita swung into a sharp U-turn and the rental car shot out of the lot, slammed into a depression at the curb, and shrieked out into a side street.

It was immediately obvious to Kit that they weren't going to get far very quickly if they took one of the north/south arteries. The traffic, especially in the rain, was slow and heavy. The same idea apparently occurred to Rita. She didn't turn, she just kept speeding west up one alley and another and another, racing between cars at the intersections, trying to lose the Pontiac. When the alleys ran out, she turned south on Altman Road. The Pontiac followed, darting around one car and another and another until it was directly behind them.

Rita eyed the rearview window. "This guy is really pissing me off. Make sure your seat belt is tight. We're going to trick the fucker."

"Just so we don't die in the process."

They sped toward the fork just ahead, where the left-hand route led around the southern tip of the island and the right-hand route led onto the MacArthur Causeway and back to Miami. Rita allowed the Pontiac to get so close behind them that Kit could see both men clearly now. She quickly dug out the videocamera, unfastened her seat belt, and shifted around in her seat, steadying the camera against the back of it as she peered through it.

The Pontiac immediately dropped back and Rita drove into the turn that would take them toward the southern tip of Miami Beach. As soon as the Pontiac followed, she shouted, "Hold on!" Then she whipped the wheel into a violent turn. The tires skidded against the wet road, the car spun on a dime, and they shot back in the direction from which they'd just come.

Chaos erupted around them—brakes screeching, cars turning abruptly onto the shoulder of the road, and the Pontiac skidding off into the trees. Kit's head was still spinning as the rental shrieked onto the causeway, headed for the mainland.

Chapter 18

The inside of the surveillance van still stank of cigar smoke, but Webster didn't notice it as much when the doors were open, admitting the sweet smells and busy noises of the surrounding woods. He wished he were elsewhere—on his houseboat, back in the hotel room with Kit, away from the general bullshit.

At the moment, he and Moreno were monitoring the activities in Hutchin's office on the TV screen. So far today, they had witnessed a sweep of the chambers and courtroom by the local PD, listened in on dozens of calls, and eavesdropped on several conversations between Hutchin and Louise Reese. The office sweep worried Webster because it wasn't clear to him how the local PD had gotten involved. The last he'd heard, some other outfit was going to do it. Other than that, though, they'd learned nothing of significance.

"Court TV is more interesting than this," Webster griped as Moreno popped a fresh tape into the VCR. "Or how about if we watch what goes on at home between Hutchin and his wife?"

"So far, nothing's gone on between them, at least not that we've seen, since they stayed at the same place you did last night. You want to patch through to Vogel's equipment and take a look? Maybe the missus went home and met her boyfriend."

"Right."

"Another call's coming through for Hutchin," Moreno said. "His private line." He hiked up the volume.

Webster, expecting this call to be another bust, simply rolled his eyes and watched the screen as Hutchin picked up the receiver. "Judge Hutchin."

"Hutch, it's Vic Blake."

"Hi, Vic. I hear your men didn't find anything."

"Nope. I still plan on questioning Agent Webster, not only about the bomb situation, but also about the other matter you mentioned. In fact, describe to me again, Hutch, what was going on when Webster grabbed your wrist."

Webster listened to Hutchin's lie, then murmured, "Asshole."

"I'll be in touch, Hutch."

"Thanks again."

The chill in Hutchin's voice, Webster thought, could freeze the balls off an Eskimo.

Hutchin hung up and sat there staring at the phone, drumming his fingers against the desk.

"Look at his face," Moreno said softly. "You can see the color rising right up his neck into his jaw and cheeks. He is one pissed-off judge, amigo."

"I was wearing my badge when I prevented Louise Reese from returning to the chambers during the evacuation. That's how he knows my name."

"They weren't talking about names."

"Yeah, well, we had a bit of a run-in last night at the Hilltop," Webster said, and explained.

"So he's after your butt."

"His problem is the one most judges have. He thinks he's God outside his courtroom."

Everything that had happened last night, Webster thought, from the moments Ryan started shrieking and stabbing his finger at Hutchin to those ugly moments out on the grounds, had been personal for Hutchin. Ryan had embarrassed the almighty judge in public, so the judge had to make this big show of concern by running after Ryan. Hutchin's real opinion about the matter lay in his empty threat about the psychiatric evaluation.

He struck Webster as the sort of man who got even with whoever crossed him. Hardly the moral fiber for a judge, he mused, much less for the most powerful prosecutor in the free world.

But their investigative report couldn't be based on psychology. A negative report demanded evidence, proof. *He's a profligate gambler. He has accepted bribes. He's involved with the Mafia.* Something along those lines.

"Ben, our boy's going back into judge mode," Moreno said.

Webster sat forward again, peering over Moreno's shoulder at the TV screen. Hutchin had the receiver to his ear. On the audio, they heard ringing, then: "Parole Office. How may I direct your call, please?"

"Lou Tucker."

"Just a moment."

"Who's Lou Tucker?" Moreno asked.

Webster shrugged. "Beats me."

"This is Tucker."

"Lou, it's Jay Hutchin."

"Jay. Nice to hear from you. Hey, congratulations. I heard the good news."

"Thanks, but I'm just on the short list."

"Scuttlebutt says you're the favored son."

"Well, I hope the gossip is true."

"So what can I do for you?"

"You remember Rico Sanchez?"

"Remember him? He's one of my cases. He did about eight months on a two-year sentence for B and E and because he was a repeat offender, they put him on parole for two years. He's got about eight months left."

"How's he doing?"

"Not bad. He reports in every week, works with his brother in the family fishing business, stays sober. I don't have any concerns. Why?"

"Well, we've been talking about implementing a new program where inmates who have less than a year left on parole would be released on the condition that they perform so many hours of community service a week for the remainder of the parole time. We have some bugs to iron out of it and I figure the best way to do that is hands on. We're going to confine it to Tango County for the time being, but I need at least two people to start with."

"Rico would be a good one to start with. Despite his recidivism, he's nonviolent."

"That's why I figured we could start with him and one other person."

"Give me a day or two and I'll have another name for you."

"Great. We'd like to get it under way before Christmas."

"Sounds terrific. Who's going to handle it if you head off to DC?"

"We'll appoint you to head the program, Lou."

Tucker laughed and they chatted on about life in general.

Webster noticed that Hutchin had a strange expression on his face, a smug, self-satisfied expression. Like the canary that had just eaten the bird. He wondered what it meant.

When they'd gotten off the phone, Hutchin's right arm came into the chambers and reminded the judge that he had a pretrial hearing in ten minutes. Webster watched him putting on his robes, that same smug expression still in place.

"I don't buy it," Moreno said, lighting one of his nasty cigars. "He'd have to get statutes changed to implement that kind of program."

"Maybe. I'm more interested in who this Rico guy is." He turned to his laptop, went on-line, and accessed the Bureau's criminal files. He typed in Sanchez, thought a moment. "Hey, Eric. What's Rico a nickname for?"

"Try Enrico."

Sanchez, Enrico.

Moments later, Enrico Sanchez's entire rap sheet came up, page after page of misdemeanors, from breaking and entering to car theft, poaching, and shoplifting. A small-time crook, Webster thought. He'd done hard time once for robbery but because no weapon had been involved, he'd gotten off lightly, a year at Indian River Correctional, a medium-security facility inhabited mostly by juvenile offenders.

By now, Moreno was seated next to him, eyeing everything, his putrid cigar burning away in an ashtray. "At least open the goddamn door if you're going to smoke that thing in here, Moreno."

"Yeah, yeah. I'll get the door, but we need more information. Did Hutchin prosecute this guy when he was state attorney for Tango County? Dade County? Where?"

Webster scrolled through the rap sheet, looking for convictions that went back six, seven, eight years. He checked several, but they'd all happened in other counties—Monroe, Dade, Palm Beach. He knew that Hutchin had been the state attorney for Dade County during the eighties, so he went back as far as 1984, then moved forward, charge by charge.

In March 1985, Sanchez was convicted for robbery and
Hutchin had been the prosecutor. In 1987, Sanchez was
charged with shoplifting. But a week after his arrest, the
store dropped the charges when restitution of $625.45 was
made for what he had shoplifted.

Webster felt a telling chill that prompted him to read
through the information again. Where had Rico gotten six
hundred bucks to pay restitution? Maybe a bleeding-heart
relative or a girlfriend had loaned it to him. Maybe this
person, maybe that person, there were a number of reasonable explanations. But what Webster felt just then had nothing whatsoever to do with reason. It was exactly how he'd
felt the night he'd awakened from a sound sleep, chilled to
the core of his soul and certain something had happened to
his parents. He was suddenly certain that Hutchin had paid
the restitution. Hutchin, an ambitious prosecutor, had understood the value of street sources for information and had
recognized such a source in Sanchez. But was it any worse
than what he and Moreno were doing?

No street address for Sanchez, just a PO box on Tango
and a phone number—a cell phone. He began to think out
loud, and pretty soon, turned around to face Moreno, who
simply listened, his eyes wide, inscrutable. He didn't respond
immediately when Webster finished and the silence seemed
eerie, unnatural, punctuated by the soft hum of the electron-
ics in the surveillance van. Moreno rolled his spent cigar
between his fingers.

"When I first started working with Banks in the cold
cases department, he used to drive me totally nuts by going
off on these tangents concerning a particular case. The tangents never made any sense to me, Ben. There was nothing
logical about them. But you know what? Those tangents
always yielded new information. That was his gift, a nose

for connections that other people just don't see. I think you've got the same gift.''

The comparison flattered Webster, but at the moment he was more interested in whether Moreno agreed with him. "So we know he can be compromised."

"Hey, paying for a street source doesn't mean he was compromised. It just makes him like the rest of us. It means he makes mistakes. Errors in judgment. The fact that he made threats about a kid who embarrassed him in public means that his passions can be stoked. We're on the right track, but we haven't quite found it yet. And you're not going to find it by barging in on this Sanchez fellow and interrogating him. That'll just tip off Hutchin."

The voice of reason. "I'm telling you, Eric, there's a connection between our investigation of Hutchin and what that kid said last night. I don't know what it is yet, but I will."

"I don't doubt it for a second," Moreno replied, and slipped the cigar between his lips and relit it.

Webster's houseboat was an Orca, smaller than the standard model, custom built for two, only twelve by forty. She had a MerCruiser 215 engine so dependable that it wasn't made anymore, a fifty-amp battery charger, twelve-volt deep-cycle batteries, power and automatic bilge pumps, a marine shore power cord, and dual-station hydraulic steering. The fuel, waste, and water capacities were 150 gallons each, the water was solar heated, and the fridge and stove ran on gas. Inside and out, she was equipped for comfortable onboard living and for the past eight months, this boat had been more home to Webster than nearly any other place he had lived.

He'd bought her for a song the day after his divorce had

become final, using part of what he'd gotten when he and his ex had sold their Miami home. The aging conch who had owned her had loved and coddled her for years. But he could barely walk anymore and knew that his need to sell her to the right person was as great as Webster's need at that time to start a new chapter of his life. They'd struck a deal. Even though Webster hadn't exactly sailed off into the sunset, the houseboat had been the right place for his transition from married man to single man.

When he checked his answering machine, he wasn't surprised to find that Vogel had called twice. He sounded tense and irritable and Webster guessed that Sheriff Blake had gotten in touch with him. Abuelita had called from her cell phone, a short message merely to inform him that she was at Kit's. The last call was from Sheriff Blake himself. His folksy southern voice sounded benign enough. "Give me a call, Agent Webster." No please, no hint what it was about, just a call from one cop to another. He could wait another fifteen minutes, Webster thought, and went into the cabin to change clothes and to think about things. He decided it was probably wisest to talk to Vogel before he called Blake.

When he came out of the bedroom, Vogel was sitting at the kitchen table, a bottle of ice-cold water and a file in front of him. To say that he looked unhappy didn't quite cover it. Veins stood out in his dark face, his mouth had flattened out like a dash.

"Hey, Bernie."

"What the hell made Hutchin so suspicious about the bomb threat that he went to the locals?"

"I was wearing my badge when I stopped his assistant from returning to his chambers."

"C'mon, it's got to be more than that."

"Yeah, Bernie. It's called a guilty conscience. He and I

ran into each other last night at the Hilltop,'' he said, and
went on to explain, again, what had happened.

Bernie Vogel certainly wouldn't buy Webster's theory
about what might be going on with Ryan, so Webster simply
stuck to the facts, relating them as they had happened. ''He
was going to take a swing at Kit and I stopped him.''

''I believe the sheriff's exact words on that count were
that you grabbed Hutchin's wrist for no apparent reason and
told him to get the hell out of there.''

''That isn't how it happened and I had three witnesses.
Kit, her son, the hotel employee.''

''Good. Let Blake talk to the witnesses and we'll simply
inform him that although the Bureau is investigating Hutchin
for the attorney general position, illegal surveillance is the
CIA's domain, not that of the FBI.''

''You lie with such conviction, Bernie.''

''It's what makes me good at my job.''

''If Hutchin knew your name, would he connect you with
your nephew?''

The question obviously caught Vogel by surprise—not
the question, exactly, but the fact that Webster knew about
his nephew. He apparently didn't realize that in the Bureau
hallways, rumor and gossip were king. To his credit, though,
he masked his emotion quickly. ''No. We have different
last names. And just for your information, Ben, my nephew
doesn't have shit to do with this.''

Webster didn't buy it, but he didn't say anything.

When the sheriff showed up a while later, the three of them
stood on the houseboat deck, under a flawless November sky,
talking like good ole boys who knew the score. Blake asked
his questions, one cop to another, and Webster let Vogel
lay it on the line, how they were investigating Hutchin
because of his candidacy for attorney general. And Vogel,

naturally, lied through his teeth about how the Bureau never used illegal surveillance tactics.

"You have any leads on who might've made the call?" Blake asked.

"None. All we know is what you know," Vogel said. "That the call was made from a pay phone on Tango."

"I've known the judge since he was a prosecutor in Tango County and I can tell you right now there aren't many men with his integrity."

"That's good to know, Sheriff," Vogel replied. "It makes our job that much easier."

"I'm real curious, though, about what happened at the Hilltop last night." His eyes seemed to slide sideways in his masklike face and paused on Webster. "I understand you were there when the Parrish kid went berserk."

Webster knew Blake had heard some version of the incident from Hutchin, but suspected he'd heard it again over morning coffee in the police department staff room. Tango was a small island, word got around quickly about public spectacles. So Webster gave his spiel, describing how Ryan had freaked when he'd met Hutchin, shouting that he was a bad man. "It undoubtedly embarrassed the judge and he was angry, rightfully so," Webster said. "But he had no business threatening the boy and his mother with a psychiatric evaluation by the courts and she got angry and grabbed the front of his shirt and then he took a swing at her and I stopped him."

Blake's masklike expression finally cracked with what might have been surprise or disbelief, Webster couldn't tell. "I see. Well, it's not really an issue since Judge Hutchin isn't pressing charges. He was merely voicing a suspicion about the bomb threat."

"What suspicion is that?" Vogel asked innocently.

"That it was engineered by the feds, so they could spy on him."

Vogel glanced at Webster and Webster lifted his brows and they exploded with laughter. "Sure. Big Brother's alive and well," Vogel managed to say in between laughs.

Blake's mask cracked a smile. "Yeah, well." He slipped his hands in the pockets of his meticulously pressed trousers and gazed out over the water. "The boy's behavior sounds sort of strange," he said finally.

"Hey, he's a nine-year-old kid. Maybe he'd had too much sugar. Maybe Hutchin rubbed him the wrong way. I don't know."

When Vogel spoke, his deep, sonorous voice sounded like the very paragon of Bureau authority. "Agent Webster acted within his jurisdiction, Sheriff. That's absolutely clear. We hope that Judge Hutchin doesn't persist in this ludicrous waste of your time and ours. That will hardly further Judge Hutchin's candidacy for attorney general."

When Blake left a while later, Vogel seemed satisfied that the matter would be dropped. But Webster felt less certain. He put nothing past Hutchin.

(2)

The light in the storage closet had burned out and Ryan didn't know where his mother kept the spare bulbs. So he and Becky stood just inside the door, their flashlights aimed at the ceiling just above Ben's head.

He stood on a ladder and was pushing cartons around on the shelves, looking for those that had belonged to Ryan's Uncle Pete. "She said they were on the back shelves," Ben said. "But I don't see them."

"Mom's not very organized sometimes," Ryan remarked.

"She's organized when she's being a lawyer," Becky said.

"Yeah, but she wasn't being a lawyer when she packed away Uncle Pete's stuff. Try the shelves on the right wall, Ben."

Ben climbed down from the ladder, moved the ladder, went up again. "I need a little more light, guys," he called.

Becky stepped over to the ladder and shone her flashlight directly upward. Ryan stayed where he was and simply turned his flashlight toward the right side of the storage room. He didn't want to venture any farther in. He didn't like the storage room, never had. He didn't like the immense darkness in here, the way shadows pooled in the corners and oozed down the walls like some weird, sticky sap. He didn't like the musty stink, that smell of mothballs and old dirt.

"Here's one," Ben said. "It's pretty light. I'm going to drop it, so watch out."

The cardboard box landed against the concrete floor with a soft plop. Ryan stared at his mother's handwriting across the top. *Pete's clothes.* Why would she keep Uncle Pete's clothes? Did she think he was coming back? Ryan pushed the box out the door and across the porch to the table, where Ben's briefcase and a pair of scissors were. He used the scissors to cut the tape on the box and pulled open the flaps.

He didn't know what Ben was looking for—and didn't think that Ben knew, either—but maybe there would be something in this box besides clothes. Oro, who had been sprawled near the table, now came over, tail wagging, thinking this was some sort of game. She poked her nose into the box, sniffing at the clothes, and began to whimper and paw at the sides of the carton.

"You smell him, don't you, girl?" Ryan said quietly, and

Oro barked and moved around the box, sniffing and pawing and whimpering some more.

Ryan dug his hands into the clothing and lifted out a heap of shirts and trousers and jeans and set them on the floor. The dog went right over to them, burrowed her snout beneath them, then flopped down on top of them, whimpering until the whimpers turned to outright howls. Goose bumps raced up Ryan's arms and he hurried over to Oro, trying to comfort her, but she was grieving for the man who had owned her during the early part of her life.

Becky and Ben came out of the storage room to see what was going on, and just stood saying nothing, as astonished as Ryan was. He didn't understand how anyone—human or animal—could carry so much sadness inside for so long. The noises his dog made hurt him and when he didn't think he could stand it anymore, he stretched out beside her on the pile of clothes and put his arm around her. Only then did she stop the whimpering and howling. She lay very still for a few minutes, breathing hard, and finally rolled onto her side.

For what seemed a long time but probably wasn't, her amber eyes locked onto Ryan's, something that had never happened before. In the past, whenever Ryan had tried to look her directly in the eyes, she turned her head or licked him or grabbed a sock or her Frisbee. But this time she just gazed back at him and he felt something familiar stirring down deep in his belly, the Other coming awake, responding.

''Let's go play Frisbee,'' he said suddenly, and they both leaped up and ran through the open screen door and out into the yard.

Ryan tossed the Frisbee for her and eventually the stirring sensation in his belly went away. It was as if the Other had gone back to sleep or whatever it did when it wasn't bugging him. The important thing was that he'd prevented anything weird from happening by removing himself from the source of the problem—in this case, his uncle's old clothes. But why should that wake up the Other? The clothes obviously had been a source of pain for Oro, but not for him. He never had met his uncle. Maybe it was Oro's pain that the Other had been reacting to.

He gave Oro a large dog biscuit and left her in the yard while he went back onto the porch to help Ben and Becky. Ben had taken down eight or nine boxes and was stacking several of them on a dolly. "Oro okay?" Ben asked.

"Yeah, I think so."

"That was pretty weird," said Becky, as she and Ryan pushed a carton apiece over to the table. "She remembered your uncle through the smell of his clothes, after all this time. She was mourning."

Mourning, grief, sadness: those were the emotions the Other had reacted to, Ryan thought, and wished he knew what it meant.

They went to work opening the cartons and emptying the ones that Ben thought might yield some precious clue. After a while, Abuelita came downstairs with drinks and a platter of snacks. "Have you found anything useful yet, Ben?" she asked.

"I don't know. I'm not even sure what I'm looking for."

"Correspondence, perhaps?"

Ryan shut out the sounds of their voices and cut the tape off a large carton that his mother had labeled *Stuff*. That meant he would find things in here that hadn't been sorted or organized in any way. Some of the kitchen drawers upstairs were like that. He pulled back the flaps and found books, notebooks, yellow legal pads, letters, old photographs, two manuscripts. He and Becky lifted things out and brought them over to the table so Ben and Abuelita could have a look.

Ryan felt like an archeologist at a dig. But instead of uncovering artifacts worn away by dirt and the passage of time, he had discovered his uncle's literary treasures. He picked up a thick packet of letters and began to go through them, setting the ones that seemed boring in one pile and others that looked more interesting in another pile. None of the letters was in an envelope, which made it easier for Ryan to decide which ones were boring and which were interesting.

A lot of the letters seemed to be from fans—people who read his uncle's columns or his books—others were requests for appearances, still others were nut letters. *On page 219 of your book, there's a misspelling.* Or: *You're a moron who knows nothing about Florida politics.*

He unfolded a letter in the interesting pile that had been written in soft green ink, on paper the years had turned yellow, and began to read.

10/10/91

My dearest Pete,

It's raining as I write this, one of those soft autumn rains that releases the fragrant smell of earth, trees, the wilderness the keys once were. This scent used to fill me with such joy and wonder. Now it just depresses me because we aren't together to share it and probably never will be.

I've thought a lot about our discussion last week. In truth, I've thought of little else. I've tried to imagine us together for the rest of our lives and it gives me a warm, beautiful feeling, the kind of emotion I can wrap around myself and hide in forever. But I can't do it. When I got married, I meant the "till death" part of it and I can't bring myself to break that vow.

One could argue, of course, that I broke the vow

when I fell in love with you. But that was something that just happened, I didn't plan it, and in the beginning, I did what I could to discourage it. But you were like an inexorable tide, a force of nature, and I got swept up in it all, Pete.

I can't see you anymore. Even as I write these words, my heart aches and I can hardly grasp the idea of my life without you in it, somewhere. But I also know that I can't continue living like this, my loyalties split down the middle, my soul in constant turmoil.

Please don't get in touch with me again. Know that I will always love you, but not in the way that you deserve.

XX

"I think I found something," Ryan said to no one in particular.

Becky heard him, but the other two didn't. She looked up, frowned, and leaned across the table. "What's wrong?" she said gently.

"I found something. A love letter."

"No, I mean, what's wrong with you?"

"Me?"

He blinked and realized he was crying.

Chapter 19

The evening loomed like a vast, empty desert in front of Hutchin, space that he had to fill and populate in some way. His wife was going out for drinks and dinner with teachers at her school and he didn't expect her home until late. In his life before last Thursday, he would have seized the time to be with Diane, if she'd been in town. But tonight was a different life, with a different set of challenges, and those challenges began with what to do for dinner.

Every so often, he ordered takeout, enough food to feed a small army, and took it over to the jail for the cops on the three-to-eleven shift. It was good public relations, especially on an island as small as Tango, and because he had done it before, who would think there was anything unusual about it?

He called Chinee-Takee-Outee and ordered enough of a variety to appeal to anyone's tastes. This Chinese place delivered, so while he waited for the food to arrive, he got out his personal file on the Poulton case and went out onto the porch.

The evening was already splendid, the sky a vast panorama of blue now bruising at the edges. The air held a thick, lingering scent from the water that surrounded Tango and it mixed with other island smells—earth, roses, gardenias, jasmine, and more distantly, the smell of barbecued fish and chicken. He rocked in the old porch swing, his hands motionless against the file, his eyes fixed on the hedge that shrouded the porch. The dwindling light touched the leaves in such a way that for moments they looked almost luminous.

He remembered a camping trip with his father when he was eleven or twelve, an overnighter into the Everglades. They had gone in by canoe and had paddled for hours, up this channel, down that channel, until they had crossed an open lake where the humid summer wind blew without obstacles to slow it down. On the other side of that lake, beyond the wind, they had found a chickee, a roofed, wooden platform that rose out of the water, and they had camped there for the night. He had awakened at one point and the moon had emerged from a bank of clouds and turned everything around them softly luminous, just as the leaves of the hedge were now, in the light of the dying sun.

Transfixed by the sight of the leaves and the clarity of his memory, he didn't move until the light had faded and the luminosity had fled as cleanly as his memory of the camping trip with his old man. Then he looked down at his hands, folded so primly on top of the file, one on top of the other, as though he were a preacher mulling over the sermon contained between the covers of this file.

He opened the file.

This was his personal file, not a legal document, and it contained numerous clippings about Diane's murder that had appeared in South Florida newspapers in the last week. The *Fort Lauderdale Sun Sentinel* articles had the clearest photos of Poulton. Hutchin's personal favorite showed a young, virile man with deeply set eyes, hair that fell across a broad forehead, nostrils that flared, as if from anger or the cold, and a hesitant, shy smile. He liked it because it made Poulton look guilty of *something*.

"Prick. You'll get yours."

What had Diane seen in him?

Another photo showed Poulton at his absolute best, wearing a doctor's white coat, a stethoscope hanging around his neck. Under this picture was a sidebar about a young child, a burn victim, whom Poulton had treated. She was one of his triumphs. She'd recovered. In yet another photo, Poulton's expression looked guarded, cautious, perhaps even alarmed.

"Bastard," Hutchin murmured.

He had a sudden, ridiculous urge to tack one of the photos to a corkboard and hurl darts at it. He used to be pretty good at darts, years ago, when his daughter was young. He had bought Barb her own darts and board, and had taught her how to hold, aim, and throw the darts so that they would reach the bull's-eye.

Other than a glimpse of Poulton yesterday, outside the courthouse after the evacuation, Hutchin hadn't seen him face-to-face. His first appearance in court, to determine whether there was probable cause for his arrest, had been before Hutchin's colleague, Judge Yerdovitch. His arraignment, when he would enter his plea, was scheduled for Monday morning at ten. Hutchin intended to see the man up close before then. Like this evening, he thought, when he delivered Chinee-Takee-Outee to the cops at the jail.

A car pulled up in front of the building and Hutchin quickly slid the newspaper clipping back into his file and set it beside him on the swing. He stood to see who it was and felt a surreal dread when he saw Paul Opitz get out and walk toward him.

What the hell's he doing here?

"Judge, I was hoping you'd still be around. You have a few minutes?"

"A few." Hutchin quickly opened the door to his office and set the folder just inside, on the floor. "What's up?" he asked as Opitz came up the steps to the porch.

"Not much. Just decompressing." He held up a flask. "How about a drink?"

"A small one. I'll get us some glasses and ice."

When he returned with ice tinkling in a pair of glasses, Opitz was sitting on the railing, straddling it like a rider on a horse. Hutchin held out the glasses and Opitz filled his much higher than the one he gave to Hutchin. He still wore his lawyer clothes, an expensive suit and a tie. He removed the tie and stuffed it in his jacket pocket.

"So what's really on your mind, Paul?" Hutchin asked, sitting on the porch swing again.

"The Poulton arraignment on Monday."

"I don't expect any surprises. He'll plead innocent."

"Of course he will. And there won't be any bargaining. Kit already informed me that her client isn't interested in plea bargains. Now that the trial is on the docket, I'd like to schedule a pretrial conference as soon as possible after the arraignment."

Opitz was really chafing at the bit, Hutchin thought. The trial was on the docket, yes, but no date had been set. Hutchin wanted very much to set that date for mid-December, to get this goddamn nightmare out of his life as soon as possible. It was entirely within his right to decide the order in which cases in his courtroom would be tried. But such speediness might draw more attention to what was already a high-profile case.

And yet, speed was what he desperately needed now. The faster the case went to trial, the less time Kit would have to prepare a convincing defense. If he won the appointment for attorney general, there might be time constraints that would make it impossible for him to sit on the bench for this trial. But he couldn't risk judicial control falling to someone else. He *had* to sit on the bench for this, had to be sure that the case was slanted toward Poulton's guilt. He had to do what he could to get a conviction.

The president's chief of staff hadn't given Hutchin any idea when the appointee would be expected in DC. But Hutchin figured it would be spring at the latest. Therefore, the Poulton trial had to begin well before the spring. Early January, he thought, would be considered fast, but not suspiciously so, considering how much media attention the case was getting. January 2, he decided, but didn't say it to Opitz.

"I'll talk to Kit and see where things stand for her. She needs time to prepare an adequate defense, Paul. And, as I've said before, we can't discuss this case without her being present."

Opitz sipped at his drink—carefully measured sips, Hutchin noticed, a pattern that followed his conduct in court. In fact, he suspected that all of Opitz's life followed this same, inexorable pattern, this dilatory rhythm whose bottom line was multifaceted—circumspection in which he weighed the odds, then action based on his conclusions.

Hutchin conducted his affairs in the same way—he hated to admit it, hated to admit that he and Opitz had anything in common except the law, but he recognized the parallel. And it made him innately suspicious of Opitz, of his motives for these seemingly casual meetings. If, in fact, there were any similarities at all between him and Opitz, then he had to believe that Opitz had an agenda that went well beyond the simple desire to win a conviction. But damned if he knew what that agenda was.

Opitz deftly turned the conversation away from the Poulton case and offered his speculations about yesterday's bomb

threat. But even his speculations involved the Poulton case.
"I figure the threat came from the usual nut faction that
rides tandem with high-profile cases," he said. "But it
spooked me. The Oklahoma City bombing is still too vivid
for me and that wasn't even related to a particular case.
There was some grumbling on the staff that we should
consider trying this case in another county if it isn't tried
soon."

So that was it, Hutchin thought. That was the real reason
for Opitz's visit. Diplomatic pressure for a very speedy trial.
"Like I said, I'll talk to Kit. You like Chinese food?"
Hutchin asked, knowing that Opitz's taste in foods ran
strictly along mainstream American lines—fast, greasy,
gross.

"Not particularly. MSG and I don't get along. Why?"

"I've got to pick up my order."

"And I need to be getting home." He raised his nearly
empty glass to the porch light. "Cheers, Jay." And he tipped
the glass to his mouth and polished off the remains of his
drink.

Hutchin was buzzed into the building by Sergeant Morris,
who sniffed the air and grinned. "Smells like Chinese.
You're a mind reader, Judge. We were just talking about
whether it would be Chinese or pizza tonight. Come on
back."

"Back" was the control room deep inside the building,
the hub where prisoners were processed and visitors were
buzzed in and out of the cell area. Thanks to the exorbitant
property taxes on the island, the jail didn't suffer from tech-
nological deprivation. It didn't suffer from any kind of deprivation. The meals were rumored to be nearly as tasty as
those of the better restaurants, prisoners were allowed to

bathe and exercise daily, the Tango Library supplied all requested books, and life in general wasn't bad—merely restricted.

But for a guy like Poulton, Hutchin thought with a certain smugness, life in jail was probably not much better than life in hell.

Hutchin and Morris laid out the Chinese feast on one of the desks, someone else brought in paper plates, and pretty soon, rumors and gossip were flying. Hutchin had learned that jailhouse rumors often held more than a nugget of truth and these rumors provided him with plenty of fodder for this own theory about the bomb scare at the courthouse.

In one version of this rumor, the bomb threat had been phoned in by one of the sick groupies whom Poulton had attracted like fleas to a dog's back, a warped fan who figured she would catch sight of Poulton when the jail was evacuated. In another version of the rumor, the threat had been phoned in by some fan of Diane Jackson's, who hungered to see the sick bastard accused of killing her. In yet a third version, the phone call was the work of a crazed group who had idolized Diane and intended to assassinate the man they believed had killed her.

Hutchin found the rumors fascinating—not for their substance, but for their common thread: that the threat had been a hoax perpetrated for a specific purpose that involved Poulton. "So when we finally get back into the building yesterday," said a lieutenant named Farmer, "Sheriff Blake tells us to put Poulton under twenty-four-seven guard, for his safety. It's like Blake believes all this conspiracy shit."

"And he's still there?" Hutchin asked, trying not to appear too interested.

"Absolutely. In the glass cage," said Morris.

"I've never even laid eyes on the guy."

"Morris thinks he has satanic eyes," remarked Farmer, snickering.

"What a crock, man, I never said that. I said he has Machiavellian eyes, not satanic eyes. C'mon, Judge, take a look. You tell me what *you* think."

In other words, Hutchin thought, he would be able to see Poulton but Poulton would not be able to see him.

His eagerness to see Poulton up close was so extreme it became a physical sensation, a kind of hungry churning across the floor of his belly, a sudden dryness in the back of his throat. Opportunity knocks, he thought.

"You need to see what you're going to be up against, Judge," said Morris.

"You make it sound like I should arm myself with garlic and a cross."

Morris chuckled. "You'll see what I mean."

So Hutchin accompanied Morris through the electronic doors, down a narrow corridor that smelled faintly of disinfectant. The silence here seemed to vibrate, as though it were a physical thing. They went into a small room where most of the wall that separated the room from Poulton's space was one-way glass. No lights in here, just the soft glow of computer consoles and a lone cop to keep tabs on Poulton's every move.

At the moment, Poulton wasn't moving at all. He sat staring at a TV tuned to CNN, a remote in his right hand, a cigarette in his left. Odd, Hutchin thought, that he smoked, him being a physician and all. The other odd thing that he noticed about Poulton was the degree of his stillness. It was as if his consciousness had vacated his body and any second now, his vital signs would stop, his bones would crumble, he would turn to dust.

"He's so still, he looks like a sculpture," Hutchin whispered.

"Yeah, he does that a lot," Morris replied.

"Does he get any visitors besides his lawyers?"

"Nope," said the sentry, a corporal. "His sister calls daily and he takes those calls, but that's about it. When he isn't watching CNN, he's reading."

"What does he read?"

The corporal shrugged. "Lotta stuff. But most of it seems to be medical books and Hollywood memoirs."

"What kind of medical books?"

"Texts," said Morris. "He had a copy of the autopsy report on Jackson's death. His lawyer brought a copy and since he's a doc, Blake gave him permission to keep it. He requested a book on obstetrics and another on forensics medicine."

Due to Diane's pregnancy, Hutchin could certainly understand the interest in obstetrics. But what was in the autopsy report that would require a book on forensics medicine? Poulton, he thought, seemed to be seeking something specific. While he sat here in isolation, his medical training hummed right along, looking for pieces of the puzzle.

"Ask him if he needs anything," Morris said to the corporal. "Get him outta that trance he's in."

The sentry flipped a button on the intercom. "Doc, you need anything?"

Poulton's head turned slowly toward the one-way glass and Hutchin got his first good look at the man who had been his competition for months. He didn't resemble the newspaper photos, not with his hair in a jail buzz cut and his eyes puffy from lack of sleep. If anything, he seemed younger than Hutchin had expected, more like a kid barely out of his teens. He had compelling, intense eyes, darkness swirling within a greater darkness.

"Another pack of smokes when you get the chance. Thanks."

"You're smoking too much," the sentry remarked.

Now Poulton ground out his cigarette, stood, grasped his fingers, and stretched his arms way above his head. Then he dropped forward, folding down so perfectly it was as if he had a hinged waist. He touched his toes, grasping the ends of his tennis shoes, the pose one that would put Hutchin in the hospital for a week with a strained back. He held that pose for about thirty seconds, then snapped upright and over into a back flip.

"Jesus," Hutchin said. "He's a gymnast?"

"Yoga," the sentry replied. "When he isn't reading or watching the tube, he's practicing yoga."

As he straightened from the back flip, he strolled over to the one-way window and pressed his face to the glass. Hutchin wrenched back, an involuntary movement that he instantly regretted. "Helloooooo," Poulton called. "I know you spies are in there. I'm going to take a wiz now, you going to watch me do that, too?"

The sentry flipped the intercom switch again. "No one's watching you piss, Poulton."

"Ha," Poulton spat, and stepped back from the window again. "So you want to know what I've discovered?"

The sentry glanced up at Morris, apparently asking if it was okay, because Morris nodded. He flipped the switch again. "Sure thing, Poulton. What've you discovered?"

"A couple of things. According to the autopsy report, Diane was between eight and ten weeks pregnant. The way OBs determine the date of conception is to take the date of the beginning of the last menstrual period, add seven days, count back three months, and advance that date to the following year. I know for a fact that Diane had her last period on August twenty-four, which would have put her most fertile time around Labor Day weekend. I didn't see her that weekend. Whoever did got her pregnant. So actually, she was about nine weeks' pregnant.''

He paced as he spoke, back and forth, back and forth, his head down, hands lost in the pockets of his shorts. ''Another interesting fact. The baby had A-negative blood, just like his father—I'm type O, Corporal—so it's likely that at some point this may have been a problem because of the Rh incompatibility. I haven't found anything in the forensic evidence yet that gives me the name of the fuck who killed her.'' He let out a short, ugly laugh. ''But I'm starting to remember things. You know how memories sometimes come back to you at odd moments, Corporal?'' He paused and glanced toward the window, expecting the corporal to respond.

He flipped the switch into the speak position again. ''Uh, sure, Poulton, I know what you mean.''

''In the last few months that I knew her, some of her habits had changed. I should've connected it to something, but hey, I was in residency, sleeping about four hours a night. So based on the change in her habits, I've reached some conclusions about the guy who killed her. You want to hear my conclusions, Corporal?''

''Go for it,'' the corporal replied.

Hutchin stiffened. He didn't want to hear a goddamn word of it, but he couldn't very well back out of here now.

''Her killer drank Scotch. How do I know? Because up until, oh, maybe the spring, she never touched hard stuff. We used to smoke an occasional joint, but sometime earlier this year, she informed me that smoking joints is illegal.'' Poulton gave another sharp, ugly laugh. ''Illegal, for Christ's sake. So this guy who killed her must be a real straight arrow on the outside, right? Never breaks the rules, drives the speed limit . . . you know the type. There were subtler signs, too. She started liking her sex rougher, liked to be touched differently. I'll spare you the intimate details, Corporal.''

"Uh, yeah, thanks, Poulton.''

"And her reading tastes changed. She used to read romances, romantic suspense, books on acting. Then I noticed she was reading legal thrillers, Grisham, Turow . . . and hey, get this, Corporal. She was reading law books. Maybe her killer's a lawyer. How's that one?''

"Maybe he was a con," the corporal said. "And she was trying to figure how to spring him legally.''

Poulton made a face. "For such a smart guy, Corporal, you say some dumb things.''

Scotch, no drugs, not breaking rules, rough sex, legal thrillers: all of Poulton's clues were right on, but there was no way in hell he could connect the dots. Hutchin had heard enough. His head ached and the small, tight room left him with a raw, tight feeling in his throat. He tapped Morris and stabbed a thumb toward the door.

As they turned to leave, Poulton shouted, "Hey," and Hutchin spun around to see Poulton rushing toward the window, his mouth lolling open as he shrieked like a banshee. The words were unintelligible, but Hutchin didn't have to understand the words to feel the power of the emotion, a tidal wave of rage and grief so utterly primal that it paralyzed him. He simply stood there, unable to wrench his eyes from the one-way window. Poulton threw himself at the window, a wild man with fingers hooked like claws, his spit smearing against the glass, his cheek squashed up against the window.

Hutchin knew that the corporal was shouting into the PA system, that Morris had hurried out, that Poulton was still shrieking. But for long, terrible moments, he felt as if he were trapped inside the violent tumult of Poulton's emotions, inside the raw, burning agony of his pain. Poulton's pain became his pain, scorching afferent pathways through his being. His head lit up with the memory of Diane on the bed, Diane as he'd pressed the pillow over her face and she had struggled, arms flailing to grab his wrist, his hands, held it there through her muffled screams, her final sucking, futile breaths.

Then Poulton began to sob, huge, gasping, pitiful sobs, and he literally slid down the one-way glass to the floor, his body crumpling until it lay in a broken heap. The door to his room exploded open and three cops rushed in with a fourth man behind them, a doctor with his medical bag.

With tremendous effort, Hutchin forced his muscles to move, his feet to uproot from the floor, and he spun around and practically ran from the room. Later, he wouldn't remember much of his passage through the jail, of who had spoken to him or what he or they had said. He wouldn't remember much of anything except his desperate need for fresh air, silence, and an end to the hard, unforgiving pressure in the center of his chest.

Chapter 20

Dr. Luke arrived during dinner, blowing in with the wind that now came off the lagoon. Even though Ryan suspected Doc had come to talk to him, he felt okay about it. He liked Doc, who liked horses nearly as much as Ryan did and had two horses, in fact, that he allowed Ryan to ride whenever he wanted.

After dinner, Doc and Ryan went downstairs and sat in two canvas chairs close to the water. The moon was rising in the distance and looked like a wedge of lemon. Somewhere just offshore, fish splashed. "Your mom, Ben, and Abuelita have some business things to take care of, so I thought it'd give us a chance to talk a little, Ryan."

"About the weird stuff, you mean."

"Is that how you think of it?"

"That's how it feels most of the time."

"Let's try a little experiment."

"Okay."

"I want you to get real comfortable. Kick off your shoes

if you want to. Settle back into the chair and just relax and listen to the sound of my voice.''

''And then what?''

''Well, sometimes when we're really relaxed, it's easier to understand things that seem otherwise confusing.''

Ryan kicked off his shoes and let his body sink back against the chair. ''Should I shut my eyes?''

''Sure.''

Ryan shut his eyes.

''Let's make sure you're really relaxed, Ryan. Feel the relaxation in your toes, your feet. Now that relaxation is moving up into your legs, so that your muscles feel almost loose, soft . . .''

Ryan listened to the sound of his voice, a soft, slow voice that reminded him of the breeze gliding through the branches of trees or through a grassy field. Pretty soon, he was so relaxed that he could feel himself at the edge of sleep.

''I want you to imagine an elevator door in front of you. At the count of three, that door is going to open and you're going to get in the elevator. One . . . two . . . three . . .''

The elevator door took shape in front of him, a bright blue door. When it opened, Ryan got on and the doors shut. He was vaguely aware of Doc's voice, talking about the floor numbers lighting up overhead and how when each number lit up, his relaxation was going to deepen. Floor number 10 lit up and Ryan kept his inner eyes on the numbers, watching as they went from 10 to 9 to 8 . . .

''When you reach floor number one, you're going to walk out into a movie theater. You're going to take a seat wherever you want and the screen is going to light up.''

Ryan felt as if he were drifting in the warm waters of the canal at high summer, when the sun burned holes through the sky and light spilled through the trees like molasses or honey. Then the elevator doors opened and he walked out into a small theater and took a seat in the very first row. The screen lit up. Doc was still talking and now images appeared on the screen.

"What do you see, Ryan?"

"A man and a woman on a beach. They're holding hands. A puppy is with them. They're happy."

"Can you describe these people?"

"I can't see their faces."

"What color is the man's hair?"

"Dark."

"And the woman's hair? What color is it?"

"Brown. A pretty brown with reddish streaks in it."

"Where is this place?"

"A beach. Bahia Honda. I think it's Bahia Honda."

It was such an effort to talk. He didn't want to talk. He just wanted to watch the movie screen.

"I'd like you to leave the theater, get back into the elevator, and watch the floors light up again. Your relaxation triples with each level that you descend. When you get off this time, you'll be in a place that's connected to what you've been experiencing."

He went down five floors now. The elevator doors opened . . .

And he steps into paradise. Music plays softly from a CD player, the light streams through the large window just above the bed, and huge potted plants soak up the sun from a skylight. She is here with him, sitting on a stool with a length of fabric draped over a shoulder, covering one breast, the rest of her as bare and beautiful as the sky itself. He is sketching her, struggling to capture the exquisite shape of her naked shoulder, the curve of her naked arm, the sweet perfection of her breast.

"Ryan, describe where you are, what you're seeing."
"Woman," he whispered.

Her head turns toward him, the light so bright against her face that it washes out details. "Are we almost done? My back is starting to ache sitting like this."

"Just a few more minutes."

"And I need to scoot soon," she adds.

"What do you do with all these drawings?" he asks.

"Hide them," she replies.

It saddens him that she hides his sketches, stashes them away as though they are something tainted, dirty, sinful. "You can leave him," he says to her.

She sighs and slides off the bench and reaches for her clothes. "We've been over this a million times. I can't leave him and I don't know how much longer I can keep this up . . ."

"Can you give me a name, Ryan? For the man or the woman?"

Ryan's heart had filled with such sadness that he began to cry. "Can't," he whispered. "Can't."

"At the count of three, Ryan, you're going to wake up feeling refreshed and happy. As these memories begin to surface, you'll be able to deal with them in an emotionally detached way, as though they are happening to someone else. The memories will become clearer and more detailed so that we can get to their source. One . . . two . . . three . . ."

Ryan's eyes opened slowly, as if the lids were gummed from sleep. Doc was still sitting beside him and now his mother stood nearby, too. "How're you doing, hon?" she asked.

"That was fun. Can I go find Becky and play now?"

"You sure can."

He hugged Doc. "Thanks, Dr. Luke. Let's do that again, soon."

"Any time, Ryan. And why don't you and Becky come over to Tango soon and we'll go riding?"

"Great."

Then he hurried off, wondering why he had felt so sad before but felt so great now.

(2)

"What do you think, Aaron?" Kit asked, sitting in the chair her son had vacated.

Dr. Luke rubbed his hand over his chin, drank from the bottle of water in his hand, and shook his head. "I'm not at all sure what to think. I've read some of the literature and I know of one psychiatrist, Ian Stevenson, who has been researching this area for at least forty or fifty years. He has investigated thousands of cases that are suggestive of reincarnation and applies such stringent criteria to every case he investigates that only several hundred have passed the muster.

"In some of his cases, children have not only recalled who they were, but how, where, and when they had died. In instances where the child was murdered in a previous life, he bears witness against his killer. Many of these kids recognized former family members and loved ones. Most of Stevenson's cases occurred in India, where the concept of reincarnation is embraced. But even in the Western world, Kit, things are changing. Have you read any of the popular literature?"

A kind of shock tore through her, as if she'd stuck her hand in an electrical outlet. She hadn't expected Luke, of all people, to even mention past-life trauma as a possibility. "Some, yes. Brian Weiss's stuff."

"In *Return from Heaven*, author and researcher Carol Bowman documents a number of convincing cases of reincarnation within the same family. Her interest in the subject was triggered by her young son's sudden aversion to loud noises during a July Fourth celebration. The end result was that he recalled a life as a black Civil War solider in which he'd been shot in the wrist—the same spot where he'd had recurring eczema that simply didn't respond to treatment. But within days of his recollection of a life as the soldier, the eczema vanished, suggesting that healing could occur through the recollection of past-life memories, especially those that were traumatic in some way."

"So you think Ryan is actually recalling memories from another life?"

"It sure looks that way to me." He reached down to pick up the cassette recorder on the ground between the two chairs. "I'm going to replay the tape tonight and make some notes. I'll make you a copy, too. The suggestions I gave him should facilitate the spontaneous surfacing of these memories and should make the emotional part of it easier to deal with."

"But what can I do to help him?"

Luke gave her hand an affectionate squeeze. "I think you're doing all the right things. Be there for him, acknowledge that his experiences are valid, and be alert for patterns, Kit."

Patterns. Hell, that was easy. She was surrounded by patterns. Today she had been chased by someone who didn't want her poking around in Diane's past; Webster, meanwhile, was poking around in her brother's past; and she was poking around in what might be Ryan's past-life memories.

The pattern with this cluster of events was related to the past.

In the next cluster, Diane Jackson had a secret lover, Pete had a secret lover. Diane had been a celebrity, Pete also had been something of a celebrity. Diane's killer managed to frame Poulton for the murder; Pete's killer had done the job so well that ten years had passed with few clues. The pattern here involved crimes.

What united these clusters? What was the common thread? Why had Ryan's episodes begun around the same time she'd taken the Poulton case?

If she approached this from the assumption that all these patterns were somehow related—a huge leap of faith— then the central question was: how did Ryan's experiences connect to Pete and to the Poulton case?

"Kit," Abuelita called from the kitchen window. "Phone. It's Rita. And it sounds urgent."

"I'll get it on the porch." She touched Dr. Luke's arm. "Don't go away, Aaron. I'll be right back."

Shortly before she'd come downstairs to listen in on Luke's hypnosis session with Ryan, Kit had shown Abuelita the videotape she'd taken today and the old woman had identified the man. He was a Cuban named Carlos Matanza whose family she'd known years ago in Miami. She'd called Rita to let her know and now Rita was returning the call.

Kit picked up the phone on the porch. "Hey, you got my message?"

"We have bigger problems right now. Poulton freaked. The jail doc had to sedate him."

Christ, I need this. "Is he calm now?"

"Sleeping."

"Then he's not an immediate threat to anyone."

"They're talking about moving him to the psych unit."

"Absolutely not. We're not copping to an insanity defense. How soon can you get over there?"

"I'm in my car now."

Rita lived at the north end of Tango and could be at the jail within ten minutes. "I'll meet you there as soon as I can. Dr. Luke's here at the house. I'll ask him for a shrink recommendation. We *don't* want Poulton to be Baker-acted." Involuntary commitment to a psychiatric unit would damage her defense.

"I hear you, I hear you. Leave your cell on."

Kit hung up and hurried back over to Dr. Luke. As soon as she explained the situation, he said he knew the right man for the job. "Jerry Clarke is a psychiatrist in private practice in Key West. He also works as a consultant for the corrections system. How soon do you need him?"

"As soon as possible."

As they went upstairs, Kit had the nearly overwhelming sensation that her life was jammed in fast-forward. She needed to tend to her son, but also had to tend to her client. She wanted more time with Webster, time to read a novel, to go for a run with Oro. And none of that included the mundane tasks like laundry, which was piled high in the utility room, or that her floors screamed for a good sweeping and the run of a mop because her cleaning lady hadn't shown up yet this week.

Webster offered to drive her over to Tango and Abuelita offered to stay at the house with Ryan. The old woman winked when she said it and whispered, "Stay out all night if you want."

"I may just take you up on it."

"Good, good," Abuelita replied, and handed Kit a black shoulder bag. "I packed a few things you might need."

Kit laughed, grabbed her laptop and briefcase, and rushed downstairs. Her only stop was to tell Ryan where she was going and what the arrangements were for the evening, possibly for the night. Her pending absence apparently didn't bother him. He and Becky were playing in the front yard, tossing a Frisbee back and forth to Oro.

The highway unrolled before them, a strip of asphalt that shot through an even greater darkness and ultimately ended at mile zero. The end of the line. She disliked the metaphor.

"I appreciate the ride, Ben."

"I've got some business on Tango and we can stop by the Bureau to drop off the videotape. I'm pretty sure the techs can grab a license plate number for that Pontiac."

"You have a case on Tango?" she asked.

"It's connected to Rico Sanchez, the guy I asked Abuelita about during dinner."

Right. The man whose name Abuelita hadn't recognized. Webster hadn't elaborated earlier and he didn't elaborate now, either. In fact, whenever she asked him a question he didn't want to answer, he offered an oblique reply, just as he'd done now. An interesting observation, she thought, and decided she could live with it.

They were buzzed into the Tango Key Jail and taken into the main area. Rita came right over and gave her a quick rundown on what was going on—none of it pleasant. Sheriff Blake was carrying on at great length while a man she presumed was Dr. Clarke stood there patiently, just listening. Clarke, wearing jeans and a work shirt, didn't look like Kit's idea of a man who dissected people's psyches. He looked like a businessman whose vacation had been interrupted.

"Were you here when the incident occurred, Sheriff?" he asked Blake.

"No, but I got a full report."

"From whom?"

"From me," said Sergeant Morris, a cop Kit knew only slightly. "We have it all on tape, if you'd like to see it."

"I would. But first, I'd like to see Mr. Poulton and the physician's report."

"Is he awake?" Blake asked Morris.

"Just coming around, sir."

"I don't recommend that you go in there alone, Dr. Clarke," said Blake. "One of my men will—"

"We'll go in with him," Rita said.

"I can't take responsibility for what he might do," Blake said.

"You don't have to," Webster told him. "I will."

Blake gave Webster a dirty look. "This isn't your business, Agent Webster."

"It is now," Kit replied. "I want all the video and audio equipment in that room disconnected while we're in there. Consider this an attorney-client conference. And please get the medical report for Dr. Clarke."

There wasn't much Blake could say to that, so with as much aplomb as he could muster, he asked Morris to fetch the physician's report, then took them down the hall to Poulton's room. He asked for Webster's weapon before they entered, then told Sergeant Morris to stand outside the door just in case Poulton got agitated.

Poulton looked bad, Kit thought. He was sitting at the edge of the bunk, his eyes puffy, bloodshot, his hair mussed. He seemed to have trouble focusing his eyes, as if the eyeballs had come unhinged from the sockets. "Steve, this is Agent Webster, with the FBI, and Dr. Clarke, a physician Rita and I have called in. He'd like to ask you a few questions."

Clarke had finished glancing through the physician's report and scribbled a note on a slip of paper, which he clipped to the front as he handed the file to Kit. It read:

Thorazine was inappropriate. While Clarke questioned Poulton, Rita videotaped it and Kit slipped out into the hall to get the tape from Morris and to find out firsthand, if she could, what had happened.

Morris was a nice enough cop and actually seemed eager to accommodate her. They went into the observation booth where a one-way window looked out into the room where Poulton and the others were. A cop sat with his feet resting on a desk as he watched the proceedings in the room. He hastily dropped his feet to the floor.

"Corporal, we need the tape of what happened earlier."

"Got a copy right here." He stood, popped a tape out of one of the VCRs, and handed it to Kit.

"What set him off, Corporal?" She asked.

"Dunno. He was just doing his usual thing, ma'am, pacing and smoking and watching the tube, spouting his theories about Diane's killer. It's all on the tape."

"Judge Hutchin had stopped by with some Chinese food," Morris added. "And I told him the sheriff had moved Poulton yesterday, after the bomb threat at the courthouse. Hutchin remarked he'd never seen the man close up and I brought him back here to take a look. Poulton couldn't see him," he quickly added, as if that were important.

Kit, instantly alert now, said, "What difference could it possibly make to the judge that he'd never seen Poulton close up?"

Morris seemed embarrassed now. He jammed his hands in his trouser pockets, glanced down at the floor, then up again. "I, uh, think Poulton has strange eyes and I wanted to show the judge what I meant."

"Strange eyes."

Kit repeated the words, perhaps hoping they would make more sense to her if she said them aloud. But the only thing that became clear was that to Morris and his fellow officers,

Poulton was like some new creature under the Ringling Brothers big tent, a curiosity, a celebrated anomaly, something to gape at, point at, to bring your buddies to see. It disgusted and enraged her.

When she spoke, she could barely contain her anger. "Corporal, get Sheriff Blake in here. Now."

"Uh, okay, hold on." He hit the switch for the PA system and moments later, Blake came in.

"What's going on?"

"Sergeant Morris here wanted to show Judge Hutchin my client's strange eyes, Sheriff, and he brought him in here while Dr. Poulton was extolling his theories about Diane's murder. In case you and the rest of your staff haven't heard, Judge Hutchin is sitting on the bench in this case. To say this is highly irregular doesn't quite cover it, Sheriff. If my client incriminated himself in any way on that tape, there may be grounds for getting this case tossed out. I suggest you rein in your staff's curiosity quotient. My client is not an animal in a zoo. Do I make myself clear?"

Blake had raised himself up to his full height, which was still several inches shorter than Kit, and his chest had puffed out like that of a crowing rooster. "Judge Hutchin often stops by the jail with take-out food for the officers on duty. I'm sure this was an entirely innocent matter. And I'm equally sure that if Dr. Poulton was incriminating himself by anything he said, Sergeant Morris would have hustled the judge right out of here. Or the judge would have left on his own accord, Ms. Parrish. And by the way, you're fortunate that the judge didn't press assault charges against you for last night."

Really steamed now, she snapped, "We're not talking about last night, Sheriff Blake."

He rolled onto the balls of his feet, then back. "Off the

record, ma'am, but I think you and your son have a personal beef with the judge.''

She didn't hear the rest of what he said. Anger roared through her head, blood rushed into her face, and she leaned right into Blake's obnoxious face, up close and very personal. ''Right now, I have a personal beef with *you* and the way you run your jail.''

Her voice sounded like an Arctic wind and he actually drew back, astonished at its vehemence, then tried to cover it up with an explosion of laughter. ''You lawyers are all alike, you know that? You defend scum for a ton of money and expect the rest of us to respect you.'' He spat at her feet and sauntered off.

She suddenly wondered if Poulton would be safe here and how long it would take to get him transferred to the Monroe County Jail. She quickly nixed the idea. Blake, for all his macho bluster, was relatively harmless and wouldn't do anything that would make him or his department look worse than it already did.

She met Dr. Clarke in the hall, as he was leaving Poulton's room. ''He's as sane as you or me, Ms. Parrish. The Thorazine that was administered was overkill. Regardless of his innocence or guilt, Dr. Poulton has suffered acute grief over the death of the woman he loved. I suspect he never expressed that grief, until today. I'm going to recommend that he be placed back into the general population. This scrutiny''—he waved his arm at the closed door to Poulton's room—''only contributes to his anxiety. If you have a few minutes, let's view this tape just to be sure.''

''I've got it right here.''

Morris showed them into a conference room and before Clarke started the tape, Rita and Webster joined them. There didn't seem to be anything incriminating on the tape. If anything, Poulton made a strong case that Diane had been killed by someone else. What Kit found particularly interesting were the habits of Diane's that had changed in the last six or seven months of their relationship. She jotted notes on Poulton's conclusions, that the killer had a distinct preference for Scotch, rough sex, and legal thrillers, that he didn't do drugs, and probably abided by the rules in his daily life. Slowly, but surely, she thought, her sense of this still faceless, possibly older man, was expanding. And sooner or later, she felt sure it would yield a name and address.

Chapter 21

The surveillance van was only two and a half miles from the courthouse and jail complex. But it might as well have been a different continent, Webster thought.

He drove north into the Tango hills for a mile, following a rutted, curving dirt road into the woods. A couple of times, he thought he saw lights behind them, a shimmering reflection against the trees in the rearview mirror. Probably a car that belonged to someone who lived along the road, deeper in the woods, he decided.

As he came around a cluster of trees, the surveillance van appeared suddenly in the moonlight, its sleek curves seeming to grow out of the darkness of the surrounding woods. He wished he had done this earlier, while Kit was at the jail. But he'd taken the precaution of calling Moreno and warning him that Kit Parrish would be with him when he stopped by. In other words, he should turn off the surveillance equipment.

"So this has to do with the Rico Sanchez thing?" Kit asked.

"It's related."

"And you can't talk about it."

"Right. But from here, I can run Matanza's name and check on the status of things with the video of the license plate on that Pontiac and do just about any other kind of check either of us might need."

Matanza: the big guy who had pursued her and Rita in Miami. "Such as?"

"Try to find out more about the Schuller family. Ryan showed me what he'd tracked down on the Web, but the information is too general."

"I didn't know Ryan had tracked down anything."

"I think he's afraid you'll just worry about him."

She laughed at that, a quick laugh that held resignation, puzzlement. "He confides more in you than he does in me, Ben. Maybe it's the lack of a father figure or something. I asked Dr. Luke if he knew anything about the Schullers. He said the name was familiar, but he's lived on the Key West side of the bridge for the last forty years. I guess that makes a difference."

As Webster parked, the van's sliding door opened and Moreno swung out, howling like a monkey. He landed in a crouch a yard in front of them, sprang to his feet, and grabbed Kit's hand. "Kit Parrish, my legal heroine. This is really a pleasure."

Webster rolled his eyes. In a dry voice, he said, "Kit Parrish, Eric Moreno, madman."

She laughed. "You're Ben's partner?"

"His lackey. I do the grunt work, he has the fun." Moreno ran his fingers through his hair. "I've been in there too long. I'm starting to bug out. Pretty quiet on the surveillance front. Anything new on the Sanchez connection?"

"Not yet. I need to run another name."

Moreno swept his arm toward the van's open door. "Be

my guest. There's bad coffee, fruit that's a bit too ripe, and some fresh croissants. I need to walk around a bit.''

He trotted off into the woods and Webster and Kit climbed into the van. "Incredible," she remarked, glancing around at all the equipment. "This looks like something out of a Clint Eastwood movie."

"Your taxes at work. Help yourself to coffee or whatever. This won't take too long."

He booted up the laptop, keyed in his access code, and ran Matanza's name. He never ceased to marvel at the amount of information that was available to him through nothing more than the touch of a few keys. Armed with just a Social Security number, he could access nearly every type of record—criminal, Social Security, income tax, credit, and, to some extent, medical.

This was the Big Brother nightmare in action, through the miracle of computers and microchips, and there were many times when his conscience screamed out in protest. But tonight his conscience was silent. Tonight, his conscience agreed that when the law fell short or failed altogether, all bets were off.

Matanza, thirty-seven and married, with one child, had no criminal record. Last year, he made thirty-five grand and change, his credit was good. He listed his occupation as a driver for Limousines in the Keys, an outfit on Big Pine, and he lived in Marathon. On paper, he sounded like a Good Citizen.

"You'll find this intriguing," Webster said, and passed the information to Kit.

He ran Rico Sanchez's Social Security number through the IRS computers, hoping to find a street address this time. Two came up—one in the fishing district at the south end of Tango Key and another, more recent address in Miami. But when he initially had run Sanchez's name, a PO box on Tango had come up. This guy, he thought, got around, but seemed to remain pretty well hidden, except for regular visits to his parole officer.

Presumably the parole officer knew where Sanchez lived.

The van's door opened again and Moreno said, "I'm primed for the next twelve . . . oh, shit."

Webster spun around and saw Kit seated in front of a silent TV screen, staring at the inside of Hutchin's office. She didn't speak, she merely sat there, motionless, her frizzy hair struck through with the pale light. It seemed to Webster that many minutes passed in total silence. Now and then, the chir of crickets or some noise from the nearby woods pierced that silence, but otherwise, the stillness was like death.

She spoke first, spoke without turning, spoke in a toneless voice devoid of any emotion. "Well, this is interesting. The inside of Judge Hutchin's office."

Moreno and Webster exchanged a glance and Moreno, without another word, simply stepped outside and shut the door. Webster sat there for another moment or two, rubbing his palms over his jeans, wondering what the hell to say to her. Then a slow, simmering anger rose inside of him and he snapped, "Christ, what'd you do that for?"

She turned her chair around, turned it slowly, the damn thing squeaking. "Correct me if I'm wrong, but the only way to get surveillance shit into Hutchin's office is when it's empty. At night, the courthouse is sealed up like a national secret. So that means you were in there when the courthouse was evacuated. And what an interesting coincidence that is. You couldn't have maneuvered that unless you knew about the bomb threat before it was phoned in."

"Look, as a potential appointee for attorney general, Hutchin comes under scrutiny by the Bureau. If the Bureau doesn't find anything in his life or background that's illegal or scandalous, then it sends its recommendation to the Oval Office and they take it from there. I'm just doing my goddamn job.''

"Like *this?*" She waved her hand toward the TV screen. "With hidden cameras? With hidden mikes and bogus bomb threats? Jesus, Ben.''

"Cut the sanctimonious crap. This is how it's done.''

"That's bullshit.'' She got up, grabbed her bag, and shoved the van door open. "What you're doing is illegal *and* unethical. I'm outta here.''

She stepped down from the van and walked off into the darkness, apparently forgetting that she didn't have her car. Webster didn't bother going after her. He moved over to the surveillance equipment and flipped the switches, turning everything back on. Outside, he heard Kit and Moreno talking; then Moreno stuck his head in the door.

"I'm going to, uh, drive her to her office. She has a car there.''

"Whatever.''

"Unless you want to do it,'' Moreno added quietly.

"Nope.''

"I'll be back in a few minutes.''

Webster went through the stack of videotapes on the desk, popped in the most recent, and watched the day's activities in Hutchin's office. Other than the call to Lou Tucker, which he had seen this morning, nothing of note had gone on. He accessed Vogel's connection to Hutchin's home and viewed the day's activities. Isabel Hutchin hurrying around the kitchen, unloading bags of groceries, talking on the phone to her daughter. Later on, she spoke to one of her coworkers on the phone and made plans for drinks and dinner later this evening. No wonder Hutchin had gone to the jail with his Chinese take-out goodies. No wifey at home.

Webster switched to the live feed, flipped back and forth

between the two cameras, but it appeared that no one was home.

Moreno returned a few minutes later. "She was pissed big time."

"That's her problem."

"It could be *our* problem if she decides to let anyone know about the bomb threat, amigo."

"I didn't admit to anything."

"Shit, Ben, you don't have to be a fucking brain surgeon to figure it once you know about the surveillance stuff."

"Hey, she has some serious doubts about Hutchin. She's not going to do anything to tip him off. Let's go check out this address I have for Sanchez. Put everything on autopilot."

"Sounds good. I need to get outta here."

They drove past Kit's office on their way south and Webster noticed that the firm's car was still in the lot and lights shone inside. No telling what the hell she was doing in there. Calling the press, her partner, the cops, the president himself. Served him right for getting involved with the sister of the missing man he was trying to track down. Or, more to the point, with a defense attorney who would be coming up against the judge he was investigating.

"Did she say anything on the drive to her office?" Webster asked.

"Just that she appreciated the ride. But as she got out, she wanted to know how I could be party to such tactics. That sort of pissed me off and I said, 'Probably the same way you can defend people you know are guilty.' "

"What'd she say to that?"

"Nothing. She just slammed the door and headed into her office." He paused. "So is that the shortest relationship on record?"

"Something like that."

Webster didn't want to talk about it and changed the subject.

The Tango address for Sanchez put them on a narrow street two blocks north of the docks, in a raucous neighborhood where Latino music blared from open windows and yards were filled with plants that grew with riotous abandon. Men and women sat around on their porches, visiting with friends, having late dinners, living much as Webster imagined they might be living in Havana.

They parked in front of a small concrete block house old enough to have stood here since before the ruling about homes at sea level being built on concrete pilings. Two dilapidated cars were parked in the narrow driveway and a plump woman in a loose dress was sweeping the sidewalk.

"Buenas noches, señora," Moreno said as they came through the gate. *"Rico Sanchez se encuentra?"*

She leaned on her broom and let loose with what sounded to Webster like a string of obscenities. Moreno listened politely, held up his badge, and the woman's tone changed completely. She stepped closer and gestured with her right hand as she spoke rapidly, but more calmly. Moreno asked her a couple of questions and handed her a piece of paper. She sketched a map, Moreno thanked her, and they left.

"That's his sister-in-law. She says Sanchez is a no-good shit *maricón* and she hopes we take his no-good ass to jail," Moreno said. "He lives at the edge of the preserve. Pretty far in, if this map is correct."

"Should we have a look?"

"I thought that was the idea."

"Just checking."

"What's our excuse for the visit?"

"The truth. What's his relationship with Hutchin?"

"We may be opening doors here, amigo."

"Hey, it's a matter of record. He got out of a shoplifting rap when Hutchin was prosecutor for Tango County by paying restitution. Where'd that money come from?"

"It's flimsy, but what the hell."

The map the woman had drawn was crude and took them so far into the preserve that Webster felt like Theseus in the labyrinth. Without streetlights and with the trees obscuring the moonlight, darkness blanketed the area. The Jeep's headlights seemed puny, the equivalence of a pair of fireflies darting about in a vast, impenetrable blackness.

Then the trees broke open and there, on the right, in the glare of the security lights that winked on, stood a ramshackle place, some backwoods nightmare straight out of *Deliverance.* Dogs erupted into frenzied barking, half a dozen of them leaping at a wire-mesh fence. "Christ," Moreno whispered. He brought out his weapon, disengaged the safety.

Webster pulled in behind a pickup truck on huge swamp tires that raised the pickup itself about six feet from the ground. He killed the Jeep's engine and he and Moreno looked at each other. Webster knew they were thinking the same thing. *If those dogs get out . . .*

The dogs kept barking and leaping at the fence, their eyes glowing like fiery red moons, their teeth glistening with saliva. Webster pounded on the door. "FBI, Sanchez. Open up," he shouted.

No answer.

Again.

No answer.

The dogs suddenly fell silent, a silence so eerie that the hairs on the back of Webster's neck stood straight up and a chill ate into his bones. When he glanced around the post at the fence, the dogs were gone. "I'm going to check around back," he said.

"That's not a good idea," Moreno whispered, and Webster turned around.

Three very large Dobermans and four very large Rottweilers stood between them and the Jeep, their teeth bared, their muscular bodies poised to leap. "Fuck," Webster whispered, reaching slowly into his jacket for his weapon. "Let's fire in front of them. Maybe it will scare them off far enough for us to make a break for the car."

"Let's just shoot the fuckers."

"Only as a last resort. Pepper the ground in front of them."

Moreno opened fire first, with Webster following moments later so they wouldn't run out of ammo at the same time. The dogs, howling and whimpering, turned tail and raced into the overgrown yard. Moreno slammed in a new clip as Webster kept firing and they stepped off the porch simultaneously, the shots echoing out through the darkness and the woods, no doubt awakening everything and everyone within miles. When they were less than two yards from the Jeep, the lead dog, a rottweiler the size of a small horse, got brave. He edged forward, snarling, testing them, and within seconds, the other dogs followed his example, forming a wide half circle behind the leader.

Moreno made a run for it and Webster kept firing, moving steadily backward, his fear so extreme that he wasn't paying any attention to how many bullets he fired. When his weapon suddenly clicked, the clip empty, he whipped around and flew toward the pickup, hurling himself into the back of it with Moreno.

The dogs surrounded the pickup like hounds from hell, leaping up, snapping at the air, trying to jump into the back of the pickup. But it was raised too high from the ground, high enough, Webster thought, so that he and Moreno might be able to leap onto the hood of the Jeep, then onto the roof, and climb through the open passenger window. He said as much to Moreno, who looked scared shitless.

"I'm filing a complaint with animal control. These dogs will be gone by tomorrow," he spat, and reloaded. "You first. I'll cover you. Don't drop your goddamn keys."

Moreno started firing again and the dogs backed off once more, but not as far this time. Webster climbed onto the rear edge of the pickup. Moreno continued to fire; then Webster leaped and landed hard on the hood of the Jeep. He went down on one knee, scrambled up the windshield to the roof, and saw the lead rottweiler race away from the pack and come up behind the Jeep, out of the line of Moreno's fire. Webster, sitting back on his heels now, squeezed off several shots and inched back on the roof, close to the open window.

"Get in there now!" Moreno shouted, firing from the side of the pickup, trying to keep the rottweiler back while Webster swung through the passenger window.

As soon as he was in, he scrambled to the driver's seat to get the key into the ignition so he could raise the window. His hands shook, his throat had gone hot and dry, and a voice in his head screamed, *Hurry, c'mon, hurry. . . .*

He grabbed his right wrist with his left hand to steady it, then a terrible sound sundered the air, and Webster realized one of the dogs had taken a bullet. "Shit, shit, shit." He got the key into the ignition, turned it, and raised the window seconds before two of the Dobermans leaped, snarling, against the glass, their claws scraping the length of it.

Webster turned on the Jeep and banged his fist repeatedly against the horn, scaring the dogs away from the Jeep and the pickup. He gunned the engine and slammed the car into reverse. He could see Moreno now, backing up until his spine was against the pickup's cabin. He frantically patted his pockets, looking for another clip, then held up his weapon, shouting something that Webster couldn't hear. But the message was clear enough: he was out of ammo.

He pressed his hand to the horn again, hoping to scare the dogs out of the way. He deeply regretted that the lead dog had been shot and he didn't want to run over any of them. But, Christ, he didn't intend to let them get to Moreno, either. He gunned the engine, swerved around the pickup, and drew alongside it, scraping the shit out of the side of the Jeep. The cars were now so close together the dogs couldn't get between them. Webster lowered the window and Moreno hurled himself inside, shouting, "Get the window up, fast, Jesus, they're coming. . . ."

Webster hit the button for the window and seconds later the dogs struck the Jeep, leaping, snarling, trying to bite their way through the glass. "C'mon, man," Moreno shouted. "Let's get the fuck outta here."

"No."

"*No?*" Moreno looked at him as if he'd lost his mind. "You're one crazy gringo, you know that?"

"So we leave and what's Sanchez going to do?"

"Wait until he thinks we're gone, then come out and probably take off."

"Exactly. And there goes our best lead to whatever it is Hutchin is guilty of."

"Look, you're convinced Hutchin is guilty of something, but I'm not."

"You will be."

Webster put the Jeep in park and, with the engine still running and the dogs still going nuts outside, he climbed over the seats to the well in the back of the Jeep. He rummaged through everything—car tools, a bag with several changes of clothes and other personal items, packages of dried fruit and bottles of water, and a black bag that held tools of the trade. He climbed back into the front seat with the bag.

"Load your weapon and shoot out that goddamn security light."

"Yeah? And how do I do that without losing my hand?"

"Through the sunroof," Webster replied, and pressed a button on the dash.

The explosion of glass from the security lights startled the dogs and they retreated, but not far. It gave Webster time to assemble the rifle and load the tranquilizer darts. "Where the hell did that come from?" Moreno asked.

"I got chased by a dog in Miami and have carried it ever since."

He stood on his seat and poked his head up through the open sunroof. The Jeep's headlights provided just enough light to see the dogs. He aimed at the rottweiler at the rear of the Jeep, squeezed the trigger, and winced as the dog fell back, whimpering.

Jesus, he'd never shot an animal in his life. But it wasn't dead, he told himself. He wasn't killing them. He was just putting them out of commission for a while.

Within minutes, all six dogs had gone to sleep. The wounded dog had apparently fled into the woods. If it could flee, he thought, then it probably wasn't hurt badly enough to die out there.

The subsequent silence spooked him. He withdrew into the Jeep, shut the sunroof except for a crack for air, and killed the engine, the lights. "Now what?" Moreno whispered.

"Let's go in."

"How long are those dogs going to sleep?"

"A few hours."

"You're sure?"

"Yes."

They followed procedure, one of them in the lead, the

other covering. Their shoes crunched over the shattered glass as they made their way up the sidewalk. Moreno stood to the side of the door while Webster hurled his weight against it. The door flew open and Webster swung into the room, weapon leveled, Moreno right behind him.

Webster knew immediately that the place was empty. Just the same, they went from room to room, three rooms and a bathroom. In the kitchen, the door to the outside swung open and shut. Webster stepped outside. Off to his right was the dog pen, the gate wide open. And directly in front of him loomed the woods, thick, impenetrable, black as pitch.

"He's halfway to Cuba by now," Moreno muttered, coming up behind Webster.

"And as soon as he hears that we've been to his brother's house, he'll be back to get his truck. And we'll be here waiting for him."

"Fuck that," Moreno said.

"One of us waits in the Jeep, the other in the back of the pickup. When Sanchez returns to the house, he'll step outside, maybe whistle for the dogs. I don't think he'll be able to see them from the porch, unless it's daylight. He'll see the Jeep, but no one inside. He'll probably think we took off or were torn to pieces. He'll head to the pickup. And we'll ambush him."

"You're one crazy fucking gringo. How long do those darts last?"

"A few hours."

"Not long enough."

"I'm not leaving, Moreno. Your only way out is on foot."

"I know, I know. Christ. But I'm going to tip the odds in our favor." He went over to a pile of junk near the dog pen and pulled out a large wheelbarrow. "The mutts go in here, we put them in the pen, lock the gate. Sanchez will think the gate blew shut. He'll be in too much of a hurry to check.''

"You're nuts. Those are big fucking dogs."

"Hey, if I have to stay here because you're pigheaded, then you owe me at least this. Besides, the second Sanchez comes through that front door to get to his truck, he's going to see his dogs snoozing. That's going to be a major tip-off that it's an ambush."

He had a good point. "Okay, let's hurry up."

It took them twenty minutes to load the dogs into the wheelbarrow and get them into the pen. Webster locked the gate and they hurried back into the house, leaving the kitchen door flapping in the breeze, just as they'd found it. They made a cursory search of the house, but Rico Sanchez wasn't the type who kept records or anything else of importance on paper. The eerie part of the whole thing, at least for Webster, was the way the eyes on the peacock feathers that covered one wall seemed to watch them, follow them.

By 10:38, Webster was hidden in the back of the pickup and Moreno was inside the Jeep. For a while, he simply lay there, gazing into the belly of the star-strewn sky. His first six months in the keys had been uneventful, business as usual. But the last week had taken such a dramatic turn into the land of the weird and the strange that he wasn't sure how he'd gotten here. Even worse, he couldn't see his way out.

So he shut his eyes and waited for Sanchez to return.

Chapter 22

"So tell me where we're going to live when we move to DC," Isabel said.

"Georgetown, Bethesda, maybe even Virginia."

"Of the three, Virginia appeals to me the most. You know, a place with some land, with trees, and more than three hundred feet between us and our neighbors."

They were lying in bed, in the dark, the windows open to the sweet night air. It blew over their damp, naked bodies, this air, cooling them, soothing them, Hutchin thought, lulling them into old, familiar marital patterns. It was easy to slide back into this way of life, he decided, and a relief to be able to do so after the long months of lies, half-baked excuses, and sneaking around.

He hadn't realized until now, until just this moment, how much energy his affair with Diane had consumed. At times, he couldn't remember what lie he had told or to whom. During the midpart of their relationship, he had kept an appointment book that helped him keep his lies straight.

Told Isabel I had to work late. Told Diane I had to get home early because Isabel was home.

Many times, he had gone home to his wife with his body smelling of Diane. His treachery then had been so great that it was everything he could do to greet his wife and then extricate himself from the situation as quickly as possible so that he could shower. So that he could wash away the traces of Diane.

He often thought of the relationship as stages of life—youth, middle age, old. And in that middle period, he had looked one day at his appointment book, trying to find out what he had told Isabel about his whereabouts on a night he'd been with Diane, and his folly, his utter stupidity, had hit him. Paper trail. And the next morning, he had ripped every page out of the appointment book, then shredded them and burned everything—the pages, the book, the paper trail.

"Barb said some FBI agents came to Amherst and spoke to a couple of her friends. They were asking questions about you."

Shit, the bastards are everywhere.

"That's not surprising. They're probably poking around in the lives of the other candidates as well." The calmness in his voice astonished him—and belied the rapidly mounting panic that he felt. "I expected some of that."

"There was also an FBI agent at the school, Hutch, talking to my principal about me."

He lifted up on an elbow, gazed down at her. "How do you know that?"

"The principal told me."

"Look, just say the word, Isabel, and I'll have my name taken out of the running."

He knew that he wouldn't and he also knew that Isabel wouldn't demand it. The freedom to pursue their individual dreams with the full support of the other constituted the unspoken part of their marital agreement.

Perhaps this was why he hadn't asked questions during that time in their marriage when she hadn't been around much, when he'd been sure she was having an affair. And maybe it was why she hadn't asked questions during his affair with Diane.

See no evil.

Speak no evil.

Hear no evil.

These three things seemed to have become the sacred writ of the marriage.

"Oh, stop it," she said softly. "I'm behind this completely."

She drew his face toward hers and kissed him and he thought: *I'm mending this marriage. We're healing wounds.*

They made love again and because she'd had a few drinks with her buddies from school and because it had been a long week, she fell asleep immediately afterward. And if she hadn't been sleeping so soundly, she might have heard the cell phone ring a while later.

He knew immediately that it was *his* phone because his played the "Mexican Hat Dance" and was plugged into the wall, recharging. His wife's played a tango and was in her purse. Hutchin bolted upright and snatched up the cell phone, disconnecting it from the charger. He hurried into the hall.

"Yes?" he whispered. "Hello?"

"Hoodge?"

Sanchez. And he sounded as if he'd just run a 10K race. Hutchin went into his daughter's room, shut the door. "Christ, Rico. You're not supposed to call me on this phone."

"*Mira, lo siento,* but I didn't know what else to do." The words gushed out of him, a stream of English and Spanish all mixed up. The feds. His dogs. He'd taken off into the woods. He was at a phone booth in the park, got there on his motor scooter, he needed money, help, something. "My scooter, it has no gas. I have just a few dollars in my wallet. You come, Hoodge."

"I'll be there in about twenty minutes. Just go into the trees and wait so you don't get picked up by the local cops."

"*Sí, sí*, I go now. I wait."

Hutchin disconnected and turned off his phone. *Fuck, the stupid fuck.*

He crept quietly back into the bedroom, dressed in the dark. His thoughts stumbled over each other, struggling to make connections, to follow the many lines of probability, the many *what ifs. What if* Sanchez talked? *What if* he spilled his guts to the cops? *What if* his wife woke up while he was gone? *What if* he got caught?

He had to make sure that he didn't get caught. He reached into a shoe box on the top shelf in the closet and brought out a long, thin knife with a very sharp edge. It had belonged to his old man, he had inherited it. Hutchin couldn't remember ever seeing this knife when his father had been alive and couldn't imagine what he had used it for. Hunting? His old man hadn't been a hunter. Filleting fish? Steak? No telling. He had found it in his parents' attic after his old man had died, when he and Isabel were cleaning out the house to move his mother into an assisted-living facility. He had kept it—not because he thought he would ever use it, but because it was part of the family history.

It took him seventeen minutes to get to the park where Sanchez was. And Sanchez, completely freaked out and consumed by fear, crept out of the protection of the trees, glanced around, and whispered, "Is it safe?"

"Just you and me." He felt the weight of the knife inside

the sleeve of his windbreaker, its sharp point sticking into his hand. "We're safe."

He hurried over to the bench where Hutchin waited and sat down. It was back in an embrace of trees that blocked the streetlights and pooled the area in darkness. But he didn't have to see Sanchez to smell his fear. It oozed from his pores, his hair, from his mouth when he opened it.

"These men, these *federales,* Hoodge, they come long after dark, banging on my door, and Rico, he gets scared, no? He takes off. But first he lets the dogs out and . . ."

Hutchin listened as Sanchez rambled, as he sweated, as he nearly wept at the thought that his parole would be violated and he would go back to jail. And in between his ramblings and sweating and all the rest of the goddamned drama, he told Hutchin about the jewelry store that Kit Parrish had visited that morning in Miami. And how his men had pursued her.

"What men?" Hutchin nearly shouted. *What fucking men?*

Sanchez looked at Hutchin as if he'd just realized he had made a major mistake, but wasn't quite sure why. "The men Rico hired. Men I know. Men I trust. Men without records. They follow this woman, they make her afraid, just as you tell me to do."

Christ, Christ. What the hell had he done? "Okay, Rico, just calm down." Hutchin rested his arm across the back of the bench and eased the knife out of the sleeve of his jacket. "You've done a great job. Did these men know why they were doing what they were doing?"

"No way. I tell them nothing about you, *lo prometo." I promise.*

"That's good. That's very good."

"And they are going to do other things, Hoodge. You will see. You will be much pleased with Rico's plan."

"What other things?"

He babbled then, babbled about hell and devils and he needed money to get off the island, to go someplace and lie low for a while, and it would be okay, right? It would be okay because Hoodge had promised him a reprieve from his parole, an end to his parole, and he would not go back to jail.

"No jail, Rico, I promise. Just tell me what else you told them to do."

He started to cry then, for Christ's sake, sobbing into his hands like a two-year-old. It disgusted Hutchin and frustrated him to such extremes that he grabbed Sanchez by the jaw with one hand and hissed, "Stop it, Christ, just stop it," and the knife slid into his other hand and his fingers twitched around it, gripping it tightly. Then he drove the blade into the base of Sanchez's neck and twisted it.

A scream leaped in Sanchez's throat, Hutchin actually heard it, but as a strange gurgling, a choking. It was as if his urge to scream had coincided with a deluge of blood in his lungs and now he was choking on it. He struggled, but it was no more than a reflex and it lasted only seconds. Then he slumped into Hutchin, his head lolling as though it were barely connected to the rest of his body. His eyes, wide open and dark, stared vacantly at a sky glistening with stars.

Staring as vacantly as Diane's eyes had stared.

Staring and empty.

The emptiness terrified Hutchin. These eyes were the eyes of death, staring back at him, stalking him. A void of nothingness loomed within Sanchez's eye sockets, an unknown so infinite and ultimately beyond Hutchin's comprehension that it seemed to mock him.

Hutchin shot to his feet—and froze. Sanchez's body slumped sideways on the bench and lay there, the knife protruding from the back of his neck.

A tsunami of perspiration swept over Hutchin's back, moisture surged from his palms. He pressed the heels of his hands to his eyes and sucked air into his lungs, his mouth. He saw Sanchez's eyes in his head, then Diane's eyes, oceans as black and fathomless as outer space.

Move. Snap out of it. Fast.

His hands dropped away from his face. From the nearby trees, he heard animals sounds, coons, frogs, nocturnal creatures, his witnesses. His leg muscles twitched, finally loosened, and he hurried to the back of the bench.

So far, none of Sanchez's blood had gotten on him, but he smelled it. The stink of it seemed to be everywhere, on his hands, in his clothes, clogged in his nostrils. It threatened to choke him, so he breathed through his mouth as he leaned over the back of the bench. He touched the knife's handle. It felt hot, scorching hot, and although he knew it couldn't be hot, it was impossible, he jerked his hand back.

Hutchin rubbed his hands against his shirt, reached again.

This time his fingers grasped the handle and he pulled the knife out. The blade made a sound, a noise like that of feet squishing around in wet shoes and socks. Bile rushed up his throat, he nearly gagged. He stumbled back, dropped to a crouch, slapped the blade against the grass, cleaning it. He slipped it back into its leather sheath, and walked quickly around to the front of the bench.

Leave him or arrange him? Which? Make it fast.

Those eyes, he had to cover those goddamn eyes. . . .

Hutchin swung Sanchez's legs onto the bench, so that he now reclined against it, and grabbed a newspaper from the trash. He shook it open, covered Sanchez's face with it. He hid those horrifying eyes.

He looked as though he were sleeping. The early morning joggers who saw him first would think he was a drunk sleeping it off. Maybe someone would call the cops, maybe not. Either way, it would look as though he had fallen asleep and been killed while he slept.

Killed for what?

A thief sees him snoozing on the bench and figures he's an easy mark. But just as he's lifting Sanchez's wallet, he comes awake, a struggle ensues.

How difficult a struggle?

Enough so that the thief stabs him in the back of the neck.

Hutchin frantically patted Sanchez's pockets, felt something in a back pocket, brought out a wad of cash. Not a very big wad, ten or fifteen one-dollar bills. He shoved the cash in his own pocket, then spun and ran into the trees, over branches, through weeds. He stumbled once, went down on a knee, and remained like that, his stomach heaving, and threw up in the grass.

Evidence, screamed Hutchin, attorney and judge.

Run, shrieked the primal heart of his brain, and he ran.

He could smell Sanchez's blood on his hands, his skin, in his hair. It pursued him, this stink, thickening in the air that he breathed until it was the only thing he could smell.

He exploded from the trees on the next block and forced himself to slow down, to walk normally, his head down. As soon as he was inside his car, he locked the doors and sat there, breathing hard, sweat rolling down the sides of his face, the stink of blood thick and terrible now. His mouth tasted of puke and when he squeezed his eyes shut, he saw the bottomless pit of those eyes, Sanchez's eyes, Diane's eyes.

He fumbled with his keys, got the right key into the ignition. On his way over the Tango Bridge, he considered hurling the knife into the water. But would salt water wear away his prints if the knife were found? He didn't know. And since he couldn't be sure, he didn't toss it.

He finally coasted into his driveway, headlights already

off. The engine ticked in the silence. He pressed his forehead to the steering wheel, anxiety eating through him.

Deep breaths. It's okay. You covered your tracks.

He raised his head and for a moment he thought he saw a shadow at the bedroom window. *Isabel? Christ, no, please be asleep, please, I can't deal with you right now.*

He waited another few moments in the car. The knife felt as hot as a poker through his clothes, scorching its shape against his ribs. The knife, he had to do something with the goddamn knife. But not tonight. Tonight he would stash it somewhere and tomorrow he would bury it in the backyard.

Stash it where? He got out of the car, shutting the door softly, and crept through the moonlight, eyes on the upstairs window. No shadows now. No Isabel. Maybe he had imagined it.

He moved along the side of the house to the backyard. A bank of clouds had swallowed the moon, but starlight spilled through the branches of the mango trees and pines, enough for him to make out the shapes of things. He stood utterly still in the quiet, in the starlight, surrounded by shapes that could have been anything. His eyes darted here, there, seeking a temporary spot for the knife.

After careful consideration, he dug near the base of the mango tree that grew at the southeast corner of the fence. He dug with his hands, dug like a dog burying a bone, and hid it under a layer of dirt, then pine needles, then fallen leaves. And when it was done, when he could feel the dirt under his nails and smell the pine needles he'd stirred up, he rubbed his palms back and forth against his jeans. *It'll be fine. It'll work.*

As he patted the dirt back into place, he replayed everything in his mind, every little detail, every nuance, every sensation about tonight. The stink of Sanchez's blood returned, swirling around him until he thought he would vomit again. And his mind, of course, returned to last Thursday night, to the moments when he had pressed the pillow over Diane's face and held it there.

A tidal wave of sorrow and terror, the two inexorably mixed and confused, crashed over him and emotion surged from the depths of his soul, something so huge and grotesque he couldn't control it, couldn't fight it, couldn't stop it, couldn't change it. It simply was what it was. And to his utter shock and horror, he began to weep and wondered how he had come to kill two people in just eight days.

He kept biting his lip to stifle his sobs and pretty soon, tasted blood on his tongue. His hands, all this time, had kept right on moving, sliding dirt into place, patting pine needles over it. His digging must have dislodged something else in the dirt because his nails scraped against a hard, solid object. He paused, frowning, then clawed at the dirt and the pine needles until he dislodged the object.

A metal box. It looked like a fishing tackle box. He unlatched it with his aching, dirty, bloodied fingers, and flipped open the lid.

Papers, folded papers inside.

Hutchin shut the lid quickly, stood, and ran the sole of his shoe over the spot where he'd found it. Then he hurried through the side door that led into the garage, turned on the light, shut the door, and set the box on the workbench. For the space of several heartbeats, no more than that, he simply looked at it, certain it was his Pandora's box, that once he opened it, he would not be able to close it again. The ills of the world would be free.

Go back outside and bury it, he thought.

But he couldn't. It exerted a kind of inexorable pressure against him, against the center of his chest, against his fingertips, his hands.

Hutchin tipped the lid open, removed the stack of folded

papers, set them to one side. He wiped his filthy hands on his clothes, then unfolded the top paper.

He stared at it, trying to make sense of it, but his brain refused to process it.

He kept staring, waiting for comprehension to kick in. Since he couldn't grasp the totality of what he was looking at, he focused on the upper part. A woman's head. A sketch of a woman's head. An exquisitely beautiful woman. Her head was turned slightly to the side, so the artist had captured her profile, which seemed to be lit from some unseen source of light. An ethereal light.

Now his eyes dropped a little lower, to the long, graceful curve of her neck, the protrusion of her collarbone, to the curves of her naked breast.

She had something draped over the other breast, a swath of fabric that looked light, almost transparent, perhaps silk. He couldn't tell what color it was, the sketch had been rendered in charcoal. His eyes dropped even farther on the sheet, to her slender waist, the posed posture of her naked, crossed legs. His gaze fixed on her ankles and feet, on her beautiful toes.

The detail, my God, the detail astonished him, detail so beautiful that it literally made his heart ache. Even the single rose in a vase in the windowsill behind the woman looked real.

Then his brain allowed him to see the entire picture, the whole sketch. An excruciating agony lit up the center of his body and he doubled over at the waist, arms clutched against him, and gasped for breath. He couldn't pull air into his lungs, couldn't get it past his mouth, his clenched teeth, over the cumbersome weight of his own tongue.

His knees buckled and he went down. The metal box clattered to the floor, the sketches fluttered down after it. Hutchin pressed his face against his thighs, into the familiar scent and texture of his jeans, and closed his mouth over his knee to stifle the wrenching sounds that surged out of him.

The woman was his wife.

His wife, nearly naked, sketched by another man.

Who?

His head snapped up, his mouth came away from his knee, and he lunged for one of the sketches, brought it up close to his face, and searched for the artist's signature.

Nothing. Unsigned.

Have you had sex with anyone else during our marriage?

Yes.

He held the sketch at arm's length, taking it in, taking all of it in at once, and knew this hadn't been just sex. This had been a full-blown affair, every bit as intense and confusing as his affair with Diane.

You lied to me.

And he had lied to her.

They were even.

But as he told himself this, that they were even now, his fingers crumpled the sketch, and he hurled it across the garage.

Chapter 23

Saturday, November 10

Ryan's eyes snapped open. He kept the covers pulled tightly against him, listening, waiting, his senses reaching out into the darkness beyond him, seeking whatever it was that had jerked him from a sound sleep.

His senses drew him under his bed. *Is the black hole growing?*

No, not that. It isn't that.

It wasn't the Other, either.

What? What is it?

He didn't know, he couldn't find it. He threw off the covers, sat up. The house. Was something wrong in the house? He listened hard to the quiet. Oro snored at the foot of his bed. That was good. If she was still asleep, that meant the threat wasn't close to him.

He could feel Abuelita's presence in the house. She was asleep somewhere, maybe in the living room. And he knew his mother hadn't come home yet. He felt her absence as surely as he felt her presence when she was in the house. His mother and Ben had gone somewhere together and that was okay. His mother liked Ben. Ben liked his mother.

Ben would take care of her. Ben would protect her.

But Ben isn't with her.

Ridiculous. Ryan had seen them leave together. Seen them leave in the same car.

Ryan rubbed his hands over his face and got out of bed to go to the bathroom. He thought about calling his mom, but it was nearly one in the morning, he didn't want to worry her. But he didn't think he could go back to sleep unless he heard her voice. So when he came out of the bathroom, he went over to the phone next to his bed and called her cell phone. It rang and rang until a message came on, which basically said her cell phone wasn't turned on. It meant she was asleep. And if she was asleep, he told himself, then she was okay.

But he knew she wasn't okay. He hurried up the hall, looking for Abuelita, and found her on the living room couch, a comforter pulled over her. Her long hair, loose now, fanned out across the pillow. "Abuelita," he whispered. "Wake up."

And she did. She woke up so fast, sitting straight up, that it startled Ryan. "What? What is it, *mí amor?*" she asked, her voice hoarse, her fingers sliding through her hair.

"Something's wrong."

"Wrong," she repeated, and swung her legs over the side of the couch. She turned on the lamp, the pale, buttery circles of light spilling over her arm, her legs, her toes, part of the rug. She squinted when she looked at him. "Wrong how?"

"I don't know. Something just doesn't feel right."

"Do you feel sick?"

"No."

"What do you feel, then?"

"Scared. About my mom. She doesn't answer her cell phone."

"It's very late, Ryan, that's why she doesn't answer."

He knew she didn't believe that any more than he did. He saw it in her face, in the small changes in her expression—the twitch under one eye, the way the corner of her eyebrow lifted, the movements of her mouth as she tried to decide what to say to him. "What would you like me to do?" she asked, finally.

"I have to talk to her."

Abuelita pulled the phone into her lap. "Ben. We'll call Ben."

She called his number, hung up, called another number and another and now Ryan was up again, moving quickly around the room. He straightened things, he couldn't help it. When he got scared, he straightened things, tidied them, organized them. Pencils with pencils, pens with pens, books by author, oh God oh God this was bad, this was . . .

Flames leap out of the floor, huge, towering tongues of bright orange flames, and the heat . . . the heat is so terrible that he feels it melting his lashes, his eyebrows, his skin, and he runs. He runs like a blind man, his arms thrust out in front of him, a long, terrible scream clawing its way out of his throat . . .

Then arms went around him, holding him, trapping him, and he felt Abuelita's magic sing through him. It calmed him and this time he didn't free himself from her grasp, he let her see what was inside of him.

It seemed that he did nothing more than blink and suddenly they were in the car. Ryan didn't remember getting into the car, but here they were. And it was real. The seat felt cold and hard beneath him, darkness filled the windshield, the windows were wide open. Oro sat between him and Abuelita,

alert, watchful. Abuelita drove too fast and her loose hair
flew around her head so that she looked like a wild woman.

"I . . . I'm sorry that you have to get up in the middle of
the night and—"

"Do you understand what happened to you back at the
house?"

"I got scared."

"Besides that, Ryan."

"I saw . . . fire . . . smoke . . ."

"Right. And what else?"

"It seemed so . . . so real."

"Exactly. It was so real you thought it was happening to
you, right there in the house."

"I could smell the smoke, the flames were hot and
bright . . ."

"When this kind of vision happens, it's difficult to tell
if what you were seeing was happening as you were seeing
it or if you were glimpsing the future."

Ryan thought about this. "How can I tell the difference?"

"It takes practice. The first step is to learn to pull away
from what you're seeing or feeling. You can't let it swallow
you. You have to disengage somehow. Then the vision or
the feeling flows through you and it's easier to place it in
time."

"It sounds complicated."

"It isn't really. It's just that we aren't taught how to do
these things."

"When I was digging in the field that night, was that a
vision?"

"No, you were actually doing the digging. But the woman
you say you saw on the bridge at Bahia Honda may have
been a vision."

"A past-life vision?"

"It's possible."

"Abuelita, until last Friday night, nothing like this has ever happened to me before. Why's it happening now?"

"Actually, *mí amor,* these sorts of things have happened to you several times in the past. But none of the incidents was as dramatic as these and they didn't happen one after another, the way these experiences seem to be doing, so they were just, well, *odd.* None of us attached any particular significance to them. But the incidents this past week have been remarkably different. It's almost as if there's a message that none of us is getting."

"What did you see when you touched me?"

"I didn't *see* anything. But I felt what you felt, smelled what you smelled. I believe the event you saw hasn't happened yet, but it's so close that perhaps we can do something to prevent it. Quite honestly, I would feel a whole lot better about all this if your mother or Ben were answering their phones. But it *is* late and it's likely they turned off their phones and are sleeping."

"So where're we going?"

"Ben's houseboat."

"And then?"

"Let's take it a step at a time, *mí amor.*"

Ryan felt a little better now that Abuelita was in charge, but fear for his mother coiled like a snake in the pit of his stomach.

(2)

When Kit came to in the dark, she couldn't remember where she was, didn't know the time, couldn't even remember the day. It was as if she had stumbled down the rabbit hole and lost consciousness on the way down.

She blinked and everything snapped into clarity. Her office, of course. She had fallen asleep in her office. When

Moreno let her off, she had headed straight into her office, booted up her computer, and gone to work, preparing for Poulton's arraignment on Monday. By law, the clerk of court had to provide written notice of arraignment to a defendant within ten days of arrest. The actual date had to be set between thirty and thirty-five days after the date of arrest. On Tango, because it was such a small county, the process often moved more quickly than that, but the speed with which things here had moved bordered on the ludicrous. Poulton had been arrested less than a week ago. That had bothered her when she'd fallen asleep and it bothered her now.

She sat up, swung her legs to the floor, and wondered if she should just drive home now. Abuelita would be in bed and she wouldn't have to face the old woman's questions about what she was doing at home. She ran her hands over her face and started to turn on the lamp next to the couch when she heard a noise in another part of the office.

Or had it been outside?

She sat there a moment, listening so hard that she could hear the rush of her own blood through her veins. *You imagined it.* Just the same, she felt around on the floor for her purse and fished out her keys. She opened her briefcase and grabbed her cell phone, which she stuck in the back pocket of her jeans.

Kit padded barefoot across the room to the storage closet. She unlocked it, turned on the penlight attached to the key ring, and shone it inside. There, standing against the wall amid other gifts that she'd bought for Christmas, was Ryan's bat. She picked it up, shut the closet door, and peered out the window, into the street, Atocha Drive.

The street was deserted, no surprise. This was the business and bureaucratic district—with the jail and courthouse at one end of the block and law and county offices at the other end, and it was the dead of night. The noise hadn't come from this end of the building or from outside. It had come from the back of the building, *inside.*

Kit moved quickly to the door, her thumb already pressing against the power button on her cell phone, turning it on. She paused in the doorway, senses straining, and then she heard it again, a noise she couldn't describe or compare to anything else because she didn't hear it clearly.

She hurried down the carpeted hall, the bat clutched tightly in her right hand, the penlight in her left hand, aimed at the floor, a beam of light no thicker than her pinky finger. Her heart did an erratic drumroll in her chest. *It's probably squirrels or mice.* Over the years, they'd had nests in the building's attic. But this hadn't sounded like mice or squirrels. This had sounded *human.*

Had she locked the rear door after she'd come in? She didn't remember. It seemed that she had, but she couldn't remember doing it and she couldn't remember resetting the alarm, either. *Check there first,* she thought, and moved swiftly down the hall, past offices, a staff room, the conference room, all of them silent, empty. She smelled something now, a foreign scent that didn't belong. But it took her a moment to identify it because it was so obviously out of place.

Gas.

There was a gas grill on a deck on the other side of the building that they used for office parties, city gas that came through an underground pipeline. Did it have a leak? Or maybe the ancient gas stove in the staff room had sprung a leak. The closer she got to the rear door, the more pervasive the smell became. *Coming from outside?*

But the rear door was shut—and locked, she noticed, and the security system wasn't engaged. When she passed it, the smell got stronger, thicker. Its origin was inside the building, she decided. A gas leak, not intruders. She hit the hallway switch. The overhead light didn't come on. Burned bulb? Blackout? No, not a blackout, not with the streetlights on outside her office window.

Bulb, she decided, and came around the corner and stopped. Thanks to the light from the window at the far end of the hall, she could see a man, a very large man, his back to her as he moved down the hall, swinging a can from side to side as he splashed gas onto the walls, the carpet, and into the rooms he passed.

Fucker, how dare you.

A strange rage seized her, an emotion borne in some dim corridor of time when man had lived in caves and defended to the death what was his, an atavistic rage. She moved with the quickness of light and the silence of a predator. Everything seemed to contract to precisely this moment, this instant, this breath. Adrenal floodgates flew open in her body, every muscle tensed. Seconds before she reached him, the bat already in the air, ready to swing down against his miserable spine and crack every goddamn vertebra, her cell phone rang.

The man whipped around at the sound of it and Kit recognized him. Matanza, the big guy who had pursued her in Miami. In the moment when their eyes caught, it occurred to her that he looked as shocked to see her as she was to see him and then there was no time to think anymore because the bat whistled down and his arm flew up.

As the bat struck him across the chest, he hit her right arm with the can of gas. Then they both stumbled back, her cell phone still ringing. Her arm turned bright with pain and the bat seemed to be slipping from her grasp and the can lay on its side on the floor, gas pouring out of it. Kit fell into the wall, lost her hold on the bat, and the man tripped over his own feet and crashed to the floor.

He leaped up and she ran up the hall, moving toward the bat that had rolled away from her. He grabbed his gas can and she shouted, "Matanza, Carlos Matanza, I know who you are!" As she lunged for the bat, something flashed in her peripheral vision. Kit's head snapped to the left and she caught a glimpse of a second man, rushing out of one of the rooms, and then he was on her.

She was never quite sure whether he kicked her or hit her, whether he used his fists or a gun or some other object. Whatever it was, the end result to her was the same. She sank to the floor, her ribs shrieking, and blackness licking at the corners of her eyes, shrinking her vision.

Even as her vision began to go, she could still hear— their exchange in Spanish too rapid for her to understand, her cell phone ringing again, the ring vibrating in her back pocket, against her buttocks, and she could hear her own moans as she tried to lift up on her arms. Then everything went black.

(3)

It swept over him suddenly, an intense urgency to get out of here. Webster took one look around—at the pervasive darkness that covered Sanchez's house, porch, yard, and at his Jeep, where Moreno was.

Webster shot to his feet, climbed out of the pickup, and ran around to the driver's side of the Jeep. He threw open the door, startling Moreno from a sound sleep.

"Moreno, wake up. We have to leave."

Moreno grumbled and slid over to the passenger side, griping about his stiff neck and what the fuck was going on, anyway? Webster had no answers. There was only the urgency, the same terrible urgency he'd felt that night decades ago, when he'd awakened in a terrible chill, certain that something had happened to his folks.

"What about Sanchez?"

"If the guy was coming home, he would be here by now." Webster gestured at the dashboard clock, which read 2:17. "He's now officially wanted for questioning."

Moments later, he sped up the dirt road, trying to sort through what he was feeling. He called Kit's cell phone, let it ring half a dozen times. He didn't get a recording or a voice message system, so the phone was on, but she wasn't answering it. Why not? He tried her office number. The busy signal indicated the line was out of commission.

"What the hell," Moreno muttered. "Where're we going?"

"Something's wrong."

Webster pressed the accelerator to the floor and the Jeep shot forward.

(4)

Smoke. It filled the hallway, roiling clouds of smoke that choked her and burned her eyes. Kit pushed up from the floor, rocked back on her heels, and nearly passed out from the pain in her ribs. Then she saw the flames at the other end of the hall, racing toward her, a living thing with a singular purpose, to consume and destroy.

She leaped up and stumbled blindly in the other direction, praying that the fire hadn't reached her office yet, that she could get to her briefcase, to the Poulton file. It was so dark and her eyes burned so terribly that she couldn't see where she was going and ran into a wall. No, not a wall. The door, the rear door. She slammed her hands against the bar, but the door wouldn't give. She slapped the wall for the security pad, squinting against the smoke so that she could see the numbers. She thought she punched in the emergency code, just two numbers, but when she hit the door bar again, the door still wouldn't budge.

They pushed something against it, to keep me in here.

Kit spun around and struck her fist against the opposite wall, again and again until she hit the fire alarm. The glass shattered, she jerked up on the lever, and the alarm shrieked shrilly. Then she ran with the bottom of her blouse folded up over her nose and mouth and as she came around another corner, a wall of fire stood between her and her office.

She ducked into the staff room, which still hadn't caught fire because there was no carpet on the floor, and shut the door to keep out as much of the smoke as possible. No windows in here; otherwise she could get out and run around to the front of the building and break the window in her office to get in. But the staff room was the only room without any windows at all.

She threw open the closet door. A blanket, there was a blanket in here from when she and Ryan had spent several days at the office while the house was undergoing renovations. She found it in the back, half a dozen gallon jugs of distilled water sitting on top of it. Kit jerked the blanket out, tore off the tops from the gallons of water, and emptied all but one of them over the blanket, soaking it.

The alarm continued to shriek, smoke now rolling under the door. Before she pulled the heavy blanket around her body, she turned off the gas that fed into the little stove. She didn't know if it would help, especially with the underground gas lines feeding into the grill outside. But it might buy her a few minutes.

She pulled the heavy blanket over her head, emptied the last gallon of water over her sneakers, then ran to the door, felt it. Warm, but not hot. The flames hadn't reached this far yet. Kit opened the door and stared at the wall of fire that moved toward her. Panic nearly forced her back into the windowless staff room, the room with no other exit.

Forget it. Go now, fast, fast fast. . . .

Except for her eyes and feet, the blanket covered her entire body. She kept it clutched tightly around her, a cocoon of saturated wool, and raced up the hall, toward the flames, faster and faster, until she plunged through them. The heat nearly roasted her alive, the fire singed the bottom part of the blanket, but the flames didn't touch her.

She burst into her office, out of the flames. The doorjamb was on fire so she swung the wet blanket against the flames, extinguishing them, then slammed the door. The room had filled with smoke from the hallway, but nothing in here seemed to be burning yet. Kit pressed the blanket against the crack under the door to prevent any other smoke from getting in, then grabbed the heavy-duty wastebasket from beside her desk and hurled it against the window. The glass shattered and the smoke began to drift out the window.

She ran over to the couch, grabbed her purse, briefcase, and laptop, and ran to the window. Sirens screamed through the darkness, police, fire trucks, she didn't know which, it didn't matter. They were all too late. Any minute now the flames might ignite a gas line and the entire building would go up, blown to Never Never Land. She climbed through the window and ran across the street, dumped everything on the grass, and ran back toward the shattered window, trying desperately to ignore the stabbing pain in her ribs.

A Jeep screeched to the curb and Webster and Moreno leaped out. ''I have to get stuff outta there!'' Kit shouted.

Windows on the other side of the building exploded from the heat, releasing huge, greasy clouds of smoke and long fingers of fire that swept up the sides of the building. Webster and Moreno raced after her and the three of them scrambled through the window. Kit tore cables out of the back of the

computer, picked up the box with the hard drive inside, and
Moreno jerked a drawer out of the desk and set the printer
and boxes of backup disks inside. Webster loaded stuff onto
a cart on wheels and they raced for the window.

Cop cars and fire trucks were already at the curb, firemen
unrolling hoses. An ambulance roared into view. The fire
alarm kept shrieking. Several cops ran over to help them
carry what they had salvaged from her office and she shouted
for them to put everything into the Jeep. Relieved of the
computer, she spun around to go back in once more, but a
cop grabbed her arm, shouting that it wasn't safe, the building might blow. Kit, seized by a kind of desperate fever to
save what she could, wrenched free of his grasp and raced
for the window.

Smoke now seeped around the blanket she had stuffed
against the crack under the door. Waves of heat rolled
through the room. She grabbed the box that held some of
Ryan's Christmas presents out of the storage closet, passed
them through the window to Webster. He was shouting at
her, probably telling her to get out now, fast, but she needed
every goddamn thing that related to the Poulton case. Insurance couldn't replace that. And it couldn't replace the box
that held Ryan's Christmas gifts or the four charcoal sketches
on the walls that Pete had done.

Webster came in after her, took the sketches in one hand,
and grabbed her arm with his other hand, literally pulling
her toward the window. "We've got what's important," he
shouted. "C'mon, c'mon. . . ."

And just as they made it through the window, she felt a
great, hot rush of air against her back and knew the door to
her office had blown inward and that the hungry flames now
consumed the room. She could almost see it in her mind,
the flames racing up the doorjambs again, leaping to the
bookcases, devouring the furniture. It sickened her, enraged

her, and beneath those emotions lay a sorrow so deep that she was afraid it would overpower her if she acknowledged it.

She and Webster raced across the street and hurled themselves into the Jeep, where Moreno threw the car into reverse. "My briefcase and laptop," she shouted. "I left them on the—"

"I got them," Moreno shouted back.

He swerved, still in reverse, between two cop cars that formed a barricade between the end of the block and the building, then slammed the gear shift into drive and sped away like a bat out of hell. Kit glanced back and saw that the ambulance, fire truck, even the cop cars, were taking off. And as she watched, the building blew, an explosion that was probably heard twelve miles away in Key West.

A huge piece of her life hurled skyward, lighting up the darkness like the Fourth of July. Something broke inside of her, she felt it, heard it, and tears welled up in her eyes and spilled down her cheeks. When the Jeep stopped, she threw open the door and stumbled out, her hair and skin and clothes stinking of smoke, her face and hands smeared with soot. She fell to her knees in the grass, rage and grief so mixed up that she could no longer tell one from the other.

Her cell phone rang, the damn thing still functioning and still on, vibrating in her back pocket. She pulled it from her pocket and rocked back on her heels and looked at the number in the window. Ryan's cell phone number. *Dear God.* She answered the call in a voice that sounded, even to her, deeply shaken. "I'm okay, Ryan. I'm okay," she said before he could utter a single word.

He started to cry, great heaving sobs that tore her apart. And in between the sobs, he managed to tell her that he and Abuelita were at a police barricade two blocks from Atocha and no one would let them through or tell them what was going on and he was scared.

Kit kept talking to him as she got up and moved quickly south, her feet moving as if of their own volition. When she saw him, he was running toward her, racing toward her with his arms thrown open, his dog galloping alongside him. And he was screaming, "Mommy, Mommy! . . ."

Her exhaustion by then was so extreme and his terror was so great that when he crashed into her arms, he bowled her over and she fell back into the grass, her son's arms clutching her around the neck. He whispered, over and over again, in a voice as harsh and hoarse as gravel, "The bad man did this, the man did it, bad man, bad man . . ."

They clung to each other in the smoky darkness and Kit squeezed her eyes shut, giving thanks to whoever might be listening that she had not lost her son.

Chapter 24

Kit had given the sheriff a statement while the paramedics were checking her over and Webster and Moreno had stood there listening to everything that was said, witnesses to her statement. Then they'd dropped Moreno at the surveillance van and followed Abuelita to her place.

At 4:30 that morning, Webster crashed on an air mattress in Abuelita's living room, Kit and Ryan shared a pullout couch, and Oro collapsed on the living room floor. During the hours that Webster slept like the dead, he woke twice. The first time, he woke because Ryan rolled off the couch he was sharing with his mother and plopped onto the air mattress. Webster didn't have the energy to move him, so he simply covered him with the blanket and slipped one of his pillows under the boy's head.

The second time he woke to something crawling up his arm, but quickly realized the sensation was too erotic to be an insect. He turned his head and saw Kit next to Ryan, her right arm extended, nails sliding up his bare arm. "Thanks," she whispered.

"I'm sorry I didn't tell you about—"

"It's okay." Her hand slid down to his in the dark, against the air mattress just above her son's head, her fingers slipped between his. "I owe you, Webster."

He tightened his grip on her hand and drifted off again. When he woke the third time, light the color of cream fell in stripes across the floor. His cell phone was ringing. He rolled onto his side, patting the floor beside him for the phone, and answered it with a dozen frogs in his throat.

"Hey, listen up. It's Moreno. Sanchez's body was just found in the Tango Park. Looks like he took a knife through the back of the neck."

Christ. "You there now?"

"Yeah."

"Tell the local cops he's our case. Don't let them touch the body."

"I've already done it. There's an APB out on Matanza, and the animal-control people have already collected Sanchez's dogs. Get your ass over here."

Webster scribbled a note to Kit that included what had happened to Sanchez, and was out of the house within five minutes, grateful that they'd unloaded Kit's office things when they'd gotten here earlier this morning. Even though he had showered when he'd gotten to Abuelita's, the stink of smoke still clung to his hair and jeans. When he coughed, he could feel the smoke still in his lungs. He couldn't face a corpse without a cup of coffee and something in his stomach, so on his way to Tango, he pulled into the only drive-through Cuban coffee shop in the keys.

A steaming cup of Cuban coffee and a warm guava turnover went a long way toward mitigating some of his fatigue, but they didn't do much for his disposition. Unless a search of Sanchez's house turned up some definite connection to

Hutchin, something more than what they'd gotten on the surveillance tapes, then that lead was as dead as Sanchez.

The spot at the park wasn't difficult to find. A crowd had already gathered and the area had been cordoned off. Webster spotted Moreno, wearing sweats and a T-shirt, talking to Sheriff Blake, who looked aggravated. As soon as he saw Webster, he snapped, "Agent Moreno tells me this homicide is a federal case. But since it happened in my county, I'd like to be kept abreast of any developments."

Webster kept his manner amiable. "Absolutely, Sheriff. I agree. We'll have the autopsy report faxed over to you as soon as we've got it."

"I'm somewhat unclear about the federal investigation this homicide pertains to, Agent Webster."

"We're not at liberty to say."

Blake's mouth pursed with disapproval. "It seems that every time I turn around, you're there. Last night at the jail, then at the nightmare on Atocha Drive, now this morning."

Webster acknowledged the remark by asking how Poulton was this morning. The sheriff shrugged. "Rather subdued, but otherwise he seems pretty normal." He then got right back on the topic. "My other question has to do with Ms. Parrish's statement last night. How does she know Matanza's name?"

"He followed her yesterday in Miami and she happened to get him on videotape. He was identified by Carmela Perez, who—"

"I know who she is," the sheriff said. "And what case is Matanza related to, Agent Webster?"

"I believe he's involved in the same case that Sanchez is. Or was."

Blake jammed his hands in the pockets of his baggy trousers. "It all sounds goddamn vague."

"Then I suggest you talk to my boss. You met him at my houseboat."

"I *know* where I met him. I'm accustomed to more cooperation from the feds than I've been getting from your little group, Agent Webster. Right now, with this goddamn explosion last night, my department is strained to the max. I don't have time for bullshit secrets."

Webster opened his hands, a gesture that indicated he was sorry, but . . . "I'm just doing my job and following orders, Sheriff."

"When you see Ms. Parrish, please tell her to call me. Everything was confusing last night when I got her statement and I'd like to speak to her again."

"Tell her yourself. She's at Carmela Perez's house. If you'll excuse us, please."

"Oh, one other thing," the sheriff said. "We found a scooter in the bushes, the kind with a little motor on the back. It was out of gas. We're assuming it belonged to Sanchez. We lifted prints off the handlebars."

"Thanks." So that was how Sanchez had gotten out of the woods and up here to the park, Webster thought as he and Moreno headed toward the area that had been cordoned off. *And then what'd he do?* Stretch out on the bench to take a nap? Damn unlikely. He glanced around and spotted a public phone on the other side of the parking lot. "Hey, Eric, go hit the redial on that phone."

"I'm one step ahead of you, amigo. The jogger made the last call to the Tango Key PD. I've already called Tango Bell about retrieving a list of calls made from this phone since eleven o'clock last night. They can't promise anything because some of their lines were damaged in the explosion."

"Sanchez called someone and was sitting on that bench waiting for the person to arrive."

"Yeah, I came to the same conclusion."

"How'd you hear about this so fast?"

"I came down here for a run and got here about the same time the cops did. I told them not to touch anything, went back for my car." He handed Webster a pair of gloves. "I've already videotaped the area and Vogel's on the way over here with forensics. Hey, you think Blake is in Hutchin's pocket?"

"No. I think he just sees us as intruders."

Sanchez lay on a bench that was up against a curve of trees, a newspaper covering his head, just as the police had found him. Webster walked around the bench once, noting the position of the body and the fact that Sanchez's shoes had a lot of dirt caked on the soles. He apparently had trekked a distance on foot before he'd turned on the scooter's motor. Webster checked his pockets, but they were empty, not even a wallet. He lifted the newspaper off his head and looked at the wound.

Clean, he thought. Sanchez probably had died as soon as the blade had gone in. Webster guessed the killer had opened the newspaper over his head so that the early morning joggers would figure he was a drunk, sleeping it off. He put the newspaper back over Sanchez's head and crouched to look under the bench. A dollar bill lay there, partially covered by leaves. Webster picked it up, smiling to himself. No wallet, but a bill.

"You thinking what I am?" Moreno asked.

"Sloppy staging. The guy was scared and tried to make it look like robbery was the motive."

Webster's thoughts suddenly leaped in a direction that seemed, on the surface, so over the top that he almost laughed out loud. But now that he'd thought it, he couldn't get the dual images out of his mind. Sanchez had been found with a newspaper over his head; Diane Jackson had been found with a pillow covering her face. It hardly qualified as an

MO, but perhaps there was some psychological reason for covering the victim's face.

Or the victim's eyes. In some weird and inexplicable way, it fit. It all fit.

Hutchin was an older man, just as Kit had speculated from the astrology charts, and probably made enough to afford the necklace and silver box. With his possible appointment for attorney general and the fact that he would be sitting on the bench for the Poulton trial, the urgency to cover his tracks must be enormous.

Big enough, Webster thought, to hire Sanchez to deter Kit from defending Poulton. In return, perhaps he had promised Sanchez something—getting off parole? That would explain the call to Sanchez's parole officer.

Sanchez, Webster guessed, had hired Matanza to do the dirty work and when Webster and Moreno had gone by his place last night, Sanchez had panicked, taken off, and then come here to call Hutchin for help. The surveillance tapes of Hutchin's home probably wouldn't show him leaving his house last night. He didn't have to go through his kitchen or his family room, where the cameras were located, to leave the house.

Webster figured that Sanchez had called Hutchin's cell phone, not his home phone, so forget having it on audio. But in a quiet house, in the dead of night, would the audio pick up a ringing phone? He would check Vogel's tapes. But even if the audio picked up the ringing, what did it prove? Nothing, a fat fucking zero. And even if Hutchin had type A-positive blood, like Diane Jackson's unborn child, and even if he were a Sagittarius—which Kit believed the "centaur" on the engraving referred to—he had *no proof,* not a shred of evidence that would stand up in court.

"Hey, Ben," Moreno called.

Webster realized he had walked off into the trees behind

the bench where Sanchez had died. He stopped and Moreno caught up with him and they started walking again. "This is one possible route the killer may have taken when he left the park," Webster remarked.

"Yeah. But you took off through here like someone had lit a fire under your shoes. What's up?"

If he told Moreno his wildly speculative conclusion, Moreno probably would laugh like hell. On the other hand, he needed Moreno's support and experience. "I'll explain on our way to Sanchez's place."

"We've already been inside."

"But not in daylight."

"Christ, Ben, we're not going to find anything."

"Probably not. But we need to take a look."

Through the ride into the preserve, Moreno listened without interruption to Webster's theory. And when Webster had finished, Moreno slapped his thigh and exploded with laughter. "That's the most outrageous bullshit I've ever heard. You're making leaps with nothing to connect them."

"But suppose it's true?"

"Good luck proving it."

"Put yourself in Hutchin's shoes, Eric. He's killed two people and he's under scrutiny by the feds because of a possible appointment that would be his professional coup. The pressure has got to be incredible. How can we crank up the heat a little more so that he'll do something really careless, something that leaves a trail?"

Moreno pressed his hands to his ears and shook his head. "Shit, I don't want to hear it. Last night I nearly get eaten by dogs, before the sun comes up I nearly get my ass fried in a fire, and now this morning the mark turns up dead on a bench. If we crank up the heat, no telling who he'll take down next."

Webster fell silent, mulling over a plan that was as vague

and undefined as the dirt road through the preserve. Now that he saw it in daylight, with sun filtering down through the immense trees, he wondered how the hell they'd gotten in and out of here without the Jeep breaking down. Eventually, the road widened somewhat and they reached Sanchez's spavined shack.

Shattered glass from the security light shimmered against the ground. Tire tracks marked the place where the Jeep had parked. Sanchez's old pickup looked abandoned. The whole place, Webster thought, looked abandoned. The front door stood open and they walked inside.

The eyes of the peacock feathers, which had sort of spooked him last night, now looked merely eccentric. Other than that, it was apparent that Sanchez had lived rather simply.

"I'll search the bedroom," Webster said.

"And we're looking for . . . ?"

"Hey, Eric, you don't have to buy my theory. Just humor me, okay? We're looking for anything that connects him— recently and personally—to Hutchin."

"Chill out, amigo. As fucked-up nuts as your theory is, it actually seems plausible to me."

Webster felt better after that, but only marginally. The longer he searched Sanchez's bedroom and makeshift study, the more apparent it became that he wouldn't find anything tangible that would connect Hutchin and Sanchez. The man's primary source of income had come from selling peacock feathers—at between twenty and fifty bucks a feather—to New Age shops in South Florida. Sanchez actually had kept good records, all by hand, in a handsome leather ledger. Webster glanced at the entries since the beginning of November, but didn't find any entry that looked suspicious. Of course not, he thought. That would be too goddamn easy.

His cell phone rang, an empty, hollow sound in the shack. "Webster."

"Vogel here. You on Tango?"

"Yeah. Why?"

"A chopper will be waiting for you and Moreno at the airport. We think we've located Matanza. He's under surveillance, but I'm not risking anything going wrong. You, Moreno, and I are going to bust this bastard and he's going to sing."

"We're on our way."

(2)

Early that afternoon, they were allowed into the war zone, as Kit came to think of it, the ruin of where she and Rita had spent their professional lives for the last ten years. The two of them, accompanied by Ryan, Abuelita, and Oro, picked their way through the debris, looking for anything that was whole or relatively undamaged. They found odds and ends, but nothing of value.

The insurance adjuster, who had already been out here and spoken to the police, had promised a speedy resolution to what usually was a long and tedious process. She and Rita had decided to rent office space down by the pier, which would give them a place to work until the insurance check arrived. Then they would decide where to relocate.

Once they were in the war zone, attorneys, clerks, and other courthouse employees stopped by to offer sympathy and, in some instances, food, as if for a wake. Even Paul Opitz did the compassionate thing—he came by with several employees and three grocery-store carts and helped them sift through the debris.

"I hear you know who's responsible for this, Kit."

They were at the rear of the destroyed building, where

part of the walls still stood, when Opitz said this. She wondered how much she should tell him, whether she should
say anything at all. But she didn't detect any hidden agenda
in this question. Opitz merely seemed curious. So she told
him basically the same thing she had told Sheriff Blake
when he had called her earlier today, about the Miami pursuit
and then about last night, how she'd caught Matanza in the
hall with a gas can. "There was a second man who tackled
me, but I never saw him. Frankly, I think they were hired by
someone who hopes to deter me from defending Poulton."

"Hey, I'm innocent," Opitz said with a laugh, hands
thrown up in front of him. "Honest."

She laughed, too, but added: "It's not your style. You'd
rather have a direct victory in court."

"I think that's a compliment, but I'm not sure."

"It is." She crouched and dug through ash and chunks
of concrete, and found a framed photograph of herself and
Pete, perfectly intact, even the glass unbroken. It had hung
in the staff room, in a montage of photos that her employees
had contributed of their own families. "Look at this," she
said softly, and held it up.

"Your brother," Opitz exclaimed. "That's weird."

To Kit, though, it was more than weird. It was as if Pete
had reached out across death to tell her something. But what?
What the hell was the message?

While she was crouched there, Ryan came over to show
her what he'd found, remnants from the gas grill that had
been on the outside deck. "What's that?" he asked, pointing
at the photo.

"An old picture of—"

"That's you and me," he said softly, his tone so adult
and serious that she rocked back on her heels and stared at
him. "When I was a writer and you were my sister. We

took that picture with a tripod and a time delay, right after I won a prize. Then I went away and came back as me.''

Kit reacted viscerally, at a level where language didn't exist. Tears surged in her eyes, she blinked to clear them, and struggled to find something to say to her son. *To bear witness:* wasn't that the term Dr. Luke had used? *Dear God, what am I supposed to do with this?* A normal mother would tell him he was imagining things. But she wasn't a *normal* mother, not in that sense, at any rate. ''What do you mean, hon?''

Benign enough, she thought, and ran her hands over her arms.

But the moment had passed. When he spoke, he was a kid again, on a treasure hunt in a field of ruin. ''Where should I put the stuff that I find, Mom?''

''In one of the grocery carts.''

He ran off and Kit gazed after him, those words, uttered in that serious, adult tone, bright and hot inside of her. *That's you and me. When I was a writer and you were my sister.*

Photos of Pete had been around her house and her parents' home for as long as Ryan had been alive. When Ryan referred to him, which wasn't often, he called him Uncle Pete or *your brother.* He knew that Pete had vanished, that he had won an important literary prize, and now, of course, he also knew that a woman had been in love with Pete. But he hadn't said anything of the sort this time. He had referred to Pete as *me.*

He tends his roses, just like Pete.

So what.

He's tidy and organized like Pete was.

Nope. Not enough.

Oro attached herself to Ryan from the day he came home from the hospital.

Well, yes, but retrievers love everyone.

He cried when he read the letter from Pete's lover.

That was tougher to dismiss. Ryan cried over the things kids usually cried about, but not like this, not by reading something. As both Abuelita and Webster had described it, the tears just spilled down his cheeks and he seemed completely surprised that he was crying.

Another detail that she couldn't dismiss concerned his knowledge of the photo itself, that it had been taken with a tripod and a time delay, right after Pete had won the Pulitzer. She couldn't recall having told him that. And if memory served her, he never had seen this particular photo. She had included it in the family collage only a few days ago and Ryan hadn't been in the staff room since his birthday in September.

It didn't prove anything. But . . . and right now it was a very big *but* . . . if it were true, it cast all the weird and disturbing incidents of the last eight days in an entirely different light and raised many troubling questions. Given that Ryan had such an immediate and intense dislike of Hutchin, she had to know the capacity in which Pete had known Hutchin. Given his apparent familiarity with the Schuller Museum, she needed to know more about the Schullers, who had owned it when Pete had been alive. And it made the woman on the bridge at Bahia Honda even more vital to her grasp of what the hell was going on.

The skeptic's path was too easy, too convenient. *Nope, it doesn't fit into my worldview, therefore it isn't true.* The tougher road was to investigate and draw no conclusion until the facts were in and the results were tallied.

"Hey, you okay?"

She glanced up at Opitz, standing in front of her with one of the grocery-store carts, and saw twin miniatures of herself reflected in his sunglasses. She looked like a wild woman, her hair a mass of frizz, her face devoid of any makeup, even lipstick. Worse, she apparently had walked the entire perimeter of the property while she'd been staring at the photo and thinking. She now stood at a corner in what had been the storage closet in her office. Only the concrete floor and a partial wall remained.

"I'm, uh, just wiped out, I guess."

Just fucked in the head, Paul. Over the top, Paul. And who were you in your most immediate past life? For that matter, who the hell was I?

Christ, she was losing it.

Now Opitz was asking her where he should put the stuff that he'd gathered and she told him to load it into one of the trash bags in the back of her van or in the trunk of the old Mercedes behind it. She knew that they chatted briefly about where she and Rita would locate for now and that her replies sounded rational. She realized, too, that for the time Opitz had been here sifting through the debris, their enmity had vanished. Their radically different views had been set aside for the moment. His humanity had come through. The problem, the good ole bottom line, was that she didn't understand what it meant. Her eyes ached, her chest ached, she needed sleep, order, specifics, answers, everything that, at the moment, seemed to be completely beyond her grasp.

And you were my sister.

(3)

Hutchin had done his best all day to avoid his wife. He had pulled weeds in the garden, cleaned the swimming pool, cleaned the files in his den. If Isabel was in the house, he went outside. If she was outside, he went inside. He simply couldn't be in the same space with her without seeing the sketch in his mind, that naked shoulder, the curve of her neck, that breast.

And every time the sketch popped into his head, his imagination ran with the rest of it, casting up images of Isabel posing naked for the anonymous artist, making love to him, sneaking away to be with him. So what if he had done the same thing with Diane; this was different. This was his *wife,* who was supposed to love him and stand by him through thick and thin, till death do us part. Somehow, when they'd talked about their infidelities the other night, it had been intellectually real, but not *emotionally* real, not like the sketch.

Around four, Isabel came out of the house in jeans and a cotton shirt, her purse slung over her shoulder. "I've got to run to the grocery store, Hutch," she called.

Finally, he thought, and didn't look up from the sprinkler head he was fixing. As soon as she left, he would dig up the knife and burn the journal and the appointment books. There would be time, plenty of time. Isabel always dawdled at the grocery store.

He waited for the sound of her car, but didn't dare look up to see what she was doing, what was holding things up. Suddenly, she stood there beside him. "Hutch?"

He glanced up at her, glanced slowly upward, from her delicate feet in the expensive brown sandals, to the exquisite ankles the artist had sketched with such precision and love, to the denim-clad legs and slender hips, to that tiny waist, those breasts, that throat, that face. But he couldn't see her face clearly. The sun burned against his eyes.

"What?"

"Is something bothering you?"

Wild, maniacal laughter bubbled up in his throat. *Bothering me? No, no, nothing's bothering me. I've killed two people and found out you weren't just fucking another guy, Isabel, you were involved with him in a full-blown affair.*

He winked an eye shut against the sun, shook his head. "Nope. Just tired."

She crouched in front of him, head cocked to one side. He saw her face clearly now, the soft, perfect blue of her eyes, the way she bit at her lower lip, the translucent quality of her skin. "So where'd you go in the middle of the night?"

The shadow at the window. He looked down at the sprinkler head. "I couldn't sleep and went for a drive." And because he knew she might seize on this and pick an argument, he changed the subject. "Why don't you pick up some fresh salmon and a bottle of wine? I'll toss the salmon on the grill."

The personal implication—that they would have dinner together this evening, at home—deflected her attention. "That sounds good. See you in a while."

She actually left this time, backing her Mercedes out of the driveway, driving up the street. Even so, he counted to sixty before he got up and ran into the yard and dug up the knife. He buried it at the bottom of a trunk in the attic, buried it under his daughter's baby clothes, photo albums, all sorts of memorabilia no one ever looked at.

Then he hurried back downstairs, retrieved Diane's journal and appointment book from his briefcase, and went into the garage for the metal box that contained the sketches. He carried everything into the backyard, dug a shallow hole, and tore several pages out of Diane's journal. He dropped the pages in the hole, held a lit match to them. They caught fire and he watched, mesmerized by the way the paper blackened and curled, by the rapidity with which the fire consumed the evidence.

He tore out pages from the appointment book, then the journal, alternating between one and the other, burning the paper in the hole. He was tempted to throw them both into the hole and set fire to the whole goddamn mess and be done with it. But the smoke would be too thick and might attract attention. So while these pages burned, he tore out the rest of the pages, and stacked them beside him, readying them for incineration. He opened the lid of the metal box and removed the top sketch.

When he looked at it this time, a strange dispassion clamped down over him. He was actually able to study the sketch, to dissect it, to see its beauty and talent separate from his wife, and couldn't resist looking at the other sketches, a dozen in all. The artist hadn't just captured Isabel in poses; he had captured her moods, her essence, her very soul. And in the act of creating the drawings, the artist had exposed the depth of his love for Isabel, a depth that astonished Hutchin, startled him, and ultimately filled him with sorrow because he never had loved her as this man had.

He couldn't burn these sketches.

He put them back into the metal box, latched the lid, tossed the rest of the journal pages into the hole. While they burned, he picked up the box, and carried it out onto the deck, where he and Isabel would have dinner later. He set it inside one of the large potted plants, leaves obscuring it from view. His hands lingered briefly against the box, against the cool metal, and that strange sorrow filled him again. Even in the best of times, he had not loved Diane the way the artist had loved Isabel.

Chapter 25

Carlos Matanza, the man who was Webster's only link to Rico Sanchez and, thus, his only very tenuous link to Hutchin, lived at the edge of Little Havana. The tidy little homes in the tidy little neighborhood had yards no larger than postage stamps, bars on the windows, and mostly wire-mesh fences that surrounded each family's slice of paradise.

As Webster and Moreno moved quickly up the street, both of them wearing bulletproof vests under their clothes, Webster caught the aroma of dinner in the air. Baked plantains, yellow rice and black beans, slices of buttery Cuban bread. Latin music drifted through the street. Kids played in the dusk of their tropical yards. Dogs barked, cats skulked through hedges, here one moment, gone the next.

They passed Vogel's van, empty now. He was covering the rear of the house, just in case Matanza tried to bolt. Webster felt strange, his body loose, rubbery, the vest too tight around his chest. He slid his hand into the pocket of his jacket, checking his weapon. He touched the radio clipped to the inside of his jacket pocket and in a low voice said,

"Bernie, it looks like the bogeyman is having dinner with the family. Over."

"Just holler if he does something weird. Over and out."

"Kids will be at the table," Moreno said.

Webster heard the trepidation in Moreno's voice. "Then it's less likely that he'll be armed and less likely that anyone will get hurt. Remember: he doesn't know that we know who he is. He probably doesn't even know that Rico is dead, since they haven't released the name of the guy found dead in the park. He's not expecting company."

Matanza's house looked like all the other houses they'd passed, a small concrete block place with a fenced yard, toys strewn across the grass, and a curved sidewalk running to the front door. The gate was open and so was the front door, Latino music pumping out loud and fast into the rapidly vanishing dusk. Two small kids, a boy and a girl, romped with a puppy in the front yard.

They walked through the gate and Moreno greeted the kids. *"Hola, niños. Carlos se encuentra?"*

"Sí, señor," the boy replied, and pointed toward the open door. *"Adentro."*

They moved up the sidewalk with the casual ease of friends arriving with food and wine and good music. The moment Webster reached the front steps, he could see into the smoky living room, where music and a TV vied for the Guinness record for volume. And there, sitting on the couch with his wife and an older couple, was Matanza, yukking it up, a beer bottle in one hand, a cigarette in the other.

"Buenas noches," called Moreno.

A pretty young woman got to her feet and started toward them. *"Sí? Puedo ayudarse?" May I help you?*

"Buscámos a Carlos." We're looking for Carlos.

"Carlito," she called. *"Sus amigos están aquí." Your friends are here.*

Matanza got up, obviously annoyed at the interruption, his eyes darting from the TV to them, then back and forth as he crossed the living room. He was a big man—not tall so much as broad, with wide, strapping shoulders and bulging biceps.

"*Sí?*" he said, frowning slightly, already wary.

Webster flashed his badge. "FBI. We'd like to ask you a few questions, Mr. Matanza."

His eyes flared with shock, panic. He glanced back at his family, then at Webster and Moreno. "I would prefer to speak outside." His English was perfect. In a softer voice, he added, "Away from my family."

"On the porch," Moreno said.

"*Carlito, qué pasa?*" asked his wife, coming up behind them.

"*Todo está bíen,*" Matanza replied. *Everything's okay.*

In a pig's eye, Webster thought.

As they stepped outside, Matanza moved with the speed of light, spinning on one leg while the other leg jackknifed and slammed into Webster's stomach. He stumbled back, air rushing from his lungs, and saw Moreno on the ground, writhing, struggling to rise, and Matanza racing past the two kids, headed for the street.

"Bogeyman's on the run," Webster shouted into his radio, and tore after him, his chest on fire.

Matanza moved like the wind, through the gate, the kids shouting after him, thinking it was some sort of game. He raced up the sidewalk, parallel to the street, and Webster pushed himself harder, harder, astonished that such a large, muscular man could run so fast.

As Matanza got close to Vogel's van, Vogel himself leaped out and slammed into him from the side, knocking him toward a row of hedges. His arms pinwheeled for balance, his feet seemed to do an erratic tap dance, then he crashed into the bushes, a giant going down.

(2)

Ryan didn't like the silence at the dinner table. His mother seemed really down and when she spoke at all, it was to ask someone to pass her something.

Even Abuelita didn't have much to say. Finally, as they were clearing the dishes, his mother said, "I've got to go out for a while, Ryan. But Abuelita will be here. You guys can stay here if you want or go over to Becky's. Her dad said either is fine with him. He'll be home all evening."

Ryan wasn't about to let his mother out of his sight now. "We'll go with you, Mom."

"Yeah," Becky agreed.

A look passed between his mother and Abuelita, a look that concerned him, he knew, and the way he had insisted all day on being with her. She leaned close to him, his mom did, and whispered, "Lighten up, Ryan. I'll be back before you go to bed. This is about work, not fun."

"You promise you'll be back before I go to bed?"

She leaned back, crossed her heart, and touched her finger to his mouth and then to hers, their solemn oath. He did the same and Becky exclaimed, "Hey, that's cool. Like a secret language or something."

"C'mon, let's get some snacks and go over to your house."

"Right now?"

"Yeah."

From the pantry, they helped themselves to snacks and boxes of Gatorade. Ryan went into his room for his backpack, stuffed things inside he thought he might need, then glanced around, certain he was forgetting something. He couldn't think of what that something might be, though, so he went back out into the kitchen. He hugged his mom.

"Check in around nine, *mí amor,*" Abuelita called after him.

"Okay, see you guys later."

He and Becky bounded down the stairs, Oro trotting after them. As soon as they were outside, Ryan headed over to the shed where they stored bikes, roller blades, his scooter, the kayaks. "I thought we were going to my house," Becky said.

"You have to do me a favor, Beck."

"I *knew* it. I *knew* something was going on."

"It's nothing bad," he said quickly, and explained as he checked the gas level in the little motor that went on the back of his scooter.

"Let me come, too."

"No, you've got to keep Oro at your house."

"She won't even go with me to my house unless you're there."

"I'll go over there so she'll follow us, then I'll leave. You have to call Abuelita at nine o'clock so she thinks I'm still there."

"So I have to lie."

"Forget it, she won't be watching the clock." He opened the rear door of the van and set his scooter on its side, behind the backseat. He covered it with a blanket and some beach towels and tossed in another blanket to pull over himself. He would be squashed, he thought, but he couldn't worry about that now.

Upstairs, he heard the shower running. His mom or Abuelita?

"Let's hurry. C'mon, Oro," and the dog ran after them as they went next door.

Ryan greeted Becky's dad, then they all went back into

Becky's room. He squatted down so he could look Oro in the eyes and held up his finger. "Stay, Oro. You have to stay with Becky for a while."

She whined and pawed the floor.

"Does that mean okay or forget it?" Becky asked.

"I don't know."

She opened the closet door and gestured Ryan over. "Go out the secret way, so my dad doesn't know." They crawled back into the deep closet, under Becky's clothes, across all the stuff on the floor. She shoved a laundry basket to one side, exposing a trapdoor in the floor. She unlatched it, pushed down on it, and it opened like a jaw, its hinged wooden ladder unfolding.

She hugged him. "Be careful, Ryan. Life would be pretty boring without you around here."

"Take care of my dog. And thanks." Then he scrambled down the ladder, dropped to the carport under her house, and gave the ladder a shove so that it folded and went up again. As he ran through her backyard toward the canal, where he could cross the seawall to his house, he heard Oro barking.

It was a tight fit in the well behind the van's backseat. He slid his pack under the backseat and lay on his side, with his legs drawn up against him. After five or ten minutes, he heard the screen door bang shut as his mother came outside. Moments later, the van pulled out into the road.

Ryan was grateful that his mother turned on the radio. It drowned out the noise he made when he stretched out his legs. He couldn't stretch them very far, though, because the scooter was in the way. He wished he hadn't brought the scooter now and wondered why he'd felt so certain that he should. His arm, folded under his head, went to sleep and he had to move again to stretch it out and then he didn't have anything to put his head on. So he had to bunch up part of his blanket and use it as a pillow, which left his head exposed. But at least he could breathe now. He could breathe and watch the lights flash past on the roof.

His mother's cell phone rang and she turned down the radio to answer it. Ryan kept very still, listening hard.

"Kit Parrish. . . . Hi, Rita. Yeah, I'm running a couple of errands. . . . Really? That's great. When did he talk to him? . . . Uh-huh. Did he give you any idea when we can expect the check? . . . After the new year. Well, what the hell. That's not so long. We'll start the new year in new offices. . . . Right, I'll talk to you later."

Errands, Ryan thought. She wasn't running errands, who was she kidding? She wouldn't have Abuelita stay at the house if all she was doing was running errands.

But even if it was nothing more than that, he was here, close to her, exactly where he was supposed to be.

(3)

He was grilling the salmon and Isabel was setting the table on the patio. Hutchin felt uneasy, tense, edgy. He kept going over everything that had happened last night, worried that he'd overlooked something, afraid that in his haste to get away from the park, he'd left something of himself behind. He went over every detail—from Sanchez's call to his arrival at the park to the long, terrible moments after he'd slid the knife into the back of Sanchez's neck—and he couldn't uncover anything that might connect the murder to him. The only possible weakness in all of it was whether Sanchez had told his hired guns the truth. *You do this for the hoodge.*

Isabel came up behind him and slipped her arms around

his waist. "Let's go somewhere for Thanksgiving, Hutch. You, me, and Barb. It's been a long time since the three of us have done anything together. We could book a cruise to the Caribbean. Or fly out to Aspen."

"Okay." That was the best he could muster, a lackluster *okay.*

Her arms slid away from him and he knew he'd hurt her. But she deserved it. She'd lied to him, she'd had an affair with the artist. Yes, he'd lied to her, too, but his affair with Diane had been different. He never had loved Diane. He'd been obsessed with her, consumed by her, but he hadn't loved her.

When the salmon was done, he put it on a plate and carried it over to the table. Isabel sat there, sulking and sipping at a glass of wine. "How big a piece do you want?" he asked.

"Small." She dished a dab of fruit salad and a bit of potato salad onto her plate and didn't bother with a slice of bread. "I've sort of lost my appetite."

He, of course, was supposed to ask why she'd lost her appetite and then she would give him a blow-by-blow description of how he'd avoided her all day and been cold and indifferent toward her. It would end with a blistering indictment of his moodiness. Thanks but no thanks. He refused to take the bait.

Hutchin sat down and a tense silence ensued, just as he'd expected. Isabel was entirely predictable, transparent, whereas Diane had been the exact opposite. He never had been able to predict anything Diane would say, do, need, or demand. Finally, Isabel blurted, "Hutchin, what the hell is going on?"

He thought, suddenly, of a dormant volcano he'd seen years ago in Mexico. He and Isabel had climbed to the rim, and when he'd peered down over the edge, into the bottomless cone, he could think of nothing else but the mounting pressure deep inside that volcano that would one day blow away the floor of the cone and spew out ash, fire, heat, lava. It had made him so dizzy that he'd wrenched back and Isabel had pulled him away from the rim.

He felt like that now, the mounting pressure fed by so many unforeseen complications and the savage heat of his own terror of discovery. If the tectonic plates in his life shifted once more, he would blow.

"Hutch? Did you hear what I said?"

He got up and went over to the potted plant where he'd put the metal box earlier. He brought it back to the table, dropped it in front of her. "I guess you could say this is what's bothering me, Isabel." He unlatched it, flipped open the lid, grabbed the top sketch, slapped it flat on the table. "This wasn't just a quick fuck and good-bye. This was an affair."

He stepped back then, his heart hammering, his palms sweaty, his breathing hard and labored, as if he'd been running, and he looked at her. Isabel said nothing. She simply stared at the sketch, one hand against it, the breeze flapping at the corners. "I . . . I . . ." she stammered.

"Truth or consequences, Isabel." His voice held the mockery of her same words that night at the Hilltop. *Truth or consequences, Hutch. Remember when we used to play that game?*

"I don't want to play any goddamn games." She tossed her napkin on the table, pushed to her feet. "We're all guilty of something. Isn't that what you said to me, Hutch? Well, okay, so I'm guilty of an affair. So are you. We both lied. We both were involved with other people—not fucking them, not just playing around, we were *involved*."

"Who was he?"

"Who was *she?*"

"It's not the same thing."

"*What?*" Isabel exploded with laughter. "What kind of macho bullshit is *that?* Of course it's the same thing."

"It isn't. You strayed first."

She rolled her eyes, pacing now, so enraged that her body seemed to shake. "Yeah? And just how the hell would you know *that?*"

"Because I know."

"Because you know." She spat the words, stopped pacing, and faced him. "So who was she, Hutch? Or maybe the tense is wrong. Maybe I should say, who *is* she?"

"No one you know." He didn't want to go there. "No one you would even want to know."

"You'd be surprised at the people I know."

"Like artists."

"Oh, fuck off. You don't have any idea what you're talking about."

"So enlighten me, Isabel. Give me a name."

"It works both ways. You give *me* a name."

They glared at each other, neither of them willing to go first. Isabel threw up her hands. "Impasse." She marched over to the counter that ran under the pass-through window to the kitchen, and opened a drawer. When she turned, he saw that she held a tablet of paper and two pens. "Since neither of us wants to go first, let's write down the names at the same time."

She slapped the tablet and pens on the table, and glared at him again, daring him to rise to the challenge. A thick, almost crippling fatigue seized Hutchin. "Forget it. Just fucking forget it. I don't give a shit who he was. Is. Whatever."

He turned away from her, squeezing the bridge of his nose, fighting the mounting pressure in his head.

"Don't turn your goddamn back on me," she shouted.

"His name was Pete. Pete Beaupre. Is that what you want, Hutch? A name? Okay, there's his name. His goddamn name."

Beaupre. Jesus. Pete Beaupre. He pressed his fists into his eyes and pressed so hard that black stars exploded inside his lids. He was dimly aware of Isabel crying, sobbing, and that she waited for him to say something—*a name, she wants a name*—and that Diane's name was rolling down his tongue, begging to be spoken, to be acknowledged, but just then the front gate clattered open.

He and Isabel glanced around simultaneously, both of them surprised that the gate wasn't locked. Kit Parrish stood there, wearing jeans, a cotton shirt, a lightweight jacket. It was as if Beaupre himself had arrived and Hutchin glanced quickly at Isabel. His wife stood there with her mouth open, the blood draining from her face.

"Sorry to barge in like this," Kit said.

Hutchin's ears rang. Neither he nor Isabel had said a word, but Kit didn't seem to notice. She came right over and stopped several feet from Hutchin. "I find it disturbing, Jay, that you observed my client last night through a one-way window while he was spouting off his theories about who killed Diane Jackson. I think it's proper at this point to request that you recuse yourself from the Poulton case. If you don't do it willingly, I'll go through legal channels."

Her gall shocked him. Just who the fuck did she think she was, anyway? "Your client said nothing to incriminate himself and I have no intention of recusing myself from the Poulton case."

Before Kit could reply, Isabel burst out with, "After the scene your son created at the motel the other night, Ms. Parrish, you should be here apologizing to Jay, not accusing him of something. Get off our property."

When Kit replied, she sounded angry. "This isn't your business, Isabel."

"It most certainly is. You're accusing Jay of what amounts to unethical behavior."

Kit dismissed Isabel by just looking away from her and turning her fierce eyes on Hutchin. "Then I'm going through legal channels and I intend to note that you threatened my son that night at the motel."

The tectonic plate deep inside of him shifted and the pressure that had mounted steadily and unbearably for the last eight days suddenly blew, vomiting the human equivalent of ash, fire, and lava—rage. "Just a goddamn minute," he snapped, and lunged for her, grabbed the back of her jacket, and jerked her around so fast that one of her loafers came off. Then he struck her in the stomach with his fist. She gasped, her eyes bulged in their sockets, and she doubled over, struggling for air. Before she could run, he brought his fist up and hit her in the jaw.

She stumbled back, tripped, and fell to the patio floor, bleeding from the mouth, her face ashen with disbelief, her breathing ragged. Her feet moved, one shoe on, the other off, and she pushed along the ground on her butt, trying to find the purchase or the strength to rise. Hutchin moved toward her, his rage consuming him, just as it had the night he'd held the pillow over Diane's face.

And when he was almost on her, she shot to her feet and swung her purse. It hit him in the side of his face and he pitched to the right, pain singing along his jaw, and the purse arched through the air and crashed to the ground just beyond him, spewing its contents. Kit lurched toward the gate and music suddenly blared, Mick Jagger singing that he couldn't get no satisfaction, the volume so high it swallowed Kit's screams.

For seconds, Hutchin couldn't imagine where the music

came from, then his wife shot past him, quick as light. He had completely forgotten about her, about Isabel, but now she hurled herself at Kit and slammed into her so hard that she knocked her flat.

Kit sprawled on the ground, maybe moaning, maybe unconscious, maybe dead, he couldn't tell, and Isabel didn't give a shit. She kicked Kit in the side, kicked as Jagger belted out what had passed for music in the sixties, her face contorted with a rage that perfectly reflected his own and that he knew was directed at Beaupre, her long-lost lover, and at Hutchin himself, her treacherous husband.

Hutchin, still dazed from the blow to the side of his head, ran over to her, grabbed her arm, and jerked her away from Kit. "Stop," he hissed. "Stop it."

Isabel wrenched her arm free and stood there, breathing hard, staring down at Kit. Then she slipped a remote control from her pocket and aimed it at the French doors, shutting off the music. She spat, "Bitch. She and her brother, the two of them ..." She looked up at Hutchin then, tears glistening in her eyes. "I ... I never loved him, Hutch," she whispered. "You were working all the time, I got lonely, I ..."

He pulled his wife against him, holding her tightly, clutching her, whispering, "I'm sorry, I'm sorry, I'm sorry. . . ."

He didn't know how long they stood like that, holding on to each other like two people on a raft that was losing air fast. Isabel broke the embrace first. "We have to get her out of here," she whispered.

"Her hands. Get her hands." Hutchin grabbed Kit's feet. "Let's carry her to the side of the house. She's too visible here."

"Her van's out on the street. We have to move it."

They carried her to the side of the house, then Isabel ran in to get duct tape. A pall of unreality clamped down over

Hutchin. How had this happened? And who was this woman
his wife had become? Not once had she screamed or tried
to stop him when he had hit Kit. She, in fact, had become
an accomplice in every way, a shocking revelation. It was
as if the abruptness of their combined rage had stripped
away every mask they had worn for the twenty-five years
they'd known each other. Only a while ago, he had thought
how predictable Isabel was, how transparent. Now he realized how unfair and glib that assessment had been.

Hutchin patted down Kit's jeans, just as he had done with
Sanchez. This time, though, he was searching for keys, not
a wallet. Her wallet lay in the mess that had fallen out of
her purse. He checked her pulse, two fingers against the
carotid. Fast, erratic. With luck, she would die on her own
and he and Isabel would be spared what looked inevitable
right now.

Isabel returned with the duct tape. Kneeling in the grass,
she cut off a piece that she pressed over Kit's mouth. They
turned her onto her stomach, pulled her arms behind her,
and taped her wrists together and did the same to her ankles.

"Where should I take her van?" Isabel whispered over
Kit's motionless body. "We can't leave it out there."

"We have to gather up everything in her purse and get
her out of here, off our property."

"To where? Take her where, Hutch? We can't just dump
her somewhere and hope she dies. It's gone well beyond
that."

Here they were, he and his wife, whispering over the body
of a woman they had just beaten up, conspiring about how
to kill her. They had no other choice, none, zip, zero, so
now they would do what they had to do and they would
both take the secret to the grave.

"Get the stuff that fell out of her purse. Make sure the

cell phone is off. I'm going to put her in the Beemer's trunk.''

"We should bring the van in here and put her in the back.''

"Too many steps. We can transfer her body later. You follow me.'' He pressed Kit's car keys into his wife's hand, then took her hand in both of his own and pressed it to his cheek.

"Let's hurry,'' she said softly, urgently. "Let's get this over with.''

Chapter 26

Too long, Ryan thought. It was taking too long.

He pressed the button that lit up the face of his watch. It was ten of nine. His mother had been inside the house for half an hour and except for a loud blast of music from the house, he hadn't heard anything. She wouldn't leave the house tonight just to visit a friend and probably not to visit a client, either. Not after everything she'd been through in the last twenty-four hours. So this trip, this visit, had to be important. So important, he thought, that his mother had told Rita a white lie—that she was running errands.

But this wasn't any errand. He threw off the blanket and sat up. Ryan pressed his face to the glass. He couldn't see anything, the bushes were in his way. He climbed over the seats to the front. The passenger window was halfway down, but he had a clearer view of the dark patio.

No music now.

He didn't see anything at all, in fact.

He considered getting out and going up to the gate and calling for his mother. But as soon as he thought it, the

Other came alive, screaming inside of him, screaming, *No, too dangerous, forget it, bad idea.* Ryan pressed his hands over his ears and squeezed his eyes shut, fighting back. The voice stopped and he opened his eyes again.

Now he saw shapes moving in the darkness, coming around the side of the house. The garage door went up, the light inside came on, and he saw a man and a woman carrying someone into the garage. He knew immediately that someone was his mother and that she wasn't moving.

Tears scorched his eyes, his hand slammed down over the handle to open the door, but it was locked. He jerked his hand away and sank down in the seat, hands covering his mouth to keep his sobs from exploding out of his mouth. *Stupid, that was stupid. You won't help her by letting those people know you're here. You'll get your chance.*

He didn't know if the thought belonged to him or the Other and he didn't care. He ran his arm across his eyes, took a couple of deep breaths, and dared to look again. The garage light had gone off, but the car's trunk lid was open, the light on, and the man and woman were putting his mother inside the trunk.

She'll suffocate. Oh God, she's going to suffocate. Or she'll freak. She hates tight spaces.

The lid shut. Without the lid, there was no light. He still hadn't seen the man's or the woman's face. But he had seen enough.

He scrambled over the seats again, to the well, where his cell phone was. He punched out Ben's number at the houseboat. It rang three times before a machine picked up. At the beep, he whispered, "Ben. Ben, help me." His voice broke and he cried as he finished his message. "Old Town, it's in Old Town, at . . ." The phone suddenly went dead.

He hadn't charged it up last night at Abuelita's. But he had another battery in his pack. He unzipped it, his hands shaking, his fear so deep he couldn't think straight. He kept digging, digging, digging, but he couldn't find the battery. It was the thing he had forgotten to pack.

Ryan shoved the dead phone down into his pack and climbed over the seats again, praying that his mother had left her cell phone in the car. As soon as he slid over the front seat, he knew she'd taken it with her. It wasn't plugged into the cigarette lighter, wasn't resting on the dash, wasn't anywhere. He sank down in the seat and moved to the passenger window again. He poked his head up.

One shape was crouched near the pool, there was enough light from the pool to see the figure. The woman, yes, it was the woman. Ryan couldn't see what she was doing. But he knew he didn't have much time.

He climbed into the middle seat and flicked the button that controlled the van's inside lights. Now they wouldn't come on when he opened the back of the van to get out his scooter. He needed to get someplace for help. But where? One of the houses across the street? He would bang on the door and scream for help. Better yet, he would start screaming for help as soon as he was outside of the van, where they wouldn't catch him.

But it was Saturday night and this didn't look like a neighborhood with kids in it, which meant that the people who lived in these houses had gone out for the night. This was Key West, where everyone went out on the weekends. Everyone except the people his mother had gone to see.

He would ride the scooter to the first public phone he saw. He would call Ben's cell phone this time. His cell phone was always on, hadn't he said that to Ryan once? But what if a public phone was two or three blocks away? By the time he got to the phone, talked to Ben, and came back, they might be gone, his mother in the trunk of their car and Ryan without a clue about where they had taken her.

I can't leave.

"Think, think," he whispered to himself, pressing his fists against his forehead.

The spare key. Of course. His mother always had a spare key hidden under the wheel well on the driver's side. When they left, he would get the spare key and follow them. He knew what to do in a car. Put the key in the ignition, give it a little gas, and keep the wheels straight. Gas pedal on the right, brake on the left. Sure, he had sat in his mother's lap a zillion times, steering the car while his mother's feet worked the pedals. No problem, except that his feet wouldn't reach the pedals. Even if he piled the blankets under him, so that he could see out the window, he knew his legs wouldn't reach the pedals.

He raised up to look again.

The car was backing out of the garage and the woman—yeah, it was definitely the woman, he could see her in the backwash of light from the garage—now hurried toward the gate. Toward the street. Toward him.

Ryan dropped to the floor of the van, slid his pack under the blankets, then flattened out as flat as he could and slipped under the seat. A spring or something dug into one shoulder and the seat didn't cover his entire body. He couldn't turn onto his side and pull his legs up against his chest, there wasn't enough room. He managed to angle his legs out toward the blankets and somehow got his feet under it. He had no way of telling if the blanket covered his legs, but it was too late to worry about it. Too late because the woman opened the driver's door and got in.

Moments later, the van pulled away from the curb.

(2)

For three hours now, they had been at Matanza, grilling him, interrogating him, trying to break him down. First Vogel, then Moreno, now Webster. The room where they sat was in the Bureau's Miami office, a small, windowless room still thick with smoke from Moreno's endless cigars. Webster had a file in front of him, ammo they hadn't used yet because it had just come in from the Key West office.

"I don't know who the fuck hired Rico. He didn't tell me, okay? I keep telling you that." He was practically shouting. "Look, man, I'm entitled to one call and you bastards haven't let me make it yet. You're violating my civil rights."

"Make your call." Webster set a phone in front of him. "But you won't get bond, Matanza. This involves arson, murder . . ."

Matanza's hand was already on the phone when he glanced up, eyes darkening. "Murder? Whose murder?"

Webster opened the file and removed the first photo. He dropped it in front of Matanza. "Sanchez took a knife through the back of the neck last night."

Matanza stared at the picture of Sanchez sprawled on the coroner's slab, his skin the color of Elmer's Glue.

Webster dropped another three photos next to this one, all of them from Kit's video taken in Miami yesterday. "So what was the deal, Matanza? Were you supposed to harm her? Scare her? What was the point of the chase?"

His voice sounded soft and beaten when he replied. "Scare the shit outta her, that's what Rico said."

"And that included burning down her office building?"

He rubbed his hand across his eyes. "Shit, man."

"The guy who killed Sanchez is going to be looking for you next, Matanza. And you'll never know how it's going to happen. Or when. So if I were you, I would think back very carefully and try to remember Sanchez's exact words to you. There may be something in what he said that will make sense to me.''

For the first time in the hours they'd been here, Matanza seemed to have some rudimentary understanding of the gravity of his situation. He frowned, rubbed his eyes again, leaned back in his chair. ''He called me very early Friday morning.''

''How early?''

''Five, six, the sun had barely come up. He said, *''Epa, amigo, quiere un trabajo?''*

''In English.''

''Do you want a job? I told him it depended on the pay. One thousand, he said. So yeah, I'm interested in a job for one thousand tax-free dollars and what do I have to do? Rico said, 'You have to scare the shit outta a gringa lawyer. The hoodge wants her to be distracted from her lawyering. No killing, just scaring, maybe some damage to her property. . . .' So Rico gave me all the information and I was waiting outside her office that morning and followed her and another woman to the airport. I had to find out the gringa's flight plan and then I had to hire a plane to get to Miami and have a friend meet me there.'' He paused. ''I won't tell you the name of my friend so don't ask.''

''I don't give a rat's ass about your friend. Go on.''

''So we follow the two gringas to Miami Beach and she gets me on tape and I had to chase her to get back the tape and then I was pissed, okay? I was pissed that I didn't get the tape. So that night I set fire to her building. But I didn't know she was in there. I swear, I didn't know she was. And my friend, he . . . he shouldn't have knocked her out. I told him, no killing, no death.''

Webster mulled this over for a moment. "What did Rico mean by 'the hoodge'?"

Matanza shrugged. "I don't know. Rico talked with a bad accent."

Hoodge, hoodge, hoodge. This was the game he and his sister had played as kids. *Sounds like . . .* Hoodge: foodge, moodge, soodge, toodge, groodge. No, no, no, no, and no.

In Spanish, *H* is silent and the only letter in Spanish that sounds like the English *H* is *J*. "Joodge," he said quietly, to himself. "Joodge, joodge, joodge. Jesus." He shot to his feet so fast that his chair toppled and crashed to the floor. "Matanza, given Rico's bad accent, what English equivalent could *hoodge* be?"

Matanza's mouth moved silently for a moment, then he said, "Judge. It could be judge."

Webster raced from the room.

(2)

Hutchin's mind no longer scrambled for answers, a plan, a strategy. His stomach no longer churned. He no longer felt like puking. Between the time that Kit had shown up and now, he had stopped fighting who and what he was. He had done what he had to do with Diane, with Rico, and now. Any man in his situation would do the same thing.

Good and evil were simply perspectives and society had drawn an imaginary boundary between them. Laws had been created that supported and helped define the consensus beliefs about what was good and what was evil. Things that didn't fit neatly into these definitions were relegated to the vast wasteland between those boundaries where most people lived their lives. The problem with these boundaries was that they were arbitrary. They didn't take into account what to do when *shit happens.*

He aimed his Beemer toward the bridge that crossed to Tango Key and glanced in the rearview mirror. The van was back there, his wife at the wheel. As long as they didn't hit traffic or get stopped by a cop, they would be fine, they would pull this off. Sometime tomorrow, Kit's van would be found abandoned in the hills on Tango and her body would wash up on shore. The authorities would call it suicide and blame it on the explosion that had devastated her office.

But the spot had to be perfect. The area around Pirate's Cove had some of the highest spots on the island, but the cove was heavily populated during the tourist season. Too risky. The hills were probably the better bet. They were isolated, wild, and the cliffs, which ran for nearly two miles along a ridge, were probably 150 feet high at their highest point. High enough, he thought, so that a body pushed over the edge of the cliff would plunge in a free fall, perhaps hitting the jutting variegated rocks on the way down.

He knew that a decent man would feel some regret that it had come to this with a woman who had been one of his brightest criminal law students so many years ago. But he felt no regret, no sorrow, nothing at all except a kind of gnawing urgency to get it all over with fast so that he could move on with his life. The irony struck him, of course, that Kit's brother had been Isabel's lover.

Had it ended before Beaupre had disappeared? He would have to ask her.

No, forget that. If he asked her that, she would ask the name of *his* lover and then the situation might slide into madness again, as it had for a few moments out there on the patio. No, it all ended here, tonight. He and Isabel would bury their ugly secrets and move on to DC.

As he started across the bridge, he heard a thump in the trunk. He couldn't tell if Kit's body had shifted or if she had come around. Either way, she wouldn't be able to escape the trunk. Either way, she was already dead.

(3)

Kit's eyes opened into darkness, a total, suffocating darkness. She immediately sensed that the space was very small, tight, sealed, and that wherever she was seemed to be moving. *A car, I'm in the trunk of a car.* With this realization, an intense and powerful wave of claustrophobia swept over her.

She squeezed her eyes shut, struggling against a panic that would crush her if it found full expression. She drew air in through her nostrils and exhaled it slowly, in and out, in and out, over and over again until she had established a rhythm that took the edge off. Only then did she allow herself to take inventory of her physical condition.

She lay on her side, hands taped behind her, ankles taped, mouth taped. Her body felt bright with pain, battered and raw, but her terror was greater than the pain and for long moments, the terror seized her so completely that it numbed her pain and paralyzed her mind.

Tears sprang into her eyes and the physical sensation, the heat and wetness of the tears, shocked her out of the paralysis. If she started crying, her nose would get stuffed up. If her nose got stuffed, she wouldn't be able to breathe. If she couldn't breathe, she would die. Nothing could be simpler or more basic than that.

Hutchin and his wife had taped her up like a package and tossed her in the trunk of a car. She felt the car's movement, heard the tires racing over ridges in a road—no, the Tango Bridge. It had to be the bridge.

She rubbed her wrists together as fast as she could, which wasn't very fast, trying to break the tape, loosen it, to get a hand free. But it was futile. The tape was wound too tightly or she was too debilitated or both. It felt like duct tape, thick and sticky, pulling at the tiny hairs on her wrists every time she moved her hands. It was easier to work with her ankles, which were stronger, larger, and didn't hurt to move.

First, she moved her legs up and down, as though she were on a bicycle, so her ankles rubbed counterpoint to each other. Since she was lying on her left side, her right leg was on top and she tried to lift it up, hoping it would strain the tape. She repeated this several times while the van sped over the Tango Bridge.

Then suddenly the bridge ended. She knew it because the sound the tires made against the road changed. No ridges and bumps now, just the smooth glide of rubber over asphalt. The car turned right, then stopped.

For a light? Let it be a stoplight. Please.

In moments, she knew she would feel the slow ascension into the Tango hills. Was that their destination? Or did Hutchin and his wife plan to get rid of her somewhere else? *And how will they do it?* A shot through the back of the head and a gentle shove off a cliff? Or maybe Hutchin would suffocate her first, as he'd done to Diane. Because, of course, he had been Diane's older lover, Hutchin the Sagittarian—the centaur who had given her the silver box.

No wonder he had gone to the jail last night. He'd wanted to see his competition up close. No wonder he had taken such umbrage over Ryan's outburst at the hotel. Even though Webster hadn't connected Hutchin to Diane, at least not that she knew about, his instincts about Hutchin had been right.

And Ryan, she thought, squeezing her eyes shut against a surge of emotion. Ryan had been right about Hutchin, too. Ryan or Pete: how did that fit into the picture? How? Had Hutchin killed Pete? If so, why?

Later, think about it later.

Her anger gave her strength and she began working her ankles again, her wrists, back and forth, one then the other. And in the back of her mind, she screamed for Abuelita to call Webster and for Webster to figure it out in time. But in the event that neither thing happened, she needed to do what she had always done, prepare for her own defense.

She wiggled her body back farther into the trunk, fighting her mounting claustrophobia, her fingers feeling around for something sharp. Although she had limited mobility in her hands, she found that by stretching her arms out to their full length, she could sweep her fingers across a larger area of the trunk's floor. Working against the inexorable ticking of a clock in her head, she kept maneuvering her body this way and that, sweeping the area with her fingers, then maneuvering again until she touched something.

Kit couldn't tell immediately what it was. The curve of a spare tire? The spine of a large book? No, it felt like leather. Small enough to move. She grasped it with her fingers, got it into her left hand so that her right fingers could explore it. A strip of metal with tiny ridges. *A zipper, it's a zipper.* She pinched the end piece between her thumb and forefinger and slowly worked it down. When the opening was large enough to slide her fingers inside, they greedily explored this new terrain, defining shapes, texture, length, width. She suddenly realized this was a tool kit, a small, portable tool kit.

The car was on the move again, that clock in her head kept ticking, ticking, and her fingers twitched and fumbled, looking for something sharp. She found what felt like a screwdriver, a flat-edge screwdriver, and worked it out of the kit—then lost her grip on it when the car turned again. She had to wiggle her body forward once more to maneuver her hands close enough to the floor so her fingers could make their sweep.

She grasped the handle of the screwdriver with her left hand and tried to press the end up through the tape, but because she was right-handed, it was too awkward. So she transferred it to her right hand, clasped it tightly. She stabbed at the tape, poked at it, ran it across the tape like a knife. It seemed that the pressure eased, but maybe that was her imagination. She had to pause now and then because the strain woke up the pain in her body.

Then the car stopped again and her breath caught in her chest, waiting for it to start moving again. *Please, please, a little more time, that's all I need.*

The car's motion resumed, but on a rougher road. They were in the Tango hills now, she thought. On a dirt road. *Fast, c'mon, you can do it.*

(4)

She played the radio while she drove and a good thing, too, Ryan thought, because it covered the noise he made as he squirmed under the rear seat to the middle section of the van. He managed to move his pack along with him and now he fitted it onto his back and lay almost flat against the floor. Something dug into his right hip.

He finally moved it out from under him and saw that it was his mother's purse. *With a cell phone inside it.* He fit the strap over his neck, so he wouldn't lose his grasp on it. The purse smelled like her, the scent thickening in his nostrils, and brought such a pure, white rage into his heart that he suddenly shot up from where he was and slapped his hands over the woman's eyes and clawed at her face.

She screamed and fought him with one hand while trying to drive with the other. The car swerved violently to the left, the right, the tires shrieking, the woman grunting, panting, screaming, scratching him, trying to grab his hair, his clothes, something. Ryan grabbed her by the hair and jerked her head back, shouting, "Bad, you're bad, you hurt my mom, you're bad!"

And suddenly the woman's arms flew up and locked around his head, jerking him into the front seat, practically into her lap. The car careened off the road, gravel pinging against the sides, and Ryan was thrown back against the passenger door. His pack must have hit the lever exactly right because the door suddenly swung open.

Just then, the woman slammed on the brakes and the door swung inward again, out again, and he scrambled for freedom. The woman grabbed his leg, hissing like a snake. "You're not going anywhere, you little shit."

He kicked her with his left leg, her grip loosened, and then his shoe came off and Ryan slid to the ground, into the leaves, stunned, but not hurt, shocked but not so shocked that he couldn't run. And run he did, into the trees, the darkness, into the smell and noises of the woods, one shoe on, the other gone, his mother's purse banging against his chest and stomach.

Phone, get the phone.

He dug out his mother's cell phone as he ran deeper into the trees. He heard them behind him, the man and the woman, people whose faces he had yet to see, and he wondered if he could circle around and get back to the car where his mother was. Maybe, he thought. Maybe.

He tripped once and sprawled in the leaves, the phone still clutched in his hand. He rolled, got to his feet, and heard their voices, closer now. Ryan pressed up against the trunk of a tree, breathing hard, and turned on the phone. He punched out Ben's cell number.

Please answer, please, please.

"Webster."

Ryan heard the drone of engines on Ben's end of the phone "Ben, it's me," Ryan whispered.

"Ryan, what—"

"Tango Key," he whispered. "They have Mom in the trunk of a car, I got away, I'm in the woods. In the Tango hills somewhere. They're after me. Come, come fast."

"Ryan, stay on the line, don't hang up. I need a landmark."

A landmark. Trees and more trees. He heard the man and woman off to his left, very close. They weren't talking, but they made a lot of noise crashing through the brush. He didn't dare speak. But he couldn't risk not speaking, either. "Have to climb," he whispered. "They're too close. Won't disconnect."

He dropped the phone into his mother's purse, grabbed on to the lowest branch, and pulled himself up, up into the folds of leaves, the forks of branches, and then he went still, eyes fixed on the darkness below.

A few moments later, they passed right under him. Ryan clung to the branches, motionless, afraid even to breathe too hard for fear they would look up. A strange feeling went through him, like electricity or maybe heat, and he realized he knew the man. It was that judge his mother had introduced him to, Judge Hutchin. *You. I hated you. Jay will pay, Jay must pay. . . .* He still didn't understand why he had said those things that night at the hotel, but he understood the emotion behind the words because the same emotions bubbled up inside him now.

I hated you from the start.

Curiosity killed the cat.

The words that drifted through him belonged to the Other, but belonged to him, too, in a way he couldn't quite grasp. He got dizzy watching them, Hutchin and his wife, and thinking thoughts that were his but not his, or was it the other way around? He shut his eyes and pressed back harder against the branch, afraid that he would get so dizzy he would fall. If he fell, he would be useless to his mother.

When he opened his eyes again, they had moved away from the tree, but he could hear them still, somewhere off to the left. He needed to get down and circle around to the other car before they left the woods. He had to get down *now*.

He climbed down to the lowest branch, his bare foot scratched and bleeding, then he dropped to the ground. Leaves crunched as he landed. Twigs snapped. He didn't think they could hear it, not over the noise of crickets and frogs, and he didn't stick around to find out. He crept away from the tree, his heart hammering, his hands slick with sweat, and pretty soon he was running, he had to get to his mother, to the car, before they did.

He burst out of the trees and stopped dead. There, on the other side of the road, sitting in the starlight like some little enchanted stone house, was the Tango Museum. He didn't know why Hutchin and his wife had come here. But he now had a landmark for Ben.

Ryan crouched at the edge of the trees, got out the cell phone, and realized he'd been disconnected. He punched out Ben's number again and it barely rang before Ben said, "Where are you, Ryan?"

"The Tango Museum. Oh God, please hurry."

He turned off the phone and ran along the edge of the trees, his senses so sharp that he could smell his own fear. He ran at a crouch. The car stood right in front of him, parked off to the side of the road, the driver's door wide open. He ran over to it, praying the judge had left the keys in the ignition, but he hadn't. Somewhere in here, though, there had to be a button or a latch that would unlock the trunk. He finally found it, down near the floor, and pulled up on it.

He ran to the rear of the car and suddenly the trunk's lid sprang open and his mother lay there, breathing hard, her legs taped together and still in the air from having kicked the lid. Her mouth was taped shut and something terrible had happened to the side of her face. It was swollen so badly that one of her eyes had nearly shut. She started to cry when she realized it was Ryan and tried to talk through the tape. Ryan peeled it off and she gasped and sucked at the air and sobbed and in between her sobs she whispered his name. He saw that it wasn't just the side of her face that was swollen, but her lips, too.

"Sssh, they're in the woods. We have to get out of here fast. Let me get your legs first."

"In my hands." Her words sounded slurred, thick.

Ryan reached behind her and took the screwdriver that she clutched. With the flat edge of the screwdriver, he sawed at the duct tape around her ankles, sawed and stabbed at it, again and again, until the tape finally gave way. He had to help her out of the trunk. She didn't seem to have the strength to do it on her own. When she stood straight up, she was shaky and he could tell she was as scared as he was.

"Hide, have to hide," she murmured.

"Your hands, let me get your hands."

He stabbed at the duct tape a couple of times and it, too, gave way, and they hurried across the road, toward the museum, their hands clutched together.

"I . . . I can't move fast," she said, and pressed a hand to her ribs.

Ryan tightened his grasp on her hand. "I'll help you. We have to get outta here."

They hurried past the old gate, across the front grounds. The museum was locked up for the night, but Ryan knew if they could get inside and remain hidden long enough, Ben would get here. He didn't think his mother could run very far. She had trouble even now, stumbling, weaving, her every step causing her so much pain that she gasped.

Just before they reached the building, Hutchin and his wife exploded from the woods and raced toward them. Ryan grabbed his mother's arm and pulled her forward, urging her to run fast, faster. They made it to the porch. Ryan grabbed one of the heavy glass ashtrays on a wicker table and hurled it at the window to the right of the door.

It crashed through the glass, triggering an alarm. He kicked out the rest of the glass, spun to get his mother, but she had sunk into one of the old green Adirondack chairs. "Get in there fast. Hide. Give me the screwdriver."

"But I don't want to—"

"Go!"

He thrust the screwdriver at her and whipped around, climbed through the window, and headed for the spiral staircase. He would hide in the room at the top . . . no, not there, where he would have only one way out. He darted across the room to the soft glow of an EXIT sign at the other end. Memories flickered way at the back of his mind, memories of this building as it used to be.

In the time before, there had been a door, but no exit sign—and no fire alarm.

Ryan paused long enough at the door to break the glass on the fire alarm and to pull the switch. The alarm started shrieking and he burst through the door and ran, arms tucked in tightly at his sides.

Chapter 27

Neither of them saw her at first. She was just sitting in the shadows, slumped in the green Adirondack chair on the porch. She didn't try to get up or to run as they approached. Hutchin thought that was strange, but realized that Isabel probably had broken several of Kit's ribs when she'd kicked her repeatedly.

He and Isabel both stopped. Kit raised her head. The right side of her face had swelled, she had a fat lip, she looked like hell. "Shit, she's not going anywhere," Isabel said with a sharp, ugly laugh. "I'll disconnect the alarm. The kid's inside the building."

"Or he wants us to think he is," Hutchin replied. "Just turn off that goddamn alarm."

Isabel climbed through the broken window and moments later, the alarm stopped. The silence seemed eerie, expectant, a strange hollowness just begging to be filled. Isabel climbed back out and hurried over. "You get her into the trunk, then we'll look for the kid."

"Do you know what's going on, Isabel? What any of this

is about?'' Kit asked. She talked slowly, unevenly, words slurring together. "It's about Diane Jackson. Jay was fucking Diane. She was pregnant by him. He suffocated her. I bet you don't know any of that, do you, Isabel.''

"What?'' Isabel whispered, and looked at him, her face pale, eyes like lumps of charcoal.

Shit, Hutchin thought. The silence had been filled. "What horseshit! She's stalling for time and trying to drive a wedge between us.''

"And what did you promise Sanchez, Jay, in return for doing a little dirty work for you? He did his part—quite well, I'd have to say, considering the ruin of my office building. And then you got rid of him, a knife through the neck. Now, that is one nasty death, Jay.''

Hutchin lunged for her and jerked her to her feet. After that, nothing was clear. He thought that her arm swung upward, but that might have been shadows flitting across his peripheral vision. However it happened, he didn't know where the screwdriver had come from or how she managed to plunge it into his stomach and jerk it out again.

His hands flew to his stomach, to the hot, sticky blood that leaked through his fingers, and he stumbled back, unable to connect one moment to the next. He thought he heard someone screaming, someone close by, maybe Isabel, but he wasn't sure. He fell into the bushes just beyond the porch and sank into them as if into a bed of feathers.

(2)

When Kit turned, Isabel was gone.

She knew that Isabel had gone after Ryan, that the only thing in the woman's mind was revenge. An eye for an eye. Kit had stabbed her husband and now she would get Ryan.

Ribs screaming, Kit somehow managed to climb through

the shattered windows, into the museum. Her voice echoed. She patted frantically at the closest wall, fingers seeking a light switch. She found it, flipped the switch, and the lights in the room blazed.

Door, the rear door is open.

Kit ran for it, one elbow pressed to her ribs to stem the pain, and stumbled outside, into a starlight that seemed brightest just beyond the ridge, 150 feet above the reservoir below. *Dear God, no, please, no. . . .*

She looked wildly around and finally saw Ryan off to her right, backing toward the lip of the cliff, Isabel Hutchin moving slowly toward him.

(3)

The woman.

As she came toward him, Ryan saw her face clearly, saw it in all its incredible beauty, and the Other roared to life and his feet stopped and suddenly reversed direction. Then he was running toward her, toward this woman, and she stopped, the murderous rage in her face gone.

He hurled himself at her, clutching her legs, holding on even as she fell back, and he sobbed, "Izzie, Izzie, I loved you so much. I brought you roses."

Even as he said the words, they rolled across the ground, Ryan still clutching her legs and Isabel kicking, clawing at him, and finally getting him off. She scrambled away from him on her hands and knees and he scurried after her, the alarm more distant now, but his cries nearly as loud and terrible.

"And that day at Bahia Honda, you . . . ran away from me. You were mad . . . and then you wrote me a letter. You didn't want to see me anymore. You . . . you loved him more. Him. Jay. Jay this, Jay that, Jay, Jay, Jay." His voice got louder, angry. He leaped onto her, leaped onto her back. "I loved you and I thought you loved me but it was all a lie."

Her arms collapsed under the weight of his body and for seconds they just lay there, Isabel on her stomach, Ryan on her back. Then he rolled off of her and got down close to her face. "You hurt me," he said, his heart so filled with pain he thought it would explode. "You hurt me so bad. Out here, by the ridge, you hit me with a shovel. Remember that, Isabel? Remember how you smacked me with that shovel?" And he rolled back onto his heels and ripped open his shirt, showing her the scar. "Right here. You hit me right here. And I went away and I . . . I . . . I watched you hit me again on the head, over and over, and then . . ." He screamed the rest of it. "And then you buried me!"

His heart exploded finally from the hurt and he doubled over at the waist and the world went black.

(4)

The chopper landed on the grounds behind the museum, its searchlight so bright that Webster saw them immediately. Kit, on her knees, held Ryan against her chest, her face buried in his shoulder. Beside them lay Isabel Hutchin, so motionless that he thought she was dead.

"Hutchin," Kit gasped. "In the bushes out front."

Webster shouted to Vogel and Moreno, telling them where to find Hutchin, then turned to Kit. Her face looked misshapen, a ruin of ugly bruises and swellings. "Ryan?"

"He passed out."

Webster felt Isabel's neck for a pulse. Strong, steady. Yet, her eyes were wide-open, unblinking. *Alive, but not here,* he thought, and wondered if she was injured or just *gone.*

He patted her down for a weapon, but found only her wallet. He opened it and glanced through her ID, her credit cards.

Only her voter's registration card held the truth. The name on it was *Isabel Schuller Hutchin.* He held it up, so Kit could see it. Mute, she simply nodded and pressed her face into the crook of her son's neck and said nothing at all. It had all been said.

Epilogue

Sunday, December 2
Tango Key, Florida

The first cold front of the season had moved in last night, plunging temperatures in the keys into the mid-forties. Up north, Webster thought, they laughed about Floridians who called the mid-forties cold. But it felt like the Arctic to him as he stood with his back to the cliff behind the Tango Museum, the wind whipping up off the reservoir below it.

A land-moving crew worked the back property of the museum, and so far, the pile of dirt they had dug up and deposited near the trees at the edge of the museum property was eight or nine feet high. They hadn't found what they were looking for, but he didn't feel discouraged. Not yet. Maybe by tonight he would pack it in, but not now.

Moreno and Vogel drove up in the surveillance van and brought out fresh coffee for the crew, then joined Webster. Moreno looked as if he had a secret, Webster thought, and wondered what it was.

"Any word on the Hutchins?" Webster asked.

"Hutchin will pull through, but the Mrs. is as still as a dead mouse," Vogel replied. "They're calling it shock-induced trauma." Vogel handed him a tiny paper cup filled with espresso. "So you really think they'll turn up Beaupre's bones?"

Webster shrugged. He made no judgments, drew no conclusions.

"Well, either way, you upheld your end of the bargain." He pulled an envelope from his pocket and handed it to Webster. "A bonus."

"To make up for all those lunches you never paid for?"

Vogel laughed and Webster glanced in the envelope. Inside were three airplane tickets, open-ended tickets, round-the-world tickets. "Jesus, Bernie. I'm one guy."

"With a girlfriend who has a kid who would probably love to see koalas and kangaroos in the flesh. Or the beaches and volcanoes in Hawaii. Or Singapore. It's a really good deal, actually. As long as you travel in one direction, you can make as many stops as you want. That comes with four weeks' paid leave. Don't say I never bought you anything, Ben."

"What expense account did it come out of?"

"You wouldn't call it in a million years," said Moreno.

"A couple different ones," Vogel replied. "But someone else contributed to it, too."

"Yeah, who? The president?"

"Paul Opitz. He was actually behind this investigation. He suspected Hutchin was crooked, but could never find what he needed to bust him."

Opitz, Webster thought. *Go fuckin' figure.*

Over Vogel's shoulder, he saw Kit's van pull in. She and Ryan got out with Oro and the boy and his dog ran straight over. "Hey, Ben, hi, Agent Vogel, hi, Agent Moreno."

"Hey," Moreno said.

"How's it going, Ryan?" asked Vogel. "How's your mom doing?"

"Real good. She brought some pastries and stuff. What's going on, anyway?"

It seemed that Ryan couldn't recall much of anything about what had happened the night here at the museum. "We're looking for some pottery shards and spearheads, archaeological stuff," Webster told him.

Kit joined them and passed out pastries from the Cuban coffee shop in town. She looked surprisingly good, Webster thought, considering that she'd broken two teeth and three ribs, one of which had punctured a lung. When Ryan ran off with his dog, she said, "Found anything yet?"

"Nope," Vogel replied.

"You will. At least, that's what Abuelita says. We'll be inside the museum. Ryan needs to use the rest room."

"Hey," Webster said, and caught her hand before she could move away. "Take a look at this." He handed her the envelope and she peeked inside and whistled softly. "Ever been to Australia?" he asked. "Think Ryan would like it?"

Her eyes lit up. "You're kidding, right?"

"Uh-uh. Courtesy of Bernie and Paul Opitz."

"Opitz?" she exclaimed, and threw her head back and laughed and laughed, a pure and wonderful sound. Then she hugged Vogel. "Any time you get tired of the Bureau and want a job, Bernie, you've got one with us. The same for you, Eric."

"I'll be traveling," Moreno said, wagging his own ticket.

"I'm not a lawyer," Vogel said.

"But you think like one."

She walked off with Ryan, and Oro trotted back over to Webster, a Frisbee in her mouth. She sat between him and

Vogel, dropped the Frisbee on the ground, and watched the land mover. Suddenly, Oro barked and ran over to the land mover, which had stopped. The driver got down and whistled. "Hey, guys, get over here."

They crowded around the most recent hole, Webster and Vogel, Moreno and the crew—and Oro. "What's that look like to you guys?"

They all looked down. "I don't see anything," Vogel said.

"Over there. To the right."

"Toss me a shovel," Webster said, and he and the driver slid down into the four-foot-deep hole, Oro sliding along behind them.

In the end, though, they didn't need the shovel. Oro dug frantically, madly, whimpering, barking at the sand as it covered her paws. When the sand finally stopped sliding and cascading, Webster saw the skeleton of a foot. Then fingers. Then another foot. Then the entire skeleton, head and all. Oro sniffed at it once, just once, and sat back and lifted her snout into the air and howled, mourning the man who had loved her as a puppy.

It was the single-most heartbreaking sound that Webster had ever heard, both a tribute and a lament of love and loss, redemption and resurrection. Then Oro climbed out of the hole and trotted off in search of Ryan, the boy who had been the man.

PRAISE FOR THE NOVELS OF
T.J. MacGREGOR

THE HANGED MAN

"Taut, tricky, and terrifying ... A dark and suspenseful page-turner."

—Nora Roberts

"A tense and provocative suspense novel."

—*Publishers Weekly*

"A gripping tale of revenge and obsession that's filled with pulse-pounding suspense, bizarre twists, and non-stop action."

—*Booklist* (starred review)

THE SEVENTH SENSE

"MacGregor combines a riveting story, memorable characters, and heart-pounding suspense in this outstanding supernatural thriller."

—*Booklist*

"MacGregor keeps the suspense rising ... in her creepy exploration of the power of human perception."

—*Publishers Weekly*

"THE SEVENTH SENSE grabbed me, pinned me to my chair, and kept me there until the last page. I loved it."

—Nancy Pickard, author of *Twilight*

"THE SEVENTH SENSE is superb. MacGregor's writing blazes through the twisting catacombs of the heart and mind, leading you deep into new terrain so fascinating you almost forget to breathe. Don't wait for Thomas Harris. Read this book."

—Steven Spruill, author of *Rulers of Darkness*
and *Daughters of Darkness*

VANISHED

"Through succinct prose and sharp dialogue, MacGregor spins a haunting tale of classified technologies that warp the delicate fabric of space-time."

—*Publishers Weekly*